SÂR DUBNOTAL

The Astral Trail

IN THE SAME COLLECTION:

Sâr Dubnotal vs. Jack the Ripper

From The Memoirs of Sâr Dubnotal

SÂR DUBNOTAL

The Astral Trail

adapted by Brian Stableford

edited by
Jean-Marc & Randy Lofficier

stories by
**Matthew Baugh, Matthew Dennion,
Micah Harris, Travis Hiltz, Roman Leary,
Josh Reynolds** and **Stuart Shiffman**

A Black Coat Press Book

Acknowledgements: We are greatly indebted to Massimo Introvigne for having located a copy of *The Astral Trail*.

English adaptation of *The Astral Trail* Copyright © 2015 by Brian Stableford.
All stories Copyright © 2015 by their respective authors.
Introduction Copyright © 2015 by Jean-Marc & Randy Lofficier.
Cover illustration by Gino Starace.

Visit our website at www.blackcoatpress.com

Table of Contents

Introduction

The adventures of *Sâr Dubnotal* were published anonymously in France in 1909. The identity of its author(s?) remains unknown even today. It has been suggested that the series might have been the work of the prolific Norbert Sevestre, but this is unsupported by any actual documentary evidence and, frankly, Sevestre's work was much better in style, characterization and plotting than *Sâr Dubnotal*, obviously written in a hurry, often loosely plotted, and rarely researched.

It is highly improbable that the unknown author of *Sâr Dubnotal* was familiar with the adventures of *Ozmar the Mystic* (1896) by Emeric Hulme-Beaman, E. and H. Heron's "psychic detective" *Flaxman Low* [1] or former theosophist and Golden Dawn member Algernon Blackwood's *John Silence* (1908), but he might have been at least vaguely aware of their existence. It is quite possible that our anonymous storyteller was commissioned by the publisher, Eichler, to create a French version of such characters, in the same way that they would later ask Jean Petithuguenin to pen the adventures of *Ethel King*, the female *Nick Carter*, in 1911. [2]

Today, the best remembered successors to *John Silence* and *Sâr Dubnotal* are William Hope Hodgson's *Carnacki the Ghost-Finder* (1913); Aleister Crowley's (writing as Edward Kelly) *Simon Iff* (1917); Violet Firth's (writing as Dion For-

---

[1] Written by Hesketh Pritchard and his mother Kate, and published in *Pearson's Magazine* in 1898-99

[2] Available from Black Coat Press, ISBN 978-1-61227-233-7.

tune) *Dr. Taverner* (1926); and Manly Wade Wellman's *Judge Pursuivant* (1938).

One thing is certain: unlike some of the authors mentioned above, whoever wrote the adventures of *Sâr Dubnotal* was not actually well versed in the Occult, and relied on dubious and often mangled sources for his plots. Some of the pseudo-esoteric mumbo-jumbo used in the series was likely inspired by Eusapia Palladino, Eliphas Lévi, Madame Blavatsky, Jules Bois, and the so-called Sâr Joséphin Péladan—whose title was appropriated by the author—spiced up with a little jargon borrowed from Friedrich Nietzsche.

As for the term "psychagogue," it is often equated with "necromancer," but its meaning derives from the Greek *psychagogos*, which referred to the god Hermes, whose role included guiding souls into the Underworld. Like the word "psychognosis," it was re-appropriated by 19th century psychologists, for whom "psychagogy" became a kind of psychotherapy; needless to say, it is used in *Sâr Dubnotal* in its original sense.

Who is Sâr Dubnotal?

The origins of Sâr Dubnotal were never spelled out by its creator, but we know that the so-called "Great Psychagogue," also nicknamed the "Napoléon of the Intangible," the "Master of Psychognosis," the "Conqueror of the Invisible," and more simply "El Tebib"—meaning the Doctor in Arabic—is a westerner, despite his stylish oriental guise.

Sâr Dubnotal was born in Mumbai. His exact age is unknown, but he is probably much older than he seems. He was schooled by the Rosicrucians, and learned the ancient secrets of the Hindu mystics. He is capable of telepathy, levitation and hypnotism.

His regular companions are Rudolph, his disciple, a European youth whom he rescued from gypsies and to whom he is teaching his knowledge; Gianetti Annunciata, an Italian medium who helps him communicate with the dead; Naini, his faithful Hindu servant and strong man; and an international trio of private detectives consisting of Frank (an Englishman), Fréjus (a Frenchman), and Otto (a German).

When confronted by a particularly difficult case, Sâr Dubnotal uses telepathy to contact the yogi Ranijesti, with whom he once studied psychognosis. Well versed in the Occult, Ranijesti had himself entombed alive in an underground cell in Benares so that he could enjoy the bliss associated with nirvana in a state of temporary suspended animation. But before descending into his tomb, Ranijesti promised Sâr Dubnotal to enlighten him any time the Great Psychagogue would find himself embarrassed by a psychic problem.

Sâr Dubnotal owns houses in Trez-Hir in Brittany, on the Champs-Élysées in Paris, and in Cheyne Walk in London. (He is therefore Carnacki's neighbor!) He also owns several yachts, including the *Brahma* and the *Derviche*. Finally, he also owns an atoll called Redemption Island, located along the Tropic of Cancer in the Pacific Ocean, where he sends villains to be reformed.

Like Carnacki, Sâr Dubnotal likes to mix modern science with more traditional occult spells and recipes, having invented such devices as a camera that can photograph astral bodies, and a telegraph that can communicate with the dead.

Publishing History

A general introduction to the *Sâr Dubnotal* series was included in our first volume,[3] and there is no need to repeat all of it here. Suffice it to say that twenty issues of *Sâr Dubnotal* were published by Eichler, starting in January 1909. They are:

1. *Le Manoir Hanté de Crec'h-ar-Van* (The Haunted Manor of Crec'h-ar-Van) (included in our Volume 1)
2. *La Table Tournante du Docteur Tooth* (Dr. Tooth's Turning Table)

---

[3] ISBN 978-1-934543-94-8.

Our previous collection comprised five linked episodes: No.1, which introduced the villainous Tserpchikopf, then Nos. 7, 9, 10 and 11. A copy of No.8, *The Astral Trail*, could not be located, but its substance was summarized in the translation of No.9.

This series-within-the-series sees Sâr Dubnotal fight a villain called Tserpchikopf, the "Bloody Hypnotist," who is also an evil mastermind with psychic powers and the leader of a criminal network called The Chessmen, where members are given names of chess pieces: Queen, Knight, Pawn, etc., Tserpchikopf being, of course, the King. It turns out that the villain is also behind the murders attributed to Jack the Ripper.

The Many Lives of Sâr Dubnotal

Sâr Dubnotal has proved himself to be a popular character, featured in many new stories published in our annual anthology series, *Tales of the Shadowmen*, devoted to heroes and villains drawn from French popular literature.

In addition to the stories reprinted in this collection, we encourage our readers to seek out *Harry Dickson and the Werewolf of Rutherford Grange* [4] by G.L. Gick in which the Sâr teams up with a young Harry Dickson to defeat a monstrous creature from beyond.

Now read on!

Jean-Marc & Randy Lofficier

---

[4] ISBN 978-1-935558-80-4.

SÂR DUBNOTAL

Chaque fascicule contient un récit complet.

THE ASTRAL TRAIL

(translated by Brian Stableford)

I: The Tutelary Spirit

"Master, I'm very sorry to tell you, on behalf of my comrades, that all our investigations have been fruitless. The Pawn cannot be found."

Those words were addressed to Sâr Dubnotal, the great master of psychognosis, and the person who had just pronounced them respectfully was Fréjus, one of his most skillful investigators.

The confession of impotence made by Fréjus did not have the wherewithal to trouble the superhuman.

Sâr Dubnotal had probably expected that failure on the part of the sleuths he employed, for he sent the delegate away with a simple nod of the head, without manifesting the slightest discontentment or surprise.

. For nearly four months the psychagogue had been occupied with an extremely important and mysterious affair that obliged him to call upon all the resources of his extraordinary intelligence and supernatural science.

As you know, after living for a long time in Chaldea and India, in the company of yogis and mages, Sâr Dubnotal, who had discovered, among other secrets, those of longevity and the crystallization of carbon, had come to Europe to put his immense fortune and admirable knowledge at the service of Progress and Justice.

Following certain circumstances that we have described in our preceding narratives, the Great Psychagogue, then on vacation at his bungalow in Trez-Hir, on the Breton coast, had

13

unmasked and arrested Comtesse Azilis de Treguilly, who was guilty of the murder of her brother-in-law and her husband, with the objective of obtaining their inheritance and remarrying a supposed Russian boyar, Prince Tserpchikopf, a most redoubtable malefactor, who had driven her to commit the crime. [5]

Unfortunately, Tserpchikopf had escaped the punishment that awaited him. A powerful hypnotist, he had, to tell the truth, formidable trumps in his hand, and he had made use of them with diabolical skill.

Once captured by Sâr Dubnotal, the wretched Azilis had succeeded in getting away with the Russian's help.

Sâr Dubnotal had instructed Naini, his gigantic Hindu servant, to take the woman to a destination only known to him and his aides, of which we shall have occasion to speak later.

Until Marseilles, the journey of Naini and Azilis had not given rise to any incident. Staying at the Royal Palace in the Cours Belzunce on a Tuesday evening, they were due to embark the following day, but on the Wednesday morning Naini had been found unconscious and Azilis had disappeared. Quickly alerted to the capture of the Comtesse, Tserpchikopf had leapt on to the same train, had succeeded in communicating with the criminal and conceived a bold escape plan.

The Hindu, a stern and vigorous man, not being easy to hypnotize, the rogues had decided to poison him with a few drops of an infernal drug fabricated with *upas antiar*, a drug that Tserpchikopf had secretly stolen from the indigenes of Malaya, and which leaves no suspicious traces in the body.

The plan succeeded, and the police thought that Naini had died suddenly.

At the hotel, Tserpchikopf had registered under the name Schönprink. The bandit possessed false identity papers, and, although momentarily suspected of having been mixed up in the tenebrous affair, he was not troubled.

---

[5] See our previous volume, *Sâr Dubnotal vs. Jack the Ripper*.

In the interval, Sâr Dubnotal had hastened to Marseilles after having telegraphed the examining magistrate to wait for his arrival before proceeding with the autopsy of Naini's body, transported to the morgue the day before.

It was then that the Pawn had made his appearance. Warned by a dispatch from that enigmatic individual that the Great Psychagogue and his associates had taken a special express train, the pseudo-Schönprink had gone to plant a bomb on the railway line between Arles and Avignon, at a place where the track crossed a bridge over a tributary of the Rhône.

The express had been derailed, and the master and his followers had only escaped a frightful death by a miracle. Continuing their tragically-interrupted journey, those heroes had only thrown themselves more ardently on their enemy's track.

The *upas antiar* had not killed Naini, but merely rendered him torpid. His master recalled him to life just as the medical examiners, convinced of his death, were about to proceed with the formal autopsy.

On the other hand, an intelligent investigation on the part of the Frenchman Fréjus had permitted them to pick up the trail of the fugitives. They had taken refuge in England, where Azilis was passing as a medium and her companion as a celebrated yogi.

The false mage Luckvrak and the fake medium Dolorosa, unmasked in the middle of an occult séance, spent a bad quarter of an hour.

Rudolph, the master's favored disciple, took possession of Azilis, but while being taken to the nearest police station in a taxi, Tserpchikopf had hypnotized his guards on the way and given them the slip.

The next day, when Sâr Dubnotal went to the police station to ask for news of the boyar, he found that the two constables had been locked up. Knowing that they had not been corrupted by the pretended Luckvrak, as the inspector was convinced, Sâr Dubnotal had defended them, and his intervention had saved them from serious disciplinary punishment.

Azilis, taken back to Trez-Hir, was embarked on the *Derviche*, a superb steam-yacht that Sâr Dubnotal had summoned from Colombo in order to take her directly to the place of detention he intended for her, to prevent Tserpchikopf from making any further attempt to rescue her.

Once the yacht had departed, the Great Psychagogue, freed from concern with the Comtesse, had devoted all his efforts to picking up the trail of Tserpchikopf. He abandoned Trez-Hir and all his staff in order to take up residence in Paris, in his magnificent house in the Champs-Élysées, which his immense fortune had permitted him to acquire.

It was, in fact, better for him to remain constantly in the City of Light, where everything led him to believe that Tserpchikopf had maintained secret relations with a notorious criminal brotherhood, and where the fake boyar had probably come to take refuge after his adventure in London

Before the arrest of Azilis, Tserpchikopf had occupied an apartment in the Rue Voltaire. He had left suddenly without paying the rent he owed and had not been seen since, but it was possible that he had found refuge with the mysterious Pawn, whose identity, thus far, all the research carried out by Otto, Frank and Fréjus, the master's three secret agents, had been unable to discover.

Every morning, one of the investigators came to Sâr Dubnotal to report on the previous day's research, and every time the report was the same: nothing.

It was impossible to discover the slightest clue. The Pawn might have been a myth, who had only become more illusory as a result of the efforts of the three investigators.

As for Tserpchikopf, one might have thought that he had disappeared in a puff of smoke. Disappeared at the end of September, they had reached the beginning of December without hearing any mention of him.

When the door of his study had closed behind the discomfited Fréjus, Sâr Dubnotal fell into a profound reverie.

The noble lines of his face had not contracted, and nothing filtered through his half-closed eyelids but a distracted gaze, as if he were deep in the contemplation of invisible things.

In contrast to the unusual luxury that reigned in the other rooms of his new and princely dwelling, the master's study presented the most severe aspect. The furniture, green in hue, was limited to a desk, a side-table, a sofa and a few comfortable armchairs, in one of which Sâr Dubnotal was presently leaning back.

Nevertheless, the study did not lack a certain style, with its decorated ceiling, from which a large green crystal chandelier was suspended, and the rare and costly drapes of the same shade with which the windows were curtained. The latter overlooked an interior courtyard planted with trees.

The side-table was not even covered by a cloth but the desk was cluttered with old papyrus, a monumental writing pad, a human skull playing the role of paperweight, and a Hindu gong.

A methodically-regulated heater spread a mild warmth through the room, which remained plunged in a half-light like that of an aquarium.

Eventually, Sâr Dubnotal stretched out his arm and pressed the button of the gong. A stroke resounded, and then two more. Shortly afterwards, a young man came in without knocking, followed by a woman dressed in the Italian style. They were Rudolph, the Great Psychagogue's principal disciple, and Annunciata Gianetti, one of his best mediums.

"I need you," he said to them. "Sit down, Rudolph, next to my armchair, and you, Annunciata, in front of the side-table."

The newcomers obeyed without unsealing their lips. One did not question the orders of Sâr Dubnotal; one obeyed them passively, whatever they might be.

"Rudolph," the psychagogue went on, "it's necessary to finish with Tserpchikopf. I can't tolerate that rogue continuing to hold me in check. Since ordinary means have failed, I've decided to make use of others.

"Are you thinking of evoking the spirit of the late Jean de Treguilly, Azilis' husband, Master?" the young man asked.

"No—not yet, at least. Jean de Treguilly has suffered too much for me to voluntarily trouble the peace that he's been experiencing since I unmasked his wife and Tserpchikopf."

"In that case, Master…?"

"I'm going to consult the astral double of my friend Ranijesti, and, thanks to him, I hope to be able to disentangle this confusion."

Rudolph understood; his eyes sparkled with admiration and enthusiasm.

Sâr Dubnotal's principal disciple was prodigiously interested in his master's psychic experiments, and saw with joy the mysterious ribbon of an astral trail opening before him, at the end of which he had no doubt that Tserpchikopf would finally fall into the power of the superhuman Sâr, a great redresser of wrongs and, when necessary, an implacable administrator of justice.

For what made Sâr Dubnotal more than a mere mortal was, above all, the faculty that he had of penetrating the invisible and directing himself there as surely as in the material world. One might have thought that he possessed a sixth sense. He undoubtedly had a precious aide in Ranijesti, the Hindu ascetic in whose company he had once studied magnetism and hypnotism, and who had had himself immured alive in an underground cell in Benares in order to free himself from terrestrial contingencies and permit his double to explore the regions of infinity.

The two friends were not separated because of that, and they continued to communicate via Sâr Dubnotal's intermediary.

It was Ranijesti that the Great Psychagogue sometimes called his "tutelary spirit," and sometimes his "invisible policeman," because he extended over him a kind of occult protection and guided him in his astral research.

In each of his numerous domiciles, Sâr Dubnotal had installed an evocation chamber where tutelary spirits could be received. He called those special chambers "green rooms" because of their uniform color.

In the Champs-Élysées, it was a study that played the role of green room, and that was why it differed so much from the other apartments of his princely residence.

As soon as Rudolph was informed of the Great Psychagogue's intentions, he took three ample green smocks from a cupboard, which Sâr Dubnotal, Annunciata and he put on. Then the Italian, a small, pale but pretty woman, nervous and thin, after having armed herself with a black wand, came to lie down on the sofa placed behind the round table.

"Annunciata," pronounced the psychagogue, in a forceful voice, while darting a sharp glance at the recumbent woman, "ask my friend Ranijesti to respond to us right away."

With these words, *la* Gianetti raised herself up, tapped the table with her wand, and fell back on the sofa as if dead.

Sâr Dubnotal and Rudolph retreated to the back of the room, after having placed a golden propelling pencil and a sheet of white velum on the table.

A strange obscurity had suddenly overtaken the green room. The curtains had abruptly slid, of their own accord, along their rods, completely cutting off the daylight.

The two psychagogues, however, were able to distinguish a kind of white mist that emanated from Annunciata's body, and Sâr Dubnotal murmured:

"The medium is entering into communication with the Hindu's double, Rudolph; the experiment will succeed."

In fact, the master and the disciple were soon witness to an extraordinary scene.

The pale wisp of vapor that emerged from Annunciata's body gradually condensed between the extinct chandelier and the side-table, and took on the appearance of a human hand.

That hand, suspended in mind-air, seemed to be made of wax: a hyaline wax illuminated by an unknown mysterious light.

"Ranijesti's hand," whispered Sâr Dubnotal.

For a moment, the phosphorescent hand floated in the dense shadow of the green rom.

The phalanges of the fingers were splayed, and emitted a subtle fluorescence. Around them, a nimbus of emerald light formed, a kind of green halo that grew and dissipated the ambient darkness.

Then the hand descended and paused immediately above the white sheet deposited on the side-table.

At that moment, the table rose slightly into the air and rotated, while the Hindu gong on the nearby desk rang sonorously three times.

"Ranijesti," said Sâr Dubnotal, in a loud voice, "since you have been kind enough to respond to my medium's appeal, permit me to ask you a question.

"I have been searching for a long time for a man named Tserpchikopf, a redoubtable malefactor and powerful hypnotist, who has so far evaded all my terrestrial sleuths, and whom I suspect of involvement in an incalculable number of crimes.

"In any case, he has tried to dispose of my servant Naini and attempted to kill me. He therefore merits the punishment I intend to inflict upon him, and I beg you, O Ranijesti, to facilitate the execution of my project. Do you know this Tserpchikopf? Can you tell me where he is hiding? Reply, I implore you, my old friend."

Instantly, the luminous hand picked up the propelling pencil, and the sound of a rapid scribbling as heard, after which the hand picked up the sheet of vellum on which it had just written, and placed it in Sâr Dubnotal's hands.

By the phosphorescent light emitted by the phalanges, the latter was able to read lines traced in red letters:

No, I do not know Tserpchikopf, but I remember hearing his name pronounced by a soul in torment.

"What is the name of the soul?"

Pawn, the hand immediately wrote on the sheet of velum that Sâr Dubnotal held out to it.

On reading the name, no longer traced in red letters but in flamboyant golden capitals, the Great Psychagogue could not suppress an exclamation of amazement.

Had "Pawn," the Pawn that his investigators had been tracking unsuccessfully for so long, Tserpchikopf's enigmatic accomplice, passed over from life to death, then?

In that case, hazard had served Sâr Dubnotal well, for it would be relatively easy to evoke the spirit of the dead man and obtain from him the information necessary to pick up the Russian's trail.

In the domain of shades, Ranijesti enjoyed a certain power, and if Pawn was not naturally inclined to surrender his former associate's secrets, the yogi's double, in order to be of service to the Great Psychagogue, would be able to constrain him to do so by force.

Suddenly, however, Sâr Dubnotal's features darkened. A doubt had occurred to him. Was Ranijesti's Pawn really the same Pawn for which he was searching? Might he not be a mere namesake?

"Ranijesti," he said, "How long has this Pawn been dead? Would you please write?"

Six years, wrote the immaterial hand.

Sâr Dubnotal turned to Rudolph, disappointment causing him to smile involuntarily.

"I suspected as much," he said. "It would have been too fortunate. We're not used to so much complaisance on the part of chance, but if it's not the signatory of the dispatch that allowed Tserpchikopf to slip through our fingers, since the Pawn sought in vain by our investigators was alive three months ago, and probably still is, it nevertheless remains the case that the spirit mentioned by Ranijesti has had some relationship with Tserpchikopf. So, nothing is lost.

"No, Rudolph, nothing is lost, and we hold the conductive thread, believe me. I have an idea, which I'll divulge to you later. For the moment, let's attend to the most urgent matter, which is to ask Ranijesti one last question. It's necessary not to abuse his benevolence, and you know that our medium suffers greatly from experiments of this sort, which it's important to abridge as soon as possible..."

Waving the sheet of vellum, the Great Psychagogue went on:

"Thank you, Ranijesti. One more small item of information, and you may return to the extraterrestrial regions of our cherished and sublime Beyond. I should like to talk to Pawn, the soul in torment you have just indicated to me. Tell me whether that can be achieved."

There was a long silence, only troubled by the slight sound of the propelling pencil rung over the paper.

When the pencil stopped, the gong rang again. The curtains immediately drew apart, daylight entered the green room, and everything resumed its normal appearance.

As mysteriously as it had appeared, the yogi's hand had just vanished, leaving only a vaporous wisp that was promptly reabsorbed after having made contact with Annunciata's prostrate form.

At the same moment, the medium shuddered and sat up abruptly, viscous drool on her lips, her irises rolled back and her features convulsed as if by an epileptic fit.

Sâr Dubnotal sketched a few magnetic passes, which had the effect of extracting the medium from the crisis provoked by the prodigious tension hat her nerves had suffered.

Then he ran to the table to take possession of the sheet of vellum.

The first impressions had been erased and had been replaced by another communication traced in red and gold letters, which did not take long to fade away in their turn.

It said:

Yes, Sâr Dubnotal, my illustrious friend, you can evoke the spirit of Pawn, and I do not think I am saying too much in affirming that he will reply willingly to the questions you put to him, for his desire is precisely to confide his troubles to an honest human being.

The poor soul haunts a steamship serving as a ferry between Dieppe and Newhaven. I do not know the name of the ship. Inform yourself. Pawn's spirit will tell you why God has condemned him to that ordeal. Try to offer him relief, noble and merciful psychagogue.

Your faithful servant in the beyond, as once on the planet
Ranijesti

Sâr Dubnotal put the piece of paper down, and said: "Quickly, Rudolph, make arrangements to accompany me immediately, with Annunciata. Don't forget to pack all the equipment I might need to operate during the journey."

It was then three o'clock in the afternoon.

At five o'clock, the two psychagogues and the Italian woman embarked at the Gare Saint-Lazare on the Paris-Dieppe express.

2. The Bewitched Ferry

In the year of grace 1889, during which the celebrations of the Exposition Universelle were unfurling in Paris, the pretty town of Dieppe, situated at the mouth of the Arques on one of the most direct routes to London from the French capital, had seen legions of British tourists pass through desirous of admiring the Eiffel Tower and the Hall of Machines, the two great attractions of the epoch.

Unfortunately, an uninterrupted series of accidents to which one of the ferries of the London-Brighton Company, which, in concert with the Compagnie de l'Ouest, maintained the passenger service between Newhaven and Dieppe, had fallen victim, had cooled the enthusiasm of the islanders, or, at least, driven them to prefer one of the two rival lines from Dover to Calais or Folkestone to Boulogne.

The ferry in question, of English nationality, was named the *Prince Edward*. It was a paddle-steamer of the same model as the *Victoria* of sinister memory, which, a few years before, had been lost, with all passengers and crew, after running on to the rocks of Ailly on a foggy night.[6]

To tell the truth, the *Prince Edward*, launched six years before, had never had any luck. Her first crossing had been marked by a strange drama.

The ferry had sailed to Dieppe without a hitch and had resumed the route to its home port by night. It had arrived off Beachy Head, a promontory situated to the north of Newhaven. The captain was on watch on the quarter-deck with the helmsman and the boatswain.

The passengers were in bed in the cabins and the crew-members resting in their quarters; the deck was deserted. Nevertheless, near the port paddle-drum, two passengers, who had probably been unable to sleep, seemed to have been engaged in an animated discussion for some time.

The captain observed them distractedly from the height of the bridge. The discussion was followed by a violent quarrel, and the two interlocutors suddenly came to blows.

They were scarcely distinguishable in the darkness. From the poop deck, the captain and his sailors could only see two

---

[6] The paddle steamer *Victoria*, captained by J. S. Clark, was employed on the run between Newhaven and Dieppe. On April 12, 1887, she left Newhaven with 94 passengers and a crew of 30 and, upon approaching the French coast, ran into thick fog. From the distance he had traveled, Captain Clark was aware that he was near the dangerous Pointe d'Ailly. He listened for the fog siren, but no sound reached him. He then checked his position and decided that he must be east of Dieppe. He then proceeded on his course when the vessel crashed on the rocks. There was a certain amount of panic but the captain and the ship's officers managed to restore order and save most of the passengers on board. Only 19 lives were lost. The inquiry revealed that the assistant lighthouse keeper at Pointe d'Ailly had neglected to light the boiler fires in order to provide steam for the fog siren.

silhouettes seizing one another, each trying to shove the other over the side.

The antagonists wrestled in that fashion for several seconds before the eyes of the alarmed mariners. The latter could not abandon their posts in order to separate them, and shock prevented them from calling for help.

The two adversaries seemed equally matched. They fell over on the slippery deck of the vessel, only to get back to their feet immediately and resume their mortal hand-to-hand combat.

Finally, the gleam of a knife flashed at the extremity of the arm of one of the combatants, and at the same time, the captain and his sailors perceived a frightful scream.

Struck in the middle of the chest by a thrust of the knife, the other passenger was thrown back on the top of the paddle-drum, and his murderer, gathering all his strength, seized him by the legs in order to hurl him into the sea.

Mute with horror until then, the captain succeeded in getting a grip on himself and uttering shouts designed to summon the crew—but it was too late.

Slashing the fingers of his victim, clinging to the edge, the murderer had just finished him off. Simultaneously, the captain heard the sound of a body falling into the water, and saw the silhouette of the guilty party running to the nearest hatchway.

When the sailors came on deck, they found no one there.

The captain had the ferry stop and put a launch into the sea, in order to try to recover the body of the victim, while the ship's lieutenant and the purser went down to the cabins to search for the murderer.

The launch did not find the body, which had sunk, and the investigations of the *Prince Edward*'s officers remained sterile. The lieutenant and the purser searched the most secret recesses of the steamer, but they did not succeed in laying their hands on the murderer, of whom their superior had only been able to give them the vaguest description.

All the passengers were lying in their bunks sound asleep, with the exception of one second-class passenger who had disappeared and, to all evidence, must have been the victim. The murderer had doubtless had time to get back to his berth and, as his traveling companions had not seen him leave the cabin or go back into it, it was impossible to identify him.

The most regrettable thing was that it was impossible to establish the identity of the dead man. No one knew him, and he had no luggage. If his name had been known, it might have been possible to unmask the murderer, who must have had some connection with him, but it was not, and no one remembered him.

At Dieppe, the embarkation had taken place at one o'clock in the morning, and no one had been thinking about anything but going to bed, without paying attention to the other passengers. Furthermore, it was probable that the victim had not left the deck.

In brief, when the *Prince Edward*, flying its flag at half mast, reached Newhaven, the mystery was still entire.

Why had the two men come to blows?

Were they French or English?

Was it a matter of a vendetta, an ambush, or a simple brawl?

Too many mysteries!

The local police, alerted by the captain before the disembarkation of the passengers, and the detective on duty at the dock, had questioned everyone, one by one, but they all claimed to know nothing about the matter and produced regular papers that established their perfect honorability.

The passengers could not be detained any longer, being in haste to get on with their affairs. In despair of any result, the case was closed shortly thereafter.

From then on, it seemed that an implacable fatality weighed upon the *Prince Edward*. The unfortunate vessel experienced the worst frustrations, without anyone being able to attribute a cause to them, except for persistent ill-luck by which even the least superstitious ended up being disquieted.

Sometimes, it was an engine malfunction, the rupture of a piston-rod or crank-shaft, damage to the propellers or the explosion of a boiler; sometimes it was the slippage of a capstan, the loss of a hawser or an anchor; sometimes it was a collision with a fishing-boat or a cargo ship; sometimes, finally, it was a tempest that the *Prince Edward* had all the difficulty in the world escaping.

In any case, it only escaped with severe damage, which kept it in dry dock for months on end, and costing the shareholders in the London-Brighton very dear.

Leaks that it was necessary to repair opened in the hull; the funnels were cracked; the bulwarks staved in; seawater invaded the scuppers, the lifeboats and the spar-decks—and all that was nothing by comparison with the human lives lost in the catastrophes.

Once, the *Prince Edward* had had to mourn the loss of four sailors carried away by an enormous wave; on another occasion, two passengers were violently struck by a cable swinging from a winch, which had fractured their skulls against the edge of the forecastle. Then, there was a cabin-boy who broke his back falling into the cargo-hold; a purser who was found stone dead near the port paddle-drum without anyone being able to determine the cause of his death; a sailor who had to be put in chains after a sudden fit of madness that cost the life of the second lieutenant, struck down by the poor lunatic; ten deaths, each more mysterious than the last, the funereal list of which grew longer with every voyage.

Bizarrely enough, these repeated accidents only occurred during the crossing from Dieppe to Newhaven, and always at the same location, off the cliffs of Beachy Head, where the drama recounted at the beginning of this chapter had unfolded.

The superstitious mariners of the *Prince Edward* did not take long to be struck by that fact, and it was soon averred among them that an evil spell had been cast on the ship.

Furthermore, several of them affirmed that they had seen the white form of a phantom emerge from the sea, climb up the steamer's port paddle-wheel and come to lean on the drum where the two passengers had fought so savagely. In addition, that wrathful apparition always coincided with a further catastrophe, which had either preceded it, or was to follow it. Thus, the sailors fled at the sight of it and dared not reappear on deck for the remainder of the crossing.

The officers, with the captain at their head, confirmed the reports of their men. They had all witnessed the phenomenon; they had all seen or glimpsed the phantom, which could not be anything other than the soul of the passenger murdered by his companion and thrown into the sea.

There were skeptics among those educated officers, intelligent and not disposed to share the prejudices of common mariners, but how could they not yield to the evidence of the facts, and what man can refuse to believe the evidence of his own eyes?

One night, a certain strong-minded passenger had ridiculed the assertions of the crew and wagered that he would stand on the paddle-drum at the moment when the fatal spot was reached.

A stupid bet! The passenger was to be the victim of his temerity.

After having tried in vain to dissuade him from carrying out his plan, he was allowed to take up his position on the paddle-drum, where no one kept him company. An hour later, the *Prince Edward* was at the jetty in Newhaven, but its flag, flying at half-mast, indicated that the skeptic's wager had had a fatal outcome. In fact, his corpse had been found lying on the paddle-drum. The unfortunate fellow's contorted features and bulging eyes revealed the symptoms of death attributable to excessive terror.

By what had that terrible fear been caused, if not the marine phantom: the "sea ghost," as the apparition was now called?

It could not be a matter of a macabre joke. Terrorized, the sailors had not quit their posts or the passengers their cabins.

Furthermore, the dead man was armed with a revolver, which he had threatened to fire at anything that presented itself, and that weapon, fallen at his feet, still had its six cartridges intact, indicating that the poor man had not had either the time, or the means, to make use of it.

This time, the existence of the sea-ghost no longer encountered any incredulity, and the resignations that had been taking place in the ranks of the crew for some time increased with frightful rapidity. The captain, the lieutenants, the purser and the first mate had to be replaced immediately by the company, and the newcomers did not take long to take their leave either.

As for the sailors and the stokers, it was diabolically difficult to recruit them.

It was necessary to put an end to it. In Dieppe as in Newhaven, everyone said frankly that the *Prince Edward* was bewitched. On that matter, the maritime population of the two ports was in complete accord. Even in high places, it could not be denied that it was time to rethink the problem. The timetable of the accursed ferry was therefore changed, and the accidents immediately ceased.

There was a breathing-space, but the steamers that the two companies had at their disposal were only four in number, and when half of them were out of service, it was necessary that the *Prince Edward* resume the former timetable.

The fatal curse, alas, had not been exorcized, and the succession of catastrophes immediately resumed. Were they going to be obliged to decommission the ship, almost new? The London-Brighton began to consider that eventuality seriously. After all, it would be less onerous to replace the *Prince Edward* than to be incessantly condemned to pay heavy compensation to the families of victims...

It was at this juncture that Sâr Dubnotal, sent forth by the tutelary spirit of his former companion in study, the yogi Ranijesti, disembarked at Dieppe with his disciple Rudolph and his medium Annunciata Gianetti.

While traveling, in fact, the master was rarely apart from his principal disciple, and his invariable rule was to take one or other of his mediums with him, in order to be able to proceed with necessary incantations and ward off any danger.

Annunciata was, in truth, an admirable instrument in his service. The Italian woman's marvelous instinct was rarely in default, and, like Sâr Dubnotal's other mediums, she could communicate telepsychically—which is to say, by means of thought—with those designated by her master.

Sâr Dubnotal sought information at the maritime station where the trains deposit and pick up their passengers, and a brief consultation with the personnel permitted him to establish without any difficulty that the ship haunted by the spirit of Ranijesti's Pawn could not be any other than the *Prince Edward*.

In fact, it had been six years since the man had died, and six years that the *Prince Edward* had been struggling against ill-fortune. In any case, no other ship of the English and French companies had been visited by a phantom.

"Rudolph," said the Great Psychagogue to his attentive disciple, "purchase three first class tickets for Newhaven, and tomorrow night, we'll take our berths on the *Prince Edward*."

At eleven o'clock in the evening, before the arrival for passengers from Paris, Sâr Dubnotal went aboard the ferry, stationed at the quay, and asked to speak for a few minutes to Captain Plough, the commandant of the ship, whom he found in the coupé.

Plough, an old sea-dog, was not exactly delighted with his appointment as commandant of the accursed ferry. He was the fifth captain who had taken command on the *Prince Edward* in six years, and if the London-Brighton Company did not immediately put its plan to decommission the fatal ship, he expected to share the fate of his predecessors, who had died at their post.

"Captain," said Sâr Dubnotal, when he had been introduced to him, "I'm one of the passengers leaving tonight for

England. I've learned the troubled history of your ship, and I want to make you a proposition. If I can contrive to put an end to the *Prince Edward*'s tribulations, would you grant me a small favor?"

Nonplussed by that preamble, Plough rolled around between his sun-tanned and clean-shaven cheeks the plug of tobacco that he could no more do without than a pretty woman can do without her adornments. His pale English eyes reflected a certain mistrust. Evidently, he wondered what the man might be who had just handed him a card bearing the bizarre name of Severus el Tebib, whose appearance presented a disconcerting mixture of Orientalism and Occidentalism.

Everything about Sâr Dubnotal's costume—the black frock-coat, the white trousers, the Hindu turban and the tie-pin in the form of a death's-head—was intriguing, but the appearance of the master psychagogue was simultaneously so majestic and so frank, and his courtesy was so exquisite, that Plough assumed a less sullen expression.

"Be more precise, sir," he said.

"I shall," said Sâr Dubnotal, calmly. "Your ship is haunted, is it not?"

"Do you doubt it?"

Without blinking, the psychagogue replied: "No."

"So?"

"So, Captain, what I'm proposing to you is to exorcize the evil spell that weighs upon the *Prince Edward*."

"You?"

"Me."

"How will you do that?"

"That's my business."

"And what's this favor you mentioned?"

"I would like you to stop your ship, Captain, for ten or twelve minutes, at the location of the previous catastrophes."

"Off Beachy Head?"

"Precisely."

Plough shook his head, and launched a long jet of saliva over the side. "Can't be done."

"Why not?"

"Firstly, because it's against regulations. What would the Company say if they knew that I'd stopped there, where I have nothing to do, unnecessarily?"

"Forgive me," said Sâr Dubnotal, softly, more amused than annoyed by the old sea-dog's naivety, "but it's a matter of a scientific experiment whose objective is the deliver you from the perennial danger of death. Far from reprimanding you, the Company will be grateful to you for having granted my wish."

"And what if some misfortune befell you, like the passenger who was found dead on the port paddle-drum?"

"I'm not a skeptic like him," the Sâr observed. "I believe in the supernatural, because I believe in God." Modestly, he added: "I have, in addition, some skill in psychognosis, and I think I will be able to rid the region where its presence is a danger to the *Prince Edward* of the sea-ghost, forever."

Plough shook his head again, but less energetically. Gradually, he was submitting involuntarily to the strange ascendancy that the Sâr was able to obtain over mere mortals. The latter's magnetic gaze, in particular, troubled him. His eyelids fluttered, incapable of sustaining the other's gaze, and he felt his will-power buckling.

"All right, sir," he ended up stammering, unable to understand the strange disturbance that was invading him. "I'll stop the *Prince Edward* at the place you desire."

"Don't forget," said Sâr Dubnotal, darting one final glance at him as sharp as an arrow.

The Great Psychagogue returned to find Rudolph and Annunciata, who had remained in the waiting room of the maritime station, in order to go aboard with them definitively.

At one o'clock in the morning, the ferry, in which a hundred passengers brought by the night express from Paris had taken their places, cast off its moorings and headed for the harbor entrance.

At five o'clock, it arrived off Beachy Head.

There was a singular effervescence on board. Plough had told the ferry's lieutenants about his conversation with the mysterious Severus el Tebib and the news had spread to the passenger cabins as well as the crew quarters.

With one voice, everyone insisted that the captain had been wrong to permit the stranger to persuade him to stop the boat at the scene of so many dramas. They were convinced that the experiment that the so-called El Tebib wanted to carry out would cost him dear, and Plough was criticized for allowing the man to expose himself to an almost certain death.

Plough had let them talk, but remained stubborn.

In truth, in fear that he would not do it of his own free will, Sâr Dubnotal had hypnotized him, with the result that the Great Psychagogue was certain of seeing the *Prince Edward* stop at the precise spot where the sea-ghost usually appeared.

The ferry did indeed stop in response to a curt order given to the chief engineer by telephone. Plough, standing on the bridge, was no longer anything but an automaton obedient to Sâr Dubnotal's will.

On hearing the electric bell ring, passengers and sailors alike, with the exception of the man on watch, shut themselves up in their respective lodgings.

Near the port paddle-drum, the great master of psychognosis, Rudolph, and the medium Annunciata were alone.

La Gianetti, bleak and indifferent, seemed to be dreaming standing up, of God knows what. That astonishing creature never paid any heed to what was happening around her. She only acted on Sâr Dubnotal's orders, as the cogs of a machine only act at the behest of its operator.

But the master and his disciple, leaning over the side, were prodigiously interested in the spectacle offered to their contemplation.

The night was bright, the sea calm. Abruptly, a nebulous form, still imprecise, had surged out of the waves, a few yards from the motionless ferry, and was gliding over the surface of the water towards the hull.

As it came closer, Sâr Dubnotal and Rudolph, as impassive as bronze statues, saw its contours emerge more clearly.

It was a human silhouette enveloped in a veil of white vapors—an extremely vague and transparent silhouette, for the eyes of the observers could see right through it. It seemed to be streaming like the body of a drowned man, and was animated by a kind of mysterious life.

"It really is a soul," murmured Sâr Dubnotal. "Pay attention, Annunciata!" he added, in a loud voice. "Prepare yourself for the incantation."

Since the subject has come up, let us say in passing that, in his *Memoirs*, Sâr Dubnotal indicates countless means by which spirits can be evoked. Among them, he says, there are some who prefer to manifest themselves to the living in a visible and tangible form.

Such was evidently the case with the sea-ghost, and the Great Psychagogue was all the more pleased by that, as he hoped to be able to communicate with it directly.

His hope was not deceived.

After rising slowly into the air, the phantom came down to the deck, close to Sâr Dubnotal and his two aides.

At that short distance, the slightest details of its fluid form were distinguishable. Had it not been for the specific buoyancy and gelatinous transparency of its body, one might have taken it for the envelope of a young man with a bloodless face and a profoundly sad an unhealthy expression.

The tears in his hollow eyes had traced indelible furrows in his fleshless cheeks, and he was uttering a continuous groan: a kind of long gasp of pain.

"Quickly, Annunciata," said the Great Psychagogue. "Ask this soul whether it is willing to communicate with me directly."

The Italian woman, appeared to be suffering less than in other experiments in which she served as a passive subject. Rigid and doubtless frozen, she was not shaking with the disquieting tremor that ordinarily overtook her at the commencement of a trance. It was in an almost natural voice that

34

she repeated the master's question, facing the phantom, whose fleshless features immediately reflected a combination of surprise and joy.

"*Yes*," he pronounced, in a cavernous tone. "*Where is this mortal?*"

"Here," replied Sâr Dubnotal, taking a step toward the apparition.

The spirit examined the psychagogue at length and ended up saying:

"*Ah, I see you! I see you, bold human, who does not fear, any more than Ulysses did, to speak with shades. Be blessed, for it has been a long time that I have been hoping to converse with a carnal being. They flee from me; my presence frightens the crew of this vessel, where I am condemned to do penitence for the sins I committed on Earth. And by virtue of the fear that I inspire in people, especially when my apparition coincides with a storm, I cause further misfortunes—me, racked by remorse, burning to redeem my crimes! Speak, human! Let the sound of your voice caress my hearing once again. Who are you?*"

"I am a psychagogue."

"*A psychagogue?*" repeated the soul in torment, with infinite delight. "*I'm saved!*"

"That depends on your own willingness to oblige," Sâr Dubnotal replied. "If you respond sincerely to my questions, I will not hesitate to set you free. If not, don't count on me for eternal peace."

The phantom raised a diaphanous hand.

"*I swear to reply to you sincerely. Speak!*"

"What is your name?"

"*Roger Lardant, alias Pawn Two.*"

At those words, Rudolph shivered, but Sâr Dubnotal nudged him with his elbow and whispered: "I believe I'm not mistaken. Pay close attention, Rudolph; the revelations of this captive are going to surprise you." Turning back to the phantom, he said: "Pawn Two, you say? What is that bizarre nickname?"

The apparition shuddered.

"*It's the codename that was given to my living person when I committed the grave sin of enrolling in a band of evil-doers. That band operated in Paris and was known as the Chessmen, because it held all the efforts of the police in check. Its leader was called the King, and his principal accomplice, who was also his lover, called herself the Queen. The two lieu-tenants were the Bishops; the two enforcers the Knights, and the rest of us, the subalterns, simple Pawns. Thus, there was Pawn One, Pawn Two, Pawn Three, Pawn Four and so on, to Pawn Eight...*

"*I was Pawn Two. We had numerous lairs, which we called Castles, and the rallying cry was 'Check and mate.'*"

"That's what I thought," murmured Sâr Dubnotal, in his disciple's ear. Do you understand now? The Pawn we're searching for couldn't be Ranijesti's, but they knew one an-other once, and I have no doubt that the leader of the Chess-men—the King, as the phantom says—is none other than Tserpchikopf."

By design, the Great Psychagogue had pronounced the name of the pseudo-boyar loudly, and the start of surprise and cry of terror that the phantom emitted on hearing that name told him that he had not drawn a false conclusion.

"*What! You know that monster, then, O human!*"

"I know him," said Sâr Dubnotal, "and I'm searching for him."

"*Why?*"

"In order to punish him."

"*Ah! The hour of judgment is about to sound for him too, then?*" exclaimed the phantom. "*Avenge me, human! Be piti-less, for it is Tserpchikopf who murdered me, after having perverted me.*

"*I had made his acquaintance by chance, when I was not thinking of evil, but step by step, he dragged me into crime, and when he saw that my conscience was revolting, and that I refused to carry out his orders any longer, he took advantage of the first opportunity to get rid of me.*"

"I know, and I also know that Tserpchikopf found that opportunity six years ago, on the dark and deserted deck of this vessel. Treacherously stabbed by him, you, Roger Lardant, or rather your cadaver, fell into the sea. As you were then in a state of sin, God has inflicted this ordeal upon you, but the honest confession of your sins and the sincerity of your repentance will soon permit you to gain the fortunate spaces where purified souls alone find eternal repose. Before then, however, can you not furnish me with more precise information about the Chessmen?"

"*My death goes back a long way,*" said the phantom, sadly. "*What has happened since then? I don't know. Even when I was alive, I knew very little about the King. Extremely wily and suspicious, incessantly fearful of treason on the part of one of us, Tserpchikopf was not very communicative.*

"*The majority of his acolytes, hypnotized by him, served him blindly. What attracted his hatred to me was that, enjoying a robust constitution, I resisted his magnetic passes and criminal suggestions more easily than my comrades.*"

"Where were the gang's general headquarters then?"

"*At the White Castle, 305 Rue Lamarck, in Montmartre, at the very top of the Butte. Of course, I don't know whether Tserpchikopf still resides at that address. We also had other refuges, like the Black Castle, 133 Rue de l'Assomption, and the Red Castle, 624 Rue de Tolbiac. Perhaps those Castles no longer exist today. In spite of its precautions, the gang had ended up much reduced. Who knows whether a single member still remains?*"

"The King still has at least one Pawn in his service," said Sâr Dubnotal.

"*Which one?*"

"I don't know. All that I know is that I've intercepted a dispatch signed 'Pawn.'"

"*Just Pawn?*"

"Yes."

"*Then the signatory must be Pawn One, whose real name is Gustave Panloude.*"

"Write down that name, as well as the addresses the phantom gave me," Sâr Dubnotal said to Rudolph. Then he asked his astral informant: "Is that all the information you have about Tserpchikopf and his accomplices?"

"*Alas, yes*," sighed the spirit. "*However, I can add that all the members of the gang bear an emblematic tattoo on their right arm representing their rank within the organization—a king, a bishop, a knight, a pawn or a queen.*"

"Good," said Sâr Dubnotal. "Roger Lardant, you have sinned primarily by virtue of imprudence. May your time in Purgatory soon finish, and may God receive you in the bosom of his mercy!"

"*Amen!*" murmured the phantom, whose immaterial form dissipated almost immediately.

For a moment, Sâr Dubnotal and Rudolph looked at one another without speaking.

"So, Master," said the young man, finally, carried away by enthusiasm, "you foresaw everything that Roger Lardant has just told us?"

"Foresaw isn't the right word, Rudolph, but I expected something of the sort We still only possess superficial information about Tserpchikopf, Gustave Panloude and the rest, but I hope those few clues might suffice..." He turned toward the bridge. "Captain!" he shouted. "Start the ferry moving again."

The *Prince Edward*'s paddle-wheels began turning again, in the direction of Newhaven.

Plough, woken up from is hypnotic sleep, did not remember anything. His lieutenants refreshed his memory, and the old captain shivered as he thought about the danger that Severus el Tebib had run on his ship.

However, as the *Prince Edward* had emerged from the adventure safe and sound, he consigned the facts to the ship's log without comment.

Sâr Dubnotal assured him that the ferry would no longer be haunted by the sea-ghost—and, in fact, we can say right now that the specter of Roger Lardant was never seen on board again, and that the *Prince Edward* ceased to be the victim of inexplicable accidents.

3. In which Sâr Dubnotal's Power is affirmed with increasing clarity

Before disembarking at Newhaven, where the *Prince Edward* was due to arrive at six o'clock in the morning, the Great Psychagogue, taking advantage of the final sixty minutes of the crossing, said to Captain Plough:

"Captain, I would like to have the free use of the first class lounge for a quarter of an hour. Is that possible?"

"Certainly," the officer hastened to reply. "With pleasure, sir."

"Let's understand one another," Sâr Dubnotal specified. "It's necessary that no one disturbs me during that quarter of an hour. I don't like anyone interfering with my affairs when I need to be tranquil."

"Have no fear. I'll give orders in consequence, and no one will disturb you."

"I'm relying on you, Captain."

With that, the Sâr summoned Rudolph and Annunciata, and then went to enclose himself with them in the lounge, which the Captain had just cleared.

What happened then?

No one on board ever knew, because no one dared infringe the orders of the mysterious individual who had disenchanted the ferry. But if someone more indiscreet than the rest had violated the order and darted a glance through the windows of the lounge, he would have witnessed an extraordinary scene.

Standing on a banquette, at the foot of which the two psychagogues were positioned, Annunciata Gianetti, her eyes closed and her arms crossed, appeared to be asleep.

In reality, she was not asleep, or if she was, she was dreaming, for her lips, agitated by a continual tremor, muttering strange fragmentary phrases.

Those incoherent words, stammered rather than articulated by the Italian woman, were listened to gravely and almost religiously, by her companions, and, far from causing them any surprise, seemed to be producing an impression of profound satisfaction and relief.

From time to time, Annunciata stopped speaking. But then Sâr Dubnotal extended a hand toward her, with a rhythmic hypnotic gesture, seeming to be unleashing subtle effluvia and, looking at her with his piercing gaze, only interrupted that singular operation when the chopped voice of his medium troubled the silence of the room again.

What, then, was happening?

On penetrating into the lounge, the Great Psychagogue had said to the Italian woman:

"Annunciata, I have need of your services again."

"I am at your disposal, Master."

"Fifty minutes from now, we'll be disembarking in Newhaven, but I fear that at that early hour, the telegraph won't be functioning yet, and I don't want to lose any time in putting my investigators on the track of Pawn One, Tserpchikopf's accomplice."

"I understand, Master. You want me to transmit your secret orders to your three agents telepsychically."

"Exactly."

The Italian woman uttered a resigned sigh.

"Put me to sleep, Master," she murmured.

Sâr Dubnotal did not hesitate. Having his medium climb on to one of the lounge's banquettes, he placed himself in front of her and set about hypnotizing her. A few rapid passes and flashes of his magnetic eyes permitted him to achieve his goal.

Annunciata extended her arms, her eyelids drooped, and she no longer moved.

"Are you asleep?" asked the Sâr.

"Yes."

"Can you see me?"

"Yes," said the subject, although her eyes were closed.

"It's necessary that you no longer see me. It's necessary that you only see my investigators."

"I see them, Master."

"Where are they?"

"In the reading room of your house in the Champs-Élysées."

Sâr Dubnotal turned to his disciple. "The worthy fellows are following their orders," he murmured. "I told them not to leave the house tonight, not to go to bed, and to be ready for my telepsychic message. It's Frank, this time, who'll serve as the antenna. Warn him, Annunciata!"

Since the discovery of wireless telegraphy and telephony, it is easier to understand how thought transmission can operate. In the same way that electrical waves spread out through space and are captured by special apparatus, the psychic fluid, launched by the marvelous instrument that is the human brain, can cross enormous distances and be captured by an identical instrument. It is sufficient to achieve that for the two "antennae," as Sâr Dubnotal called them, in speaking of his operators, to be capable, one of emitting a sufficiently powerful current and the other of registering accurately and replying if necessary.

The Italian woman and the Sâr's investigators were admirable psychic antennae and excellent at the human telephony that has no other inconvenience than being extremely tiring for those who undertake it.

Without needing to have the order repeated, *La* Gianetti uttered a strident cry:

"Frank…! Frank…! It's me, Annunciata!"

"Can he hear?" the Sâr interrogated, after a few seconds.

"Yes," stammered the medium. "He can hear me and is replying to me."

"Good. Rudolph, reread in a loud voice the information given to us by Roger Lardant, alias Pawn Two, regarding his former colleague in the Chessmen, Gustave Panloude, alias Pawn One—the information you recorded in your notebook."

The young man swiftly took his notebook from his pocket and did as his master had asked.

"Perfect," said Sâr Dubnotal. "To you now, Annunciata. The communication is well established, isn't it?"

"Yes, Master."

"Well, repeat to Frank what you've just heard, and add that my keenest desire is that he and his comrades immediately set out on campaign again, armed with this information, and don't rest until they've picked up the trail of Gustave Panloude."

The medium obeyed, and it was then that, fixed in her singular attitude, she began to utter words seemingly devoid of meaning, and which, if intercepted by indiscreet ears, would have told them nothing.

"Frank...! Frank...!" she stammered. "Yes... ferry... at sea... *Prince Edward*... Newhaven."

"..."

"...No, no! That's not it... Pawn One... not dead... alive, very much alive!"

"..."

"The Chessmen... He's the King..."

"..."

"*Him*, of course...! Tserpchikopf!"

"..."

"No, only Pawn One... Gustave Panloude... The Castles..."

"..."

"Several... White Castle... Black Castle... Red Castle..."

"..."

"The White, general headquarters..."

"..."

"305 Rue Lamarck!

"..."

"Black Castle, 133 Rue de l'Assomption... Red Castle, 624 Rue de Tolbiac..."

"…"

"Immediately... Immediately!"

"…"

"Check and mate."

"…"

"The Bishops, his lieutenants... The Knights, his enforcers..."

"…"

"Yes, that's all… for the moment."

"…"

"Pardon me... I forgot..."

"…"

"Tattoos... Right arm…emblems of title…"

"…"

"That, I don't know... Wait!"

With those last words, Annunciata turned her closed eyes toward Sâr Dubnotal.

"Is that all?" the latter asked.

"Not quite, Master… Frank is asking when you're returning to Paris."

"Tomorrow morning. Tell him that he and his comrades will have to give me a report on their new investigations immediately."

"Understood," murmured the medium, who transmitted the end of the telepsychic message and fell silent.

The Great Psychagogue, observing that she was exhausted, hastened to extract her from the hypnotic sleep by passing his thumbs back and forth over her eyebrows.

Woken up, Annunciata darted a fearful glance around, surprised to find herself standing on the banquette, no longer remembering what had happened.

Her master reassured her briefly, while Rudolph helped her to get down from her perch—for she was now so weak that her legs almost refused to carry her.

When she had recovered from the shock, Sâr Dubnotal said:

"The quarter of an hour's respite for which I asked Captain Plough is almost up, and the *Prince Edward* ought to be ready to enter port. Come, my children."

He was not mistaken; twenty minutes later, the ferry went into Newhaven docks and moored against the quay.

Sailors and passengers crowded around the master and his aides to congratulate them. Sweeping the aide with an imperious gesture, Sâr Dubnotal leapt on to the quay, followed by Rudolph and *La* Gianetti.

A few minutes later, all three went into the nearest hotel, from which they did not emerge until the evening, to re-embark for Dieppe.

4. The Great Psychagogue's terrestrial sleuths go into action

That night, Otto, Frank and Fréjus, Sâr Dubnotal's three investigators, had been on the alert in his reading room, in accordance with his instructions.

Having nothing better to do to while away their insipid sentry duty, they were discussing the relative merits of the secret polices of Berlin, London and Paris, in the service of which they had been before entering that of the Great Psychagogue.

Otto, a vigorous and thickest young Teuton, claimed that Germany was the cradle of the world's most skilful policemen.

Frank, a pure-blooded Englishman, energetic and massively build, riposted that Scotland Yard, London's famous police force, had never been and never would be equaled.

As for Fréjus, a jovial and witty little Frenchman, he brought his two friends no accord by telling them that they were wrong to bicker, because the Parisian Sûreté, thank God, was worth more on its own than the other two organizations put together.

Whatever they said, though, deep down, they were beginning to have serious doubts about their professional capabilities, because they had been searching Paris for three months trying to find Pawn, the signatory of the dispatch sent to Tserpchikopf, and had always came back empty-handed. They were beginning to despair of obtaining a result.

Pawn remained undiscoverable.

It was five o'clock in the morning when Frank, who was yawning as if trying to dislocate his jaws and stretching as if trying to break his bones, uttered an exclamation.

"By Jove!"

At the same time, he stood up in a single motion, put his hands to his forehead and struck the pose of a man who has just been afflicted with a sudden attack of migraine.

"What? What's the matter?" asked his colleagues, very surprised.

Instead of replying, the Englishman uttered a guttural appeal, and his arms, coming apart, remained extended.

"Annunciata…! Annunciata…!"

It required no more for Otto and Fréjus, both initiates in the practice of telepsychy, to understand what was happening. They knew that, in order to transmit his orders from one end of the world to the other, Sâr Dubnotal had no need of the telegraph or the telephone, and that he by-passed them whenever it was necessary, or if it was a matter of grave urgency. Furthermore, they had both served the master as psychic antennae themselves in order to be informed automatically of what he wanted to say to them.

But that experiment was extremely wearing, they knew, and Sâr Dubnotal rarely had recourse to it because he did not want to squander the psychic reserves of his mediums or inflict unnecessary fatigue on his aides.

So, while Frank remained in automatic conversation with Annunciata, their anxiety and heir perplexity were extreme.

Obviously, something grave must had occurred since Sâr Dubnotal's departure with his disciple and the medium.

What? The Frenchman and the German were still reduced to conjectures in that regard.

Frank was speaking in such a jerky voice, and the questions he was asking the invisible Annunciata were so bizarre
that his friends did not understand a single word of the strange
exchange of which hey only intercepted one half.

However, a name that returned frequently to their
friend's lips—the name Pawn—informed them that the
telepsychic message that Frank as receiving had to do with the
Tserpchikopf affair.

"Are we ever going to be finished with that accursed
Slav?" whispered Fréjus, in Otto's ear.

"Just as long as nothing happens to the master," sighed
the German

"Oh, that's the least of my concerns," the Frenchman replied, confidently. "The master is above the enterprises of a
Tserpchikopf, even if he is the King of Hypnotizers! But listen, Otto—Frank is taking about Pawn again."

It was true. "Pawn One?" said the Englishman, surprised.
"Are you sure, Annunciata? Why One?"

"..."

"Oh—right! I understand now," Frank continued, after a
pause during which he seemed to be lending an ear to his distant correspondent.

"There's more than one Pawn, isn't there? Pawn One,
Pawn Two, Pawn Three… the whole sequence?"

"What is he saying?" Otto and Fréjus wondered, increasingly intrigued.

"Pawn Two's dead, Annunciata?"

"..."

"And Pawn One is alive?"

"..."

"What are you saying?"

"..."

"Uh oh! Damn! Do we have to track him too?"

"..."

"Castles? How many?"

46

"..."

"Which is the main one?"

"..."

"Good—the address?"

"..."

"And the others?"

"..."

"Right! But when?"

"..."

"There's a password? What?"

"..."

"The Bishops... the Knight...yes... but who are they?"

"..."

"That's all? No sign of identification?"

"..."

"Ah-ha! That's useful to know. And when shall we have the pleasure of seeing you again, Annunciata?"

"..."

There as a fairly long silence, and then Frank exclaimed:

"All right—I understand!"

"Well, you're lucky then!" said Fréjus, seeing his friend return to reality. "Personally, I don't understand any of it. Pawn One, Pawn Two, Pawn Three... the Castles, the Bishops, the Knights, the King, and God knows what else. Check and mate? Well, Frank, are you playing a game of chess with Annunciata, or having a serious conversation?"

Frank began to laugh. He had recovered from his emotion and retained a very clear memory of the enigmatic conversation he had just had with Annunciata Gianetti.

"No," he said, "I wasn't playing chess, but it won't be long before we're playing it with Tserpchikopf, unless I'm much mistaken."

And in a single breath, he told his amazed colleagues what Annunciata had just explained to him about the Chessmen.

"Apart from Tserpchikopf, who's the King," he said. "the gang consists—or, rather, consisted, for the facts date

47

back six years—of a woman, the Queen, two lieutenants the Bishops, two enforcers, the Knights, and eight men, the Pawns, numbered one to eight: Pawn One, Pawn Two, Pawn Three, and so on.

"It had headquarters in houses called Castles, sited respectively firstly, the White Castle at 305 Rue Lamarck; secondly, the Blue Castle at 133 Rue de l'Assomption; and thirdly, the Red Castle at 624 Rue de Tolbiac.

"The signatory of the dispatch is named Gustave Panloude, alias Pawn One. Each of the bandits has a tattoo on his right arm, the emblem of his title: king, queen, bishop, knight or pawn. Finally, their rallying cry is 'Check and mate!'

"Do you understand now?" the Englishman concluded.

"Of course," said Fréjus. "Unless we're stupid, it's clear enough for us to be edified henceforth. So, we have to get back to searching or this lascar?"

"Right away," said Frank. "That's the master's order."

"The order will be carried out wholeheartedly," said the Frenchman, enthusiastically. "Oh, we'll make that scoundrel Pawn One run! But this time, I think, we'll get him. Scotland Yard, eh?"

"Yes, by Jove!"

"When do we leave?" asked Otto.

"Right now!" Frank replied. "If we want to conserve the master's esteem, we need to deliver at least one of the rogues to him tomorrow evening, when he gets back."

"I'll go to Montmartre, to the Rue Lamarck," said Fréjus, who generally directed the trio's operations in France, as Frank took charge of them in England and Otto in Germany. You, Scotland Yard, go to the Rue de l'Assomption, in Auteuil, and you, Otto, to the Rue de Tolbiac at the Glacière.

"We'll meet up at midday on the Place du Châtelet. For the moment, it's just a matter of knowing whether these Castles still exist, and a few minutes' discreet conversation with the neighbors will suffice to inform us of that. If one of the lairs still contains a few members of the Chessmen, we'll make arrangements subsequently to surround all three. Until then, comrades!"

With that, the three investigators left the Champs-Élysées and separated, leaving the house under the guard of the giant Naini, the most devoted of servants.

At the agreed time, the three sleuths met up again on the Place du Châtelet, on the bitumen island, near the tramway office of the Montrouge-Gare de l'Est line. Their crestfallen expressions did not bode anything good.

"Well, Scotland Yard?" said Fréjus, addressing Frank.

"Damn these accursed Chessmen!" cursed the Englishman. "Do you know what I found at 133 Rue de l'Assomption?"

"How should I know?"

"An immense investment property, unfinished! The old building was demolished last year and a new one is being constructed to replace it. I interrogated the neighbors, but all they were able to tell me is that the tenants of the old block had moved long before the owner thought of demolishing it. Those tenants, a man and a woman, were named Dogson, it appears. When they chanced to stay at home, individuals of passably suspect appearance visited them. After their departure, strongly reminiscent of a flight, there was a police raid, the precise reason for which the neighbors never found out."

"At least that concords with the information the master gave us," said Fréjus. "That couple, Frank, were surely none other than Tserpchikopf and his mistress, the Queen of the Chessmen. Let's see whether Berlin has had any better luck than you..."

Berlin, otherwise known as Otto, shook his head.

"No," he said. "At 624 Rue de Tolbiac, I hit a brick wall. The house is falling down and hasn't been inhabited for six years. There, too, there was a police search at that time, and the tenants, a childless household named Lapostolle had decamped at the double."

"Lapostolle... Tserpchikopf again," said Fréjus, irritated. "And it was also Tserpchikopf who must have lived at 305 Rue Lamarck under the false name of Tommy Sicklodge. There, the neighbors remember a scandal of which the house was the theater five or six years ago. One night, number 305 was surrounded by the police, but it was too late. Tommy Sicklodge and the beautiful young woman who passed for his legitimate wife had escaped via a hidden door. The so-called aristocrats were involved, it appears, in fabricating fake bank-notes, and the police found proof of it there.

"In sum," Fréjus went on, after a few moments' reflection, "we're no further forward than we were this morning. The Castles really existed, but the Chessmen had a final run-in with the police and transported their hearth and home else-where. Perhaps it even dispersed after the capture of some of its members."

"What if you were to go to the Sûreté?" suggested Frank. "Your former colleagues would doubtless like nothing better than to clear up any uncertainty."

"I've already thought of that," replied the ex-member of the secret brigade of Paris. "But what good would it do us? If the law has sent a few Chessmen to prison, Tserpchikopf and Gustave Panloude are still free; we already have proof of that. Those are the ones we have to find and capture..."

Increasingly downhearted, the three friends went back on foot to the Champs-Élysées via the quays of the Seine. What was Sâr Dubnotal going to say the next day on learning the pitiful result of their investigations?

A crowd formed at the entrance to the Pont de la Concorde by an accumulation of idlers extracted them from their sullen reflections. Out of professional habit, they mingled with the curiosity-seekers, who were forming a circle around a railway delivery truck laden with crates and voluminous trunks. The horse drawing it had just collapsed.

The driver was trying to get the poor animal back on its feet, which was striving to do so itself. White with frost, the pavement was slipping away beneath it and its hooves kept skidding. Blows of the whip, the oaths of the furious man, cries of encouragement from the crowd, and naïve or facetious advice from experts or humorists, all failed to work.

"Let's go," said Otto, uninterested in the scene.

Frank was about to follow him when Fréjus stopped them both, grabbing their arms.

"Oh-ho!" he murmured. "What do I see there? Look, Otto, and you to, Frank—there, on those trunks in the truck: that sign!"

Frank and Otto hoisted themselves up on tiptoe in order to dart a glance over the shoulders of the idlers. Not seeing anything in particular, however, they turned to look at Fréjus in surprise.

"What? At least be precise..."

"Those black trunks..."

"So what?"

"You don't see it?"

"In truth, no."

"You don't see that they all carry a white circle with the figure 1 painted in red?"

"Yes, but what's extraordinary about that?" asked Otto.

"Listen, my old friends," said the Frenchman, mysteriously. "We've been arguing for a long time to determine which of the three of us has the most flair. Well, I'm about to prove to you by A plus B that the French Sûreté has the edge over all the other police forces of the globe."

"Prove it!" said the German and the Englishman, tranquilly.

"Patience," murmured Fréjus, with a wink. "Firstly, Otto, you're as strong as an ox—give me the pleasure of helping that driver to get out of difficulty."

"You want me to lift up his horse?"

"Precisely."

"All right!" said Otto, cheerfully.

He cut through the crowd of idlers, got hold of the animal's bridle and, thanks to his uncommon strength, succeeded after a few attempts in getting the animal to its feet.

Fréjus had slipped through behind him.

"Bravo!" he cried. "Hey, driver, he's strong, isn't he? By the way, you'd better go back to the stables—your old nag's got doddery knees."

"I'll go back after I've taken my load to the Gare de Lyon and not before," grumbled the man, more annoyed than grateful for Otto's exploit. "Too bad for the dirty beast, who never misses an opportunity to fall over."

"As you please," said Fréjus, simply. Then he called his friends and, spotting a cab, hailed it.

"Gare de Lyon, Coachman! Take it easy—no hurry."

"Right!" said Otto and Frank, after he had invited them to in him in the fiacre. "What's got into you? Why are we going to the Gare de Lyon?"

Fréjus laughed sardonically. "If I'm not mistaken, London and Berlin will be well and truly sunk today."

"How?"

"You'll see."

The fiacre rolled smoothly over the icy roadway. As Fréjus appeared, still determined not to explain himself, his companions turned up the collars of their overcoats and huddled in the corners of the cab, feeling chilly.

Otto and Frank were quite intrigued. They strongly suspected that there must be some connection between the Tserpchikopf affair and their present cab ride, but it escaped them completely. Nevertheless, by dint of reflection, they ended up conceiving a suspicion.

"I think I can guess your plan, Fréjus," said Otto.

"Me too," said the Englishman.

It was the Frenchman's turn to be astonished. "Bah!"

"Yes, Fréjus," Otto went on. "Frank and I don't have your alert intelligence, but you'll admit that that doesn't prevent us acquitting ourselves honorably on occasion. You proceed by inspiration, while we need to reflect, but in the final count, the result is the same."

"What's my plan, then?"

"You want to know who owns the black trunks."

"And to know why they all carry that mysterious white circle with the figure 1 painted in red," added Frank.

"Pardon me," said the Frenchman, laughing. "You're getting warmer but you're not there yet. The truth is that I already think I have the key to the enigma, and I'm simply going to make sure that my hypothesis isn't erroneous."

"You believe you already know who owns the trunks?" exclaimed Otto.

"*Ja, Mein Herr.*"

"And you think you know why they're ornamented with that cabalistic symbol?" said Frank.

"*Yes, sir,*" said Fréjus, in English.

"Damn!" muttered the Englishman and the German, in unison, resuming their reflection.

Fréjus, amused, winked at them maliciously and repeated: "Sunk, Berlin and Scotland Yard!"

"Not yet!" said Frank, suddenly, raising his head proudly. "This time, old chap, I have it!"

"Me too!" exclaimed the German.

"Let's hear it!" mocked Fréjus.

"It's obvious," said Frank. "The owner of the trunks is, or ought to be, an accomplice of Tserpchikopf."

"And the cabalistic symbol designed on the trunks," said Otto, "the white circle with the figure 1, means Pawn One."

The Frenchman shook his companions' hands. "Indeed," he agreed. "At least, that's my thinking, and I'm glad to see that you share it, comrades. Decidedly, you're almost my equals." He burst out laughing, and finished: "But admit that, without me, you'd never have thought of picking up this trail—in consequence of which, the Sûreté wins."

"This time," said Otto, cheerfully.

"By way of revenge," said Frank. "And let's not forget, Fréjus, that we might be mistaken. What will you look like if the trail is false?"

"We'll soon know," said Fréjus, with a grimace of anxiety. "Evidently, that would be a great disappointment for me. My opinion is that hazard has served us well and that it won't take us long to feel the collar of Pawn One—which is to say, Gustave Panloude."

"That's where I recognize my Frenchman," said Otto, "and where I'm his superior. Instead of seeing things as they are, he's already carried away, and if we let him go, his impetuosity will lead us to do something stupid."

"What's that?" asked Fréjus.

"You want to capture Gustave Panloude right away?"

"Of course!"

"And let Tserpchikopf escape?"

"Damn it!" Fréjus swore. "That's right. It would be better to follow the one until he leads us to the other."

"If we really are dealing with Gustave Panloude," Otto remarked, "of which we're not yet sure, it's probable that he's going on a journey. He's having his bags taken to the Gare de Lyon by the delivery truck and he's on his way there, or will go there, directly. The first thing to do, therefore, is make sure of his identity. Until then Frank and Fréjus, no more arguing!"

"Otto's right," said Frank, "Let's first establish his identity."

"That's easy," exclaimed the petulant Fréjus. "When the owner of the trunks comes to reclaim them, we'll pronounce either Gustave Panloude's name or his codename behind him, and if he turns around, we can conclude that he and the Pawn really are one and the same."

"Undoubtedly," said the sage Otto, "but he'll be alerted, and following him will become impossible."

"Wait!" said Frank. "I think we can get around that difficulty."

"How?" asked Fréjus.

"You're too curious, my friend," said he Englishman. "Just now you had to have your ear pulled before you'd explain. It's my turn to affect a mysterious air. Let me handle it. I'll guarantee to get us out of difficulty without the man with the trunks suspecting anything."

Shortly thereafter, the fiacre deposited the three investigators in the courtyard of the Gare de Lyon. They strolled back and forth while awaiting the arrival of the delivery truck, which only got here half an hour later.

The truck pulled up at the sidewalk outside the hall, in front of the dispatch section, and a correctly-dressed individual with the brim of a felt hat pulled down over his eyes and a warm fur coat, with a dark moustache and beard, neither fat nor thin, of medium height and wearing a pair of dark glasses, came out of the waiting room and gave orders to the driver of the truck and the station porters who had come to unload it.

"Hurry up," he said to them. "I'm taking the four-ten express. It's three-fifty, and all this luggage has to be checked in."

"Do you have your ticket?" asked one of the employees.

"Not yet, because I was wondering whether my luggage was going to arrive in time. I'll go get it and I'll join you in the registration office."

With that, the man with the dark glasses went into the hall, where Sâr Dubnotal's investigators, who were lurking not far away and had overheard the conversation, hastened to follow him.

The man joined the queue of travelers at the ticket-window.

"This is the moment to try my experiment," Frank whispered in his companions' ears. "Let's get a little closer to the fellow—and whatever happens, stay calm, and don't give the game away."

Frank stopped behind the suspect individual and abruptly, in a hoarse voice with a strong British accent, said to Fréjus: "Oh, I regret not having been able to finish the game, Monsieur, for you can be sure that it would soon have been check and mate."

The man in the queue could have received an electric shock and would not have started more violently. He pivoted on his heels abruptly, and darted a glance from behind his dark glasses in the direction of the Englishman. But Frank impassively lit a pipe he had taken from his pocket, while Fréjus, who had understood what his friend wanted to do, replied politely: "It's quite possible, after all, Monsieur, for you're very good at chess."

Reassured by the apparent indifference of the trio, the individual hastened to buy his ticket, and the sleuths were able to hear him ask for a direct ticket from Paris to Tunis.

"Come on!" said Frank, in a low voice, to Otto and Fréjus.

They drew away tranquilly, talking about this and that, but when they reached the external veranda, their feigned placidity gave way to an extreme excitement.

"It's him!" Frank said, breathlessly. "It's Gustave Panloude, alias Pawn One. I'm certain of it now."

"What now?" asked Otto.

"We follow him, of course," said Fréjus.

"Gently!" said Frank. "He's going all the way to Tunis!"

"He could go to the Devil and I'd stay with him."

"What about the Master?" said he Englishman. "We need to inform him. The Marseilles express is leaving in a few minutes."

"Have I time to send a telegram to Naini?"

"Yes, but hurry," said Otto. "We need to disguise ourselves before getting tickets. Run to the station office and send a *pneumatique* [7] to the Master. Naini will receive it and give it to him as soon as he arrives. He'll be able to send us telegraphic instructions either at Marseilles or Tunis, *poste restante*."

"I'll be back in a minute," said Fréjus, hurrying off.

Shortly afterwards he rejoined his friends, who were waiting for him anxiously. "The *pneumatique*'s gone," he said.

The three sleuths plunged into the station's public convenience, from which they emerged almost immediately, completely transformed. They had exchanged their overcoats,

---

[7] Pneumatic post was a system designed to deliver express letters through pressurized air tubes. A major network of tubes was in use in Paris until 1984, when the service was discontinued.

replaced their bowler hats with caps taken from their pockets, and made up their faces. Frank had put on a pince-nez, Otto a monocle, and Fréjus spectacles, which rendered them unrecognizable.

At four-ten, they took their seats in a corridor carriage of the Marseilles express, which released a whistle-blast and pulled out punctually.

In the next compartment, the presumed accomplice of Tserpchikopf, far from suspecting their presence, was placidly reading a newspaper.

Without appearing to do anything, Otto, Frank and Fréjus made arrangements to take turns keeping him under surveillance.

If he was Pawn One, the wretch had every chance of falling imminently into Sâr Dubnotal's net.

5. A Disturbing Disappearance

"Anything new, Naini?" asked Sâr Dubnotal of the gigantic Hindu, who had come to meet him at the Gare Saint-Lazare, summoned by a telegram sent the previous evening from Newhaven.

"Yes, Sahib," replied the faithful servant, respectfully, holding out the blue *pneumatique* to the psychagogue. "Yesterday morning, your agents left the house, and I received this at the Champs-Élysées in the evening."

Sâr Dubnotal immediately opened the message that Fréjus had went to the house and read:

Master,
As a result of circumstances it would take too long to relate here, Otto, Frank and I have acquired the conviction that a certain individual followed by us is none other than a member of the Chessmen.

In our opinion, he must be Gustave Panloude, alias Pawn One, for his luggage bears a conventional sign representing a pawn marked with that number.

The individual having bought a ticket to Tunis and a seat in the four-ten Paris-Marseilles express, we decided to go with him.

It's quite possible that he is going to join Tserpchikopf, and that it's in Tunis that the latter has taken refuge.

We shall arrive in Marseilles at midnight. Tomorrow's ferry will not raise anchor until four p.m., so you will have time to end us a telegram poste restante.

In any case, you will still have the resource of sending a dispatch to Tunis, where it will arrive before us.

Respects,

Fréjus.

The Great Psychagogue slipped the sheet of paper into the pocket of his frock-coat without a muscle in his face having quivered.

"My coupé?" he enquired, simply.

"It's waiting outside in the courtyard," Naini replied.

Sâr Dubnotal turned to Rudolph and Annunciata, who were with him, and said:

"We're going to call in at the Champs-Élysées, but we'll only stay there long enough to change clothes. After that, we'll go the Gare de Lyon, where we'll take a train for Marseilles."

"Very well, Master," said the disciple, while Annunciata Gianetti, as indifferent as usual, followed on the heels of the two psychagogues. They went through the lobby, down the staircase and, guided by Naini, did not take long to find heir carriage.

Joseph, Sâr Dubnotal's coachman, helped Naini up on to the seat beside him, and then whipped his horses, with a supercilious glance at the idlers who stopped, petrified by the sight of the magnificent horses, the escutcheoned coupé and above all, the "Nabob's" majestic and colossal Hindu. The title in question, employed at hazard, was applied to Sâr Dubnotal, whose silhouette the idlers perceived inside the vehicle.

On the way, the Great Psychagogue stopped at a post office in order to send a dispatch to his investigators, whom he simply instructed to be prudent and to wait for him to arrive in Tunis before attempting anything against Tserpchikopf and his associates.

Sâr Dubnotal hoped to leave Marseilles the next day, only twenty-four hours behind his aides. Unfortunately, although the first part of his journey was briskly completed and he arrived in Marseilles with Rudolph and Annunciata that same evening, it was all the more disappointing to learn in the later city that the next ferry to Tunis would only be sailing two days later, the Compagnie Fraissinous only maintaining a thrice-weekly service between the two ports.

"That inconvenience is regrettable, Rudolph," he said. "We'll try to charter a private steamship tomorrow, because if we let him get too far ahead of us, I'm afraid that Gustave Panloude might give our investigators the slip and Tserpchikopf, alerted by him, might contrive some devilry of his own against them."

"Fréjus isn't mistaken, Master? The man he's following really is Pawn One?"

"I presume so. My sleuths' flair is too subtle for them to make such a gross error. The only thing I fear is that Gustave Panloude might catch wind of the trap. The Chess King is a terrible adversary, Rudolph!"

"No match for you, though, Master. You'll soon have him checked and mated."

"I'm counting on it, but until I can engage him in the end game, he has a margin of operation. The powerful hypnotist is also an unscrupulous rogue. If I'd foreseen my investigators' sudden departure, I'd have rendered them resistant to the influence of magnetic waves with a few counter-passes. Remember the two policemen in London that Tserpchikopf hypnotized, and his bold escape!"

"Otto, Frank and Fréjus are prudent, Master; they'll use extreme precaution to avoid giving themselves away."

"I know. The audacity and bright genius of the French, the sane and cold reasoning of the English, and the profound sagacity of the Germans are in my service in their three persons. But once again, Rudolph, they're dealing with Tserpchikopf, and that enigmatic Slav, whom we can already call the 'Bloody Hypnotist,' is probably the most dreaded criminal of our era. There's not a minute to lose in catching up with them—and if possible, as I say, I'll charter a special steamer."

The next day, Sâr Dubnotal set forth in search of a fast ship that could take him to Tunis—but he did not find one, even though he was unconcerned about the expense.

It would doubtless have been easy for him to vanquish the resistance of the ship-owners by his habitual means, but his respect for legality, when there was no urgency, prevented him from doing so.

Thus, he resigned himself to being patient for another day and taking the regular ferry departing the following day.

The crossing was effected in good conditions.

As he had asked his investigators to meet him at the ferry dock, Sâr Dubnotal hoped to find them there on reaching Tunis. His disappointment, and Rudolph's, were considerable when they did not see Otto, Frank or Fréjus among the crowd gathered on the quay to watch the boat come in.

Rudolph, Annunciata and he waited in vain for an hour. Still not seeing anyone, they hired a cab with the aim of going in search of their aides.

"We'll go from one hotel to another until we've located them," Sâr Dubnotal decided.

The comfortable and decent hotels where the three sleuths might have booked rooms were not very numerous, in spite of the size of the city. Piloted by the coachman, Sâr Dubnotal and Rudolph presented themselves at each in turn, and ended up finding the one in which Otto, Frank and Fréjus had registered, having no motive for falsifying their names, since none of the members of the Chessmen, including Tserpchikopf, knew them.

That did not get Sâr Dubnotal any further forward, however, because all the proprietor of the Marabout Bleu—that was the name of the hotel, which was on the Avenue de la Marine—could tell them was that the three investigators had only made a brief appearance in his establishment.

"I don't know what that signifies," he added. "The gentlemen, who arrived by ferry the day before yesterday, booked three rooms and left a deposit. There were only two of them then, but the third came to join them at lunch time. After their meal, all three of them went out, having promised to be back for dinner. Well, I'm still waiting for them!"

Without letting his extreme anxiety show, Sâr Dubnotal booked three more rooms for Rudolph, Annunciata and himself, using the name of "Severus el Tebib," paid for the dinner that his aides had ordered the previous evening without doing honor to it, and then retired to his room, after having asked the hotelier to bring him the previous week's newspapers.

"Rudolph," he said to his disciple, who had come to join him in response to his instruction, "all this is unclear, and I confess that I fear the worst eventualities. This sudden disappearance of my investigators is strange. The fact that only two of them came to the hotel at first leads me to think that the third must have been following Gustave Panloude in the meantime. Since their comrade rejoined them shortly afterwards, he must already have known where Pawn One was staying.

"Evidently, his mission had gone straightforwardly, as all three had lunch tranquilly, which they wouldn't have done if any complication had emerged. In that case, they would have renounced the delights of the Marabout Bleu and, content to swallow a few of my tonic pastilles, would have been in haste to leave.

"On the other hand, they expected to come back to the hotel that evening, since they ordered dinner. We must conclude, therefore, either that their quarry left Tunis during the

61

afternoon and that they followed him—a hypothesis that I reject *a priori*, because in that case they wouldn't have neglected to leave one of them behind in order to inform me—or that something bad has happened to them."

At that moment, the newspapers requested by the Sâr arrived.

The Great Psychagogue picked them up swiftly and murmured:

"One thing that occurs to me, Rudolph, is that if Tserpchikopf really is in Tunis, he might have resumed, with the aid of a new Azilis, the experiments in pseudo-magic in which he was indulging in London when I unmasked him. So, I'm going to scan the 'Theaters and Concerts' section of the local papers to see whether any so-called yogi is exploiting the credulity of the worthy Tunisians. If there is, there's every chance that the yogi in question is our friend Tserpchikopf, concealed under a new pseudonym."

Rudolph took half of the stack, and the two psychagogues set to work, riffling through the papers, attentively reading everything relating to local attractions, not forgetting the news items, in which Sâr Dubnotal often found clues precious to the progress of his enquiries.

Suddenly, the young man uttered an expression of surprise.

"Oh, Master, read this article," he said, holding out a copy of the *Dépêche Tunisienne* to Sâr Dubnotal.

Sâr Dubnotal cast his eyes over the indicated column, and read:

MACABRE JOKE

Yesterday evening, a decrepit and abandoned building in the Rue Bab-Souika in the indigenous quarter was the theater of a farce of more than dubious taste.

At eight o'clock, a child, livid with fright and covered with sweat, literally ran into the legs of a policeman on duty on the Place Bab-Souika. Interrogated as to the cause of his hectic flight, the young Arab, whose teeth were chattering, told him that he had witnessed an atrocious crime.

The child was crossing the Rue Bab-Souika, dark and deserted at that hour, when a trickle of light escaping from the aforementioned building attracted his attention. He stopped and climbed up the wall of the façade in order to dart a glance into the interior courtyard, from which inarticulate cries were coming.

Immediately, he experienced such a fright that he jumped back down into the street at the risk of breaking his bones and then ran away like a madman. What he had just seen in the torch-lit courtyard was a man, tied to the trunk of a palm-tree and gagged: a poor fellow that three natives were attacking savagely with knives and clubs.

The victim, a European, it seemed, was rather oddly dressed in a long black frock-coat with a Hindu turban and white trousers. Stabbed and stunned, reduced, at any rate, to impotence, the man was no longer moving At the back of the courtyard was another European, of whom the child only had time to perceive the silhouette. Assuredly an accomplice of the indigenes, he was sniggering diabolically on seeing them belabor their victim.

The policeman who had just received this grave deposition ran to the station to fetch reinforcements and a patrol, guided by the child, did not take long to break down the worm-eaten door of the Arab dwelling.

How amazed, and then overjoyed, the policemen were when they discovered, tied to the tree, not the cadaver of a white man, but a mannequin stuffed with straw and, indeed, dressed in a black frock coat with white trousers and a Hindu turban. The mannequin having been stabbed repeatedly, the sincerity of the child was evident. He really had believed that he was witnessing a murder, which, fortunately, had only been simulated by the mysterious quartet, who had run away before the police arrived.

One wonders what motive the sinister tricksters were obeying in organizing that macabre scene. Perhaps they hoped to frighten the person who discovered the mannequin. In any case, their hope has been disappointed, for the child was not disturbed for long.

The police are actively searching for the authors of the macabre farce.

Sâr Dubnotal folded up the newspaper, slipped it into his pocket and stood up.

"Rudolph," he said, in his grave and musical voice, "that news item opens horizons to me that you certainly don't suspect. The exclamation that you uttered on reading it, however, tells me that the child's story has intrigued you greatly. You recognized me in the description that he gave of the mannequin in the frock-coat, turban and white trousers, didn't you?"

"Yes, Master, and that's why I hastened to show you the article."

"You did well, for I repeat that I attach a great importance to it. Don't interrogate me. The enigma will be elucidated of its own accord when the time comes. Only know that I don't accept the reporter's explanation, and that, in my opinion, it's a matter of something very different from a joke."

The Great Psychagogue reflected momentarily, and continued in a resolute tone:

"I need to see that child—whose name, unfortunately, the *Dépêche Tunisienne* failed to supply. Do me the service of running to the newspaper office, where someone can doubtless furnish you with further information, which will allow you to discover the young native's address. In any case, the police will be able to inform you. You only have to pass yourself off as an English reporter, and they'll immediately put themselves at your disposal.

"Then try to persuade the child to come with you to the Marabout Bleu, where I'll be waiting. If he won't come, I'll go to see him, but I'd prefer the conversation to take place here. We'll be more tranquil... and hurry, Rudolph!"

"Yes, Master."

64

The young man left the hotel immediately. He returned three hours later with a native child. It was the one in question, whom he had discovered without difficulty after a rapid inquiry, and who had agreed to go with him in return for an honest gratification.

"The Arabic tongue and its derivative dialects had no more secrets from Sâr Dubnotal than any of the European languages.

"What is your name?" he asked the boy in Sabir.[8]

"Ibrahim," the child replied.

"Good. Ibrahim, I've heard about the adventure you had yesterday evening, but I'd like to obtain a few extra details from you. Will you give them to me? I'll pay generously."

"I don't know very much, Sidi,[9]" stammered the child, slightly alarmed to discover in his interlocutor a faithful portrait of the famous mannequin. "I was very frightened, Sidi, very, very frightened, and I only darted a rapid glance into the patio."

"The mannequin's attackers were three Arabs?"

"Yes, Sidi, so far as I could tell. They were wearing large burnooses and babouches."

"And the other man at the back of the courtyard was European?"

"Yes, Sidi."

"Can you describe that individual to me?"

"No, Sidi, I barely glimpsed him."

"And the Arabs—did you recognize them? Were they tall or short? Could you identify them?"

"Oh, no, Sidi. I ran away right way without looking back. I was very, very frightened…"

Sâr Dubnotal addressed a few words to Rudolph in Hindi. The latter took Ibrahim by the shoulders and forced him to

---

[8] Pidgin language used as a *lingua franca* in the Mediterranean Basin from the 11th to the 19th century.

[9] Masculine title of respect, meaning "master" or "sir" in several Arabic languages.

look the Master full in the face. For a moment, the Great Psychagogue remained motionless and silent before the child held by his disciple. His large pupils were shining with a singular gleam, which gradually fascinated Ibrahim.

Evidently, his intention was to hypnotize the boy, and the magnetic fluid did not take long to operate upon the child, whose eyelids fluttered and whose whole body quivered, shaken by a spasmodic frisson.

"Ibrahim," said Sâr Dubnotal then "I want—I want, you understand?—you to see again the scene that you witnessed yesterday evening. I want you to relive it, and answer all my questions."

By virtue of a simple phenomenon of suggestion, the child, fallen into a profound hypnotic trance, had become a passive instrument of the Sâr.

Although psychognosis is relatively little known to the public, there is no one who has not heard about the experiments that the illustrious French physician Charcot carried out on the hysterics of the Salpêtrière.[10] Those experiments in hypnotism, magnetism and suggestion, repeated by other scientists, have established formal proof that the subject can accomplish all the actions demanded of him by the operator. No one should be astonished that Sâr Dubnotal, for whom hypnotism was mere child's play, had no difficulty in obtaining from Ibrahim a reconstruction of the sinister comedy of the Rue Bab-Souika.

The child immediately believed himself to be transported back to the terrace of the Moorish house and, crouching in front of Sâr Dubnotal, leaning forward as if to fathom the

---

[10] The French neurologist Jean-Martin Charcot (1825-1893) endorsed hypnotism for the treatment of hysteria, using it to conduct a number of experiments. The process of post-hypnotic suggestion was first described in this period. Extraordinary improvements in sensory acuity and memory were reported under hypnosis.

depths of an imaginary patio with his gaze, he described the scene exactly as it had transpired.

Sâr Dubnotal let him do it. When the child had finished, he said:

"Good, Ibrahim. Now, don't move. Look long and hard at the three Arabs attacking the man tied to the tree."

"I see them," replied the child. "Allah! But, Sidi, they aren't Arabs. No, no, I was mistaken! They're *roumis*, Christians disguised as believers."

"Describe them to me, one by one," the Great Psychagogue ordered.

"One is tall, vigorous, and athletic. He has a clean-shaven face and I can see a wisp of blond hair sticking out of his turban."

"A portrait of Frank," observed Sâr Dubnotal, coldly, signaling to Rudolph to listen closely.

"The second is a small dark-haired man, as brisk and nimble as a squirrel," Ibrahim went on, in a blank and hesitant voice. "He's making prodigious leaps around the mannequin. He's a Frenchman, because I can hear him swearing and blaspheming in that language."

"Fréjus," murmured Sâr Dubnotal.

"Finally," said Ibrahim, "the third has blue eyes, a pink face, a thickset body and broad shoulders."

"Otto!" said the Great Psychagogue.

Petrified by amazement, Rudolph listened in silence without yet understanding where Sâr Dubnotal was going. The only thing that was clear to him was that the three pseudo-Arabs were the Master's three investigators.

But why were they dressed up in that fashion? What were they doing in the patio of that ruined house? What was the significance of the savage and stupid scene in which, armed with daggers and clubs, they were furiously attacking a mannequin representing Sâr Dubnotal? And who was their associate, the European glimpsed by Ibrahim at the back of the courtyard?

The last enigma was immediately clarified, thanks to the subject's gift of second sight, which, on the Great Psychagogue's order, gave a description of the individual in question.

"I can see him too!" stammered the child. "He has a red beard, little eyes shining like carbuncles, a sardonic and malevolent expression. Oh! He's sniggering, and giving orders to the fake Arabs who are attacking the Sidi in the frock-coast and white trousers."

"What is he saying to them?" asked Sâr Dubnotal.

"He's speaking French; I don't understand."

"You don't need to understand. Simply repeat the words he's pronouncing! I want it!"

"He's shouting: '*Death to Severus el Tebib! Hold hard, friends! Strike! Strike harder! Kill him, the filthy dog! The Chess King will show him that one doesn't attack his company with impunity!*'"

"Tserpchikopf!" exclaimed Rudolph, his surprise reaching a peak. "It's Tserpchikopf! Oh, Master, explain to me what this means!"

"Haven't you guessed?" said Sâr Dubnotal tranquilly, while rubbing the child's eyelids. Extracted from his trace, the latter cast fearful glances around him. "Haven't you deduced that Tserpchikopf, doubtless alerted to the intentions of my investigators, has made arrangements to hypnotize them and make them the passive instruments of his vengeance?

"Otto, Frank and Fréjus have received an order to kill me, Rudolph. Yesterday evening, in that deserted house in the Rue Bab-Souika, Tserpchikopf was proceeding with a kind of dress rehearsal of the scene of my murder, a performance that permitted him to make sure that my investigators, having become his unconscious accomplices, would not hesitate for a second to strike me down.

"That's why the mannequin was made in my image, why the three pseudo-indigenes were belaboring it with dagger thrusts, why the man at the back of the courtyard was laughing diabolically on seeing them strike my effigy with so much ardor."

"And why your aides haven't reappeared at the hotel, Master!" Rudolph stammered, understanding everything now and shivering with horror.

Still calm and collected, Sâr Dubnotal gave a handful of copper coins to young Ibrahim, delighted with the windfall, and thanked him.

When the child had gone, the Great Psychagogue said to Rudolph, who had finally recovered his composure:

"Go to your room, with Annunciata, my friend. Barricade yourselves in, and don't open the door to anyone during my absence."

"Are you leaving, Master?" exclaimed Rudolph, amazed.

"Don't worry," Sâr Dubnotal said to him, smiling. "I'm not leaving Tunis, and I hope to be able to return to the Marabout Bleu this evening."

"Why not take me with you?"

"Because you'd be more of a hindrance than a help, Rudolph. Go, my friend. Above all, don't open the door to anyone, least of all my investigators, if they turn up before I return. In any case, I'll ask the hotelier to tell them that you and *La* Gianetti have gone out with me and that all three of us are looking for them. If they can get close to you, Rudolph, you're doomed, for they're possessed by murder madness, and their rage will only be assuaged by our blood."

"But, in that case, Master, you're exposing yourself to a terrible danger. What if you encounter them in the city?"

Sâr Dubnotal shrugged his shoulders disdainfully.

"What have I to fear?" he said. "And isn't it necessary that I return them to reason?"

"That's true, Master. Your formidable power and your invulnerability will permit you to accomplish that miracle."

"*Au revoir*, then, Rudolph."

"*Au revoir*, Master."

Left alone, Sâr Dubnotal undressed, anointed his body with a perfumed oil contained in a little gold phial, got dressed again, and went to find the hotelier to give him the necessary instructions.

The Great Psychagogue had hidden something in his pocket, but nothing about him revealed the slightest preoccupation.

That exceptional being, that superhuman whose name belongs henceforth to History as well as to Science, seemed informed in advance of the outcome of his perilous enterprise.

6. The Attack

Tunis, the White City, the Mantle of the Prophet, as the Arab poets put it, offers an impressive spectacle with its houses the color of alabaster, staged like an amphitheater on the hill overlooking Lake El Bahira, with its palaces, its arcades, its picturesque souks, its Kasbah, the slender silhouettes of its minarets, the green cupolas of its mosques and the variegated population of Muslims, Jews and roumis in its streets.

The Great Psychagogue was, however scarcely interested in all that enchantment when he left the Marabout Bleu hotel and set off on foot toward the native quarter, where he thought he had the best chance of encountering his investigators. He went rapidly up the Avenue de la Marine, went through the Porte de France, after having asked for directions to the Rue Bab-Souika, and headed for the street in question, looking as he passed by at the indigenes who were rubbing shoulders with him.

The narrow and tortuous alleyways into which he plunged were encumbered by numerous mercantile displays set up in the open; Africans, Jews and Berbers offered him Kairouan carpets, damascened weapons, sculpted vases, rich burnooses, pastries and a thousand other objects and delicacies as he passed by, which he refused with a gesture of his head.

At that time of year, the souk quarter presented a very animated aspect. The barbers' shops and Moorish cafés, abundantly distributed along the streets, were overflowing with clients. Sâr Dubnotal darted rapid glances into them, as well as the dance halls where belly-dancers were writhing and the audiences were particularly numerous.

Absorbed by his research, the grandmaster of psychognosis had not perceived that he had been followed since leaving the hotel by a tall and well-built Moorish woman. The woman in question, clad in the national fashion in broad white silk trousers, a *haïk* or veil, and a dark mask that hid almost all of her face except the eyes, had an almost masculine stride. She marched behind Sâr Dubnotal at a distance of a few paces, stopped as soon as he paused, and recommenced following him immediately.

If he happened to turn round, the woman struck an innocent pose and, leaning over a display of gods, set about haggling for trinkets.

One preceding the other, Sâr Dubnotal and the Moorish woman arrived at the Rue Bab-Souika. At the corner of the street, the spy took cover, leaving the Great Psychagogue to examine at his ease the old building where Ibrahim had seen Tserpchikopf launch the hypnotized Otto, Frank and Fréjus against the mannequin, armed with daggers.

Sâr Dubnotal only inspected the exterior of the house. Apparently convinced that going inside would serve no purpose, he slowly retraced his steps.

At that moment, the Moorish woman darted into a side-street. When the Great Psychagogue reached the intersection of the two streets, she had disappeared. Scarcely had he emerged into the Place Souika, however, whose shops he wanted to search, than she reappeared in his wake.

This time, she was not alone. She was accompanied by a man.

Bizarrely—which did not fail greatly to intrigue the indigenes circulating in the square—the man was a roumi.

A roumi escorting a Muslim woman was not an everyday sight in the streets of Tunis. The Bedouins widened their eyes and wondered whether the world had not turned upside down.

The Arab woman and the roumi, moreover, seemed oblivious to the curiosity they were provoking in the crowd through which they were passing. It was not until they heard the insults and the threats that were escaping from all lips that they began to notice the attention of which they were the object. Until then, they had only concerned themselves with staying behind the Great Psychagogue, without ever losing sight of him.

The anathemas and maledictions that rained down on them finally troubled them. The roumi—a man in dark glasses, a felt hat and an astrakhan coat, in whom, had they been there, Otto, Frank and Fréjus would immediately have recognized the traveler they had followed, presuming him to be Gustave Panloude—turned round to face the most furious of the Bedouins, and simply pronounced one word:

"*Tebib!*"

As if by enchantment, the rumor died down and the crowd dispersed. A "*tebib*" (or *toubib*) is a physician, and a physician, especially a white physician, is venerated by the indigenes. He can speak to women with impunity.

Nevertheless, the woman and the roumi did not abuse their advantage. They drew apart.

The so-called *tebib* retraced his steps, while his companion continued to follow Sâr Dubnotal.

The latter still had no suspicion of anything. The rather comical scene that the man in black-tinted spectacles, the Moorish woman, and the indigenes of the Place Bab-Souika had just played out had escaped him.

As his investigations had now been crowned by success, he was thinking deeply about Tserpchikopf, and not at all about his personal safety.

Tserpchikopf was decidedly destined to reserve surprises for him incessantly. Since Sâr Dubnotal had abandoned his studious retreat in India in order to launch himself into the vertiginous whirlwind of worldly life, he could not remember having encountered a case more disconcerting and troubling.

In Tserpchikopf. Sâr Dubnotal had encountered an enemy almost of his own stature, a true power of Evil, as he was a power of Good.

He did not fear him, but he nursed legitimate apprehensions for the unfortunates upon whom the Slav had designs. Such a scoundrel, combined with such a powerful hypnotist, would have been capable of sowing terror from one end of the Earth to the other, if Sâr Dubnotal had not set about thwarting his schemes.

Certainly, the Great Psychagogue had not yet got to grips with Tserpchikopf. Every day brought new complications in the infernal confusion. Nevertheless, he had the firm conviction that the astral trail indicated by Ranijesti and Roger Lardant would not be followed in vain, and that, sooner or later, it would lead to the capture of the Chess King.

Then, again, had not his intervention, in sum, had the most fortunate results? Had it not served to clear up the mystery of the haunted manor of Crec'h-ar-Vran? Thanks to Sâr Dubnotal, the soul of Jean de Tréguilly was savoring eternal bliss; Azilis, his guilty wife, was expiating her crimes in solitude; the last male descendant of the Comtes de Tréguilly, Albert, the son of Jean, and the grandson of Hector, had entered into possession of the share of his heritage captured as a result of the unspeakable maneuvers of his unworthy stepmother.

Thanks to Sâr Dubnotal, again, the impostures of Tserpchikopf when he had passed himself off as a mage had been unveiled.

Thanks to him, finally, the spirit of Roger Lardant had ceased to frighten the crew of the ferry *Prince Edward* and to drive the unfortunate ship to its ruin.

I haven't wasted my time, Sâr Dubnotal thought, *and if I can free my aides from the suggestion that has annihilated their will, I'll have nothing to regret.*

So saying, the Great Psychagogue emerged from his meditation and pursued his investigations with more ardor. He visited several more shops in the Place Bab-Souika, but still with no success. Nowhere did he perceive the familiar faces of his aides, whom he would have recognized even in a hood or an Arab burnoose.

However, he felt the menace of an indefinable danger hanging over him. Something told him that there was peril in the air.

What peril?

That, he asked himself in vain. He had looked around, but all he saw was completely inoffensive indigenous idlers.

Finally noticing the veiled woman, however, he thought she looked suspicious, with her overly large stature and the rapid gleam that had shone in her eyes before they were rapidly lowered.

He was about to move toward her in order to examine her more closely when she became lost in an eddy of the crowd.

Thinking that he had attached to much importance to the woman's suspicious appearance, Sâr Dubnotal lost interest in her and went into the last café in the square that remained for him to visit.

In addition to a large room where the customers, squatting on mats, were silently drinking coffee, the establishment included an interior courtyard where beverages were similarly served.

In the room, Sâr Dubnotal only saw two or three grave Arabs, who greeted him with a solemn "*salaam*" without getting up. Passing into the flag-stoned courtyard, surrounded by arcades, he saw that it was empty.

He was, in consequence, about to go back into the street when a kind of cloud passed before his eyes. That cloud presented the blurred and vaporous appearance of a Hindu, and although it did not take long to dissipate, the Great Psychagogue was able to recognize the immaterial features of the astral double of Ranijesti, the man walled up in Benares.

The unexpected apparition of the yogi was certainly a presage of danger, and it was probable that the critical moment was nigh.

The Sâr never carried a weapon. To protect himself, he only counted on his indomitable bravery and his astonishing science.

Retreating to the far side of the patio, his eyes fixed on the exit door, and he waited.

Suddenly, his alert hearing perceived a prolonged whistling coming from the main room of the café, to which hoarse clamors immediately responded.

The Great Psychagogue redoubled his attention.

The clamors continued to resound, and abruptly, a frenzied group surged from the door to the café and rushed into the patio. The group consisted of four men and a woman. Sâr Dubnotal recognized three of the men at the first glance; they were Otto, Frank and Fréjus.

Dressed as Arabs, they were brandishing long daggers and uttering howls of fury. The fourth person completely unknown to Sâr Dubnotal, was none other than the pretended *tebib*, the man with the dark glasses. As for the woman, you will already have guessed that it was she who, as the Moorish woman, had been spying on Sâr Dubnotal so cleverly.

The woman and the fake doctor stopped just outside the door, but Otto, Frank and Fréjus ran toward heir master, daggers raised.

The latter waited for them, his feet firm.

Condensing all the magnetic fluid at his disposal, and transformed, so to speak, into a lyre of quivering and vibrant nerves, he darted his fulgurant gaze at the three excited men and multiplied passes design to break their savage surge,

Fréjus, more nervous than the others, was the first one to be tamed. A single flash of the wide eyes aimed at him was sufficient to render him harmless.

Otto took a few more steps and, subjugated in his turn, dropped his weapon at his feet.

But Frank, against whom all of Sâr Dubnotal's psychic force had turned, resisted his passes much better, and, at the paroxysm of his rage, leapt at his master's throat and struck him with the dagger.

With what marvelous lotion had the Sâr rubbed his body? At any rate, in the same way that two electric currents of the same polarity repel one another, the blade of the dagger and Sâr Dubnotal's epidermis repelled once another; an invisible force threw Frank's arm backwards and, instantaneously, the latter emerged from his hypnosis, while Sâr Dubnotal grabbed his wrist.

"Wretches!" said the Great Psychagogue to his flabbergasted disciples. "What were you going to do?"

While Fréjus, Otto and Frank looked at one another, haggardly, as if emerging from a frightful nightmare, Sâr Dubnotal returned his attention to the door.

To his great regret, he observed that the Moorish woman had fled. Only the fake *tebib* was still in the courtyard. His spectacles had fallen off, and he seemed petrified by fright. Suddenly hypnotized by the very man he wanted to murder, the wretch was no longer capable, thanks to Sâr Dubnotal's will power, of taking a step or sketching an action.

Two hours later, Sâr Dubnotal returned to the Marabout Bleu hotel, where his disciple was waiting anxiously.

"It's me, Rudolph!" he shouted through the keyhole of the solidly barricaded door.

Recognizing his voice, the young man removed the furniture stacked behind the door, drew the bolts, turned the key and opened up.

Imagine his surprise and joy on seeing the Great Psychagogue's three investigators come in behind Sâr Dubnotal, accompanied by an unknown man.

To tell the truth, Otto, Frank ad Fréjus had expressions like whipped dogs. Since their departure from the hotel the previous day, after lunch, they had passed through tribulations, without being aware of them, which, now that the truth had been revealed to them, put a blush of shame on their faces and a grim desire for reprisals in their hearts.

Oh, they were certainly no longer thinking of singing the praises of Scotland Yard, the Parisian Sûreté or the secret police of Berlin! They only wanted one thing, which was for no one to pay any more attention to them.

The grandmaster of psychognosis, taking Rudolph to one side, rapidly explained what had happened. Then he showed him the unknown man and said:

"May I introduce you to Gustave Panloude, alias Pawn One, former member of the Chessmen. This man, henceforth in my power, has made me the most extraordinary revelations about his leader, who is indeed Tserpchikopf.

"The Hypnotist is an adversary ten times as redoubtable as we had imagined. And yet, Panloude has not been able to document me entirely on that monster's past, for he has only been under his orders for eight or ten years.

"You'll know all that later, Rudolph. For now, I'll hand the floor to Panloude, who will tell you himself how our investigators allowed themselves to be beaten hands down by Tserpchikopf."

Panloude was visibly reluctant to talk, but the imperious gaze of Sâr Dubnotal suddenly rendered him as loquacious as could have been desired.

"It's quite simple," he said. "All the way to Tunis, to which the Chess King had come in order to rob the Bardo Palace and steal the jewels of the Beylical crown,[11] and from which he had telegraphed instructing me to join him, I had not the slightest suspicion of the surveillance of which I was the object.

"I was to take my luggage to a house in the Rue El-Khedive, where Tserpchikopf was waiting for me. At least, that was what had been agreed between the chief and me. Fearing that I might be followed, however—not without reason, as you know, Messieurs—the King had disguised himself as a Moorish woman and stationed himself on the landing-stage.

---

[11] The *Beylik* (or Kingdom) of Tunis was founded on July 15, 1705, after the Husainid Dynasty led by Al-Husayn I ibn Ali at-Turki defeated the Turkish Deys.

"He did not acknowledge me, allowing me to unload my luggage and hire a cab to take me to the Rue El-Khedive. Seeing one of these Messieurs following me, he followed him in his turn, and acquired the conviction that he wanted to arrest me.

"When that one had seen where I went, he returned to look for his comrades. Tserpchikopf, who was still following him, went to position himself in the path of the three men, in a deserted side-street. Seeing the Moorish woman address a signal of intelligence to them, the Messieurs stopped, very surprised.

"Tserpchikopf immediately hypnotized them. That's all!"

"Not all," said Sâr Dubnotal, "but the rest we already know. We know how the wretches were forced to stab a mannequin made in my image, as they would have murdered me if I hadn't take my precautions, and how the fake Moorish woman, seeing fortune turning to his disadvantage, was able to disappear, just in time... For we still don't have Tserpchikopf, my dear children!" the Great Psychagogue concluded.

"Death to him!" roared Otto, Frank and Fréjus, in chorus.

Sâr Dubnotal and Rudolph could not suppress a frank burst of laughter.

"Perfect," said the Master. "But before we run into Tserpchikopf again, I intend to give you a serious bath of counter-hypnotism... Fifteen minutes of effluvia each! That precaution will permit you henceforth to confront the scoundrel on equal terms."

After a few seconds of reflection Sâr Dubnotal continued:

"We're going to leave Tunis. We have nothing more to do in the White City, from which Tserpchikopf has surely fled following the arrest of his accomplice. Launched by Ranijesti on an astral trail, we've succeeded in taking a Pawn from the Chessmen. Gustave Panloude, passed whether he likes it or not, into our camp, will help us to capture others..."

From then on, the implacable struggle engaged by the grandmaster of psychognosis against the Chess King entered a new phase.

You will see in due course [12] what exciting vicissitudes it was still to cause Sâr Dubnotal to undergo. We shall also talk again about the revelations of Gustave Panloude, and the reader will understand why the Tserpchikopf affair was always considered by the Great Psychagogue as one of the most exciting and most mysterious cases with which he had ever been called upon to occupy himself.

---

[12] In Volume 1 which concludes the saga.

This story, featuring an encounter between the Great Psychagogue and Captain Nemo, is also a sequel of sorts to John Peel's tale "Twenty Thousand Years under the Sea"(published in Tales of the Shadowmen *No. 4) in which Nemo comes across H.P. Lovecraft's mythical sunken city of R'lyeh and threatens to unleash Cthulhu upon the world...*

Matthew Dennion: *Clash of the Titans*

Pacific Ocean, 1865

The tension inside the *Nautilus* was almost palpable. Of all the adventures the crew had ever experienced, this was the most terrifying. Captain Nemo grabbed his handkerchief and calmly wiped the sweat from his brow. He knew every member of his highly-trained crew was performing their assigned tasks with the utmost precision. The Captain was also well aware that, given their situation, each crew member was watching him closely. They looked to him for leadership and strength; currently, they needed both.

"Is the cachalot still in pursuit?" Nemo asked, stroking his beard,

"Affirmative, Captain."

"Excellent! Maintain speed. We must avoid the whale until we reach our destination."

"Aye, Aye, Captain."

Nemo scanned his crew.

"Have faith men," he added. "We will see the demon vanquished before this night is through, or die trying!"

A chorus of "Aye, Aye, Captain," echoed through the bridge.

A few minutes later, Nemo entered the observation deck where the Great Psychagogue was staring at the behemoth.

The Captain approached Sâr Dubnotal. Together, they stood in silence for a moment.

The bull sperm whale pursuing them was massive. The size of the beast was far from its most terrifying aspect. Its entire body was horribly scarred. Welts covered its head where giant squids had wrapped their tentacles around it in a vain attempted to escape being devoured. Harpoons had left puncture marks all over its body. In some instances, the weapons were so deeply embedded that they still protruded from the whale's flesh.

The most haunting aspect of the creature was its ghostly white color. In the dark depths of the ocean, the whale appeared as a gargantuan specter. Most whales were just whales, but this one was different; this beast seemed more a force of nature than an animal. This whale was—Moby Dick!

"Captain, I would like to thank you again for agreeing to utilize the *Nautilus* for this mission," said the Sâr. "I know that, by attacking the whale, you have placed your crew in great danger, but this may well be our only opportunity to stop this monster."

"My crew understands the danger," nodded Nemo, "and they know that more than our lives are at stake. If we do not stop this demon, no one else will. The seas themselves, and perhaps the entire world, are in danger!"

"Indeed! I used have to my psychic abilities to enrage the beast. He should be ready to attack anything that he sees when we reach our goal. Let us return to the bridge; we are nearing our destination and we must be prepared for the coming confrontation."

As they entered the bridge, a crewman called out:

"Captain! We have a visual on the site."

The Sâr looked out of the viewing deck. Seeing the eerie structure ahead of them sent a cold shiver through his spine. He thought that, if Moby Dick and the *Nautilus* were to have a final battle, this would indeed be the perfect arena for them to meet.

Simply viewing the cyclopean structures protruding from the sunken city began to create a small sensation of pain in his head. It was as if the city existed in dimensions that a human mind could not comprehend. Sâr Dubnotal had beheld many horrors in his time, but nothing he had seen compared to the nightmare city of R'lyeh!

A collective gasp went through the bridge as a dark shape seemed to emerge from the ruins. Massive bat like wings slid up from the sides of the buildings. These were followed by a horrifying head. The skull appeared to be shaped like that of human, but massive tentacles protruded from where a mouth should be.

The Sâr whispered his name in awe:

"*Cthulhu.*"

Nemo remembered how he had once stumbled upon R'lyeh and sought to explore the strange city. During their underwater mission, he and his men had come across the horrible form of the sleeping Cthulhu. Perhaps for the first time in his life, he had truly felt fear.

Since that encounter, Nemo had sought to better understand what he had discovered. His quest for occult knowledge had led him back to his native India, the streets of Benares, and, finally, the mystic Sâr Dubnotal, who had revealed to him the true nature of Cthulhu. The Sâr had explained that, one day, the stars would align properly for the monster to escape from his dark prison. He would then raise R'lyeh from the depths and, in doing so, extinguish all life on Earth. He had further informed Nemo that the stars would reach this alignment within two years. It was then that the two men had devised their current plan.

"What's the position of the whale?" asked Nemo.

"Less than a mile behind us, Captain!"

Nemo turned to see Sâr Dubnotal sitting on the floor, meditating. He knew that the Great Psychagogue was straining his psychic abilities to the breaking point in order to keep the whale sufficiently enraged.

"Sir something's happening!" a crew member suddenly screamed.

Aside from being astounded at the size of Cthulhu, Nemo was taken back at what happened next.

R'lyeh itself had begun to rise off of the ocean floor!

The Captain realized the time had come to execute their plan.

"Navigate directly past the head of that demon!"

The *Nautilus* shot past Cthulhu without the horror even seeming to notice the ship, but even the Great Old One had to take notice of what happened next, as an enraged Moby Dick slammed into his torso.

Nemo ordered the *Nautilus* to turn around. He watched as the whale dug its teeth into Cthulhu's face. The Old One then focused his own awesome rage upon the animal.

Nemo and Sâr Dubnotal's plan had come to fruition!

The most powerful animal in the world had attacked the dreaded monster and stopped him as he attempted to raise the sunken city. Sâr Dubnotal was not sure if Moby Dick could defeat Cthulhu, so, in order to assist the whale, Nemo ordered that all of the *Nautilus*'s weapons be fired on Cthulhu. Meanwhile, the Sâr used every spell he knew to incapacitate the monster. He instructed the crew to pray to whatever deity they worshipped, for it was all that they could do as the unstoppable force of nature battled an immovable god...

Following in the footsteps of Rudyard Kipling, Talbot Mundy, Louis Jacolliot, Paul d'Ivoi and Henri Vernes, to name but a few, Travis Hiltz conjures up the lure of a magical India-, with its impenetrable jungles, its lost temples, its fabulous jewels, its man-eating tigers and its sinister death cults in a tale that sees Sâr Dubnotal team up with Mowgli, Indiana Jones' father and a cast drawn from Jules Verne's The Steam House...

Travis Hiltz: *The Treasure of the Ubasti*

India, 1895

The jungle stood like a fortress beside the grasslands. Tree limbs overlapped, dense and wild, forming a thick canopy that left the ground below in perpetual twilight. The air was heavy with an approaching storm and the jungle was hushed, as though any sound would attract the storm's attention.

Off in the distance, a sound came; it was the 'chuff-chuff' of a locomotive. It grew louder and closer, managing to raise a cloud of dust even in the pre-monsoon damp.

Out of the dust cloud came a creature, like none other in all of India, perhaps unique in all the world.

It was a massive metallic construct, resembling the result of a mating between an elephant and a steam locomotive. Wheels set into the bottom of its feet allowed it to travel along the dirt road. Its eyes were lanterns, its upraised trunk blew plumes of steam. In a howdah, perched upon its back, sat an engineer, steering the mighty creature towards the jungle. Behind the metal elephant was attached a bulkier version of a railroad car.

The steam elephant traveled up the road and into the jungle, easily pushing aside the tightly packed foliage that lined the path. Both elephant and carriage were battered. Bullet holes leaking steam pockmarked the creature, and scorch marks marred the carriages' paint. The noise scattered the jungle's various denizens.

As the metal pachyderm came to a halt, a set of steps unfolded from a side door of the carriage and four men stepped out. The first was Banks, the stout, grey-haired English engineer who was the creator of *Behemoth*, the fantastic, steam powered elephant. He was followed by Sâr Dubnotal, the Great Psychagogue, a practitioner of the mystic arts, dressed in the turban, loose tunic and trousers of a native. He had a neatly trimmed beard and a cultured face. Next came Dr. Henry Jones, a young American academic recently arrived in India to study at the University of Bombay. He also sported a beard, though one only in its infancy. He wore a khaki ensemble and a pith helmet. Lastly, came Captain Hood, late of her Majesty's army, a thin, middle aged man in the attire of a seasoned hunter.

Banks immediately wandered off to check on his elephant, tutting sadly to himself whenever he spotted a bullet hole in its steel hide. He then began to instruct the crew on repairs. The other three peered about the newly-made clearing, Jones with a mix of awe and anxiety, the other two calm, yet alert.

"Beautiful," Jones breathed, in a thick scottish accent. "I never get tired of looking at this country."

"After hiking three days in the rain with a heavy pack," Hood muttered, "it loses a bit of its charm."

"Come, my friends," Sâr Dubnotal said, briskly. "We still have a ways to go. Once on the trail, we can discuss the scenery. Captain Hood, if you would see that our luggage is ready?"

"Back in a mo'."

"I don't think he approves of me," Henry said, quietly to the Sâr.

"Captain Hood approves of few people," the mystic replied, patting his friend's arm. "Unless they have served in the army or killed a tiger."

"It's the hat, isn't it?" Henry asked, taking off his pith helmet and peering at it accusingly. "It's the sort of thing you think you should wear on a journey like this, but now that I'm wearing it, I feel a bit of a prat."

"Henry," the Sâr said, patting his friend's shoulder. "I hate to say this about such a gifted academic, but you think too much. We have been drawn together for a purpose, and each of us has a part to play. Without your knowledge of ancient language and history, I would not have been able to piece together the clues to the Cult of Ubasti, their intentions and the location of their stronghold."

"Ready," Hood said, returning. "Banks says he'll wait three days, then has to head north."

"So, we had best make the most of our time," the Sâr said. "Let us be off."

The three shouldered knapsacks and began walking along the narrow path, leaving Banks to tend to the *Behemoth*. They trudged along for hours, pushing their way through the thick undergrowth, on occasion forced to hack through it.

"Bit too quiet for my tastes," Hood muttered, wiping his sweating forehead with the back of his hand. "Even when there's a tiger in the neighborhood, the jungle doesn't get this quiet. Feels like the whole area is holding its breath, waiting for your thugees to leave."

"Actually, while the Thugee and the Cult of Ubasti have several traits in common," Henry Jones said, fanning himself with his hat, "they have quite different rituals of worship."

"The Cult of Ubasti is no mere gathering of assassins," the Sâr added, turning to look at his companions. "They are a dark force, nearly as old as civilization itself."

"Well, the ones we encountered in Bombay were dangerous, but I think you may be overstating it..." Henry began.

"No, I do not." The Sâr paused, as if unsure how to proceed, and then steepling his fingers together spoke again. "I would be remiss if I led you into this without explaining the dangers we face. You are both aware of the legends concerning the fabled 'lost cities' that dot Africa, and how these cities are believed to be outposts of fallen Atlantis?"

Both his companions nodded.

"Well, Atlantis had a sister city, as dedicated to the dark arts as Atlantis was to the gathering of knowledge. This other city was Lemuria, and like Atlantis, it, too, was wiped from the Earth by a cataclysm, leaving behind only a handful of outposts as its legacy. These outposts are scattered across the face of Asia and they are the birthplace of Ubasti."

"Atlantis?" Hood muttered, shaking his head. "Maybe, old fellow, you've been spending a bit too much time with those yogis of yours..."

"Lemuria?" Henry interrupted, stroking his beard thoughtfully. "There are mentions in several old texts... supposed to have been visited by Prester John..."

"Yes, Lemuria and the followers of Ubasti have been content to exist in the history books as rumor and legend," the Sâr said, resuming walking. "But, as dedicated as they are to staying hidden, my teachers are dedicated to seeking them out. When rumors reached the yogis that the Ubasti were gathering in India and that some great treasure had come into their hands, I was sent to discover their plans."

"We still don't have any clue as to what this 'treasure' is though," Henry shrugged, walking along with Sâr. Hood followed, several paces behind, unsure which of his companions he found the most baffling.

"Captain Hood's skepticism is well founded," Henry said, reluctantly. "We are following crumbs—not even something as substantial as crumbs. We are chasing dust motes in a Sun beam."

"Were those dust motes that attacked us at the university?" the Sâr asked. "The Ubasti are very real and very dangerous. I do not know what this treasure is, but if the Ubasti have it, that is reason enough to cause me worry. We must find their stronghold."

"Um... Sâr...?" Henry began and then merely pointed down the path.

The mystic paused, his gaze following where his companion was pointing.

Sitting on their haunches were three gray wolves, silent, and statue still. Their gazes curious and intent.

Henry felt his mouth go dry. Never having seen a wolf this close before, he had a mental image of them appearing to be just large dogs. Their coats were rough and matted and their eyes were polished obsidian. God had not created these animals to fetch anyone's slippers. The wolf is a hunter, and Henry had the sudden realization that he and his friends were prey.

The men took several slow, anxious steps back down the trail, before realizing there was another trio of wolves behind them as well. Captain Hood slowly raised his rifle.

"No," the Sâr breathed.

"Sâr," Hood muttered back. "I've had the courtesy to trust you when it comes to mystical mumbo-jumbo. I'd think you'd at least return the courtesy in matters of the hunt..."

"I do not believe they are hunting us," the Sâr replied, quietly. His eyes closed and his forehead furrowed in concentration. "They are... not hungry, but curious. There are... men... in their jungle that they do not understand."

"They look like they're waiting for something," Henry suggested, looking around nervously.

"Waiting for what?" Hood asked.

"Maybe for him!" Henry replied, pointing up into a nearby tree. A branch fluttered with movement and, suddenly, a figure leapt to the ground and stood between the trio and the wolves.

He was a boy, in his late teens, his naked skin tanned walnut brown. His midnight black hair hung to his shoulders. Around his neck, he wore a strand of leather on which hung a crude sheath for a hunting knife.

The boy looked over the group with piercing eyes, curious and hostile.

"What in the world...?" Hood breathed, his rifle hung loose in his grip.

"Who are you?" The youth suddenly demanded. His tone was halting and accented, as though English was a language that he had not quite mastered. "Why have you come here?"

"Um...?" Henry replied.

"Bloody Hell," Captain Hood added.

"Mowgli of the gray brothers, I presume?" Sâr Dubnotal said, steepling his fingers together and making a slight bow.

The naked boy's hand went to the handle of his knife.

"How do you know my name, man?" he snapped, shifting into a defensive crouch.

"I am Sâr Dubnotal, and I know a great many things that are hidden to others. I know that men have come to this jungle. Men of evil intent."

"All men are evil," Mowgli snorted back. "No man sets foot in this jungle with anything but evil in his heart. You know no other way."

"This is going to be difficult." Hood muttered. "Especially if he commands those wolves to attack."

"Yes, but we need young Mowgli as an ally," the Sâr replied. "With every second we spend arguing..."

"Wait, just...wait, a moment," Henry exclaimed, his hands raised in what he anxiously hoped was a reassuring and peaceful gesture. "We don't mean any harm to you. Other men have hidden something here... in the jungle... your jungle. They will use it to hurt others, man and animal. We must find it. Once we've found the place... we'll gladly leave."

Despite the precariousness of their situation, the Great Psychagogue could not help but smile at his friend's awkward attempt at diplomacy.

"Henry," he said, quietly, laying a hand on the young scholar's shoulder. "Your efforts are well intentioned, but..."

"An old place?" Mowgli interrupted. "Made by men?"

The Sâr looked from Henry, then back to Mowgli, before answering.

"Yes, we believe that is where they are."

"They have taken refuge in the Cold Lair. They stir up the Bandar-Log to make war with the jungle." Mowgli said, with grim determination. "Come."

He abruptly turned and stalked off, down a path that lead deeper into the jungle. One of the wolves followed him.

"What just happened?" Hood asked.

"My good Captain," the Sâr chuckled, making an 'after you' gesture to Henry, "apparently we have, for the moment, gained a guide. The enemy of our enemy is, for the moment, our friend."

"*Go study in Bombay,*" Henry muttered to himself, as he walked. "*It'll be an adventure.* Never should have listened to Drummond."

The expedition was hard-pressed to keep up with their new guide. He and his wolves sprinted along, undaunted by the thick foliage or the tiny, uneven path. In fact, Mowgli only appeared to use the path so that the expedition didn't lose sight of him as he ran neck and neck with the wolves and even took to the trees during those times that the path was strewn with hidden roots and stones, or was swallowed up by the surrounding jungle.

The men struggled to keep up. Henry and Captain Hood were soon drenched with sweat and struggling for breath. The Sâr's skin shone with a light sheen of sweat, but he seemed otherwise unfazed by the exertion. They staggered down the path and finally caught up with Mowgli in a small clearing. The wolves were nowhere to be seen and the wild boy was lounging on a sturdy tree branch.

"Men are slow creatures," Mowgli chided.

"You get that way," Henry wheezed, "when you no longer have to chase your dinner."

"May I ask," the Sâr said, taking a sip from a canteen, then passing it to Henry, "what is this 'Cold Lair' you are taking us to?"

"A dead place," Mowgli replied, gravely. "Fit for only white hoods and the Bandar-Log. Come. You do not want to be walking the Cold Lair at night."

He leapt nimbly to the ground and trotted off.

Sâr Dubnotal shrugged and followed. Hood and Henry groaned and limped along behind.

After another mile, the already thin path had all but disappeared.

"Walk carefully, my friends," the Sâr warned, quietly. "We are approaching something... dark and evil."

Hood adjusted his grip on his rifle.

"My god!" Henry breathed, pushing aside some branches. "Look!"

The others soon joined him, peering through the break in the foliage.

"Why...it's a city!" Hood exclaimed. "A city in the middle of the jungle!"

"Gentlemen," said the Sâr smiling grimly. "Welcome to the Cold Lair."

In its earliest days, the city had been polished marble, but the dust of ages and the elements had turned it gray. Despite the cracks, crumbled corners and overgrowth, it still had a sense of majesty and wonder. Only a small portion of the old city was visible, as the jungle crept over the balconies, courtyards and towers in an attempt to reclaim the clearing.

The quartet pushed through the undergrowth and into the Cold Lair. They walked nervously and kept their voices low. Mowgli hung back, reluctant to follow the party.

"It's all a bit intimidating," Hood muttered. "Bit like walking into a cathedral."

"It's ... amazing!" Henry breathed. "Look at those carvings on that wall! Those are 5th century if they're a day."

"Henry," the Sâr said, placing a hand on the young scholar's shoulder. "Archeology later. Stay alert. I doubt we will be able to walk about undetected for long. We must find where the Ubasti hid their treasure."

"Below," Mowgli said, swinging down from the trees and joining them. "The old ones who built Cold Lair hid their precious things in the tunnels below. That way, they were kept safe from other men and the Bandar-Log."

"You keep mentioning these Bandar-log," Hood grumbled, peering about nervously. "Who are they? Some kind of native guards?"

"We must move carefully," Mowgli warned. "If we can reach the tunnels before... there! Move quickly, men!"

The jungle boy leapt and scrambled up a vine-covered wall, leaving the three men looking about, expecting the worst.

"I don't see... oh..." Henry said, spotting a small, furry head peering at them from a stone balcony "Is that them? The Bandar-Log?"

"It's a monkey," Hood grumbled. "Foolish boy! Take more than a couple of monkeys to scare me off."

The two heads were soon joined by a dozen more, all peering intently at the trio.

"I've got a bad feeling about this," Henry said.

"There must be dozens of them!" the Sâr exclaimed.

From every doorway, balcony and dried up well in the ancient city they came, dozens of small furry, screeching bodies, rushing like a wave. The noise they made was almost deafening. Even standing close together, the men had to shout to be heard.

Captain Hood brought the rifle to his shoulder and, with each shot, a monkey fell. Henry Jones fumbled for the pistol in his belt and managed to get off one shot before the Bandar-Log reached them. Unfortunately, all it did was clip the ear of a nearby statue.

"We're dead if we stay in this courtyard!" Hood yelled, firing off two more shots, then pausing to reload.

As the monkeys got close, he turned his rifle around and used it as a club to beat them back. It was as though the threatening clouds had burst and, instead of rain, unleashed a downpour of ravenous animals.

"Where can we go?" Henry asked, frantically firing. Not until the horde of monkeys was upon them did any of his shots find their targets.

"To the left!" the Sâr responded, dodging the multitude of furry bodies. "There's a doorway!"

The trio backed up, firing and then swinging their weapons to keep the monkeys at bay. The trees off to their right rustled. Mowgli and his wolf brothers burst out, plunging into the middle of the army of monkeys. The jungle boy's knife slashed left and right, while the wolves used their powerful fangs to grab hold of the creatures, like terriers hunting rats, but even their fierce efforts made only the smallest dent in the monkeys' vast numbers, and they were soon lost to sight amongst the multitude of thrashing, furry bodies.

Desperate to reload his pistol, Henry yanked at his belt, ripping it loose. With no hope of retrieving the scattered bullets, he used it as a makeshift whip to drive the Bandar-Log back.

Sâr Dubnotal merely dodged the monkeys as he made his way towards the alcove he had spotted. His movements seemed unhurried and purposeful, without any apparent urgency. Fast as the Bandar-Log sprang, he was never there. He also didn't seem to strike the monkeys, merely his arm would reach out and push them out of his path.

One particularly large specimen broke through the expeditions' defenses and landed on Hood's back, sinking its teeth into his shoulder. Hood stopped to grab it and yank the creature off, but that was enough time for the other monkeys to wash over him like a wave.

"Hood!" Henry yelled, fighting to reach him.

Sâr Dubnotal reached out and grabbing hold of Henry's arm, propelled the young scholar the rest of the way to the sheltering alcove. Its hard packed dirt floor lead to a crooked flight of marble steps.

"Mowgli!" the Sâr shouted. "To me! We have found a way into the city!"

The jungle boy, his tanned skin crisscrossed with scratches and bite marks, scooped up two of his gray brothers, one wounded, the other dead, and plowed through the storm of monkeys. He growled at the remaining wolf, and it broke for the safety of the jungle.

While Mowgli rushed to safety, the Great Psychagogue stood his ground, his hands pressed together as if in prayer and his brow furrowed in concentration. He took a deep breath and opened his arms wide.

"I am El Tebib," he intoned, "Chosen of the White Lodge and Doctor of the World's Pain!"

He brought his hands together with a thunderclap and a wave of force poured forth, scattering the army of Bandar-Log like butterflies in a hurricane.

The shriek of the monkeys was momentarily drowned out, and Mowgli and the remaining wolf staggered into the corridor.

The silence that followed was deafening. The Sâr's body swayed for a moment, weakened by the effort, and then moved a bit unsteadily to where Captain Hood lay, sprawled on the blood-smeared marble flagstones. Hood's clothing had been torn near to rags and was damp with blood. He still had a grip on his rifle. His eyelids fluttered as the Sâr attempted to get him to his feet.

"Come, my friend," the Sâr said. "We must move. Even if the Bandar-Log do not attack again, we can be sure the Ubasti know we are here."

Hood gave a weak groan and stumbled along, guided by the mystic. Henry rushed out, as they approached the alcove. He offered Hood a sip from his canteen than wetted his handkerchief and dabbed at the man's wounds.

"He looks worse than it is," the Sâr reassured them.

"Then, I must look horrible," Hood muttered, as they lowered him so that he was sitting upon the floor, his back against the marble wall. "'Cause I feel miserable... Where...?"

"We're out of the courtyard," Henry explained. "We've found a flight of stairs that lead down. Mowgli went ahead."

"Ah," Hood nodded, a bit unsteadily. "What's our next move?"

"Next move?" Henry asked, dumbfounded. "I think our next move is leaving here alive..."

"Henry," the Sâr said, his voice quiet but firm. "We must continue."

"Are you serious?" Henry exclaimed. "That attack by the monkeys…"

"…Tells me that we have gotten close enough to make the followers of Ubasti nervous," the Sâr explained.

"Yes, they're so afraid they've decided to slaughter us," Henry pointed out, his voice rising. "Even if Hood's wounds aren't as bad as they appear, he won't be up to anymore running or fighting..."

"So, leave me here," Hood interrupted, quietly.

His companions looked at him worriedly.

"Come now," Hood continued. "I took Her Majesty's coin long enough to know how this works. You lot need to go on. The Sâr's right. Jones, you've got to keep going. Besides, you'll need someone to hold this tunnel. No point going and finding this treasure if you can't get out again."

Henry kept quiet, but looked skeptical.

"You should be safe here," the Sâr nodded. "The Bandar-log seem to have no interest in going into the buildings. We'll leave you the canteen and whatever we can salvage from the first-aid kit."

"I'll need more ammunition," Hood said.

Henry and the Sâr rummaged through the remains of the knapsacks. They scavenged enough ammunition to reload Hood's rifle and enough bits of cloth to bind everyone's wounds.

"Shouldn't we get moving?" Henry asked, nervously.

The Sâr nodded. "I do not like leaving without Mowgli, but the longer we stay..."

The mystic was interrupted by the thud of a body hitting the ground near them. It was a native man, dressed in black robes and turban. His face was bruised and bloody. Mowgli stepped out of the shadows. There was a fresh gash across his chest and the beginnings of a black eye. He carried another unconscious black-robed man over his shoulder.

"The way below is clear," he said simply, tossing his burden down next to the other and going to tend to his injured wolf.

"Then let us finish this," Sâr Dubnotal said.

The stairway was claustrophobically narrow, and the further the trio descended, the darker it grew. At the bottom was a tiny chamber with a dirt floor. Three doorways, no more than holes in the wall, led further down into darkness. They felt the weight of the city above them and tasted the age in the air.

"Very homey," Henry grumbled, "if you're a mole."

"Nearly there," the Sâr murmured, his eyes closed as he ran his hands over the dirt walls. "I can feel a bright spark, struggling amongst the evil that seeps through the walls—the treasure!"

"You keep talking about this treasure," Henry said, peering over his shoulder, "but have been awfully vague about what it actually is."

"Gold," Mowgli nodded to himself. "When men kill, there is always gold."

"My information is vague," the Sâr admitted, "but I do know it is an artifact of great age. Possibly an oracle of some kind..."

"So, we don't know what we're looking for?" Henry protested. "You see, in archeology, when you go looking for something, you tend to either have some idea what it looks like, or at least don't have people trying to kill us so we can look for it at your leisure."

"Unfortunately, this item is more in the category of 'I will know it when I see it,' " the Sâr reassured him. "These tunnels seem to stretch all beneath the city."

"There is a room of treasure through here," Mowgli said, pointing towards the smallest of the three openings. "I have been before. "

"If it's so precious, would the Ubasti just toss it on the pile with the rest of the loot?" Henry asked.

"Where better to hide a book, than in a library," the Sâr replied, peering into the passageway. "Looks to be a tight fit. Can you lead the way, Mowgli?"

"Yes," the jungle boy nodded, "but, once there, be cautious."

The trio quickly moved into the passageway, which almost immediately grew even narrower. Soon, they were walking hunched over, shoulders rubbing against the dirt walls. By the time they reached the far end, they were crawling on all fours in the dark. Henry, the last one in line, tumbled out onto what he thought was a pile of gravel. The Sâr found and lit a torch. The young scholar was shocked to discover it was in fact a pile of rubies.

"Oh my!" he exclaimed.

In the circle of light cast by the torch, both men saw that the chamber was the resting place of the wealth of kings. The floor was carpeted with coins and gems of various sizes. Bits of armor, weapons and artifacts of gold decorated the room. In a corner huddled three skeletons, all wearing crowns and the tattered remains of royal finery.

In silence, they began to move deeper into the treasure chamber. Henry and the Sâr moved towards the center, while Mowgli kept to the edges of the room. His knife was out and he scanned the piles of wealth as if fearful that they would rise up and attack him.

"Walk carefully," he warned, in a low voice. "The white hoods watch over this room."

"What are these white hoods?" asked the Sâr. "Ceremonial keepers of the chamber?"

"Cobras," Henry rasped, tugging at the Sâr's sleeve. "The white hoods are bloody enormous cobras."

The Sâr realized that there was only one way Henry could have acquired that knowledge and slowly turned. Even forewarned, the mystic was unprepared for what he now faced.

A half-dozen bone-white cobras, each looking to be roughly ten feet long, had emerged. They stood eye-to-eye with the creatures.

"Good Lord!" Henry breathed, fumbling with his gun as he stumbled backwards.

The Sâr planted a palm against his friend's back, holding him in place.

"Do not move," he murmured. "You cannot possibly move faster than they."

The Great Psychagogue raised his hand, but before he could proceed with whatever mystical ploy he had in mind, Mowgli leaped between the two men and the cavern's deadly sentries. In a steady, clear voice, the jungle boy began to hiss.

The snakes hissed in reply. The Sâr and Henry stood by, stunned as Mowgli seemed to have entered into conversation with the cobras.

"Your Ubasti have powerful magic," Mowgli muttered over his shoulder to Sâr. "The white hoods refuse to hear any of the animals' words of peace. They will not let us pass without a fight."

"What?" Henry whispered. "But we can't..."

"Quiet," the Sâr said, in a soothing tone. He reached into a nearby pile of treasure and rummaged around for several moments. With a nod of satisfaction, he pulled up a small golden lamp.

"Unless there's a genie in there..." Henry began.

The Sâr tilted the lamp and there was a slight sloshing noise from within.

"A different kind of magic, this time," the Sâr reassured him.

He pried open the stopper and poured the contents of the lamp on the ground, forming a line between his party and the white hoods. The flick of a wooden match ignited a two feet high wall of flame separating the party and the snakes.

The cobras abandoned their posts, all hatred of man overridden by their fear of fire. They recoiled and scattered, burrowing into piles of treasure and various small openings in the chamber walls.

Henry's knees buckled and he plopped down on an ancient chest, struggling to catch his breath. He pulled out a ragged, dirt-smeared handkerchief and patted at his forehead. Meanwhile, Mowgli and the Sâr grabbed a gold threaded tapestry and beat out the fire.

"We must search quickly," the Sâr said, tossing aside the charred remains of the tapestry. "The Ubasti will come to verify our deaths at the hands of the white hoods."

"I suppose it's too much to hope that the snakes crawled back up those holes and immediately fanged their masters?" Henry asked, getting slowly to his feet. "Have you had some miraculous epiphany about what we are looking for yet?"

"Most likely an oracle," the Sâr replied, calmly sorting through piles of treasure. "A brazier of some kind. In some cultures, the oracular spirits would speak through a severed head..."

"Possibly something the size of a small packing crate, shipped from Cairo?" Henry asked.

"An oddly specific guess, Henry..." said the Sâr, turning.

Henry was standing by a small, wooden crate. Battered and travel-worn as it was, it still was younger by a century than any other item in the chamber.

"I noticed it because it looked so out of place," Henry explained. "They couldn't very well just have tucked the treasure under their arms to get it here?"

"Quickly," the Sâr said, snatching up a golden sword and using it to pry open the crate. He and Henry began frantically pulling away the straw the treasure was packed in.

"Men are approaching," Mowgli said, appearing at the Sâr's shoulder. "From all sides."

"We have it, Henry," the Sâr breathed, removing a golden helmet. It was roughly bullet-shaped and, when worn, would have covered the wearers' entire head. There was a slight fin at the top and the front was blank and featureless, except for two eye holes which appeared to be covered by a film of gold.

"There's no seam in the metal," Henry breathed in awe. "The craftsmanship is astounding!"

The Sâr held the helmet up until he was eye-to-eye with it and stared into its shiny countenance. The helmet seemed to pull in the feeble light in the chamber and reflect it back ten-fold.

"Henry...?" the Sâr said, in a quiet, anxious tone. "Can you hear that?"

'What? Hear what?" Henry asked, looking around franti-cally. "I don't...?"

"It's... like the roar... of the ocean..." the Sâr muttered, starring glassy-eyed into the eye of the helmet. "The ocean is... calling my name..."

"Oh, dear," Henry muttered. "Sâr Dubnotal! Sâr Dubnotal!"

But the Sâr pressed the helmet against his forehead and began to rock back and forth.

"What do I do now?" Henry asked.

"Surrender the helmet or die!" a voice replied.

Out of the shadows came a dozen men, dressed all in black turbans and clothing. Some in long robes, others simply in loincloths and sandals. All had rubbed ash into their skin to further camouflage themselves, and all had a fanatical gleam in their eyes.

Henry noted with a fraction of relief that they carried no firearms, among the multitude of makeshift weapons they wielded.

An older man with a hunched posture hobbled forward, leaning heavily upon a gnarled wooden staff. He raised his arm and pointed a skeletal finger at Henry.

"Scholar," the old man rasped. "If you wish to ever feel the Sun upon you again, return the Helm of Nabu to the Ubasti!"

"The Helm of Nabu...?" Henry stuttered. He looked fran-tically around the chamber. The Sâr was either lost in some kind of communion with the golden helmet or had completely cracked under the strain. Mowgli was nowhere to be seen. Somehow, it had all fallen upon his shoulders.

"'Er... no!" Henry snapped, quickly drawing his gun and hoping the old man didn't notice the slight tremor of his hand." You and your band of cutthroats will move away and allow us to leave or, so help me, I will shoot!"

The old man looked at Henry for several heartbeats, then limped forward, until his chest was pressed against the muzzle of the gun.

"Shoot," he snarled. "Show me your warrior spirit!"

Henry froze. Aside from the fact that he hadn't the faintest idea if there were any bullets left in his gun, he had the creeping realization that he was most likely about to commit a rather elaborate form of suicide. Hundreds of miles from home, lost in the jungle, surrounded by men and beasts that would end his life without a second thought, his only allies were either wounded, had fled or were busy communing with an ancient headgear.

Henry's eyes met those of the old man and, in that moment, he knew he was not capable of shooting a man in cold blood. Even more worrisome, he could see that the old man knew it too.

The resolution to this impasse was Mowgli.

With a growl, the jungle boy sprang up out of a pile of treasure, and, knife flashing, leapt at the Ubasti.

Even the old man turned, distracted by the struggle, giving Henry enough time to reach a conclusion to his moral struggle. He turned the gun around and used the butt to club the leader of the cult unconscious.

"So this is what my life has come to," he muttered, racing over to the still entranced Sâr. "Beating up old men."

The Great Psychagogue had not moved, despite the battle raging around him. Although Henry noticed that his lips were moving, and his eyes didn't seem quite as glazed. It looked like, instead of being in a trance, the Sâr was engaged in conversation with the helmet.

"Sâr?" Henry said, laying a hand on his friend's shoulder. "We need your help. Can you hear me? I don't have the faintest idea how to get us out of here or, for that matter, how a head piece named after an Egyptian wizard fits into any of this."

"Then, it is agreed," nodded the Sâr.

"What?"

"I wasn't talking to you, Henry," the Sâr said, standing up. "Nabu and I have come to an agreement."

The mystic looked tired, as if the events of the day were finally taking their toll. Despite the sweat, grime and weariness, he managed a slight smile.

"You may find this a little disconcerting, Henry," the Sâr said, as the helmet resting in the crux of his arm began to glow. It was soon too bright to look at, and when Henry put up his hand to shade his eyes against the glare, he realized that he could see the bones in his hand.

After the events of the day, he found it almost a relief when he sank into unconsciousness...

"Didn't expect you back this soon," was the next thing he heard.

Henry opened his eyes. He was standing, not terribly steadily, but still standing, and Banks the engineer was in front of him, looking puzzled and concerned.

"Are you all right, Mr. Jones?" Banks asked.

"I... er... don't know?" Henry replied, peering about in a daze at the English engineer and his metal elephant. He pinched himself and, when things around him didn't change, shrugged resignedly.

'You look a bit... dear lord! What happened to Captain Hood? And who is that naked child with the wolf?"

Banks rushed off to gather the *Behemoth*'s crew to help tend to the wounded Hood, leaving Henry to try and make sense of things.

Sâr Dubnotal spoke with Mowgli briefly, and the wild boy nodded, gathered up the wounded wolf and vanished into the jungle.

"He is a good lad, and will grow into a noble man, I believe," said the Sâr, rejoining Henry. "Maybe one day, he'll choose to rejoin man's world..."

"Sâr?" Henry asked, quietly.

"Yes, Henry?"

"What... what just happened to us?"

"For the moment, the schemes of the Ubasti have been thwarted," the Sâr explained. "I was able to... come to an agreement with Nabu, and it was he that saw to our rather dramatic escape from the Cold Lair."

"Nabu? The advisor to the pharaoh Khufu? Are you telling me that, not only is that his helmet, but that the legends that he was some kind of...wizard or alchemist are, in fact, true?"

"Well, yes and no, Henry," the Sâr said. "Nabu is... complicated. There is a great deal more to him... and his helmet than is in the history books."

"I can't say I find your referring to Nabu in the present tense at all comforting," Henry said, casting a nervous glance at the golden helmet. It seemed to be looking back at him, in a stern, disapproving manner. "But I'm too tired for further debate. I'm just glad this whole thing is over."

"Actually, my part in these events is not over yet..."

"What do you mean?"

"I hope that, with Captain Hood's influence, we can convince the military to keep a closer eye on the Cold Lair," said the Sâr. "Between Mowgli and the British Army, the Ubasti may seek safer havens. I must commune with my masters on recent events and then travel on. My part of our bargain entails seeing that Nabu reaches a certain temple in Mesopotamia in time for a rather important meeting. You are welcome to join me..."

As they spoke, the storm finally broke, delivering the promised deluge. Everyone raced for the shelter of the *Behemoth*.

"No, thank you, Sâr Dubnotal," Henry said, as he ran. "Any traveling I do from this point on will be in order to find some peace and quiet. I'm not cut out for the life of an adventurer. I'm going to accept that offer from the college in the States. I'll meet a nice woman, settle down, get a dog and work on my thesis on the Holy Grail. No more adventures for me."

In our introduction, we mentioned several other characters, created around the same time, rivaling Sâr Dubnotal in power. Here is an opportunity to meet two of them. What kind of supernatural threat could possibly bring together such occult masters as Sâr Dubnotal, John Silence and Thomas Carnacki? Josh Reynolds' answer is to take a page from William Hope Hodgson's The House on the Borderland—*Hodgson, after all, being Carnacki's creator—and craft the terrifying tale of...*

Josh Reynolds: *The Swine of Gerasene*

October 31, 1911

The house hunched on the edge of a spur of rock that jutted out of a vast, circular chasm, downstream of a river that no one cared to name. The circular body of the house, now crumbling and overgrown, was covered in an encrustation of curved towers and pinnacles that, in the fast fading light of dusk, resembled leaping, snapping tongues of flame. Or so the two men who looked down at the house and its chasm from an overhanging bluff fancied.

"In Kraighten, they say that this house was built by the Devil," the taller of the two men rumbled in a voice akin to the crash of the rocks that occasionally fell from the cliffs into the chasm below. Beneath his overcoat, he was clad in a finely tailored hiking outfit, offset with a brightly colored sash about his waist, and on his head was a pure white turban. He held a walking stick in one hand, and the other rested on the Webley at his waist in its military style holster.

"Which one?" the other man said. He was dressed in black, and his clothes were of an archaic cut, like something from the days of gaslight and hansom cabs. His topcoat was from that era as well, and it was shiny in places with age and wear.

"Humor, John?" Sâr Dubnotal said, frowning.

He glanced at his companion, his aura and expression radiating disapproval. The other man smiled slightly. Unlike Dubnotal, he radiated a strange serenity that reached out through his eyes and voice to calm those whom he addressed.

"Laughter chases the Devil away, my friend," John Silence said. "And I fancy that there is more than one infernal presence in that decrepit structure. I can feel them, pressing against my mind and spirit." He touched his brow with two fingers. "I can taste them, in the back of my mouth, and I can smell them." He made a face. "I'm surprised that you can't."

"Some of us are not as psychically gifted as you," Dubnotal said. "Your mind's acuity puts my own to shame. And I am the greatest psychagogue my order has yet to produce."

"I fancy there're those who'd argue that point," Silence said softly. "There's a young girl in the Highlands—Crerar, I think her name is—who displays the first flickers of what I think will become a formidable psychical prowess when she reaches maturity. And, of course, there's that Vance fellow in London. His sensitivities easily rival my own. If he could learn to control his emotions, he would be an investigator second to none."

His pale, gentle eyes were locked on the house. A number of cars occupied the overgrown courtyard that sat before the crumbling ruin. He and Dubnotal had followed a trail that stretched from the shattered foyer of a certain house on Cheyne Walk to western Ireland. They had come close to their quarry in Cardiff, and then again in Dublin. Each time, the individual they pursued had slipped away, taking his captive with him.

"I cautioned him against involving himself in this affair. This Count Magnus is no Crowley or Karswell, to be taunted. He is more dangerous than either. Thomas was a fool to confront him so openly," Dubnotal said, following Silence's gaze.

"He saved that Baines fellow though," Silence said. "Surely that makes this misfortune worth it?"

107

"Yes, and because Baines was marked by the Brotherhood of Gerasene, Thomas, in saving him from his fate, took his place. We might have had time to prevent this, if he hadn't confronted Magnus at the Savoy like some hero from a two-bit penny dreadful. That is what his ill-considered heroics have gotten him." Dubnotal made a fist, and his dark eyes blazed. "I warned him, John. I warned him!"

There were a thousand and one esoteric societies, clubs, sects and orders in London. And among the most sinister was the enigmatic Brotherhood of Gerasene. Originally formed by a pig-farmer from Yorkshire, the Brotherhood had blossomed into something unpleasant. It attracted those inclined to greed, envy and brutality to its circle, and none more greedy, envious and brutal than the creature who called himself Count Magnus. His origins were a mystery—a medium in Berkshire claimed he was an antediluvian sorcerer-king; an Oxford don of Silence's acquaintance theorized that he was a 17th century Swedish mystic of ill-repute, come back to stalk the world; an elderly theatre owner in London swore that Magnus was the same trickster who had led the Tong of the Black Scorpion to its destruction in Queen Victoria's day. Magnus now controlled the Brotherhood, whatever his past.

And when the Brotherhood had set its sights on an unlucky fellow named Baines, it had attracted the attentions of Thomas Carnacki, the Ghost-Finder. Carnacki had extricated Baines from the Brotherhood's schemes, but at great cost. A few weeks after Baines had been safely delivered to a resort, to take the waters and recover from his horrific experiences, the front door of Carnacki's Cheyne Walk house had been kicked in, and his assistants clubbed and thrashed mid-meal. Carnacki himself had been kidnapped by the Brotherhood's hired thugs. That was why Sâr Dubnotal and John Silence had pursued Magnus from London to Dublin, and now to this remote outpost in the western wilds of Ireland. Both men were acquaintances of Carnacki, though in different ways—to Silence, Carnacki was something of a protégé, but to Dubnotal, he was merely a neighbor, an asset, a useful tool in Dubnotal's own war against the forces of darkness. Or so the Great Psychagogue insisted.

"So why are you here? Looking to tell poor Carnacki 'I told you so' to his face, then?" Silence said, smiling slightly.

Dubnotal frowned and glared at the older man, but only for a moment. He shook his head and turned away.

"I am here for the same reason you are," he said, after a moment.

Silence extracted a pocket-watch from his waistcoat and popped it open. "Then, I'd suggest haste. The evening shadows grow long, and it *is* Samhain, after all. Not an auspicious night to be confronting... whatever it is that's waiting for us."

"In Wales, they call the day after this night *Calan Gaeaf*," Dubnotal said. "They say that a tailless black pig roams the countryside, devouring all whom it encounters."

"Good thing it's the last of October, rather than the first of November, eh?" Silence said.

"One will be edging into the other by the time we get down there, I'm afraid," Dubnotal rumbled. "We must hurry."

They descended towards the chasm and the house carefully, moving along overgrown paths and through curtains of tangled greenery. They had come prepared for a hike, having come to their current location by boat, and then by train. The choked wilderness of vines, arthritic trees and moss-blanketed rocky outcroppings was all that remained of a once-great garden estate. It had not seen the attentions of a gardener in close to the century or more. Their coats snagged on briars and their shoes slipped in deep troughs of mud or soggy earth. They were forced to stop more than once, when they heard the sounds of movement, deep in the greenery, or above them, or below them.

Whether the sounds were caused by animals or sentries set by their quarry or something else entirely, neither man could say, nor did either give voice to an opinion. Both men had been in similar situations, and they knew enough to save their breath for the descent. When they at least reached the ruin, the Sun had long since disappeared and the only light was that provided by the Moon, and the electric torches both men carried. They turned off the latter as they reached the crumbled walls of the forecourt. There was a man on guard, strolling through the cars, with a halo of cigarette smoke above his head. He had the look of a dock worker, or professional pugilist, and he held a shotgun loosely in his hand.

Dubnotal shed his coat, handed Silence his walking stick, and drew his Webley. He pressed a finger to his lips and stepped through a hole in the wall. Silence frowned, but made no attempt to stop the other man. Dubnotal slithered through the cars, moving as silently as a cat. As Silence watched, the Great Psychagogue hefted a chunk of stone and tossed it. The guard turned, suddenly alert, as stone rattled against stone. Dubnotal shot forward, and slammed the butt of the Webley down on the back of the man's head. The guard fell and Dubnotal caught him, and rolled him beneath a car. He motioned for Silence to join him.

"I thought for sure you would kill him," Silence murmured as he gave Dubnotal back his coat. When he made to hand him his stick, Dubnotal waved it aside.

"You keep it," he said, "And I never kill, unless it's necessary. Every death weakens the great web of life." He hefted the pistol. "Besides which, this is mostly for show. Thomas is a better shot than I am."

"Thomas couldn't hit the broad side of a barn," Silence said.

Dubnotal grinned. "My point exactly," he said.

He nodded towards the entrance, and they continued on. There was no door, though there were signs that there had once been one. The entryway was covered in mildew and mould and it stank of wet stone and animals. There were great gaps in the roof, allowing in moonlight and the walls sagged abominably. There were a number of footprints in the carpet of fungus that covered the flagstones of the floor. They followed the footprints to the stairs that led down into the cellars of the ruin.

The cellar of the ruin was a huge, multi-room expanse, and like the ground floor, was encrusted with a century's worth of mould. The feathery bristles of the faintly phosphorescent patches that clung to the stones stirred in an unpleasant fashion as they descended. A strange smell hung on the air, like a pig sty or an animal lair. Strange sculptures of fantastic design crouched in niches and in corners, adding to the eerie air of the place.

A voice, deep and raspy, echoed through the cellar. It seemed to come from everywhere and nowhere at once. Silence pointed towards a faint glow that pierced the gloom. Dubnotal nodded and they crept through the brick and stone archways, moving swiftly, but carefully. Things moved in the darkness around them, things which grunted and clawed at the stone softly as they watched the two men pass by. Neither Silence nor Dubnotal paid any attention to the phantasms. They had seen too much in their respective careers to be shaken by unseen prowlers.

"This squalid ruin is but a tattered reflection of the glory upon the other side of the border, my friends," the voice intoned, each word echoing through the cellar like a gunshot. "It is a tombstone, marking wonder and mystery. The gate is shut, and the lock is rusted. But we will force it open and fling it wide, so that Our Father, the Hog, might enter this world to run riot upon it. He snuffles at the door even now, and his children wait in the shadows to be called to our celebration."

The speech continued in that vein for several minutes. Dubnotal and Silence reached the light even as a wave of applause greeted a pause in the recitation. They came to a large, domed chamber, where ribs of wood and brick held up a roof of stone. Water dripped from somewhere, creating tiny rivers of running wetness which curled between the stones of the floor. The swinish smell was stronger here, and it seemed to permeate everything.

A crowd of cowled and robed shapes stood in a semi-circle around an altar composed of a heavy flat stone set atop two others. Behind the altar, an immense circular trap door had been set into a hump of rock that rose at an angle from the floor and slumped against the wall. Several of the cowled figures held staves topped by flickering lanterns and before the altar stood the man whom Dubnotal and Silence had pursued from Kensington to Kraighten.

Count Magnus wore heavy robes, and a wide-brimmed curate's hat. His face was obscured by a steel mask and his hands were hidden by thick gloves. He gesticulated as he spoke, causing his robes to flap and flare.

"In this place, our master has set his hoof," he said. "And in this place, we shall call him forth from the roaring paddock!"

A small, dwarfish shape capered and bounced about Magnus with seemingly childish glee. Its all-concealing hood rippled with loud squeals as Magnus spoke.

"I have made the Black Pilgrimage, and in the ruins of one world, I beheld another and the Hog, that cunning Swine of Gerasene, came to me and spoke of the world to come, when he would show mankind new ways to shout and revel and *kill*!"

The hooded figures bellowed in appreciation, and as the noise rattled the stones, Dubnotal and Silence moved swiftly, striking and grabbing two of the Brotherhood from the back of the crowd. They dragged the unconscious cultists back through the archway and swiftly stripped them of their robes. Then, disguising themselves, they joined the crowd. No one had noticed the disappearance and sudden reappearance of two members.

Magnus continued to speak:

"Our chosen sacrifice was taken from us by the trickery of itinerant magus of little account, and thus, my servants have claimed him in recompense. In the dark places where man may not go, they have prepared him for what is to come. And now, they shall bring him to the stone of sacrifice."

As he spoke, he raised his hand and the lanterns sparked and crackled, as if some strange pulse had passed between them. The lanterns dimmed. All was silent for a moment. Then, with a grinding shriek, the trapdoor began to open.

Silence grabbed Dubnotal's arm. He staggered and the latter reached out to support him. "What is it?" he hissed.

He had his answer, even before Silence could form a reply. A wave of pure, unadulterated psychic foulness struck the defenses of his mind, tearing at his thoughts and soul for a moment before passing on. From within the yawning maw of the trapdoor, a fetid wind blew forth. It bore with it the stink of ages, of lightless caverns and spilled blood. Shapes moved within the darkness. Hunched, squat shapes that grunted and squealed abominably as they ascended from whatever noisome vaults lurked beneath the deep cellars of the house. On their backs, they bore a pale shape, clad in a tattered suit, smeared with phosphorescent muck. At a sweeping gesture from Magnus, they began to carry their burden towards the altar stone.

"Thomas," Silence murmured, "He's in one piece, at least; I—hsst!" He made a surreptitious gesture towards the front of the crowd, where Magnus' hunched familiar was slinking through the forest of robed legs, pausing only to occasionally snuffle at a hem or sleeve. Dubnotal frowned.

"Ready yourself," he said. "Get to him as quickly as you can. Time is as much our enemy here as Magnus."

"And you?" Silence asked, gripping the walking stick tightly. The creature was drawing closer. It seemed to be in no hurry. Then it stiffened and its cowled features turned in their direction. It gave a querulous snort and began to move directly for them.

"I? I will be making a bit of a scene," Dubnotal said, with a grim smile.

Carnacki's unconscious body was laid atop the altar and he was bound to the stone by thick ropes by the softly grunting creatures. In the semi-darkness, neither Silence nor Dubnotal could get a clear look at them.

"Now my brethren, we have only to wait. In a few moments, the Great Swine will rise from the depths and take his due, and give unto us his blessings," Magnus said, lifting his hands in benediction.

Whatever he was about to say next was interrupted by the sudden, loud squeal of his familiar as it pointed a stubby limb at Dubnotal and Silence. The crowd of cultists drew back with a communal gasp. Dubnotal reacted swiftly. He leveled the Webley and snapped off a shot. It struck the dwarfish creature dead in the centre of its mass, and the force of the bullet knocked it from its feet and sent it tumbling backwards.

The echoes of the shot had barely faded before Dubnotal roared out an incantation and the gloom was rent asunder by an explosion of light. Revealed by the flare of light, a horde of grotesque swine-things shrieked and squealed, cowering back. Taking his cue, Silence darted from the stunned crowd of celebrants and scrambled towards Carnacki's bound form.

A swine-thing gurgled and clawed at him, its tiny eyes still watering from the blaze of light that had swept the cavernous chamber. He pivoted and made the Voorish Sign inches from the creature's face. It squealed and jerked back hard enough to send it tumbling back into its fellows. As it fell, he caught the edge of the altar stone and vaulted over it, and Carnacki, putting the stone between him and the swine-things.

"Thomas," he hissed insistently. He slapped him. "Wake up!"

Carnacki's eyes fluttered. "Ugh—what—John," he mumbled, his bleary gaze fixing on her. "What's going on? What are you doing here?"

"Saving your hide," Silence barked.

He hefted Dubnotal's stick from within his borrowed cloak and swiftly drew the silver blade he knew to be concealed within its handle. Dubnotal had gotten the idea after a chance meeting with an American by the name of Pursuivant. The American had claimed that the sword-cane he carried had been forged by Saint Dunstan. He began slicing at the moldy ropes which held the occultist fast to the stone table.

"Is that Sâr Dubnotal?" Carnacki said, twisting around. "I say, is this a rescue?"

"Yes to both," Silence said, "Now stop squirming, this is difficult enough."

Dubnotal had stepped from the crowd of robed and hooded celebrants and dispensed with his disguise. He let the borrowed robes collapse to the damp stones as he stalked towards the gathered pack of swine-things. The squealing, snorting creatures glowed with the same faint phosphorescence that they had smeared on Carnacki's clothes and they gnashed cracked and yellowed tusks at the Great Psychagogue.

"Back," he roared, "Back, spawn of the lightless gulfs!"

"Stop him," Magnus rasped, flinging out a hand. "The sacrifice must not be interrupted!"

The small, cowled shape rolled to its feet and gave a squeal far out of proportion with its stature. Robes flaring, it scrambled towards Dubnotal on all fours, seeming no worse for wear for having been shot. Dubnotal spun about as the creature leapt for him and ducked aside. It crashed down where he'd been standing and whipped around with an ear-splitting screech. It drew a knife from within its robes and slashed wildly at the mystic.

"Oh no, my little friend," Dubnotal said as he backed away, out of its reach, "A fellow by the name of Doctor Omega warned me of letting you get too close, and you as well, Count Magnus. Or should I call you *Greel*?"

"Silence," Magnus thundered. He started towards Dubnotal. "Do not speak that name."

"Names have power, do they not?" Dubnotal said, "Even those names not yet assigned a soul, eh Magnus? Are you afraid that if I speak that name, the hounds of time will catch your putrid scent? Criminal, warlock, warlord, butcher and fugitive from all that is good and holy I call you, whatever your true name. You and your homunculus are damned thrice over, in this epoch and those yet to come."

Magnus snarled and clawed about in his robes for a pistol. Dubnotal shot a look towards Silence as he sliced through the last of Carnacki's bonds. The Great Psychagogue dove to the floor as Magnus drew his weapon and fired. It resembled an old fashioned flintlock, but it made a sound like a kettle boiling over, and the air stank of lightning as Magnus fired. The rock was scorched where Dubnotal had been standing. He sprang to his feet and Magnus turned, tracking him.

"You shall not stop me here, Rosicrucian, even as you failed to stop me in London," Magnus snarled. "The vessel has been prepared, and the great swine comes, even now!"

Odd, black puffs of something very much like smoke had begun to rise from between the flat stones which made up the floor around the altar. The cavernous cellar began to shake with a strange, oscillating rhythm, and an eerie ripple of ugly crimson light flashed through the cracks between the stones that made up the walls and floor. The swine-things began to grunt and squeal where they cowered and several struck the ground with hairy fists in time to the relentless, pounding rhythm. Slowly at first, and then more loudly, the members of the Brotherhood joined in, stomping their feet and making strange piggish calls.

"I bargained a life for a life," Magnus said, his voice carrying throughout the cellar, over the noise made by beast and man. "In that place of cold fire, where I had been condemned by treachery, I struck a deal—life for life! I shall tend the Hog, as a swineherd must, and in return—life! My veins thrum with the stuff of the outside, and I am eternal. I am Ouroboros, travelling from Reykjavik to Raback, from China to Chorazin and back again. I am a god, in the service of gods."

He took aim with his strange pistol and fired again. Silence grabbed Carnacki and jerked him off the altar just in time.

Magnus' familiar pounced onto the altar a moment later and squealed down at them. The sound was filled with equal parts triumph and promise. Silence shoved Carnacki aside, as the thing clawed for them with the blade it held. Carnacki scrambled aside. He caught hold of the loose knot of thick ropes that Silence had severed and snapped them at the hooded creature. It whirled with a brain-piercing squall, and lunged off of the altar after Carnacki. He dodged aside and flung a loop of rope about the creature's bulbous, cowled head.

Speedily, he crossed to the other side of the altar from it and yanked the ropes tight, dragging the creature back against the rough stone.

"I say old man, care to give me a hand?" he shouted, as the thing clawed helplessly at the improvised noose around its throat.

Silence saw at once what Carnacki had in mind. He circled the altar, his silver blade bared. The homunculus saw him coming and redoubled its struggles. It whined like a beast in a trap as he lifted the blade.

"Hurry John, the little blighter is stronger than he looks!" Carnacki shouted.

Silence steeled himself and made a single, smooth thrust. The creature shrilled once and went limp. Magnus howled out a curse in a language neither man recognized. He fired his weapon at Silence, but Dubnotal crashed into the latter, knocking him from the line of fire.

Magnus continued to fire, as all three occultists, and they sought cover behind the altar. He ranted and roared, and his weapon sizzled and snarled in accompaniment.

"He's mad," Carnacki said, "Utterly barmy. I mean, I knew he was bad when I bearded him at the Savoy, after that business with Baines, but this just ain't cricket."

"No, it isn't," Dubnotal said, glowering at Carnacki, who shrugged helplessly. "You were rash—no, worse, a fool!" the Great Psychagogue snarled.

"Enough, we have other concerns at the moment than Thomas' appalling lack of common sense," Silence said, peering around the altar. "He's trying to keep us trapped here."

On the other side of the altar, the swine-things were racing to and fro about the chamber, like confused pigs. Magnus was shouting. The cultists were milling about nervously, unsure as to whether they should interfere or not. No one seemed to want to get too close to the altar, or the black smoke which was billowing from beneath it.

"We're pinned down, chaps," Carnacki said. "I don't suppose you have such a thing as a Webley about your person, what? Or a set of brass knuckles?"

Dubnotal touched the floor and then jerked his hand away, as if he'd been scalded. "Weapons would be useless against what is coming," he said. Nonetheless, he handed his Webley to Carnacki, who clutched it as if it were a totem. Dubnotal reached into his coat, and began fumbling for something. "Luckily," he continued, "Some of us think before we act."

"Well think quickly," Carnacki said as he looked at the billowing black cloud that rose about them. "Last time I faced that monstrosity of Magnus' I almost lost my soul, not to mention my life. I'd rather not go through that again, if I don't have to."

The red glow seeping up from the cracks had grown brighter now, and the air felt close. The floor shivered, and something that might have been titan footsteps sounded, somewhere far below them.

"He is here!" Magnus cried, "The Hog has come!"

The black smoke had risen to thigh level, and the red hell-light had begun to flash faster and faster and the chamber suddenly shuddered as something vast and unseen unleashed a monstrous grunt. The swine-things squealed, as if in reply, and a second thunderous grunt followed the first.

"What about the Incantation of Raaaee, or the Saaamaaa Ritual?" Silence said.

He looked pale, in the eerie light. The smoke bulged and stirred, as if something were rising from beneath it. The stones of the cellar ground against one another, as if the ruin were changing shape, becoming something else. The chant of the cultists had reached a crescendo, as had the shrieks of the swine-things.

"No time," Dubnotal said. He finally retrieved the item he'd sought—a strangely angled sliver of ruby which flickered with an internal light. "Something climbs towards us, out of dark gulfs. We must knock it from the path, before it reaches our sphere." He licked his lips and held up the sliver. "Desperate times call for desperate measures."

"What the deuce is that?" Carnacki said, peering at the crystal.

Silence said, "Is that—?"

"It is," Dubnotal said grimly. "A sliver of the gem known as the Blood of Belshazzar, which was retrieved from the fire column of Kor before it found its way to the lands of men. Within its facets lurk the flames of the Faltine which are hot enough to burn the very stuff of reality. The reflection of those cosmic fires—the fires of creation itself—was captured in the gem, and a flicker of it yet lurks in this sliver." He looked at the others. "We must cauterize this wound in the body of our world. The holy spark of the Faltine will burn away the foulness that holds this place in its grip."

"And how do we do that?" Carnacki asked.

Dubnotal rose to his feet. "I hope your marksmanship has improved, since I last saw it demonstrated," he said, adding, "When I throw this, shoot it."

"And then?" Silence said.

"What is it you Englishmen say—ah, yes—leg it," Dubnotal said.

Then, without another word, he threw the sliver towards the greatest concentration of smoke. Carnacki rose to his feet and snapped off a shot.

The sliver exploded, and the cellar was abruptly awash in heat and light. The curling plumes of smoke caught fire, as did the swine-things, who screamed and began to stagger and stumble blindly towards the trapdoor. Magnus cursed, and threw up his hands. The unseen presence in the smoke yammered and squealed and the ruin shifted and shook, as if, thwarted in its desires, it intended to smash down the house and crush all within out of spite.

The cultists were screaming and running for the stairs. Unlike the swine-things, they weren't burning, but Carnacki had swiftly emptied the Webley at their feet to encourage them. Between the gunshots, the shaking of the ruin and the sudden, blinding light, the Brotherhood of Gerasene had had enough for one night. They began to push and shove as they fought their way up the stairs. Dubnotal, Carnacki and Silence followed more slowly. The three men paused at the top of the steps, allowing the cultists to scramble past and out.

The cleansing fires of the Faltine washed over the ancient brickwork of the cellar, searing away the mould and fungus. Crackling flames enveloped the altar, blackening the stone and causing it to crack and shift. The body of the homunculus burned and as they watched, it collapsed in on itself. Of Magnus, there was no sign. The heat and light pierced the gloom on the other side of the trapdoor, and they could see the writhing shadows of the swine-things, as they were consumed by the cosmic inferno. Flames crept across the roof of the cellar and the floor, devouring the mould and strange statuary alike.

As they left the cellar behind, the ruin shifted about them, with a momentous groan. Dust shifted down, and the roof began to slump. A wall collapsed behind them, showering them with dust as they reached the courtyard. All of the cars had gone. Even the man Dubnotal had knocked unconscious was gone.

"Looks like the only thing holding this pile together was the fungus," Carnacki said, glancing back as dust expelled by the house's slow collapse billowed around them. "I'd say it's about time, what?" he coughed.

Neither Dubnotal nor Silence replied. Carnacki fell silent, and the three men watched as the house slowly folded in on itself and then, noisily and with much complaint, sloughed into the yawning chasm. Smoke and dust rose from the heart of the collapse, and for a moment, the twin columns mingled to take the form of a great swine. Then, as the Sun crept over the horizon, it dissipated.

Carnacki handed Dubnotal back his Webley, butt-first.

"Many thanks, old thing," he said. "I thought I was a goner for sure." Dubnotal said nothing.

"Think nothing of it, Thomas," Silence said, brushing dust from his sleeve. "If we don't watch out for one another, who will?" he added.

"Still, it was dashed kind of you to come to my rescue like that, and after you'd told me not to get involved in the first place," Carnacki said, nudging Dubnotal's arm with the revolver.

Dubnotal took the weapon, holstered it and, ignoring Silence's smile and Carnacki's bewildered expression, simply said, "I told you so."

Louis Feuillade and Arthur Bernède's Judex is the hero of a popular 1916 serial, in which the cloaked avenger (whose real identity is Jacques de Trémeuse) exacts his revenge on the evil banker Favraux who ruined his family. In this story, Judex, who has impersonated Favraux's secretary, Vallières, finds the time to protect Paris from another, more unworldly menaces, with the help, of course, of Sâr Dubnotal...

Matthew Baugh: *The Gargoyles of Notre-Dame*

Paris, 1913

"I feel a spiritual presence," Gianetti Annunciata said. "It is drawing closer."

Vallières glanced around the circular table which held a crystal ball, a lit candle, and a stack of tarot cards. To the distinguished, white-haired man's left sat Madame Beaudin, a plump, matronly woman who held his hand. Next to her was her attorney, Monsieur Moubray, then her companion, Mademoiselle Denault, followed by the tall, turbaned figure of Sâr Dubnotal. Finally, at Vallières' right hand was the medium, a beautiful Italian woman with a wealth of dark hair.

"Is it Raymond?" Madame Beaudin asked. She sounded so eager that Vallières' heart went out to her. He had no use for spiritualists and it was difficult for him to watch his employer's clients defrauded by such charlatans. Then again, it was difficult for him to see them defrauded by Favraux, his employer, but that was a necessary evil. The man, who only called himself Vallières, had spent a lot of time and effort infiltrating Favraux's financial empire. One day, very soon, he would use all that he had learned and the corrupt banker's many victims would be avenged. But that was still in the future. For now, he was playing a role, and that meant accompanying a wealthy client to this absurd ritual.

A white mist began to gather over the table.

Ectoplasm, Vallières thought. Without seeming to, his keen eyes searched for the source of the mysterious substance. He was surprised when he couldn't find it; Annunciata and her cohort must be exceptionally skilled.

"Celeste," the medium said. Her voice had changed to the deep and cultured tones of a Frenchman with the trace of a Gascon accent. The gray-haired man marveled at her talent for mimicry.

"Raymond; it is you!"

"Why have you summoned me?" the medium asked.

"I... I have to ask you a question. The bank has come to me with some investments. It will cost forty-thousand francs, our whole savings, but Monsieur Favraux has guaranteed me that there will be a great profit. Isn't that so, Monsieur Vallières?"

The gray-haired man fought to keep from grimacing. He knew that his employer's investment opportunity was a sham and had been glad when she had asked to consult some friends before signing away her money. He had been disappointed to learn that the chief person she wanted to consult was her late husband. Unable to say much without giving himself away, he simply nodded his head.

"The banker's secretary?" Annunciata asked in the man's voice. "No, you are deceived."

Vallières' eyebrows drew together. He was not what he seemed to be, but there was no way for the medium to know that. He remained silent, trusting that this was part of the ruse on the widow.

"What do you mean?" Madame Beaudin asked with a confused expression.

"No matter," Annunciata said. "Celeste, you must not invest a cent in Favraux's schemes. Not now or ever."

The woman gasped and Vallières felt the tension in his muscles relax a bit. A glance at the lawyer showed that he was also relieved to hear those words.

"But... why, Raymond?" the widow said.

"You asked and I have answered. That is all I can say."

"Very well, my dear," she said, gathering her courage. "Now there are some other…"

"No!" boomed the bass voice from the pretty woman's mouth. "I answered one question because I loved you in life and love you still. But I have passed beyond the concerns of this world and you must accept that."

"You… you're leaving me?"

"Use your own wits and the advice of those you can trust, Celeste. Do not call me again by this medium or another for I will not come."

The widow sank into her chair, looking stunned. As she did, Annunciata's gaze shifted to the Sâr and she spoke. The voice was harsher this time and more guttural. Gone were all traces of Gascony. The new voice sounded vaguely German.

"*El Tebib!*" she growled, "if you wish to find me, you must go to the holy place where the grotesques gather. To-night, as the midnight hour strikes," she said. "You must face your foeman's wrath and lust."

Sâr Dubnotal's bearded face reflected surprise, then anger. He rose and faced the medium with one palm thrust toward her.

"Enough!" he said in a low voice. "By Mitra and thrice-great Viritrilbia, I command you to release her!"

The deep voice growled and a cold breeze swept through the room, scattering papers and extinguishing the candle.

The medium spoke and it was Monsieur Beaudin's voice again.

"You must not go alone," she cried. "There is another who must accompany…"

The sentence ended in a cry of pain, this time in the woman's own voice. The wind stopped and the tarot cards shot into the air and scattered through the room. A pair of the cards fell onto the back of Vallières' hand.

In the dimness that followed, the gray-haired man found the gaslights and turned them up. In their glow, he looked bewildered while Madame Beaudin and her companion huddled together in fear; Sâr Dubnotal supported a very pale Gianetti Annunciata. He noticed that he had unconsciously held onto the tarot cards and glanced at them. One was *The Magician*, and the other *Justice*.

He hesitated a moment, shocked, then tucked the cards into his jacket and moved back to the others.

"Forgive me, my friends," the Sâr said, as he helped Gianetti to her feet. "A powerful force has interfered with our séance; fortunately, the danger to you is over. Please, go home now for I must tend to Mademoiselle Annunciata as well as… other business."

The group was distraught and confused, except for Vallières who, gently but inexorably, led the others out of Sâr Dubnotal's apartment and into the Avenue de l'Opéra. But as the doors closed, the gaze he cast behind him was anything but gentle. Something was happening here, and he would be back to discover what it was.

It was half past eleven when Sâr Dubnotal stepped out of his building and into a waiting taxi. Down the block, the man who had been Vallières was instantly alert. No one looking at him now would have recognized the kindly old man. A white wig and makeup had been stripped away to reveal a charismatic, youthful face partly obscured by the collar of his long cloak and the shadows of his wide-brimmed hat. The mysterious man sat behind the wheel of a powerful modern sedan, which slipped out after the taxi into the moonlit streets of Paris.

He followed without headlights and at a distance; for traffic this time of night was almost non-existent, and he didn't want the Sâr to know he was being followed. He used parallel streets when he could, and hung back when it became clear where his quarry was going.

He waited until the taxi had crossed the Pont d'Arcole onto the Ile de la Cité before he followed. He saw Dubnotal disembark onto the steps of the Notre-Dame Cathedral and dismiss the cab. As he watched, another man stepped from the shadows to greet him, a priest in a black cassock and a red sash. The two shook hands and spoke in voices too low for Judex to understand. After a moment, they walked to the entrance of the South Tower. The priest unlocked the door and the two men entered.

As the door closed, Judex was already in motion. Moving silently and almost invisibly under the cover of night, he reached the door quickly. He checked to make certain he wasn't being observed then quietly opened the portal and slipped inside. He could hear the two men's footsteps clanging on the narrow spiral stair as they ascended the 387 steps to the top.

The man in black followed and his footfalls made only the faintest whisper of noise. When he reached the top, he paused, listening to the two men who had stepped onto the tower's narrow walkway.

"…and you are certain this is the place that was meant?" came a voice. It sounded like a man past the prime of life and somewhat out of breath. Judex assumed it must be the clergyman.

"Where else?" replied a voice he recognized as the Sâr's. It was deep and resonant, and not the least winded. "The message said 'the holy place where the grotesques gather.' I knew at once that it had to be the Cathedral and its *Galerie des Chimères*."

"I do not understand," the priest replied.

"I have an enemy who I have been pursuing for months," Dubnotal said. "He has challenged me to come here tonight."

"My son, I owe you a great debt, but I cannot allow your fight to enter this holy place."

"It is not my choice, Monsieur l'abbé. Herr Doctor Von Meyer does not respect sanctity of any kind. Whatever he is planning, it would happen tonight whether I had come or not."

"If that is true, then I can only pray you are able to stop him."

"Thank you," Dubnotal said. "Fortunately, I will not face him alone."

"I don't know what I can do to help," the priest said.

"Thank you," Monsieur l'abbé," the Sâr replied. "But there will be another to help me. Perhaps he is already here."

He glanced around, and Judex withdrew deeper into the darkness. His fingers brushed the handle of one of the Steyr automatic pistols he carried. His brow furrowed as he wondered who this man was and what sort of game he was playing.

"Is there anything different here?" the turbaned man continued. "Anything unusual?"

"Only these," the priest said, gesturing at a pair of hideous statues. One had the head of a tiger and the wings of an eagle, the other had a satyr's face and bat wings. Beyond that, Judex couldn't make them out.

"New gargoyles?"

"Actually, they're *chimerae*," the priest said. "We have them on loan from the cathedral in Vyones. They've had some damage from the German shelling and had to move their statuary and relics to safer locations."

"Very sensible," Sâr Dubnotal said. "If you don't mind, father, I'd like to be alone to commune with your gargoyles and *chimerae* for a while."

"I do not understand."

"I believe my enemy will strike at me tonight. If that happens, I don't want you to be in harm's way."

"But, what about you?"

"I've taken steps to protect myself," the Sâr replied. "Come back at dawn. If I am successful, I will be able to tell you much more."

The priest hesitated, then nodded. "Very well. I don't like this, but I do trust you, my friend. May Our Lady and all the saints and angels watch over you tonight."

When the priest had gone, Sâr Dubnotal took a long look around the interior of the tower. "He's gone," he called. "You may as well come out; I know you're here."

Judex didn't believe that the man could have seen him, but he saw no reason to remain concealed. He stepped from the shadows, his long cloak folded around him.

"Ah!" the Sâr said, a thin smile forming on his lips. "You are a stealthy one. But are you one of the Herr Doctor's agents, or the one Gianetti predicted?"

Judex raised his left hand. With a stage magician's flourish, he made the tarot card seem to appear in his hand. Then he tossed it to land face up near the mystic's feet so the word *Justice* could easily be read.

"That tells me what you are," Dubnotal said, raising an eyebrow. "I still don't know who you are."

"I call myself Judex."

Judging by his expression, Sâr Dubnotal was hoping for more of an answer, but Judex wasn't inclined to give him one. The man in black relied on knowing more than his enemies— more even then his potential allies. He likes having enough information to be the master of the situation. Unexpected happenings, like the séance, and mysterious people were a frustration and always a potential source of danger.

"Very well, Monsieur Judex," Dubnotal said. "Did you hear what I said to the abbé?"

"That a rival magician with a German name sent a message to draw you here and strike at you? I heard that."

"You sound skeptical, my friend," the mystic said.

"I don't hold with mummery and hocus pocus," Judex replied. "I may not know how you managed everything at the séance…"

"So you *were* there!" Dubnotal's eyes narrowed in thought, then opened wide. "Of course! You were the old man, Vallières. That is an impressive disguise, Monsieur."

Judex kept his face blank with effort. The man's shrewd deductions had rattled him more than he wanted to show.

"If you're going to continue this guessing game, I'll be on my way." Judex turned to go.

"Please," Dubnotal said. There was something in his voice that made Judex pause—a trace of vulnerability in his confident façade. He turned back to face the mystic.

"Stand vigil with me until midnight," he said. "If something happens, I will need your help."

"And if nothing happens?"

"Then you have my word that I will never trouble you again."

Judex nodded. "Until midnight."

"Thank you, Monsieur," Dubnotal said. "Then it is time to prepare."

He took a piece of chalk from his pocket and began to draw patterns on the floor of the tower.

"Come into the circle," he said.

"What is it?" Judex said.

"A form of protection," Dubnotal replied. "It will shield us against any magical attack."

"Thank you, but I'll see to my own safety," Judex said. He drew back into the shadows and watched as the Sâr continued his drawing. First, he made a large circle, then at each of the points of the compass he wrote something in Hebrew. Halfway between each set of words he drew a five-pointed star, then a smaller circle within the first. He drew four more Hebrew letters at the cardinal points and finally two interlocked triangles, forming a six-pointed circle, with himself in the center.

"What do you do if you need to counter-attack?" Judex asked. He found himself both amused and vaguely troubled by the mystic's preparations. He seemed so sincere about his mummery.

"I have this," Dubnotal replied. Reaching into his jacket, he produced a short, straight dagger with a three-edged blade and a hideous, demonic face on the pommel.

"This is a Tibetan *phurba*," the mystic said. "It should suffice against anything my enemy can send at me."

Hearing footsteps on the spiral stair, Judex faded back into the shadows. A few moments later the door opened and a tall, dour looking man in the dark cloak of a sacristan emerged, followed by three younger assistants. The sacristan nodded curtly to Sâr Dubnotal and led the group to the platform where the four bells in the tower hadn't been rung since before the days of Quasimodo. They took their seats and began working a system of foot-pedals to get the huge bells ringing. Judex glanced across to the South tower where the massive Bourdan Emmanuel hung silent. The colossal bell was only rung on high holy days.

The clamor of the bells was deafening but mercifully brief. As the twelfth stroke rang out and then began to fade away, Judex heard a new sound—the scrape of stone on stone. He turned to the two grotesques and saw something that chilled him to the core. The two hideous statues from Vyones were moving. Their eyes were lit with a hellish glow and their limbs had gone from stony immobility to fluid, animal grace.

The sacristan crossed himself and his helpers froze in horror as the monsters moved toward Sâr Dubnotal. They reached the edge of the circle and stopped as if they had encountered a wall. Inside his ring of protection the mystic raised his strange dagger and began to chant something in some language Judex didn't recognize.

The cat-headed gargoyle opened its mouth in a silent roar. It bared terrible fangs at Dubnotal and swung a taloned paw. The claws struck sparks of blue flame as they encountered the invisible barrier and failed to reach their target. Judex noted that the creature's other hand was missing, apparently broken off sometime in the past.

The second grotesque, which he now clearly saw to be a bat-winged satyr with the upper torso of a leering, horned man and the lower body shaped like the hindquarters of a goat, didn't waste any effort on the barrier. It turned toward the cringing bell-ringers and began to stalk them.

"Stay back!" Judex shouted as he drew his pistols and emerged from the shadows. He fired both weapons and the bullets struck the monster's torso side-by-side.

Surprised, the gargoyle stepped backward and clutched its chest. Then it moved its hands and a triumphant leer lit its face. The bullets had barely made a mark on the solid granite of its body.

"Run!" Judex yelled to the terrified men. "Get to the stair; I'll hold this thing here!"

He fired as he spoke, this time striking the creature in the forehead. Again, the damage was negligible, but the shot managed to focus the gargoyle's attention on him. He lost track of the ringers and Sâr Dubnotal's fight as it sprang at him. Judex dodged by the narrowest of margins.

As the creature turned on him again, Judex shot it point blank in one glowing eye. He heard the bullet ricochet away with a whine as the gargoyle's clawed hand caught the front of his shirt. With frightening ease, it picked him off his feet and tossed him away. The force of the throw carried Judex out of the tower into the open space, two-hundred feet above the ground. His back struck something solid and he lost his grip on one of the pistols. He grabbed frantically and his hands caught something. With a start he realized that he was hanging from a gargoyle, one of the Cathedral's many hideous waterspouts. With a surge of effort, he managed to pull himself atop it and lay there, gasping.

The monster didn't give him a moment to rest. It lunged at him. Judex had managed to hold onto one of his pistols and fired once at point blank range to no effect. As the thing's stone fingers encircled his throat, he grasped his wrist and heaved backward, thrusting his foot into its midsection as he did. The improvised throw worked; using his leg as a lever he thrust the monster up and over. Judex struggled for a moment to keep from joining his foe in its plunge into space. A moment later he rose and looked down.

"Impossible," he whispered.

The gargoyle hadn't struck the ground. Somehow—defying physics and common sense—its outspread wings had caught air, and it glided beneath him like a monstrous bat. It swung away from the tower and gained altitude.

Judex knew that, if the gargoyle gained the tower again, his chances of beating it were next to nothing. Taking careful aim he fired all his remaining bullets in quick succession. The first punched a hole in the monster's wing. Like the rest of the monster's body, the membrane was stone—or stone-like flesh—but here it was thin enough to puncture. The second and third bullets also made holes from which fine cracks extended. When the fourth shot struck, a large chunk split away and the gargoyle's flight became erratic. The final bullets fairly shattered the wing, sending the monster down to the cobbles with a shattering impact.

He stared down on the broken remains of the monster for a moment, then clambered back into the tower. The ringers were gone, he saw, and Dubnotal still stood in his protective circle, though he was too busy dodging to do anything else. Apparently, the cat-headed gargoyle was helpless to pass the barrier, but nothing prevented him from tearing up boards, metal rods, and loose pieces of stonework and using them as missiles.

"Judex, look out!" the Sâr cried. It was an unnecessary warning and one that cost the mystic dearly. The monster hurled a chunk of rock the size of a big man's fist. The projectile caught the Sâr in the torso and sent him reeling out of the circle, the *phurba* falling from his grip. The monster's lips pulled back from its fangs in a snarl of pleasure, and it stalked toward him.

Reflexively, Judex raised his pistol before remembering it was empty. The gargoyle had turned its back on him in its single-minded desire to kill Sâr Dubnotal and he used that. Racing after the monster he leaped on its back, locking his legs around its waist and one arm around its neck. He used the other to hammer at its head with the pistol.

The creature staggered, but quickly recovered. It was immensely strong and his weight impaired it no more than a housecat's would have slowed him. Worse, his hammering blows with the pistol barely scratched its head. The gargoyle flexed its wings, crushing him between them. Judex gasped in pain, but tightened his grip. Then the creature reached back, over its head. He felt the talons pierce his cloak and clothing to tear into the flesh of his back as it gripped him. Then the thing pulled him loose with frightening ease and slammed him down.

Ignoring his pain, the man in black tried to roll away but the monster was too fast. It placed a knee in his belly, crushing the wind out of him. The monster's talons dug into his chest muscles as it pinned him to the tower floor. Judex struck at it with the pistol and managed to break off one of the thing's fingers, but it swung the stump of its other arm, smashing the weapon out of his grasp. The cat's head lowered, fangs bared and Judex thrust up both hands in a futile attempt to hold it back.

As the mouth opened, ready to tear out his throat, Judex heard chanting from behind the creature. Sâr Dubnotal had risen and held the *phurba* in his hands as he murmured strange words. As the jaws descended on his throat, he saw the Sâr let go of the ritual knife. Amazingly, it did not fall but hovered for a moment before shooting toward the gargoyle's back. He heard the rasp of iron against stone then the monster reared back, its face a mask of pain and rage. It toppled to the side, as stiff and unmoving as stone should be.

As Judex rose, he saw Dubnotal kneel by the fallen gargoyle to inspect it. The handle of the *phurba* projected from the monster's back, between its shoulder-blades.

"Is it...dead?" he asked.

"Yes," Dubnotal replied. "At least, as much as that word can be applied to a creature like this. I should have recognized these gargoyles sooner. They were the work of a stonecutter named Reynard. Legend says that his wrath and lust were so great that they somehow animated the creatures and that neither magic nor the protection of holy symbols was any use against them. It is as I feared, my enemy has discovered the ancient magic of Averoigne and will be almost impossible to stop."

Judex shuddered and took a deep breath to steady himself. He had seen things this night that he didn't want to believe but, having seen, he couldn't turn his back on them. Evil such as this couldn't go unchecked, even if it meant delaying his own plans of vengeance.

"You saved my life, Sorcerer," he said.

"No more than you saved mine, my mysterious friend."

"If you need me again, will you be able to reach me?"

"I will." Dubnotal turned his attention back to the gargoyle for a moment. "The authorities will come soon," he said. "I will stay to deal with them, and to see to the final disposal of the gargoyles, but it may be best if you are gone when they arrive."

But when he looked up, Judex had already disappeared.

Paul Féval, the wonderful and prolific author of The Black
Coats, *once described Paris as a "jungle." This is to be taken
almost literally in the following story by Travis Hiltz, in which
three determined hunters, including Sâr Dubnotal, are going
after a pack of savage beasts...*

Travis Hiltz: *The Hounds of Saint-Augustin*

Paris, 1915

The morgue was a low ceilinged, dimly lit room. The
walls of dark stone seemed to absorb light and trap it. Two
men stood, looking down upon the body that rested on the
slab.

One was a tall man, with piercing grey eyes, and an
American-style mustache. He wore the kind of plain, brown
suit and overcoat, popular amongst those on a policeman's
salary. His companion was slimmer and more fashionably
dressed in grey. His suit and neatly trimmed beard gave him
the look of a European aristocrat; clashing with that impression was his tanned skin, white and gold sash and white turban.

Both men studied the corpse, the man in brown with a
stony face, the man in grey with keen interest and curiosity.

The two gentlemen were Inspector Maigret of the Paris
police and Sâr Dubnotal, the Great Psychagogue and occult
investigator.

After several minutes study, the Sâr looked up at the Inspector and nodded. Maigret then covered the body with a
sheet and the two men stepped away from the slab.

"So?" Maigret muttered.

"He was attacked by some kind of animal," the Sâr replied, glancing back over at the covered corpse. "A tragedy,
certainly, but why contact me?"

"A prominent banker, mauled to death by a wild animal," Maigret said, nodding. "On the Rue Saint-Augustin."

"Really?" the Sâr said, raising an eyebrow in interest.

"And with a half-dozen witnesses around. None of whom can tell us what sort of animal it was."

"They couldn't identify it…?" the Sâr asked.

"They didn't see it. *At all*," Maigret said, putting his hat back on. "We need to move along. The medical examiner will be back from lunch soon and I don't think my office will be quiet enough…"

"Your superiors do not know you are consulting me?" Sâr Dubnotal asked, a slight smile appearing on his face.

"Monsieur le Préfet does not approve of amateur detectives, or those that claim to dabble in the Occult…"

"Claim to dabble…?" Dubnotal muttered, frowning.

"But," Maigret said, attempting to draw the other man back to the matter at hand, "I have encountered a few unusual cases and learned that not all can be solved from behind a desk or walking the streets. There are two other bodies like this one, and we are no closer to piecing together what happened. My friend Chantecoq recommended you. Would you hear me out and see if there's something you could do to help?"

"Of course," Sâr Dubnotal nodded. "To begin with, I know a place we can talk."

Several blocks away was a small, discreet café, run by an equally small, discreet man, who seemed familiar with the turban-wearing occult investigator and quickly had the two men settled in a back, private room.

"So," Sâr Dubnotal said, as he stirred his tea. 'Three men, killed by wild animals in the middle of Paris, and no witnesses…"

"Oh, we have witnesses," Maigret interrupted, drawing out several sheets of paper from his inside coat pocket. "Just none that can swear to what kind of animal it was, or even that they saw it…*ghost wolves*, the press wants to call them…We are fighting to keep it quiet, but one more attack, they'll have it in headlines tall as I am."

He passed the papers to the other man. Sâr Dubnotal sipped his tea as he read, his forehead furrowing in thought. Maigret fidgeted, waiting for the mystic to say something. He spooned sugar into his coffee, stirred it and then left the cup neglected and anxiously unfolded and refolded his napkin.

"These three victims," Sâr said, looking up. "There appears to be no connection between them…?"

"None we've been able to find," Maigret shrugged. "A banker, the head of a manufacturing firm, and a doctor. Besides being prominent citizens, the only things they have in common are where and how they died."

He brought another sheet of paper out and unfolded it on the tabletop. It was a map of the city. He traced a line on the map.

"The Rue Saint-Augustin." The policeman explained.

"What about this street might connect these three men?" Sâr Dubnotal asked.

"That muddles the case more than it narrows things down." Maigret said. "The rue Saint-Augustin roughly goes from the Bourse [13] to the Opéra."

"Ah, the perfect route for a wide range of illegal activities ranging from the merely indiscreet to the blatantly unlawful," the Sâr mused, studying the map. "It hardly seems a location where a pack of wolves could prowl undetected by passersby…"

"Hence, all this whispering about *ghost wolves*," Maigret grumbled.

"I think you are correct," Sâr Dubnotal said, putting down his cup and pushing back his chair. "Something unusual is occurring in the rue Saint-Augustin and I would provide whatever assistance I can. If you could escort me to one of the crime scenes, we shall see what we shall see."

---

[13] Paris Stock Exchange.

They took Inspector Maigret's car to a side street, between a small stone church on one side and several neglected looking shops on the other. A policeman let them through to the still cordoned off crime scene.

The two men walked up to a bloodstained patch on the pavement.

"Not much to see, I'm afraid," the Inspector explained. "But the other two would be even less helpful. The doctor was attacked while crossing the street and there's some dispute about where the gentleman from manufacturing was coming from when he was attacked."

"Was the body moved by these supposed supernatural wolves?" Sâr Dubnotal asked absently, as he kneeled down to study the bloodstain.

"No, it's believed the victim was either going to, or coming back from, his mistress' home, so his acquaintances are reluctant to be more specific about his last nights' activities."

The bearded mystic shrugged and ran a finger across the blood-crusted pavement. His other hand went to his forehead and he closed his eyes.

Maigret thought the mage was having a dizzy spell, as the Great Psychagogue began swaying back and forth. The Inspector leaned in to support his colleague, when he heard the other man murmuring under his breath.

Maigret straightened up, stuck his hands in his overcoat pockets and waited. After a couple minutes, he began to regret not drinking his coffee, back at the café. He was contemplating sending the policeman on duty to fetch him a sandwich, when Sâr Dubnotal stood up, rubbing together the fingers that had touched the bloodstain and frowning.

"Most strange," he muttered. "There are…traces here, but they do not make sense. Something is wrong…"

"What?" Maigret asked, moving closer, until he was practically standing at the Sâr's shoulder.

"There are psychic traces, an… energy left by all living things."

He glanced over at the Inspector and smiled slightly at the other man's baffled expression.

"Think of them… like… fingerprints," the mystic continued. "Unique to the individual, appearing where they have been, and indicating what they have come in contact with. Strong emotions leave a stronger trace, so an incident of violent death will leave a stronger impression on an area."

"I see… I think," Maigret muttered, peering about, as though being in the presence of an occult expert would somehow imbue him with the ability to see this energy. But the street continued to look as dark and drab as before.

"It's very clear that your banker died a most violent death, but the traces left by these *ghost wolves* are…puzzling, to say the least."

Sâr Dubnotal paused and stroked his beard in thought. Maigret sighed, shrugged, and began to pace behind the mystic, looking for he knew not what, but convinced that the Psychagogue's very presence here would make some new clue spring out.

"I don't believe these phantom beasts are ghosts," the Sâr continued absently. "Their psychic traces are most assuredly those of some kind of animal, but the traces they leave feel wrong… whatever these creatures are, something has been done to them, something most unnatural…"

"I don't pretend to understand half of what you said," Maigret said. "And, to be honest, I'm not quite sure how much of what I did understand, I believe, but it seems to me we don't know much more than when we started."

"We have learned a few things of interest," the Sâr told him. "We may not have gained many answers, but we now know what questions we need to ask. Sometimes, that can be just as important."

The Inspector looked dubious, as he led the bearded mystic back to his car. He nodded to the policeman as they drove off.

It was several blocks before he realized that Sâr Dubnotal was lost in thought and not going to volunteer any further opinion without prompting.

"Can we track these… ghosts… creatures…whatever they may be?"\he asked.

"Individually, you or I would have little hope of solving this mystery," Sâr Dubnotal said, after a pause, looking straight ahead, into the night.

He sounded more as if he was thinking out loud, rather than answering Maigret's questions.

"You are quite capable at investigating criminal matters and I am, without sounding too self-praising, an adept at all matters concerning the unseen world, but I feel that, in this case, we are missing something…"

"How so?" Maigret asked, his tone gruff, but giving the impression he was not taking the other man's statement as a personal slight. "I admit, there are aspects that I feel a bit out of my depth on…"

"But, you have thoroughly investigated the victims and any possible connections between them; I have studied the scene, and have gathered information concerning the super-natural elements… As two, we are strong, but as schoolchil-dren are taught, the strongest structure is a tripod. There is another element we need: someone skilled in tracking animals. We need a hunter… I know where we may find one."

"In Paris?" Maigret muttered.

The Psychagogue would say no more, except that he would contact Maigret the next day. The Inspector drove the Sâr back to his home on the Champs-Elysées, then returned to his own apartment on the Boulevard Richard-Lenoir for some much needed sleep.

Maigret spent most of the next day at his office, catching up on paperwork and fending off numerous reporters and city officials that were demanding information on the recent kill-ings.

It was late in the afternoon when he received a message from Sâr Dubnotal, inviting him to meet for drinks.

Together, they arrived at a modest apartment in Montmartre and were greeted at the door by a slim middle-aged man with a graying beard and an inviting smile. The turbaned mystic gave him a respectful bow. The man then ushered them into an obviously bachelor sitting room, took their coats and then left them to fetch drinks.

"Is that your 'hunter'?" Maigret asked, settling back into a plush wing-backed chair.

"Monsieur d'Arnot...?" Sâr chuckled. "No. He is a talented pilot, but not particularly adept at woodcraft. I contacted him, as he is a close friend of the person I believed could help us."

"Gentlemen," d'Arnot said, coming into the room with a tray. "May I introduce... Monsieur John Paul Clayton IV."

Maigret gave the young man, who followed their host, a questioning look, while helping himself to an offered drink. Sâr Dubnotal looked obviously nonplussed.

"I'm thinking you were expecting someone else," the young man said, with a smile, as he sat down and helped himself to a drink.

He was of medium height, broad shouldered, with an athletic build. His black hair was a bit longer than was fashionable and his skin had the coloring of someone who had spent years under a tropical sun. His movements were smooth and graceful, reminding the police inspector of a dancer, until one saw his dark eyes and realized this man was indeed the hunter they were looking for.

He wore the uniform of a soldier in the British army, but wore it so casually, that one realized that young Clayton could have been wearing anything from a tuxedo to work clothes.

"I was hoping to speak with your father...?" Sâr Dubnotal began.

"Unfortunately, Lord and Lady Greystoke had to return to the 'family estate'," John Clayton said. "He asked me to meet you in his place, as I have several more days of my leave."

"Monsieur Clayton…" the Sâr began.

"Jack," The young soldier interrupted. "Or, depending on what sort of help you are looking for, Korak."

"What…?" Maigret muttered, puzzled.

Sâr Dubnotal gestured the Inspector to silence and then explained about the recent murders and how they felt that the addition of someone familiar with hunting wild beasts could prove essential to the investigation.

Jack Clayton nodded thoughtfully and took a sip of his drink.

"Well, I'm not quite in my father's class, when it comes to tracking," he said, with a slight smile, "but, I think I can help. Where do we start?"

They left Monsieur d'Arnot and took the Inspector's car to the rue Saint-Augustin, to the most well preserved spot. Jack Clayton got out of the car, unbuttoned his uniform jacket and tossed it into the backseat. He rolled up his shirtsleeves, as he approached the faded bloodstain.

Maigret leaned against the hood of his car, rummaged in his coat pocket and brought out a pipe. Sâr Dubnotal touched his arm and shook his head. Maigret frowned, but tucked it away and settled in to wait.

The young soldier crouched down besides the blood stain and ran his fingers across it. He then scraped at it with a thumbnail, bringing up flakes of dried blood and dirt. Clayton sniffed his fingertips and then licked them. After a moment lost in thought, he made a face and spat. He then bent down till his nose was less than an inch away from the pavement.

The other two men watched in puzzled fascination.

Jack Clayton had faded away, to be replaced by the other name he was known by—Korak. Gone was the polite young English soldier, and in his place was a primal being, more suited to the wilderness than the streets of Paris. He crawled about for several more minutes, running his fingers in the cracks between the cobblestones, before getting to his feet and brushing off his hands.

"Very odd," he muttered.

"So, we are all in agreement," Sâr Dubnotal said, sardonically.

"This man was killed by an animal," Clayton said, peering thoughtfully at his fingertips as he rubbed them together. "But there was something... wrong about them... and they are not *ghost wolves*, they are dogs."

"Dogs?" Maigret asked, straightening up. "How do you know that?"

"I found this," Clayton replied, digging a small tuft of hair from his shirt pocket. "I found strands from at least three different dogs. That, and their scent still lingers."

"Then what did you find odd?" Maigret asked, at last lighting his pipe.

"The scent of dog is still distinct," Clayton said. "But, there is another scent, underneath. I can't place it, but it's... unnatural... I have hunted a great many animals and this scent is like nothing I've ever come across before."

He shook his head. "I wish I could describe it better than that."

"You've given us more than we had before," Sâr Dubnotal said. "Every piece gives us a better view of the puzzle."

The three men stood, quietly, anxiously pondering this new bit of information and what came next.

"I will be the one to say it," Maigret said, gruffly. "We still don't have enough information, and the only likely way to get it is another attack."

The other two nodded grimly.

For two days, the hunters waited, pondered and hoped for some new clue that would not involve a brutal murder.

Jack Clayton spent that time pacing, re-reading the same couple paragraphs of a novel, and pretending he had any interest in the gourmet meals d'Arnot provided for the two of them.

Then, on the third day, the phone rang.

"It's happened," Maigret said. "I've sent a car to pick up Sâr Dubnotal and they will then fetch you."

"I'll be ready," Clayton replied.

Within minutes, he was bundled into the backseat of a police car, alongside the Great Psychagogue. Despite the circumstances, the mystic was impeccably dressed in a bottle green suit along with his ever-present white sash and turban.

"What happened?" Clayton asked the older man, already knowing the answer.

"Another death," the Sâr replied. "A professor at the Sorbonne, an elderly man. There were several witnesses, one was wounded, but it appears the professor was the main target. I was told no more than that."

Clayton nodded and then spent the rest of the drive, peering out the window. The thrill of the hunt mixed with awareness that for them to acquire a new clue, a new piece of this horrific puzzle, someone had to die.

The car brought them to a narrow boulevard, a common short cut from a nearby theater to a street of cafés and bars.

A policeman spotted Sâr Dubnotal's distinctive attire and lead the two men to Inspector Maigret. They had to wait several minutes, as the broad-shouldered detective was directing his men.

"Take two men and comb those side streets," he barked, gesturing. "Any further people claiming to be witnesses, bring them to me. And above all, keep those damn reporters back!"

Looking about, Maigret spotted his two fellow hunters, gave them a nod in greeting. He then shooed away the remaining policemen, and steered Clayton and Sâr to a quiet corner.

"We need to find something solid," he muttered. "There is no way to keep this quiet any longer. By morning, news sellers all across the city will be screaming about it from the rooftops."

The other two nodded with grim determination.

"I can go about my own investigations away from the crowd," Sâr Dubnotal said. "I will return to the car. Why don't you escort Monsieur Clayton to the body."

Maigret cast a quick glance at the young soldier, nodded and walked away. Clayton followed after him, letting the burly Inspector navigate the crowd. It parted, allowing Jack his first view of the body.

He was no stranger to death, even violent death. Living in Africa, as well as living in his father's shadow, it was a part of life, as ever present as the sun in the sky. Jack had hunted, he had fought to stay alive, and then, as a soldier, he had seen war. This was different. No worse than anything he'd seen before, but it was just brutal, with no purpose. It was not done for food, survival or any necessity. It was motivated by darker emotions. Clayton shook his head, saddened by the depths men could sink to, rather than repulsion at the violence.

The body was that of a slender man, in his late sixties. His suit was several years behind in fashion, but had been well kept. His thin face was contorted in pain and fear and long-fingered, gloved hands still clutched a cane with a round brass head.

Jack Clayton drew in a deep breath, letting the cloak of civilization drop away and letting Korak, the hunter, come to the forefront. His eyes took in every harsh detail, his nostrils flared, drawing in a multitude of scents.

He stood, statue-still for several minutes. Maigret was unsure if the young soldier was too stunned by the scene to function, or if, like Sâr Dubnotal, his methods were unfathomable to him.

"He was killed by dogs," Clayton muttered, absently. "Three of them."

"We found paw prints in the blood," Maigret added, quietly.

"He fought," Clayton said, a brief, grim smile appearing on his features. "He made them pay a steep price for his life."

"The witnesses were by his side when the attack happened. They saw no attacker," Maigret explained. "They heard noises, but could see nothing... he was killed by ghosts in the middle of the street...!"

"Not ghosts," Clayton said, matter of factly. "They are dogs... just dogs, but something... something was done to them... it has pushed them into a savagery that borders on insanity."

Both men lapsed into silence, immune to the chaos around them.

"Can you smell that?" Jack asked.

"Smell what?" the Inspector asked. "Between the blood and the surrounding neighborhood..."

"It's mingled with the dog's smell," Clayton continued. "Can't place it, but it's there... it's like... something..."

He turned and peered at Maigret, but seemed to be looking through him, rather than at him, chasing a thread of an idea.

"I need to speak with Sâr Dubnotal," Clayton suddenly decided, turning away from the body.

The turbaned mystic sat in the back seat of Maigret's car, as serene and at ease, as though he was merely waiting for a traffic light to change. Clayton joined him, while the Inspector sat in front.

"There is nothing supernatural about these dogs," the Sâr announced, as soon as they had closed the car doors.

"They have been treated with a chemical of some sort, turning them savage," Clayton added. "They are saturated with it... whatever it is..."

"But, how can it be?" the Sâr asked, more to himself than the other men. "They come and go unseen... How are they summoned? In the midst of this city, how do they find their targets? No witness can even describe them..."

They are invisible," Maigret suddenly exclaimed, with quiet conviction. "The Griffin formula!"

"What?" Clayton asked, puzzled.

"There were reports, years ago, of a ghostly figure terrorizing an English village," Maigret explained. "It was, in fact, a scientist that had created an invisibility formula, which had the side effect of turning him insane. Griffin is believed to have died, but there have been other incidents over the years that have been attributed to be different individuals attempting to recreate Griffin's formula...."

"Invisible dogs! Of course!" Sâr Dubnotal muttered, stroking his beard in thought.

"That would explain the chemical smell," Clayton nodded. "As well as their bizarre, savage behavior. This is the work of a madman!"

"In that, there is no dispute," the Sâr said.

"And now, we have the connection between the victims," Maigret said. "Someone attempting to recreate this invisibility formula would need money, equipment and other scientists to consult with... the killings were attempts to frighten the others into helping him, or silencing them, once he'd gotten whatever ne needed from them."

"The important thing is," the Sâr said. "can we track this madman?"

"Can we indeed?" Maigret asked, gruffly.

"I have the scent," Clayton said. "It will not be easy, but I believe I can track the dogs."

"I should be able to follow the psychic traces," Sâr Dubnotal added. "These dogs are drowning in madness; they will leave a trail."

"How do we begin?" Maigret asked.

"Allow me to find the start of our path," Clayton said, shrugging out of his jacket. He and the Inspector returned to the body. Maigret communicated with his men and the other policemen on the scene.

Clayton rolled up his sleeves and crouched next to the body. He dabbed his handkerchief in the blood in order to have a fresh source of the scent with him. He breathed in the scent of the dogs and the strange chemicals they were saturated with. He felt Maigret standing close behind him.

"Have they moved the body?" Clayton asked, peering questioningly at the blood soaked corpse. "Something is different..."

"No, they've tried not to touch it," Maigret replied, after a quick consultation with one of his men.

"That blood wasn't on the head of the cane before. It's not fresh; it's as old as the rest of it."

"The old man tried to fight off the dogs," Maigret muttered, after several moments' thought. "That cane would have made a handy weapon… so, that's… dog's blood…?"

"They leave a trail!" Clayton said, looking up at the policeman. "When they bleed, it becomes visible again!"

He quickly got to his feet and, steadying himself with one hand on Maigret's shoulder, used his other hand to slip off his shoes and socks.

"We need to move," Clayton said, tying the laces of his shoes together and slinging them over his shoulder. "Can you follow me?"

"I'll have Sâr Dubnotal to help guide me. On your way!"

Maigret gave instructions to the nearest policemen and then quickly made his way back to the car.

"Games afoot," he muttered, climbing into the front seat and starting the car. The headlights came on in time to see young Clayton go jogging through the crowd and down a side street.

What followed was a surreal game of "Follow the leader." Korak raced along the darkened Paris streets, hunched over to scan the street for more traces of the dogs, startling pedestrians by pushing past them, pausing to sniff at various objects and at one point, leaping over a parked roadster's hood.

Maigret grumbled under his breath as he struggled to keep up with the feral Englishman. The streets grew narrower and more cluttered with refuse, pedestrians, and those citizens that dwelt in the shadows of Paris, due to poverty or intent.

Even with the cacophony of the Inspector leaning on the horn, as well as getting into shouting matches with irate passersby and other drivers, Sâr Dubnotal kept calm and focused in the back seat.

"He's heading east," the Psychagogue said, quietly. "The traces are getting stronger... getting near... I do not like this... we are walking a dangerous path."

"Should I have brought some men with us?" Maigret asked, swerving to avoid a pair of drunken workers.

"No, we three can end this. I feel we are going to walk into chaos. Bringing more guns would not help that situation."

Feeling little comfort at that statement, the Inspector, frowned and hunched further over the steering wheel.

Korak jogged through the streets and alleys of the city, pausing to investigate a scent or some other bit of spoor, then rushing forward, following the trail.

Jack Clayton was completely gone now, and Korak the killer had taken over. Paris had become just a different kind of jungle: streetlamps in place of trees, buildings instead of hills and cliffs, and late night revelers instead of monkeys. There was prey and nothing else mattered. The hunt was the hunt.

He ran around a corner and skidded to a halt. The alley was narrow and cluttered with piles of refuse and the almost overwhelming odor of dogs.

Maigret's car halted at the mouth of the alley and he scrambled out. Korak held up his hand, warning the Inspector to silence.

The young man crept forward, then knelt down in front of pile of soaked newspapers and rags.

Maigret moved forward came to a stop, when the rags began to growl. It was the sound of a dog, but as Maigret approached, all he saw was a nightmare.

He could make out the vague outline of a dog's body, sprawled amongst the trash, but all he could distinctly see were its eyeballs, what looked to be its nervous system and a few organs.

As the crazed animal slowly bled out its last moments, its body became visible, but not all at once, rather in a slow, sporadic process, where it was revealed a bit at a time, as if it was being assembled by ghostly, drunken workers.

"Wretched animal," Maigret muttered, joining Korak.

The young Englishman shook his head sadly and reached a hand out towards the bizarre half-formed dog. It growled, feebly back, its lower jaw and teeth, slowly coming into view, but was too weak for more than a shallow pretense at its previous savagery.

"You and I have no need to fight," he said, in a low, soothing tone. "You have been ill-served, but your suffering is over."

The dog lowered its partially visible head and sniffed Korak's palm. He brought up his other hand and grasped the dog's head. With a swift, sure movement, Korak snapped its neck. Death was instantaneous.

"I would like to have words with whoever would treat an animal this way," he said, getting to his feet.

Maigret took a step back, seeing no sign of the young English soldier in those dark eyes. He was standing in this dirty, crowded alley with a being born of the jungle.

"Let's go find him, then," the Inspector gruffly replied.

There was a moment of grim understanding between the two men, and then they made their way back to the car. Sâr Dubnotal had a slightly pained look upon his usually serene face and one hand rubbed at his temple.

"We are quite close," the Great Psychagogue said. "We must move, not just swiftly, but carefully. The psychic traces are… harsh… the dogs are suffering… screaming…"

"Then let's stop talking," Maigret said, climbing behind the wheel. "Lead me to the bastard."

Korak squeezed past the car, paused at the mouth of the alley to test the air, and then ran off down the street.

The neighborhoods grew ever more dark and dismal, as they traveled. The colors faded, the windows were dark and contained broken glass.

Desolate buildings squeezed together into one huge squalid, grey hovel.

The slum ended and Korak came to a halt, standing in a thin patch of grey, dry grass, staring angrily at a dark, dilapidated warehouse.

Maigret turned off his lights and backed the car into a side alley. He and Sâr Dubnotal quickly joined the Englishman.

"There.! Korak said, pointing.

"Even I can smell the dogs from here," Maigret muttered, drawing his revolver. He then patted his overcoat pocket, reassuring himself that his extra bullets were still there. "Let's finish this."

Korak nodded, pointed to the far corner of the warehouse, where it slouched against an equally decrepit shed and then vanished into the shadows.

The Inspector and the mystic exchanged a glance.

"I prefer to use the front door," the Sâr said, with a sardonic smile.

"I'll see if I can find a door on the other side."

Maigret crept around the warehouse, squeezed down a narrow gap between it and another equally unkempt building, and found a side door. It was locked, but hung crooked and seemed to be kept in place by dirt and wishful thinking. The Inspector slid his hand through a gap in the frame and fumbled around till he reached the lock. He gently eased the door open a few inches and peered inside.

The interior was equally grim and cluttered. A few battered oil lanterns generated pools of sickly light. These oases were decorated with wooden crates, bits of broken equipment and castoff furniture.

Deep in the inky shadows at the back of the warehouse, Maigret spied a thin line of light, indicating another door. Snatches of fearsome, bestial noise told him that he had found where the dogs were kept.

He slid into the warehouse and stealthily crept towards the door, skirting the pools of light, keeping to the shadow.

So, focused was the detective on reaching whatever makeshift kennel was behind that door that he did not notice an oaken table leg floating up off a dusty workbench and drifting after him.

Maigret was now within a few feet of the dark door; behind it could be heard the breaking of wood and the wild barking of angry dogs. As he ran forward to join in on what must have been Korak's attack, the ghostly table leg came down on the back of his head and, with a grunt, he collapsed to the grimy floor.

It was at that same moment that the front door of the warehouse blew in, as though struck, by hurricane winds, and Sâr Dubnotal came strolling through.

The table leg dropped to the floor and there was the sound of hurried footsteps.

"Truly, you believe you can hide from me?" the Sâr said to room. "From one who has been called the conqueror of the invisible!"

His arms rose in a dramatic flourish and a wave of force, like heat haze, washed across the room, toppling furniture and equipment and causing a mini-tornado of dust and dirt.

There was a grunt, followed by a string of curses as an unseen body was hurled against the sidewall. With a second gesture, Sâr Dubnotal directed the dirt tornado towards it. Where it struck, it revealed the form of a man, short and stoop-shouldered, now plainly revealed by its coating of dirt.

The until recently invisible man staggered about, spitting and cursing.

Meanwhile, Maigret slowly got to his feet, rubbing his injured head. Catching sight of the strange, dirty apparition, he rubbed his eyes. When it didn't go away, his deductive mind pieced together what had occurred and he strode angrily over and punched the dirt-covered phantom full in the face. There was the satisfying crunch of unseen cartilage, followed by a scream of pain, as the invisible man fell to his knees.

"Understandable and effective," the Sâr said, joining him. "But was it necessary?"

"Lost my gun when he hit me, so shooting him was not an option," the Inspector replied.

The Sâr shrugged and then knelt down to retrieve his fellow hunter's hat. He handed it to the bigger man.

"Korak?" he asked.

Maigret turned, looking towards the back door. The noise of the terrible animals had risen in pitch and ferocity. Both men jogged across the warehouse, Maigret falling behind to retrieve his gun, as well as plant a kick across the invisible man's temple.

"Stay down," he warned, rather unnecessarily, his mystic colleague thought.

The Inspector caught up to the Great Psychagogue, moved past him and cracked the door open with his shoulder.

Inside, Korak was locked in bizarre combat. He was rolling about on the floor, engaged in a fierce struggle with empty air that growled hatefully at him. Across the room, Korak's knife seemed to be floating several inches above an every widening pool of blood.

Near the door, the decapitated body of another dog was slowly creeping into visibility.

Maigret, feeling a bit unsteady from his blow to the head and recent exertions, leaned against the doorframe as he raised his revolver and struggled to get a clear shot at the remaining invisible dogs, unsure how many were left. Korak seemed to be fighting two, while a third, partially visible due to the amount of blood it was smeared with, dragged itself along, as its back legs appeared to be broken.

Sâr Dubnotal moved so that Maigret could brace his gun arm on his shoulder.

"On the left," the mystic said. "When Korak shifts his leg."

The young hunter struggled to his feet and caught one of the dogs in a headlock. He shifted his weight, pinning the dog against his hip. A trio of gouges suddenly appeared on his thigh. Korak kicked out wildly. As soon as he drew back his leg, Maigret fired.

There was a brief burst of visibility as the dog's skull cracked and its brain splattered.

Korak twisted his arm, cracking the dog's neck, then spun, and used the carcass as a makeshift club on the surviving dog.

"It's done," Sâr Dubnotal intoned, as the dog's spine cracked and it rasped its last breath.

Maigret nodded, exhaled and sank to perch on a dusty crate.

Korak tossed aside the dog's body and rubbed at the blood on his cheek with the back of his hand. His shirt was in ribbons and he was smeared with blood. Besides the claw marks on his leg, he had a cut above his right eye and deep bite marks on his shoulder were bleeding steadily.

"You look a sight," the Sâr said, walking up to him and offering a paisley handkerchief.

"To be honest," Clayton said taking it and wiping his face and bloody knuckles. "Most of the blood is not mine."

He looked about, sadly at the half formed corpses and gradually increasing pools and spatters of blood.

"These animals will suffer no more," he muttered. "What about their master?"

"We should probably fetch him," Maigret said, getting to his feet with some effort.

The trio returned to the main room of the warehouse. There was a vague imprint, where the invisible man had fallen and a smudged trail where he had dragged himself across the floor. They found his body behind a stack of crates. All that was visible was his skeleton and nervous system. Traces of blood and bile were smeared around his mouth of his skull and down his rib cage.

"Such a waste," Sâr Dubnotal muttered, sadly.

"I don't suppose we'll be able to find out who he was," Korak added.

"We might," Maigret said. "Not that I think it matters much at this point."

"What now?" the Englishman asked. "What about this place?"

They contemplated the corpse and their squalid surroundings for several moments of thoughtful silence, before Sâr Dubnotal spoke.

"Amongst my abilities," he said. "I have a well developed psychic capacity and, at this moment, I am getting a premonition of a fire, a most terrible fire, that will render this building and all its contents to ash"

"That's a shame," Maigret nodded grimly. "I'll need to find a telephone before my men file a missing persons report on me. Thank you again, gentlemen for your help with this investigation."

He dropped his revolver into his coat pocket and shook hands with both men, before hobbling outside.

"Um…what do we do now?" Jack Clayton asked.

Sâr Dubnotal merely smiled and opened his hand revealing a box of matches the Inspector had handed to him.

An hour later, the trio was gathered by Maigret's car, watching the blaze and the efforts of the Paris fire department to ensure that it didn't spread to the surrounding buildings. Jack Clayton sat on the running board, a blanket thrown over his shoulders, the two older men stood on either side of him.

"Not a triumph," the mystic noted, philosophically, "but, an ending."

"We found the truck he used to transport the dogs," Maigret said, absently. "Quite a bit of blood in it. Most likely we'll have to burn it as well, what with the threat of it being contaminated with rabies…"

"Rabies…" the Sâr mused. "That should cover some of the more… unusual aspects of this case." He gave a brief shiver in remembrance and huddled deeper into his overcoat. "It's been a long night; I could do with a cup of tea and a smaller, cheerier, more confined fire. How are you faring, Monsieur Clayton?"

"Tired. I need a bath, and something stronger than tea to drink. I think it'll be more restful if they ship me to the front lines, after this leave."

The Great Psychagogue chuckled and the Inspector nodded in silent agreement.

Past the police and fire department vehicles, and the dozens of policemen and fire fighters, past the crowd of curious and morbid onlookers, was parked a sleek, black touring car with curtained windows.

Two men sat across from each other in the spacious back seat.

The older man leaned back and moving aside the curtain with a finger peered at the blazing inferno.

"It is night," he sighed.

The other man, younger with receding black hair and intense eyes, shifted anxiously in his seat.

"It is merely a matter of refinement, Colonel," he said, speaking with a pronounced Hungarian accent. "With further study and some additional elements…"

The older man let the curtain close, leaned forward and turned his eyes, even more intense than that of the dark-haired man, eyes that seemed to soak up the flickering light from the nearby fire, and directed them at his fellow passenger.

"The matter is closed, Boroff," he said. "You were given the opportunity. Your assistant has *paid the law*. We will speak of it no more. Perhaps we will allow young Drago to test his own theories concerning this *superconn*; perhaps we will settle for the invisibility of the shadows."

He sat back and closed his eyes.

"Paris is no longer welcoming," he murmured absently. "If you wish to further your studies, might I suggest Marovania?"

"If it is the will of the father," Boroff muttered.

In this second story pitting Judex and Sâr Dubnotal against Herr Doktor Von Meyer, the action moves to the blood-drenched front lines of the Great War. This time, the two heroes are forced to team up with a very superhuman fellow, Philip Wylie's "Gladiator", in order to prevent Meyer from raising a supernatural apocalypse...

Matthew Baugh: *What Rough Beast...*

The Trenches, 1916

"Monsieur Danner?"

Hugo looked up from his novel. The nurse was an angular woman in her 30s who he had never particularly liked. He knew the feeling was mutual; with so few beds to spare for the wounded, she didn't think much of accommodating one uninjured Legionnaire.

"There is a man wanting to see you," the nurse said. "Will you follow me, please?"

He put down the book and rose with the ease of a gifted athlete in perfect health. He was handsome, with his tanned skin, and his hair and eyes so dark that many of his compatriots mistook him for a "Red Indian." More than that, there was a sense of power about him, as if his personality was charged with electricity that made him the center of attention.

With a sour look, she led him through the rows of cots crammed into the ruined church that now served as a field hospital. Outside, the day was sunny and there was no sound of the fighting in the trenches, not five miles away. She left him in the shadow of an oak where an elderly man dressed in formal black waited. On the lane, just beyond the tree, stood an expensive Peugeot touring car.

"Legionnaire Danner?" the white-haired man asked, extending his hand politely. Hugo shook it, trying to size up his visitor. He was probably in his sixties, and possessing a quiet dignity that impressed the younger man. He wore no sign of rank or service.

"My name is Vallières," the man said.

"Do I know you, Monsieur?"

"No," Vallières said, "and there is no reason that you should. I am not a terribly important person; outside of the mission I have been given."

"And this mission concerns me?" Hugo asked.

"It does... At least, if you truly are the one they call *le Colorado*."

"I come from Colorado, in the United States," he replied. "Some of the men in the Legion called me that as a nickname."

"I have heard some remarkable stories about *le Colorado*," Vallières continued. "They say that you single-handedly resupplied your post during the recent German offensive. You carried 1000 kilos of food and ammunition on your back through no-man's land."

Hugo shrugged.

"Is it also true that you went into the trenches alone and, when your rifle was broken, slew scores of men with your bare hands?"

Hugo didn't respond. He wanted to like the white-haired gentleman, but he wondered where this was going.

"You were shot?"

"More times than I could count."

"And bayoneted?"

"The *Boches* did their best. They managed to shred my uniform, for all the good it did them."

"You were not wounded?"

In response, Hugo stripped off his shirt revealing lean, hard muscles and unmarked skin.

"Why, then, were you in the hospital?"

"Exhaustion."

Vallières shook his head in wonder. "If all of this is true, then you are the man we need."

"It is true," Hugo said.

"Forgive me, but this is so remarkable. Can you show me something to convince me?"

Hugo walked over to the man's automobile. Taking a solid grip with both hands, he strained to lift the vehicle. The weight didn't bother him, but it was tricky balancing the big car, and he wanted to be careful not to damage it. After a moment, he found the right stance, and his feet sank ankle-deep into the grassy lawn as he raised the car over his head.

"How do you do that?"

"They grow us strong in Colorado."

Vallières smiled. "I think, rather, it has something to do with your father, the medical scientist, Abednego Danner."

Hugo scowled as he lowered the vehicle to the ground. He hadn't made a secret of his strength in his service with the Foreign Legion, but had never said a word about the treatment his father had used on him in the womb. He felt suddenly vulnerable, something uncomfortable for him.

"What else do you know?"

"You were liked in your hometown, even though your parents kept you rather secluded. You left to attend Webster University in Missouri where you excelled at American football. You left there…"

"I left when I accidentally killed another player in a game," Hugo said. "Monsieur Vallières, where is this leading?"

"Forgive me, Monsieur Danner, but it was necessary to investigate you. I regret that I have crossed the bounds of discretion, but I assure you, there is no need for concern. Your private history is safe with me; even should you refuse to accept my offer."

"What offer?"

"There is a mission you are needed for. It is most urgent and only you have the power to accomplish it."

What kind of mission was this?

Vallières had dropped Hugo in an abandoned farmhouse close to the front. He'd obtained the American's release from the hospital with a set of orders signed by General Broulard and brought him to this remote place.

"Wait here," the old man said. "You will be joined by three others shortly. Two men and a woman."

"Agents of the French government?" Hugo asked.

"Not exactly," Vallières said with an enigmatic smile. "I am a patriot, but trust me when I say that this is a greater matter than nation against nation. You will understand soon enough."

Hugo looked into the old man's eyes and saw the strength there. He could tell that he would not get any more from Vallières, except through force. He decided that he would rather trust that the man was an ally.

Vallières showed him where provisions and an oil lamp were kept, and the best way to blank out the windows so the enemy would not see his light and call down fire on him. Then he bade him good luck and drove away.

Hugo waited, impatiently, for several hours. There was some furniture still in the house, though most of the belongings had long since been looted. There were a round table and a few chairs, plain but made with painstaking craftsmanship. Hugo wondered about the hand that had carved them. He imagined a farmer, skilled with mallet and chisel, and the family he shared meals with, and wondered if they were still alive.

He made himself as comfortable as he could and ate some of the provisions, finding the bread stale, but the cheese good and the wine excellent. For a time, he tried to read his novel, but without much success. He was too anxious to focus his mind on anything for long.

Just past dusk, he heard the sounds of a car coming down the lane. Hugo extinguished his lantern and watched as the vehicle came to a stop and two shadowed figures emerged.

With the confidence born of invulnerability, Hugo opened the door and stepped out. The visitors walked into the light from the doorway and, if they were afraid, he couldn't

160

see it. The first was a man as tall as he was; he wore a European suit but with the beard, turban, and sash of a Sikh. The woman looked to be well into middle age, though still very attractive. She had a wealth of black hair, shot with gray that framed a pale, lovely face.

"You are the people I am to meet?"

"Yes," the man replied.

"I was told to expect three."

"We are all here," said a voice from behind him. Hugo spun to see another man, this one dressed in a long black cape and matching slouch hat that partially hid his features. He had not heard or seen any movement, but the stranger had managed to enter the cottage.

"How did you…?"

"Pardon me," the turbaned man said, "but it would be more practical if we finished this conversation inside. Your light may be seen."

Hugo stepped aside, letting the man and his companion pass, then followed and shut the door.

"Now, perhaps you can tell me what this is all about," he said. "And who are you?"

"I am Sâr Dubnotal," the turbaned man said. "My companion is Mademoiselle Gianetti Annunciata. Our mysterious friend uses the name Judex."

Hugo scowled, puzzled by the men's odd pseudonyms. Still, this was secretive business and spies, he supposed, must have codenames. "Gentlemen, Mademoiselle," he said with a nod. "If someone can tell me what we are here for, I'd appreciate it. I've been on pins and needles all day."

"Of course," Sâr Dubnotal said with a polite smile. "Each person here has certain abilities that are needed to prevent the unleashing of a terrible weapon."

Hugo felt his heart begin to pump faster and his mouth tightened in a grim smile. This was the sort of thing he'd been looking for: a true challenge, a chance to make a difference.

Dubnotal produced a folded map and spread it out on the table. It showed France and the western front was clearly indicated by a red line.

"As you know, the war has been static for some time, with each side entrenched against the other. There have been offensives and counter-offensives, all without any real result. But recently something new happened, here."

The Sâr placed his finger on a point that Hugo judged to be about 20 miles north of the farmhouse.

"For the last three nights, the bodies of the fallen have risen from the trenches and walked."

Hugo glanced at the man's face, incredulous, but the turbaned man seemed completely serious.

"The dead walking? That's preposterous!"

"I have heard the reports," Judex said, his shadowed features grim. "They say that the soldiers walk or crawl in the same direction. It doesn't seem to matter whether the dead belong to our forces or the Germans. Some soldiers have tried to shoot them down, but short of blowing them to bits, nothing stops their macabre pilgrimage."

"Our enemy has strange powers, and strange allies," the Sâr said. "I have taken the liberty of procuring ammunition that should be more effective." He produced two boxes of pistol cartridges from his jacket and set them on the table.

Judex opened a box and took out one of the bullets to examine. It shone a bright pale color in the lamplight.

"This is silver?"

Sâr Dubnotal nodded.

"Your best target with these is the heart," he said.

Hugo stared at the men in disbelief. "Are you serious?" he demanded. "This story is insane! It's obviously nothing more than hysteria, or shell-shock."

Judex had taken out a pair of Steyr automatic pistols and was changing out his load.

"You're actually going into combat with silver bullets," Hugo said, feeling more disgusted with each moment.

162

The dark-clad man looked him in the face with such intensity that he took half a step back before he caught himself.

"Monsieur Danner," Judex said. "My homeland is threatened and I plan to fight. I believe, as you do, that we will face only mortal soldiers; silver will kill them as surely as lead. On the other hand, if our friend is correct, I do not intend to go into battle unprepared."

He handed his second pistol and a box of shells to Hugo, who tucked them in the pockets of his jacket.

"Thanks."

"For what? A man like you has no need of guns." Judex turned back to Sâr Dubnotal. "Where are we going?"

"Here." He indicated a spot on the map some distance behind the enemy lines. "This is a ruined fortress here, the ancient Château de Joiry. It is said to be haunted, and to contain passages that descend into Hell itself."

Hugo felt a stab of anger at this the man's melodramatics, but said nothing.

"Currently the Château is in the hands of Herr Doctor Von Meyer of Leipzig," Dubnotal said. "He is a powerful occultist with dozens of disciples, and may be the most dangerous man in Europe. He is the seventh son of a seventh son, and is 49 generations removed from the master magician, Simon of Tyre. More than that, he remembers the knowledge of every one of his incarnations."

Hugo's patience snapped.

"Look," he said. "You can believe in whatever kind of hocus pocus you want; that's your business. But, for pity's sake, get to the point. Is this man a mastermind? Then tell me where he is and I'll kill him. Show me his weapon and I'll break it to pieces. But, please, don't ask me to believe this nonsense about sorcery and past lives."

The Sâr seemed unperturbed by Hugo's outburst.

"I do not ask you to believe anything, Monsieur Danner," he said. "I simply offer information; it is up to you to decide how to use it. There is one more thing I must show you. If you will be seated around the table and join hands..."

"What is this, some kind of séance?" Hugo asked.

"Gianetti is one of the most gifted spirit mediums of our age," the Sâr replied.

Hugo nearly refused, but the appeal in the woman's dark eyes, and Judex's stern expression swayed him. He sat opposite Judex and joined hands with Gianetti on one side and Sâr Dubnotal on the other. The turbaned man began to chant quietly, using words that belonged to no language Hugo recognized.

A thin, faintly luminous mist was gathering on the table and dribbled off the edges. It thickened as Hugo watched and he seemed to see tiny figures moving through it. Slowly the insect-sized forms resolved into human beings—men in tattered uniforms—who trudged and crept through a landscape sculpted of mist."

"He calls them," Gianetti said in a hollow voice.

"Who?" Sâr Dubnotal asked.

"Von Meyer calls the dead to his home."

"Why does he call them?"

"That he may use their flesh and bone to sculpt a weapon; a colossus that will sweep away the forces of his enemies."

"By what power does he call them?"

"By the words of the grimoire."

"What grimoire?"

"The book of Nathare of Vyones."

The Sâr caught his breath. Even in the dim light, Hugo could see that his face had gone pale.

"Does he build the same abomination that once laid waste to Ylourgne?"

"He does, and no weapon forged of man shall be able to stop it."

"Show me!"

Gianetti gasped in pain. Her eyes rolled back and Hugo felt her hand spasm and grow cold. He looked at her in alarm, but the spell passed in a moment. When his gaze returned to the table, the scene had changed. The tiny soldiers lay in heaps while robed men and nude man-like things hewed the flesh from their bones with knives and cleavers. The flesh they gathered in a cauldron that simmered with a deep red glow while the bones they placed in a vat of sickly pale hue.

As quickly as the two vessels filled, huge bestial man-things ladled their contents into buckets which hooded men carried into another area where they dumped the contents on a great pile in the shape of a colossal, partially fleshed skeleton.

"The Colossus," Gianetti said. "Made from the flesh and bones of ten-thousand dead men. He will—"

Her words ended with a shriek of pain as she leapt to her feet, her limbs twitching with epileptic frenzy. Hugo and Judex both reached for her, but the Sâr's voice stopped them.

"She is in the power of our enemy," he said. "If you touch her, she could come to great harm. Please, leave this to me."

"*El Tebib?*" Gianetti's voice had changed into a deep and cultured male voice. "*El Tabib, ist dass Sie?*"

"I am here, Von Meyer," Dubnotal replied. Hugo was amazed at how calm he remained.

"*You seek to spy on me, my old friend,*" Gianetti said. Her limbs no longer twitched but Hugo saw that her feet hovered several inches over the floor. The sight sent a shiver of dread through him. He glanced at Judex, wondering if the same fear he felt had penetrated those unreadable features.

"Release the woman," Dubnotal said in a clear, reasonable tone. "She is an innocent; your conflict is with me."

"*An innocent?*" Gianetti threw back her head and peals of masculine laughter came from her mouth. "*El Tebib, don't you know how much joy it gives me to torment an innocent? The jaded are so tedious, but the naïve can provide us with such exquisite entertainment.*"

Hugo saw the Sâr's hand dip into his pocket and emerge with a thick piece of chalk. Out of the corner of his eye he saw that Judex had drawn his Steyr, but made no move to point it at the woman.

"Danner," Sâr said. "Seize Gianetti."

Hugo leapt forward, his arms closing firmly around the woman's slender form. She struggled with inhuman strength, clawing and biting, but might have been trapped in a steel vice for all the good it did her. His only concern was to keep her from harming herself in her frenzy.

Dubnotal didn't waste a moment. He bent low and used the chalk to draw an even circle around Hugo and his captive. Then he drew strange glyphs, fourteen in all, evenly spaced around the outer edge. When he completed the last one, Gianetti screamed in her own voice and went limp in Hugo's arms. As gently as he could, he powered her to the wooden floor.

"What did you do?" Judex asked.

"I did not think he was so powerful," the turbaned man said. "He reached out with his psychic powers and overwhelmed her mind. The circle should protect her, but…"

He stopped as the woman's body convulsed violently and her mouth began to foam. Hugo caught her arms to keep her from hurting herself.

"She's like ice," he said.

The Sâr stepped carefully into the circle, taking care not to scuff the chalk. He knelt next to Gianetti and forced her eyes open with his fingers.

"Von Meyer is trying to break through my defenses," he said. "I must save her if I can."

"What can we do to help?" Hugo asked.

"Thank you, my friend, but this is something only I can do," Dubnotal replied. "While Meyer is distracted here, the two of you must go to his base. The colossus must not be allowed to rise."

Hugo gazed at the dark terrain far below. In the light of the full Moon, and from an altitude nearly a mile, the French country looked serene and beautiful. It was hard to imagine that this was the same land that was the battleground for tens of thousands of men in the daylight.

He rode in the front seat of Judex's plane, a Morane Type-L spotter. His mysterious companion, ever prepared, had hidden it in the old barn by the farmhouse. He and Sâr Dubnotal must have been planning this even before they contacted him.

His reverie was broken by the roar of diving engines and the whine of bullets. He felt a series of mild stings across his back and saw holes appear in the fuselage around him, then the aircraft rolled sideways and several dark shapes shot past.

Biplanes, he realized. *The Germans have found us.*

He strained into the darkness and counted three of the planes circling to come at them again. Judex didn't seem interested in a fight. He turned them away from their pursuers and began to climb toward a bank of clouds, clearly hoping to lose them.

It was a good strategy, but Hugo quickly realized that it wouldn't work. The German planes were faster, and could climb better than the Morane. It was only a matter of moments before they were strafed again.

As the planes began to fire, Judex took the Morane into a dive, picking up speed. The Germans followed as he dodged and wove in an unpredictable pattern. Abruptly, the aircraft rose into a steep climb, losing speed rapidly but rising out of the line of fire. It took only a moment for the pursuers to adapt and begin the climb behind them, but, as the Morane came close the stalling point, Judex turned the rudder and the nose dropped. In an instant, they were screaming toward the ground.

The Germans scattered to avoid the diving plane and, with a half roll, Judex leveled out heading back in the direction they had just come.

For a moment, Hugo thought they had escaped, or gained a few precious moments, but the squadron leader was an unusually talented flyer. He was back on their tail in an instant, firing his twin Vickers machineguns. Several shots struck the engine, for it stuttered and caught fire. Hugo could see Judex fighting with the controls, but the aircraft didn't respond. Despite his best efforts, the plane went into an uncontrolled spin and plummeted toward the ground.

The spinning, tumbling fall disoriented Hugo, but he knew he had only seconds to act. He reached behind him and grabbed the fuselage, his fingers tearing through the heavy canvas to find a solid grip on the plane's metal skeleton. He pulled himself from the cockpit, shredding his safety harness as he did, and made his way, hand over hand, back to Judex's seat.

He had just a moment to register the disbelief on the Frenchman's face before he ripped lose his harness. Gathering his ally in his arms, Hugo kicked out into space.

Once he was away from the plane, Hugo managed to orient himself. They were approaching the ground rapidly and he barely had the time to get his feet under him before they hit.

The Moon had risen to the peak of the sky, but its light barely penetrated the heavy canopy of forest. As far as Hugo was concerned, that was a good thing. It meant that the German planes couldn't see to strafe them on the ground, and even search parties on foot would have trouble finding them.

Judex stirred where he lay and opened his eyes.

"How are you feeling?" Hugo asked.

"Alive," he replied, rising cautiously to his feet. "Nothing seems to be broken, which is remarkable."

"I cushioned your fall the best I could."

"And how are you?" Judex asked.

"I'm right as rain. Jumping out of an airplane doesn't seem to be that much for me."

Judex smiled and shook his head. "Did you know you'd survive?"

"I suspected as much, but I couldn't be sure. That's not the sort of thing I do for a lark, you know."

"Your strength is an amazing gift."

"I suppose so," Hugo said. "I keep hoping I'll find a way to use it that'll make a real splash in the world, but no luck. I think I'd have been a lot happier without it."

"What do you mean?"

"I didn't have any real friends, or even pets, when I was a kid. My mother was afraid of my strength; afraid I'd kill someone. When I got away from home I thought it'd be easy to make my way in the world, but all I seem able to do is break things and terrify people.

"I thought the War would be the perfect chance to put all that destructive power to use. The thing is, as many Huns as I kill, it doesn't seem to bring the conflict any closer to ending, and the people around me still die."

"You have lost friends," Judex said. It sounded like a question, but Hugo could tell that the man already knew the answer."

"One friend, yes. Another American named Tom Shayne. He was a swell guy until the Huns dropped a shell on us. It deafened me for a bit but there wasn't much left of Tom...

"I kind of went crazy then. I went into the trenches and wore myself out killing them. Can you imagine? It's like stomping cockroaches until you're so tired you can't lift your feet. That's when they put me in the field hospital. You know the rest."

Judex was silent for a moment, then he took a small flask from his coat and passed it to Hugo. He caught the aroma of strong brandy and took a swallow. The liquor warmed his stomach but did nothing to lift his spirits.

Judex took the flask back and raised it.

"Tom Shayne," he said, then took a small drink and put the flask away. The sincerity of the gesture touched Hugo.

"Did it help?" Judex asked.

"What?"

"Taking vengeance on your enemies."

"Not really," Hugo said, after a moment of thought. "Tom's still gone, and I hate the bastards more than ever."

Judex was silent and Hugo could see that his words had stirred something deep within the man.

"Perhaps for revenge to truly make a difference, it must be applied carefully."

"Are you saying I shouldn't have killed those bastards?" Hugo asked, feeling a surge of indignation.

"No," Judex replied. "I would never deny any man his just vengeance. It is only that, if it is to achieve true justice, revenge must be applied as carefully as a surgeon's scalpel."

"Is that why you do this?" Hugo asked.

"This mission?"

"More than that. You have some amazing skills, and your own airplane, and there's this hat and cloak. What is all of this for?"

"Yes," Judex replied. "There is a man I must punish, not just for what he has done to my family, but for all those he has ruined."

"Maybe when this is over, I'll help you," Hugo said.

Judex smiled and nodded, but it seemed to Hugo that he was still troubled. The cloaked man pulled out a map and a compass and spent a few moments getting his bearings.

"Joiry is that direction," he said, pointing into the woods. "If we start now and walk through the night we should be able to reach it before dawn."

"We can do much better than that," Hugo said with a grin. "I can outrun a race car if I want to."

Half an hour later, the two men stood on an outcropping of rock where heavy forest opened enough for a clear view of the starry sky. The ruin of Joiry Castle stood on a jagged escarpment overlooking the countryside. An unhealthy red light shone through some of the gaps in the ancient stonework.

"There," Judex said pointing to a narrow trail that ascended the rock face. "Movement on the rocks."

Hugo followed the gesture. In the light of the full Moon, he made out an irregular trickle of human shapes shambling up the path.

"Men," he said, "but there's something wrong with the way they're moving."

"I wish I had my field glasses," Judex said with a rueful smile. "I'm afraid I left them on the plane."

"We were in a bit of a hurry," Hugo replied, returning the smile.

"The walkers aren't being challenged, but the forest has been cut back at the base of the rocks. I don't see a way to reach the place by stealth."

"There's no need," Hugo said. "There's no way they can keep me out of that place. You stay here; I'll go and smash their super-weapon."

"We should both go."

"No offense, but for all your skills, you're just a man. There's no danger for me, but you'd likely be killed."

"No danger?" Judex fixed an intense stare on him. "My friend, you are powerful, but it is foolish to make such an assumption. We need a strategy."

"I don't," Hugo said. "I hope you take my advice and keep to cover. *Au revoir*, my friend. I'll bring you Von Meyer's head on a bayonet."

He made a huge leap, which cleared the treetops and took him to the edge of the woods, then he ran toward the cliff-side path. Hugo heard shouts from the ruins and, a moment later, the sound of rifle fire. He barked out a laugh as a lucky shot caught him in the abdomen, the bullet flattening against his unyielding flesh.

Hugo slowed for the narrow, winding footpath. He could make out the figures ahead of him now, soldiers in German and French uniforms marching together in single minded determination to reach the Château Joiry. Some of the men bore terrible wounds. A one-armed German, half his head a wreck, marched almost proudly, while another followed at a slower pace, limping but otherwise untroubled by his missing right foot. Hugo felt the fear tickle his spine from bottom to top. He knew that the walking dead couldn't harm him any more than the living, but the sight of them was horrifying. He decided to bypass the macabre procession as much as he could. He stopped running and looked up to where the trail doubled back

171

to pass over his head. Gathering himself, he leaped to the next section, then repeated the process, using the switchbacks like a set of stairs.

A few shots caught him before he reached the top, but they barely registered. The joy of battle was on him as he came over the edge, and he was disappointed to see only a dozen terrified German soldiers and two men in black hooded robes.

He raced toward them contemptuous of their rifles. When he reached them, he drove his fist through the first soldier's chest like a spear. Hugo felt a brutal satisfaction as he saw the others blanch with fear. Several of the soldiers continued to fire, but most turned and tried to flee into the keep. Hugo grabbed a man and pitched him far over the side of the escarpment. Seconds later, he sent two more screaming after him.

By this time, all of the others had abandoned their weapons and were scrambling over each other in a frantic attempt to get through the narrow door. Hugo picked up a discarded rifle and hurled it like a javelin to impale one of the men. He caught two more by their necks and banged their heads together with such force that their skulls exploded in sprays of red. He pushed through the throng, lashing out with his fists, crushing a spine, collapsing a ribcage, ripping an arm from its socket and discarding it.

Ignoring the three surviving men, Hugo surged forward and caught the robed leaders and pinned them against the parapet wall, one in each hand.

"Where is your leader?" he yelled at one of them.

"*Ich verstehe nicht!*" the man cried, his voice frantic.

"Wrong answer," Hugo said. He tightened his grip, just a little, and was rewarded by the crunch of the man's trachea and, an instant later, the pop of his spine."

"Your turn," he said to the other hooded man. "Where is the Herr Doctor Meyer?"

"*Der Meister?*" the terrified German pointed to an archway that had once been a door leading to the inner castle. "*Er ist dort, durch diese Tür.*"

"Thanks, pal," Hugo said. He slapped his palm against the man's brow, turning his head to a mix of red jelly and bone shards.

He gave a glance at the three surviving soldiers, who huddled against the wall, paralyzed by fear. He nearly turned back to kill them, but something in him didn't want to.

"Not worth my time," he said, then headed through the arch into a broad stair that spiraled downward. The passage was dark but, as he descended, he discerned the reflection of a ruby glow. A moment later, three guards appeared around the bend, carrying torches that gave off the unnatural glow. They were roughly human in shape, but with distorted, dog-like faces and hooved feet.

Their inhuman appearance startled Hugo, only for an instant, but enough for them to leap on him, attacking savagely. They were strong—much stronger than men—but that was nothing to Hugo. Their claws slid harmlessly across his flesh. He grabbed one by the hip and shoulder and found that its flesh was unnaturally touch and rubbery. With a powerful wrench, he pulled the creature to pieces. He lifted the second and slammed it into the stone wall with such force that the ceiling threatened to cave in.

The third monster backed away from him, growling uncertainly. Hugo sprang forward swinging his stiff-fingered hand horizontally, like a sword. The blow caught the creature in the side of the neck, releasing a fountain of gore. The doglike head fell from the body to roll down the stairs.

Hugo emerged into the room he had seen in Gianetti's vision. Black robed men and naked fiends paused at their grim work so stare at him. One man, tall and bearded, his robe embroidered with strange occult symbols, stood at the far side of the room, supervising. Hugo knew instantly who he must be and strode toward him.

He was met by a surge of inhuman bodies as more creatures like those he had killed on the stair leapt on him. Others joined them: a bat-winged reptilian creature shaped like a giant ape, a small-toad-skinned man with tentacles lining his mouth, and many others whose bizarre appearance Hugo barely registered before they were on him.

Hugo flailed at them as their fangs and claws shredded his clothes and left scratches on even his steel skin. This was like the trenches again, except these things were far stronger than men and did not die easily. Like ants, they continued to attack long after taking wounds that would have killed a human being. Still, for all their ferocity, he smashed them down, one by one, until the floor of the chamber was steeped with a mix of blood, ichor, and foul smelling fluids.

Then the small demon with the tentacled face rose up with a bowl of pale liquid which it dashed into Hugo's face. It blinded him and he swallowed a bitter mouthful. A moment later, he felt weak and dizzy.

Hugo tried to throw his tormenters off, but his muscles wouldn't obey him. Under the unrelenting attack of the demonic horde, he sagged to the ground and darkness claimed him.

He awoke in a different room, a huge chamber that must once have been the great hall of the castle. The ceiling had partially collapsed and he could see the moon through the aperture.

Hugo was bound to the wall by heavy chains that held his arms over his head; his feet dangled above the stone floor. He tried to test the chains, but discovered that his muscles were paralyzed. The room was dominated by a gigantic human form, the colossus of Gianetti's vision now completed.

"Master!"

He had just enough mobility to glance toward the voice. It was the toad-skinned creature which, with the winged ape-thing and two of the robed men, stood near him, apparently acting as guards.

"Master," the creature repeated, "he awakens!"

The man Hugo had seen earlier stepped up to him. He was tall and massively built, with close-cropped red hair and a full beard. The softness of his body was offset by his eyes, which were a pitiless blue that made Hugo think of an Arctic sky.

"*Wer sind Sie?*" the man asked.

"Go climb a tree," Hugo replied in English. Speech was easy for him so he reasoned that paralysis rather than weakness was what held him motionless.

"Who are you, *Engländer?*" The man's English was slow and heavily accented but Hugo could understand him.

"What's it to you, Herr Doctor Von Meyer?"

"Ah..." Von Meyer smiled at the sound of his name. "If you know that, then you are an ally of the Frenchman, Dubnotal. Was he the one who gave you such power?"

"Nuts to you."

"Are there more like you?"

"A whole regiment," Hugo said. "The 'Fighting Colorados,' they call us."

"But they only sent you?"

"One man is more than enough to take care of a freak show run by a two-bit sideshow magician."

Von Meyer's face darkened and he smashed Hugo across the face with a backhanded blow. He hardly felt the impact, but the sorcerer yelped in pain and nursed his hand.

"Ghouls," he yelled, "*Bestrafen Sie ihn!*"

Two of the dog-like men moved forward, heavy iron bars in their hands. They began to beat his torso with powerful, measured blows. After some time, they stepped back, breathing hard, and Hugo laughed.

"You are a challenge," Von Meyer said. "We must see if there are more vulnerable areas." He barked an order to the ghouls. They stepped away to return a moment later. One carried a sledge hammer, the other held a glowing poker. Hugo closed his eyes, tightly, and braced for what was coming. The red hot metal pressed against the skin of his eyelid and he felt the heat. It was unpleasant, but no worse than what a normal man might feel when the water in a shower grows too hot.

He could feel the ghoul trying to wedge the point of the implement between his eyelids and strained to prevent it. It seemed to go on forever, then the iron withdrew and he felt rubbery hands grasp his ankles and spread his limp legs.

Hugo opened his eyes in time to see the second ghoul swing the hammer in an upward arc to strike him squarely in the testicles. It wasn't a damaging blow, he knew, more what an ordinary man might feel if flicked with a fingertip, but he no longer felt like laughing. Half a dozen strikes later his eyes were watering and the creatures released him as Von Meyer stepped forward.

"You see?" the sorcerer asked. "Nothing can withstand the intelligent application of force. Even a diamond can be split when one knows how."

Hugo glared, but kept his mouth shut. As strong as he was, he knew that the man was right. Eventually they would break even his superhuman body and, long before that, the pain would break his spirit.

"Are there others like you?"

"No," he said, seeing no harm in the answer.

"Did you come alone?"

He thought of Judex waiting in the forest. It had been foolish to leave the man behind.

"I did. Sâr Dubnotal wanted to send others with me, but I thought I could do this myself."

"Perhaps," Von Meyer said. "Just the same, I have sent some of my ghouls out. They will sniff out anyone within five miles of the castle and tear them to pieces."

Hugo said nothing.

"I shall enjoy learning more about you, my friend," Von Meyer said. "A man who can slaughter ghouls and demons may be of great use to me. For the moment, though, I have far more important things to attend to. I leave you to the tender care of my creatures."

For the next quarter of an hour, the ghouls applied their ingenuity to the most vulnerable parts of Hugo's body. In the background, he could hear the sound of chanting in some language he didn't recognize.

Then it stopped.

As if someone had thrown a switch, the chanting, the torture, all sound in the movement in the great chamber went away.

Hugo opened his eyes and saw that everyone was staring at the colossus. The gargantuan body took a breath, then another, then opened its eyes; the same ice-blue eyes of Von Meyer's face.

The creature rose to its feet—Hugo guessed that it was at least 100 feet tall—and stretched its muscles. The thing raised its face to the sky.

"*Meine Stunde ist gekommen!*" The voice was the sorcerer's, but augmented by a chorus of 10,000 others. The giant laughed and strode from the castle, sending demons, ghouls and black robed men scurrying to avoid the falling debris as it tore through the walls.

Many of the fiends followed in its wake, but one man, the ape demon, the little toad skinned man, and two of the ghouls remained to continue their work on Hugo.

As he waited for the torture to resume, Hugo saw something like a shadow move from the shelter of the wall and come up behind his tormentors.

Judex!

The caped man came silently, his pistol drawn. When he was almost close enough to touch, Hugo saw the nostrils of one of the ghouls twitch. The creature spun, only to receive two slugs in the chest from Judex's Steyr. The pistol spoke again and the second ghoul joined the first on the floor.

The ape-thing sprang at the man, but he side-stepped and it caught only his cloak, pulling it loose. He fired a bullet into the demon's heart and the creature dissolved into foul greenish smoke.

The little demon sprang at Judex then, tackling him to the ground. Though only four feet tall, with a scrawny build, the toad-skinned horror seemed to have inhuman strength. It slapped the pistol away and began to strangle him. Fortunately, for all its strength, the creature only had the mass of a child. Judex spun to the right, throwing it off balance, and swept its feet from under it with his leg.

The demon lost its grip and was thrown nearly a dozen feet. It sprang back up in an instant, but Judex was just as fast. He dove for his pistol and rolled to his feet in one smooth motion. As the demon leaped, he fired two shots, and it burst into flame and vanished.

Judex turned, gun still in hand and strode toward the black-robed man who was the last of Hugo's tormentors. He placed the muzzle of the weapon against the man's forehead.

"There is an antidote for the paralysis drug, is there not?" he asked in a calm voice.

"How did you get in?"

The antidote the lackey had produced seemed effective. Hugo had recovered his movement in a matter of moments and easily broken free of the chains.

"It was not hard," Judex replied. "I overpowered one of the walking dead and took his uniform. I copied the unfortunate creature's gait and entered the castle unchallenged."

He paused for a moment.

"I saw what you did to those soldiers outside."

"Do you have a problem with that?"

"It was not necessary. They could not have harmed you."

"They were enemy soldiers," Hugo said. "They're responsible for killing Tom, and thousands of other good men."

"They were soldiers in war. Our own troops have done as much."

"Why are you criticizing me? I hate those sons of bitches and I'll avenge my friend's death every chance I get. I'd think you, of all people, would understand that."

"We have different ideas," Judex said, "but now is not the time. We have to stop the giant."

"I don't think even I can do that," Hugo replied.

"We must try."

The colossus was moving fast, but Hugo was faster. He carried Judex through the woods at the same breakneck pace, only stopping when they reaches a clearing a quarter of a mile ahead of the giant's path.

"Stay hidden," he said. "A silver bullet won't do anything against that monster." Hugo moved to the center of the clearing where an ancient glacier had scattered an assortment of granite boulders. He lifted one that must have weighed five tons and, as the colossus entered the clearing, threw it.

The rock sailed at the giant's chest, only to be batted away like a tennis ball. The monster bellowed out his eerie chorus of laughter and stomped with a colossal foot. Hugo saw it coming, but not in time to dodge. The weight stunned him and drove his body into the ground like a tent peg. He thrashed and struggled himself free of the earth, only to feel a great hand scoop him up and lift him high.

He drove his fist into the palm of the hand, piercing the flesh and breaking a metacarpal bone thicker than his torso. The colossus cried out and flung him to the ground with stunning force. Hugo lay there unable to move, waiting for the final attack that would snuff out his life, but it didn't come.

"Can you stand up?"

Judex was at his side, helping him to his feet.

"I was afraid you were dead," he said.

"Too close."

Hugo shook his head to clear it and became aware of the sound of howitzer fire around them. "What's happening?" he asked.

"Several German artillery placements have begun to shell the creature. That was what distracted him from you."

"The Germans? But he's one of them."

"All they see is a monster," Judex said. "They do what anyone would do."

"Can they kill him? Is it even possible?"

Judex shook his head. "I don't know, but we must try to help them."

The big guns were still firing as the two arrived. Dozens of soldiers tried to augment them with small arms fire. The Germans had set up their position in an old stone church and the attached parsonage. As they watched, the colossus tore open the roof of the smaller building and scooped out a handful of screaming infantrymen. He raised the soldiers to face level, then caught one with his other and popped him into his mouth. Hugo looked away as the giant began to chew.

One of the howitzers fired. Hugo turned back to see an explosion open a gaping hole in the monster's chest. For a moment he felt a surge of hope. Then the wound began to knit itself closed and, in moments, it had disappeared.

The colossus laughed and tossed away the remaining soldiers. He strode to the big gun seized it by barrel and lifted it like a toy. He tossed the howitzer into the woods and set about stamping on the gun crew like ants.

"Keep him busy," Judex said. "I have an idea."

He darted away in the direction of the buildings leaving Hugo to stare incredulously after him.

Keep him busy? That's insane.

Judex ducked into the old church but the colossus saw him. He abandoned lone survivor of the gun crew and moved toward the building.

Hugo muttered a string of curses and looked around for something to use as a weapon. His gaze settled on an officer's staff car. He raced to it and hoisted the big vehicle to his shoulder just as the giant bent to peer in the church windows. He threw it with all his might and caught the colossus on the jaw, staggering him.

"Here I am!" Hugo shouted, throwing a German motorcycle good measure.

And here we go, he said to himself as the giant rose and began to move toward him. He raced toward it, avoiding a clutching hand and running between the towering legs.

He pushed himself to the limit as the colossus gave chase. With its long legs it could cover ground faster, but it couldn't turn or stop nearly as fast as he could. He moved into the woods, darting through clumps of trees like a rabbit while the giant stumbled after him, leaving a trail of destruction.

It must have been a dozen times that Hugo narrowly dodged a trampling foot; then he saw something ahead of him. He only caught a glimpse but he could tell it was a little town, with people in the streets. He couldn't lead the abomination there.

Hugo hesitated as he tried to change his course. It was only for an instant, but that was enough. A mammoth hand scooped him up. He struggled against the grip and managed to apply a variation of a wrestling hold to one of the fingers. He pulled as hear as he could and heard the gratifying snap of tendons.

The giant let out a bellow of pain and threw him with such force that he nearly blacked out. The ground shot past at blinding speed until he came to earth with shattering impact.

Hugo lay still for several moments before he could raise his head. His entire body throbbed with pain unlike anything he had ever known.

He looked around and realized that he had been thrown back to the artillery placement at the church. The colossus apparently wanted for all of his victims to be in the same place. Colossal footsteps echoed through the forest as the monster approached. Hugo rose, his limbs barely able to support him, but he wanted to fight, or at least to die on his feet.

The colossus came into sight, towering above the tallest trees. When it saw him, its mouth twisted into a bestial leer and it headed in his direction. Hugo found himself watching his approaching death with an odd sense of detachment. He was too weary to be defiant, angry, or even frightened.

The voice of a howitzer sounded and, a second later, a wound appeared in the giant's chest. Hugo waited for the hole to close, but it didn't. Instead, black blood began to flow from the wound as a look of confusion spread across the colossal features. It raised its head and ten thousand voices shouted as one, "*Nein!*"

The colossus collapsed with the sound of a toppling building. Hugo followed a moment later, sinking to his trembling knees. He heard someone calling his name and turned to see Judex and several German soldiers racing toward him. Then he breathed deeply and let darkness carry him away.

He woke in the same field hospital. His old nurse seemed a little more pleased with him this time, now that he was covered with cuts and bruises. The second day, Sâr Dubnotal came to see him.

"Is he dead?" Hugo asked.

"Von Meyer?" The Sâr stroked his beard thoughtfully. "It is possible," he said, "though with a thaumaturge of his power it would be foolish to assume so."

"I know that Judex found a way to kill him—the giant—but how?"

"He remembered what I said about the silver bullet and went into the church to try to find something made of that metal."

"He must have succeeded. What was it?"

"I believe it was a statue of St. Dunstan. He gave it to the gun crew and it became their bullet."

"So I own my life to the enemy?" Hugo chuckled bitterly. "At least, now I know there's some use for religion."

"I have a note for you," Sâr Dubnotal said, and passed him a folded piece of paper.

My friend,

I am grateful that you survived. What you did took great power and greater courage and I am proud to have fought by your side.

182

As for your generous offer to help me in my mission, I fear I must decline. The vengeance I seek must be dealt out coolly and precisely and you are a man of passion and turmoil.

A man of your gifts has much more to offer than to act as an instrument of revenge or a weapon of destruction. I hope that you discover a way to build up rather than tear down. More than that, I hope you find peace.

Judex

The nurse announced that Hugo needed his rest so the Sâr shook his hand and left. He didn't rest though. He remained awake staring at the note and wondering if there could be anything in his life that would mean more than death and destruction.

For the life of him, he couldn't think of a thing.

Micah Harris has often regaled the readers of Tales of the Shadowmen *with untold adventures of Becky Sharp, the anti-heroine of William Makepeace Thackeray's satirical novel* Vanity Fair. *In this new chapter, the indomitable Miss Sharp crosses path with Sâr Dubnotal to battle the beautiful but singularly evil Helen Vaughan, protagonist of Arthur Machen's ground-breaking novella,* The Great God Pan...

Micah Harris: *Slouching Towards Camulodunum*
(from an idea by Mark Schultz)

It is probable that, upon mature consideration, after weighing the good and evil, I shall one day destroy this paper, or at least leave it under seal to my friend D., trusting his discretion, to use it or to burn it, as he may think fit.
Robert Matheson, Med. Dr.

Bath, 1917

I. The Encounter on Great Pulteney Street.

The man in the turban, with the olive complexion and a beard the texture of a tightly coiled vine, summoned images of a remote landscape, both arid and lush, and seemed to have stepped out of one of the paintings of the nearby Victoria Museum, inspired by *The Rubaiyat of Omar Khayyam*.

As with the *Rubaiyat*, Sâr Dubnotal might well have come from a Platonic overrealm of unchanging forms. His turban, puffy white trousers, and gold embroidered sash gave his countenance an antiquity that was belied only by his fashionable Edwardian frock coat and cravat.

El Tebib—as he was known in the East—and his massive Hindu manservant Naini sat in an enclosed black carriage drawn by horses dark as pitch and driven by a soberly dressed man in a black top hat. Like a preternatural shadow without a source, the somber conveyance loomed in the midday sunlight that brightened Bath's Great Pulteney Street.

The carriage sat by a row of homogeneously designed Georgian homes, which, along with the series of similar houses across the street, gave the impression of a single image repeated infinitely in a vast, open corridor of mirrors. The object of Sâr Dubnotal's quest had thought herself hidden among these residences indistinguishable from each other.

But little in this terrestrial sphere was hidden from the Great Psychagogue.

"Look, Naini." Sâr Dubnotal did not break his austere emerald gaze, nor move other than to slightly peel his forefinger up and then smoothly lower it. His manservant's powerful frame was cloaked in even more conservative Edwardian attire than his master: charcoal frock coat and trousers and black Stetson hat. Naini nodded, his hand already on the carriage door's handle, awaiting the next command.

They watched a petite, shapely Gibson girl tentatively making her way down the row of houses on the opposite side of the street. An abundance of strawberry blond hair spilled from beneath a broad brimmed hat, the shadow of which veiled her eyes. Under a dark vest, she wore a high, white collared blouse clasped at the throat by a thin tie. Her full-length skirt was the cut favored by the "new woman": straight and sensible.

Sâr Dubnotal, still without breaking his stare, raised five fingers to signal Naini to hold. The woman answered the physical description of their quarry, but she seemed not to know where her home was. But, of course, the similarity of a row of houses could disorient even those most familiar with the street.

Then the woman's chin raised alertly at a melodious chanting in the air. Sâr Dubnotal recognized the words, but he was compelled to keep his attention riveted on the woman herself and so let the chant recede into the background. She was now heading briskly towards the specific house they were watching. With the stakes so high, they could ill-afford to hesitate any longer.

Sâr Dubnotal flicked his wrist in the woman's direction and Naini went into action. The pair expected no resistance for *El Tebib* had planned the abduction for the heat of the day, when the wealthy would be seeking fashionable salons indoors. Still, speed was paramount, as well as stealth. To that end, the giant was both quick and strangely ephemeral, as though carried along on the summer breeze stirring in the heat of the brick and mortar canyon that was Great Pulteney Street. His stealth was aided by the woman hesitating uncertainly before the house. She looked up at an open window from which the chanting came.

As she was about to mount the front steps, Naini moved in behind her, one muscular arm lashing out about her waist and pulling her to him while his other hand pressed a cloth dabbed with chloroform over her nose and mouth.

The woman immediately went limp. The coachman cracked the whip and the carriage lunged forward to meet the Hindu. In the next moment, Naini was lifting the woman into the carriage and the receiving arms of Sâr Dubnotal. Then, before the door was closed behind him, the coach was already bolting down Pulteney Street towards the bridge.

"It is her, master?" Naini asked.

"I have never seen Helen Vaughan before," Sâr Dubnotal said, looking down into the beautiful, creamy face. He began to search her pockets.

From there, he produced a small packet of papers bound by twine which ran through a ring. *El Tebib* loosened the string and examined the jewelry. It was an ancient bit of Roman work. He found it significant that the front of the ring was shaped into a satyr's head. On the inner side of the band, his keen eye could make out a script in Latin: *DEVOMNODENT-MAVORS CAMVLOS*.

He cupped the ring, feeling strange eddies in the mystic fluids. Turning his attention to, and shuffling through, the papers, he came at last to a document of identification. He gave a sigh of accomplishment—together with the ring, there was little room for doubt as to the woman's identity.

Yet Sâr Dubnotal could not completely relax, for a spur of uncertainty remained lodged in his mind. His keen ear, which retained detailed information from even ambient noise, allowed him to recall the words to the song he had heard on the street:

Old King Cole was a merry old soul,
And a merry old soul was he,
He called for his pipe, and he called for his bowl
And he called for his fiddlers three.

Sâr Dubnotal initially had thought that the voice belonged to someone who shared Helen's dwelling, and that it had helped her recognize her own house, after a brief moment of disorientation. Yet, she had hesitated on the front steps, looking up at that open window instead of striding into her rightful home.

They crossed the bridge and soon were at the rear entrance of the Psychagogue's temporary lodgings near the Victoria Museum. Naini swept the woman into his arms, then effortlessly carried her up the back flight of stairs to their flat.

The driver dismounted, removing his black hat to reveal blond hair. His face, though now in early middle age, seemed, over their long association, to have partaken of the effulgence of Sâr Dubnotal's own timelessness.

"You look troubled, master," he said. "Why?"

"Rudolph," said the Psychagogue, "I am no longer sure that this woman is Helen Vaughan. In our haste, we may have taken an innocent. Or much worse—Helen Vaughan knew we were in Bath searching for her, and is now long gone, while we have wasted time stalking an impostor...

"Let us ascend," he continued. "Naini should have her well restrained by now. We will come to the truth of this matter by whatever means necessary."

Upon reaching their floor, their ears were assaulted by shrill screaming that would soon summon the local constabulary if allowed to continue. Sâr Dubnotal raced down the hall:

one thing they did *not* need was a red blooded English bobby bursting upon the scene to rescue this lovely flower of British womanhood, bound and at the mercy of him and Naini—"dark heathens" both.

Now he heard Naini screaming along with the woman. Reaching the still open doorway, the Great Psychagogue and Rudolph saw the Hindu standing beside the woman, whom he had successfully bound in a wooden chair, holding a bleeding hand. The same blood smeared the woman's mouth, open wide in wailing.

"Rudolph! See to Naini's wound! Take him to his room, then summon our new friends with haste," *El Tebib* ordered as he crossed the room, plucking away the skull ornament that pinned his cravat. He stuffed the freed article of clothing into the woman's mouth as she desperately turned her head from side to side, all the time bellowing. Then, Sâr Dubnotal tore asunder her high collar, undid her tie, and tied it around her head, securing the gag.

The woman was now looking up at him, her eyes widening as she fully took in his strange, austere appearance for the first time. This initiated a new round of bellowing, but, this time, it lodged and rumbled in her throat.

When she was spent, the Great Psychagogue asked, "If you are through screaming, Miss Vaughan, might we talk now?"

Still eyeing him dubiously, she nodded "yes." He began to remove the gag, and, before he could pull his cravat from her mouth, she had regurgitated it into her lap. Gasping for air and vehemently shaking her head, she shouted:

"I am *not* that *bitch* Helen Vaughan!"

"Exactly what the real Helen Vaughan would say in this position. My great tutelary, Ranijesti—blessed be he!—to whom nothing is lost in this world or the Empyrean beyond, and who is beyond reproof of error, says otherwise."

The woman's features trembled between an expression of rage and utter bafflement: "Your great Rooney-jesty— *what*?"

Sâr Dubnotal's eyes narrowed and his nose lifted in the air at this slurring of his master's name. "Ranijesti—that Bodhisattva who even now enjoys foretastes of Nirvana from his cell submerged in the earth of India…"

"You think I'm Helen Vaughan because a man *in a hole in the ground* on the other side of the globe told you so?" the woman responded, incredulity and contempt in her voice.

Sâr Dubnotal drew himself up and glared down at her. "Ranijesti directed us *where* to find Helen Vaughan. *This*," he produced the pack of papers bound with the ring, "says that you are the object of our quest. So, instead of bantering metaphysics, let us limit ourselves to the more mundane evidence, shall we?

"I adjure you to tell me why you are carrying these papers. If it's because you think you may have killed Helen Vaughan and taken her identity, let me disabuse you: Helen Vaughan does not die so easily and remains a present danger. On the other hand, if you are her willing accomplice, planted to misdirect us while she escapes, I will see that you will bear the full expiation for this crime—after you have told us where to find her."

"You, swarthy fool!" the woman snapped. "Your head is as brown as a hen's egg, but apparently nothing grows inside it! It was Helen Vaughan who murdered *me*—or, at least, came close—and took *my* identity. Not the other way around. *She* switched our papers! If you would ever withdraw your turbaned head from the 'Empyrean,' you might notice there's a war going on. With the Huns at the gate, I could ill afford to risk moving about England without some form of identification, and this was the only one available to me.

"I was at her home today because I have been searching for Helen Vaughan for two years to exact my own revenge on her, and to take back something that witch took from me. I did not know I was even on the right street until I heard that accursed song coming from the window…"

"If you are not Helen Vaughan, then who are you?" Sâr Dubnotal asked.

"My name is Rebecca Sharp!"

Sâr Dubnotal studied the woman whose initial conflagration of outrage had now cooled to simmering indignation. He was not yet certain she was not Helen Vaughan and this tale of woe but a fabrication. He could no longer wait for Rudolph to return with their colleagues who could settle the matter. If she was an impostor, the real Helen Vaughan was free—though perhaps not yet far beyond Bath. A few minutes might make all the difference in her slipping beyond their grasp.

He began to move to the back of the woman calling herself Rebecca Sharp.

"What—what are you doing? Get off!" she demanded as he took her head between his hands. She thrust her head from side to side to try to wrench it free as he pulled back her blonde locks to examine her scalp. He ran his index finger along a long groove there.

She flinched and bellowed with indignation: "How *dare* you! *Don't touch me!*"

Sâr Dubnotal did not answer, but crossed the room to open a drawer from which he took a large pair of scissors.

The woman's eyes bulged as he approached her with the sharp object. "What are you going to do?" she gasped out.

"Only the science of phrenology can quickly resolve the enigma you present, Miss Sharp—if that is who you are," the Psychagogue answered. "I have noted an irregularity in your skull—of which you seem very protective. Helen Vaughan is the Devil's child, and that may be your father's mark."

"You're mad!" she gasped.

"Even so, I have studied various specimens of human skulls in the development of my phrenology skills—skills for which, if I may say, I have demonstrated a high aptitude. Your skull shall now testify for or against you. To that end, your head must first be sheared…"

The woman screamed in face of this new humiliation and again struggled against her restraints, lifting the chair legs off the floor in her paroxysms, as the Great Psychagogue moved in to fulfill his declared purpose.

Suddenly, the door thrust inward. Sâr Dubnotal looked up to see Rudolph, Naini, and the two men he had joined in their quest. One shouted out, "Stop! Whoever she may be— this woman is *not* Helen Vaughan!"

"Finally—someone *sane*!" Becky cried out. "Now will one of you help me rescue my child—something that this turbaned buffoon sabotaged!"

II. What Lurked Within The Artists' Gallery.

Becky Sharp delicately gnawed the broiled chicken breast and surveyed her new and exceedingly colorful surroundings. She was eager for some distraction from the bitingly disappointing report that the two men who had interrupted her head shaving had brought back from Great Pulteney Street. Helen Vaughan had once again absconded with her child. More, the condition in which she had left the house made it clear that she would not be returning.

For that, Becky hated Sâr Dubnotal. But she hated Helen Vaughan far more, and she desperately needed allies in what she had thought was a personal war with that wretched woman. The revelation that she was not a lone foot soldier in that battle gave her more hope than she had had for two years.

She was no longer in the room in which she had been bound, but in the largest one in the flat. Its dimensions were necessary to contain Sâr Dubnotal's entourage, along with a number of guests who had traveled from all over County Somerset to break bread with the renowned Psychagogue.

Becky had bathed and now wore a fresh dress from the wardrobe of *El Tebib*'s medium, Gianetti Annunciata. Frankly, the woman gave Becky the creeps: her pale visage suggested the disturbed, emaciated faces of medieval iconography. Becky did not relish wearing a gown—no matter how resplendent—that had rested against the flesh of a conduit to the dead. She couldn't help an occasional, writhing shrug of her shoulders, thinking that she had felt a residual ghost creep over her skin.

Naini, had recovered and apologized for his role in her mistaken abduction. Becky had not apologized for the bite.

In a corner of the room, a dwarf, perched on a box atop a stool, tossed some chicken to the enormous dog that lay before him. He wiped his greasy fingers on the dog's coat and affectionately tousled the fur of its neck, saying, "*Bon Eustache. Bon chien.*"

Whatever was inside the box thumped against its lid and sides, as though trying to kick through. The dwarf glared harshly at Becky when he saw her staring at this unexplained phenomenon to which no one else at this bizarre soirée was paying attention.

In the middle of the room, before a draped painting on an easel—to be debuted at Sâr Dubnotal's salon that night, before being displayed at the Victoria—two men from the Order of the Golden Dawn were attempting to engage the Great Psychagogue on a topic that was apparently paramount with them. A blond man named Rudolph stood beside *El Tebib*. Becky had noticed that he seemed to make a point of being always as close to Sâr Dubnotal as possible, never removing his adoring eyes from the pompous fakir.

"Sycophant," Becky hissed under her breath, continuing to chew her chicken, watching and listening to the conversation between Sâr Dubnotal and these men, one of whom spoke with a heavy French accent, the other with an Irish lilt.

"But what about the dream?" the Frenchman said haltingly in English. He was thin, bearded, with a long face. He wore a cabby's hat atop his head, and sloppily put together evening wear. Yet, Becky had heard some gossip that he was actually from the wealthy Toulet family of Paris.

"I have written down my impressions," the Irishman said, producing a leaf of paper from inside his coat. He was handsome in a bookish way, but his disheveled hair added a distracted quality to his appearance that didn't seem appropriate in an academic—absent-minded or not.

As Sâr Dubnotal looked at the papers with a patronizingly air, Toulet spoke again: "I, too, have shared this dream of

Monsieur Yeats from across the Channel. The *same recurring dream*, between two men who had never met until recently."

Sâr Dubnotal muttered aloud the lines as he cursorily read: " '*Widening gyres*' umm-hmm. '*The rough beast... hour come round at last...* ' Ah, I recognize the motif begun with the gyring falcons. Very nice."

"The dream began with me over ten years ago," Yeats said. "A figure of something half-man, half-beast. I thought of a sphinx…"

But the Great Psychagogue was no longer listening. He brusquely returned the paper to the Irishman. "I am sorry, Mr. Yeats, but the novelty of a sphinx sashaying about the deserts of Palestine must yield to a much more pressing affair of mine. But, please, if the Order of the Golden Dawn should ever need my assistance in the future, feel free to call on me again. Rudolph, before escorting these gentlemen out, make sure that they have my card."

Becky bristled at Sâr Dubnotal's approach, but her feelings were assuaged by the fact that a contingent of artists from the Victoria who were attending the soirée—and who were not part of the Psychagogue's usual crowd—had taken his cue and were also walking towards where she sat. Her father had been a painter, and though her childhood had been impoverished, it was the only time she had known a sense of security. This left her favorably disposed to men who wielded the brush.

Joining the group that was forming around her were the two men who had saved her from a head shaving: Villiers and Clarke, occult investigators who were compiling a mammoth repository of such cases, originally begun by Clarke alone, entitled *Memoirs to Prove the Existence of the Devil*. Helen Vaughan, they had learned, was not the last chapter in that book, as they had believed.

"Miss Sharp, if you have sufficiently recovered your wits after our unfortunate misunderstanding, we would like to question you about your relationship with Helen Vaughan," Sâr Dubnotal said. "All of these men with me—and little Jacques Courbé in the corner there—have seen their friends suffer catastrophe through their association with her. We have united in a single purpose: to purge this Earth of her vile stain—this time, forever."

"If that is the case, you will find a willing ally in me, gentlemen," Becky said. "Please. Be seated. All of you. I'd like to know the natures of all your grievances. Then I will tell you how my life was nearly destroyed by an ill-considered alliance with the witch."

"Introductions are in order, first," Sâr Dubnotal said. "You'll recall Messrs. Villiers and Clark…"

"Given the circumstances of our meeting," Becky said, looking *El Tebib* in the eye, "I dare say I would be hard pressed to have forgotten them."

Becky thought she could see a hint of a blush in the Psychagogue's face, but he did not deign to acknowledge her veiled rebuff and continued the introductions.

"This gentleman," he continued, "is Francis Aytown, whose own exhibit just closed at the Victoria. What was it called again, Mr. Aytown?"

"*False Impressions of a Hungarian Count*," Aytown said. Becky gave Aytown a slight smile and nod of the head.

"And this is Mr. Randolph, from America." Becky saw a man whose face shone with a mild fanaticism—but one of a benign, even *mirthful*, spirituality. This was no decadent *bon vivant* from the *fin de siècle*. She was intrigued.

Sâr Dubnotal, seeing her interest, seized the moment: "Mr. Randolph is conversant with the powers of good that radiate from the Empyrean void, though he and I conceive of these powers differently…"

The smiling Randolph beamed at her and said, "I see them as an electrical current…"

"…while *I* see them as currents in the fluid," Sâr Dubnotal said. "It is through the fluids that the parasitic larvae swarm, for corruption can only spread through that which is wholesome, fouling the fluids with their rot—"

"Sir, must I remind you that I am trying to eat while you prattle on about secretions and maggots?" interrupted Becky indignantly. "It's revolting!" She looked at the chicken breast she still held in her hands and set it down—loudly—on her plate. "You're about to put me off broiled chicken for life!"

The men about Sâr Dubnotal all squirmed uneasily— except for Randolph, who appeared bemused.

For a moment, *El Tebib*'s lips pressed tightly, then he relaxed and continued. "An unfortunate aside. Forgive me, Mademoiselle. Your rebuff is an appreciated reminder to stay focused on the business at hand. If you are sufficiently recovered, I will continue:

"This New Englander is Richard Upton Pickman. His current showing is entitled *Back Into the Fabulous Darkness*."

Becky coldly regarded Pickman, his evening attire immaculate except for an asymmetrically gloved hand. "I loathe the dark," she pronounced curtly.

Sâr Dubnotal knitted his brow; he understood Becky's grudge against him, but wondered what she could possibly have against Pickman.

"The man beside Mr. Pickman," he continued, "is Monsieur Pierre Rodin—whose great-grandfather Henri's canvases of graveyard tableaux were a source of inspiration to our Mr. Pickman. I trust, Messrs Pickman and Rodin, that what is on that draped canvas will not revolt the delicate Miss Sharp further?" Though addressing the men, it was Sâr Dubnotal's turn to look Becky in the eye so that she wouldn't miss the caustic sparks that shone there.

"Indeed not, sir," Rodin said. "What is on that canvas is more in the nature of a portrait. I have recovered a lost technique of great-grandfather's—you haven't visited what the locals call the Judge's House in Benchurch by any chance? Any of you? No? The eponymous judge was rendered by great-grandfather in the same manner as this painting. It is my great pleasure to share his advance on the *trompe l'oeil* with you all tonight."

"We will look forward to it," Sâr Dubnotal said and continued the introductions: "Also from New England, though by a different route than Pickman, is Mr. Charles Delaware Tate."

Becky immediately liked the slim, handsome Tate. "And are you also showing at the Victoria, Mr. Tate?"

"I'm afraid not, Miss Sharp. "I came here on a pilgrimage, you might say: a long delayed visit to pay my respects at the empty grave of my mentor, Basil Hallward."

"Now, as to these men's grievances concerning Helen Vaughan," Sâr Dubnotal continued, "they had a peer who, when barely more than a boy, fell into the salon which she presided over in the 1880s under the alias of Mrs. Belmont. His name was Aubrey Beardsley, and, like so many to fall under her sway, his life—while still a young one—was cut short."

Pickman spoke up: "Gentlemen, let us be careful to keep our heads lest our quest degenerate into a Salem-style witch hunt. I do want to remind you all that Beardsley's consumption may have been inchoate *before* he met Helen Vaughan."

"Then she sped it on," Aytown snapped. "Many with his affliction live far past 25 years. Are you defending her, Yankee?"

"My dear Pickman," Sâr Dubnotal said, raising his hand. "Villiers and Clarke have shown you their record of the trail of death she left in London. That her association with Beardsley was concurrent can leave no room for doubt."

"I've always suspected she had a hand in poor Basil's disappearance," Aytown said. "And Dorian's fate, too. That portrait could have only been painted under such a malign influence as hers."

"Apparently Lord Henry does not share that opinion," Pickman retorted. "He was intimate with both men, yet remained Helen Vaughan's friend until her demise."

Again, Sâr Dubnotal raised his hand commandingly and aborted Aytown's retort. "Mr. Pickman, need I remind you that Beardsley's death is not the only crime laid to Helen Vaughan's charge? Her maleficence is well documented in Clarke's book. Hers is an evil truly not of this Earth. My late associate Robert Matheson was a medical doctor of sober mind who described via sealed document—which I was instructed to burn or use upon my own discretion— Helen's true ungodly form revealed at the moment of expiration.

"I believe his discovery that she had somehow managed to reincorporate was responsible for the seizure that took his life three and a half years after her death, though, of course, this can never be proven.

"And you may add to all this what she did to poor Jacques over there."

Sâr caught the mischievous gleam in Becky's eyes, the trembling of her pressed lips and the oscillating spasms of her cheeks.

"No, Miss Sharp," the Psychagogue added. "Before you ask, she did *not* shrink him.

"When he was with the circus, Jacques was in love with a perfectly proportioned midget ballerina named Minuette, who would pirouette on a specially prepared saddle atop a pony. Helen Vaughan saw her, proclaimed her adorable, and Minuette was accepted for the first time into the society of 'big people.' Helen would even buy matching outfits for the two of them and have her sit on her lap during her soirées. Minuette resented Jacques's warnings as an attempt to keep her within the fringe society of the circus freaks.

"Of course, by the time Helen was through with her, Minuette was destroyed. Brave Jacques stormed Helen's home in the midst of one of her decadent gatherings atop his previous Eustache, who, like the current one, could be most vicious when his master required it. Jacques himself was armed with a sword, and did not wield it in vain. What followed was... the epitome of 'too horrible to tell.' Let us leave it at that for the nonce.

"Now, Miss Sharp, you know all our grievances. If you will, please tell us yours."

"I shall gentlemen, but before I divulge my story, I think it expedient that we eliminate the traitor sitting here with us."

An almost audible muteness struck the men around the table. Their eyes darted reflexively from side to side despite the restraint they were exercising to not look from face to face.

Becky slammed one hand on the table and pointed with the other: "*J'accuse*! Pickman is Helen Vaughan's spy!"

"What? This is extraordinary!" a clearly stunned Pickman blurted out.

Only Aytown smiled at her revelation. Randolph appeared to be trying to keep an open mind while Charles Delaware Tate, with a slight nodding of his head, seemed to already find her charge plausible. Only Pierre Rodin joined Pickman in protesting his innocence:

"Why—this is an outrage! You've never even met the man before tonight, have you?" Rodin said.

"I do not require a prior acquaintance," Becky said, looking Pickman in the eye. "Pickman knows I'm telling the truth, and if you wish to succeed in your quest to destroy Helen Vaughan, I suggest you see that he never leave this room alive."

Pickman's face twisted with outrage and he stood to his feet, Rodin following his lead: "Clearly, I'm not safe in the same room as this woman! Don't anyone attempt to stop—"

Sâr Dubnotal, who had risen with Pickman, clamped his hand to his shoulder and exuded an inexorable pressure which returned the New Englander to his chair. The Psychagogue then relaxed his grip, and Pickman shrugged off his hand, looking up angrily at him.

"Never touch me again, sir!" he said.

"Believe me, Sâr, you will soon feel that once was enough," Becky said. "In fact, once you hear what I have to say, you'll want to make for the nearest W.C. and *wash* that hand."

"Why you revolting minx!" Pickman sprang across the table at Becky, hands spread and grasping toward her throat. Immediately, Aytown and Tate were on top of him.

Becky did not flinch but smiled, "Oh, dear, now you'll *all* want to make for the water closet. Queue starts on the right…"

They dragged Pickman back across the table, pulling with him the cloth that he clawed into and sending the dishes, cups and cutlery clanging to the floor.

"You're losing your touch, Sâr," Becky said gleefully. "I thought the first trick you magical chaps learned was pulling a table cloth free *without* dislodging the china."

Meanwhile, Naini had bolted across the room and his strength decided the struggle. The Hindu slammed Pickman back into his chair and held him by his shoulders as the Psychagogue pointed at Becky:

"Woman, shut your mocking mouth—unless you're ready to tell us the basis of your accusation. As far as any of us still know, your 'child' is a fabrication. Perhaps it is you who are in league with Helen Vaughan. Do not make me regret having risen to your defense—if you have played me false…"

Rodin, who had stood by during all this, helped straighten his friend's disheveled, evening clothes. The skirmish had, of course, captured the attention of the whole group. Eustache the hound growled in the corner and the hair on his back rose. Jacques snapped at him while grasping the back of his neck.

Sâr Dubnotal turned to the others who were moving tentatively from across the room toward the site of the altercation and commanded in a voice that none dared resist: "All of you, stay back. Return to enjoying your meal."

The Psychagogue then saw Rudolph, who had sent Yeats and Toulet on their way, standing in the doorway, eager to hear whatever his master's orders might be.

Sâr Dubnotal made a quick, slight shake of his head. "Rudolph, please close the door on the other side and lock it until you hear expressly from me to the contrary. Naini, stand before the door on our side.

"Miss Sharp, as you have ruined my soirée, and, I am certain, reduced cook to tears, you had better have evidence to support your charges, or it will not go well with you."

"I think I know what you're capable of, Sâr," Becky said.

The Psychagogue expelled his breath from bloated cheeks. "Your evidence, Miss Sharp—*s'il vous plait.*"

Becky sat back in her chair and dropped her hands into her lap, clasping them together and giving them all a demure look as she said, "Why, I don't exactly have it on my person…"

"Then why do you continue to look so revoltingly pleased with yourself?" Sâr Dubnotal thundered.

"It's on his!"

Now it was Becky's turn to rise suddenly from her chair and stretch across the table. She seized Pickman's gloved hand. He shouted indignantly at this new affront, grabbing at and then repeatedly and painfully striking Becky's hand with his other one.

But Becky refused to yield, continuing to wrench the glove from Pickman Fortunately, Sâr Dubnotal once again came to her aid and grabbed Pickman's assaulting hand. A few more tugs and Becky pulled the glove free. She fell back into her chair and waved the glove over her head, shouting: "*Vive la France! Vive l'Empereur!*"

Pickman quickly clasped his hand over the other to cover an exposed claw, scaly as a rat's tail. Sâr Dubnotal grabbed the covering hand, but Rodin sprung to his friend's defense. The Psychagogue drew up and expanded his shoulders, sending the effete Frenchman falling backwards and tottering.

Then he returned to yanking Pickman's covering hand free, while speaking to Rodin behind him, "Do not attack me again, sir. Your actions make clear you have taken Pickman's part in this affair—pray, do not make your position even more fragile than it already is."

Rodin stayed put, but struck out verbally: "You condemn him for a deformity he cannot help!"

"No," Tate said, looking down at the claw with his discerning blue eyes. "I was surprised to learn that Pickman was showing at the Victoria—or anywhere—since he vanished from the States without a trace a year ago. I do not know what his choice of subject has been since arriving here, but his paintings back in New England are full of rat-like, man-size creatures. A photograph taken from his studio the night he disappeared showed that he was working from models!"

"What? Impossible!" both Randolph and Aytown exclaimed.

"I tell you... *it was a photograph from life!*" Tate said, his teeth clinched. He then looked at Sâr Dubnotal. "A motif of his paintings was that of the Changeling. Ghoul spawns who become human cuckoos, while the ghouls take the human infants to raise as their own."

"Yes! Changelings! You're intimately familiar with the practice, eh, Pickman?" Becky said triumphantly. "Was that why you hit it off so well with Helen Vaughan, another Hellspawn bastard like yourself who took *my* child for her own?"

Pickman remained silent, but kept his defiant expression, registering no remorse, though he no longer denied the accusations.

"You will, of course, tell Miss Sharp where we can find Helen Vaughan and her child," Sâr Dubnotal said, his tone making it clear that he was implacable in this regard.

A woman's shriek trilled through the room, and all attention immediately riveted on Gianetti Annunciata who stood, pointing at the draped painting.

Becky smiled at the defeated Rodin while pointing at the Psychagogue: "It would appear *his* medium doesn't care for *your* medium."

"There's blood seeping through the covering!" Annunciata shouted.

"Yes, but in the final analysis..." Becky said with an inquisitive cock of her head and a mocking sideways stare at Rodin, "...is it *art*?"

"Will you ever stop your mocking mouth, woman?" Sâr Dubnotal said, as he made his way to the painting. "Must I remind you how grave is the situation for your own child?"

"You scarcely need to remind me of that, sir! My situation has been grave for two years! If I appear giddy—hysterically so—it's because, for the first time since she was taken from me, I have real hope that I might reclaim my daughter!"

Sâr Dubnotal now approached the veiled painting and carefully touched the red fluid on the canvas's drapery. Examining his wet fingertips to make certain that it wasn't merely wet oils, he then pronounced: "It *is* blood."

He took the drapery over the canvas and swept it away, discarding the stained material as eloquently as a matador does his cape. A collective intake of breath was heard around the room.

Perched on the easel like a vulture biding its time, piteously looking down on its prey, was the medieval representation of Death: a robed and hooded skull, a scythe grasped at the ready in skeletal hands. From the edge of its blade, the blood seeped.

Sâr Dubnotal indignantly turned on his heel to face Pickman and the blanching Rodin over whose now pale face a sickly glaze of perspiration glistened.

"Pickman!" Rodin shouted. "The painting has betrayed us!" In the next instant, he was bolting for the door, but the giant Hindu caught him. He beat and struck at him heedlessly—and futilely.

"Bring him here, Naini!" Sâr Dubnotal ordered.

Rodin's heels scraped the floor as the Hindu pushed the artist along, then planted him before the Great Psychagogue.

"Is *this* that advance on the *trompe l'oeil* you promised us this evening, Monsieur Rodin?" *El Tebib* demanded. "Or is it merely harbinger of something else to follow? Why were you so adamant about leaving the room? There is something more, is there not? A fate that you and Pickman have planned for all of us here, but which you do not wish to share?"

Rodin slapped moist palms over his face, his nails clawing wretchedly into his flesh. "Yes!" he shouted. "Yes! I beg of you—it is not too late, we can *all* still flee."

"But at least *someone* must die, yes? No matter where we scatter. Once begun, I dare say the Grim Reaper's work cannot be turned back." Sâr Dubnotal surveyed the room: "You have all heard his confession. Will any of you dare come between me and the administration upon this person of the same judgment he would have dealt us all?"

Mutely, all shook their heads, though there was a sick horror in their eyes at the bleeding scythe and the contemplation of what must now follow.

"Rudolph," Sâr Dubnotal shouted so that he would be heard through the door, "come to me. Naini, quickly take Monsieur Rodin to the walk-in closet—no, the small room that connects with the W.C. I suspect that arrangement will facilitate leaving the facilities as clean as we found them when we remove hence. Ah, Rudolph, here you are… Take the canvas and go with Naini. Lock in both artist and painting, Naini. I suspect you will know when it's time to open the door again."

Rodin sagged toward the floor. Naini caught him in his arms. Rudolph came forward, balking at his first reach for the canvas. Then, grasping it by the edges, he walked briskly behind the Hindu, careful that the side with the image of the Grim Reaper was not against him.

"Rudolph, when your part is done, return and again lock our door on the other side until you hear from me."

Now Sâr Dubnotal approached Pickman who glowered defiantly at him. The Psychagogue, in turn, held Pickman in his own, commanding stare. Invisible to the others, inexorable currents of mesmerism from the Sâr were assaulting Pickman's psyche with magnetic waves of force.

"I adjure, you, Pickman, to tell us where we will find Helen Vaughan. You *will* tell me. I sense your resistance, the awakening of defenses buried in your brain in so deep a strata of tissue that you yourself have forgotten that they sleep there… Sleep to be awakened for just such a moment as this."

Becky noticed that the hair on Pickman's head was rising as though from a static charge. Then the cutlery began to tremble and Becky saw that his other hand—the "human" hand—was now drawing up into a claw with the same scaling beginning to manifest like a vile stigmata.

Pickman bellowed, leaping to his feet, and Sâr Dubnotal fell back, as Becky and everyone else retreated.

Pickman's body was warping, bursting the seams of his coat, sleeves and pants. His chest expanded, firing buttons like shrapnel from his shirt—and exposing a breast of scabrous flesh.

A snout thrust out from Pickman's face; his jaw seemed to have dislocated, and fangs jutted out from his lower gums and over his upper lip. His face and body had grown increasingly hirsute, sickly gray shoots spreading into tangled brambles of hair.

Now he stood completely revealed: Pickman—the Ghoul!

Eustache tore free from Jacques's grasp, leaving hair in his master's tiny clutching fingers. The dog hurled itself at the Ghoul, the weight of its body slamming into Pickman like a catapulted frozen side of beef. Yet the monstrosity did not stagger, but grappled at the exposed fangs frenziedly ferreting at its throat.

The Ghoul sank its claws into the hound's sides, causing it to yelp in high pitches of pain, and cease its gnawing. Pickman raised Eustache over his head and hurled him at the crowd huddling on the far side of the room. They scattered as the hound flew towards them. But Eustache fell short, landing on his side in a slide. Still skidding, he righted himself, nails tapping a frantic staccato in an attempt to regain traction.

Jacques was already running toward the Ghoul, his short sword drawn. The rest of the group were surging against the door, shouting and beating on it. But Rudolph remained on the other side, holding the key, unyielding in his word to his master.

"Back, Jacques!" Sâr Dubnotal commanded, and the angered dwarf, while simmering with displeasure, obediently turned to see to his dog.

Only Becky and Annunciata had not run for the door—Annunciata lay in a fainted heap by Rodin's bare easel, and Becky had retreated to a corner, brandishing a steak knife.

"Pickman!" Sâr Dubnotal's voice resonated powerfully as he gestured at the hissing, screeching Ghoul. "Your true self is revealed. You can no longer remain here, for the light has revealed the darkness. Hear me, Pickman! Depart hence! Go to your own place! I bind you to the plane of Leng, into the region of unknown Kadath—there to perform expiation if it may be that something human remains within you!"

The Ghoul screeched in indignant agony at its humiliation, the screech rising into the unbearable pitch of nails dragging across slate as the room's lights began to drop. Pickman seemed to be drawing the darkness to him in a desperate attempt for succor. Up went a group cry from fear that they would be plunged into the darkness, locked in the room with that thing. But even more quickly than the lights had begun to dim, they rose—into a brighter splendor than they had cast over the chamber before.

And Pickman, the door still locked, was gone.

Sighs of relief were expelled over the room, ending in a moment of silence, pierced immediately by a shrill scream from the corner. Becky charged at Sâr Dubnotal with her knife, shouting:

"What have you done? You took him from me—the one man who could have told me where to find my child!"

She collided into him, knife raised. Sâr Dubnotal grabbed her thin, delicate wrist, easily disarming her and sending the knife clanking to the floor.

He now grasped both wrists together as Becky writhed in violent spasms: "You're as much a beast as that thing! You have just handed my child over to Helen Vaughan's corruption that will surely transform her into the same bitch of Hell as she is! This is on *your* head, Sâr Dubnotal! Do you hear me? I'll never forgive…"

"*Miss Sharp!*" Sâr Dubnotal's voice resonated like the sharp crack of a frozen river breaking at first thaw; it struck her like a slap. At once, she ceased her struggles and fell limp, sobbing. She would have collapsed to the floor, but the Great Psychagogue caught her up and cradled her.

"I did not mean to see it; I did not mean to see it. I had no choice…" she mumbled lowly over and over as though in a fever.

"Miss Sharp," the Psychagogue said gently. "I understand that I have given you little reason to trust me. But I do know that your burden is great, that you are in maternal agonies that I cannot begin to fathom. I am your friend, Miss Sharp, though I have not seemed like it. And apart from destroying Helen Vaughan, I wish nothing more than to reunite you with your child.

"But even I, the greatest of Psychagogues, cannot foresee all things. My desire to wrest the truth from Pickman, the unwise use of the magnetism as coercion, blew out what I thought were defenses, but were instead psychic barricades he had set up to restrain the beast within. I could not open the door and unleash the Ghoul upon the city, which meant I was jeopardizing the lives of everyone in this room—including yours. If anyone was to be left to save your baby, Pickman had to be dispatched immediately. Your burden is already too great; I am so sorry for any additional grief I have caused you."

Becky raised her tear-streaked face up at this great man who cradled her, and for the first time, her expression softened as she looked at him.

"Now, dry your eyes," *El Tebib* said as he gently sat her down next to the recovered Annunciata. Distraught as she was, Becky maintained enough of her wits to immediately slide down the couch away from her. "And when you have sufficiently regained your composure, we all still earnestly desire to hear the circumstances of your relationship with Helen Vaughan."

III. The Testimony of Rebecca Sharp.

"I suppose that when I take my dying breath, I will still be cursing the night I first laid eyes on Helen Vaughan. If only I had not walked into that tavern, choked with soldiers just about to head off to France. But foresight is a luxury those struggling to make it through the day can ill afford.

"I am not proud to say that I was there to barter my flesh with men who knew it may be their last night in their homeland forever. You must understand, gentlemen, how dire my circumstances were. I was with child; I dared not approach the father—and, please, do not ask why. Suffice it to say, the circumstances of our parting meant any future reconciliation quite out of the question.

"Nevertheless, I could not let our child die or be born sickly and weak for lack of nourishment. So I was in that tavern, surveying the room for the means to insure I would eat that night, and that was when my eyes were compelled to linger on Helen Vaughan...

"No one else in the tavern saw *it*, or they most certainly would have immediately fled the establishment for France and the comparative safety of the trenches.

"At her shoulder was an impish little satyr, and it was revolting: the sallow skin of its man's torso with pink dugs stretching thin to the waist, the veins bulging on the purplish, pulsating sacks at the base of its horns, the jaundiced eyes that stared with utter contempt at the mass of humans about it, the nastily tangled fur of its legs...

"It was the same type of beast I saw at Pickman's elbow this very evening. That was how I knew he was allied with Helen. And I reasoned that his glove concealed that which, unlike that satyr, would otherwise be visible and which he did not wish to be seen...

"I can see the inevitable question in all your faces: 'how is it that you perceived something that we talked about—and that walked about us—and we could not?' I do not know for certain, gentlemen, but I strongly suspect that it has something to do with the lingering effects from my pregnancy. Though I had seen such things before that night in the tavern, I had no such visions before I conceived.

"I'm certain that it had nothing to do with the father. My body went through a preternatural change in its make-up—again, do not ask—some time before I met him."

She allowed herself a slight, wry smile. "Believe me: you would all be astonished by how my youthful beauty belies my true age.

"It would seem entirely logical, then, that the heightened state of a human body, no longer merely '*a little lower than the angels*,' would have its own brand of prenatal quirks and unexpected side effects. Some women get flat feet; I saw monsters.

"I had not asked for this burden, but it was what caused me to linger my gaze longer than I should have on Helen Vaughan. To take note of a face that would have otherwise remained indistinct amidst the constant shifting of persons in the low lighting of the tavern.

"Well, I found my Jack for the evening, and we retired to the alley behind the tavern to transact business. Unfortunately, this soldier was not so intoxicated that he disregarded my swollen abdomen which my clothing had so far concealed. With a look of shock and revulsion on his face, he began to beat me and did so until I lost consciousness.

"When I awoke, Helen Vaughan was over me, palpating my body—trying to ascertain that I was still alive, she claimed, though I'm sure now she was trying to take any money or valuables off my person. I have no doubt that she would have strangled me in my weakened state and then continued her pillaging, except that my eyes opened on her ring, and I blurted out in my confusion:

" 'The goat man on your ring—was it he at your shoulder?'

"Her hands hovered over me. 'You saw him?' she asked after a moment.

" 'In the tavern.'

"Astonishment froze her facial features, and it was only when her hands dropped to my person and touched my abdomen again that her halted expression resolved into the sweet-est, solicitous-of-my-health, smile.

" 'My sister,' she said.

"She gathered me up, took me to her own run-down lodgings, and nursed me back to health. During this time, she asked me repeatedly the identity of my baby's father, but I would not expose him to her so that she could blackmail him or charge him a ransom for our child. After a time, she mentioned it no more.

"I was not stupid, gentlemen. I knew she was trouble, but I had no other friend. I shudder now at how much like Helen my latest reversals had made me; I have never been a saint, but I had believed the love I had of one man, and the love I had for the one whose child I bore, had somehow redeemed me. Now, with no chance of recourse to either, I quickly warmed to Helen Vaughan's considerate ministrations. I found my bitterness and rage, tempered in a furnace of helplessness and despair, commensurate with whatever black, vile abscess festered inside her where a human heart would beat—at least to the point that when I was sufficiently recovered, we began to work as a team. Helen would seduce the soldiers and bring them to her private place and, together, we would rob them. I struck many of them over the head until they lost conscious-ness—repeatedly so, if need be--each time seeing the face of the soldier who had so beaten me.

"I am not proud of my behavior, gentlemen. But unless your life has ever ebbed into so dark a place that no beam of light can penetrate it, pray, do not judge me.

"With the money we had thus accumulated, Helen suggested that, since my delivery was now near, we move to her home village of Caermaen. Though a scandal had caused her to flee from there—the cause, I suspected, of the nasty scar around her neck of which she would never speak—she assured me that many years had passed, and her appearance was much changed.

"There, Helen often took me walking along what had been her favorite childhood haunt—the Roman road. It was on such a promenade in the winter months that I went into labor. And it was Helen who delivered me there as the pains of labor came nigh to wrenching me out of this world. My agonies sent me teetering on the edge of it, and the nightmarish one that enveloped me.

"As I pushed, I saw on my breast a horned succubus, leering into my eyes. I could actually feel its weight on my chest, choking my breathing—that's how close I came to its hellish abode. As Helen tore my child from my body, I could see behind her, surrounding us, a crowd of horned, wretched, twisted things. I could make out every detail of their perverse anatomies: from the crusted matter caking the rims of their yellow eyes to the sickening pinkness of the dugs rowed over their foul abdomens. *And my child, not I, was the subject of their intent focus!*

"Like that of a crowing cock compelling what ghosts have walked the night back into purgatory, my child's first cry banished those monsters from the periphery of our world and returned them completely to their own sphere. The darkness that had hung over the whole dreadful proceedings suddenly passed, and I could feel a soothing sense of normalcy rush over me in the twitter of winter birds and the wind in the trees that surrounded us.

" 'Helen,' I weakly croaked out, hearing my child's continuing cries, 'I... want to see... my baby.'

"But helpless on my back as an upside down tortoise, I could see only an empty sky, and now even the child's wailing had suddenly gone silent.

"My heart thudded mightily against my ribs as I tried to wrench myself up from the ground, but I was too weak after my ordeal.

" '*Helen!*' I shouted. '*Bring me my baby!*'

"Only then did she lean into my field of vision, but without my child. As she switched my papers with her own and slipped her ring on my finger, she said in mockingly sweet tones:

" 'Relax, Becky, darling. It's a girl.'

"And then, I saw the large fragment of ancient Roman masonry rushing down upon me.

"You now understand, Sâr Dubnotal, the origins of that groove you found atop my head. My skull was sufficiently crushed, or you can be sure that Helen would not have left the job half-done. Nevertheless, I possessed a resilience she could not suspect, and I retained enough consciousness to hear that witch chanting to my child as she walked down the old Roman road:

"Old King Cole was a merry old soul

"And a merry old soul was he;

"He called for his pipe, and he called for his bowl

"And he called for his fiddlers three.

"And then the red mist that hung over my eyes darkened, and I knew no more.

"I know not how many days passed before I was found on that deserted road. Fortunately, no one checked my papers or recognized the ring until I was taken to a doctor, for Helen was not remembered fondly by the good people of Caermaen. I was told that, as I laid unconscious in hospital, I was saved from suffocation by pillow at the hands of some grieved parent whose child Helen had ruined years before.

"The village doctor, who had no love for Helen either, still insisted that any punitive action be delayed until my swollen features healed enough to see if they could be recognized. He realized that I might be Helen's victim, that she could very well have schemed to switch our papers, in hope that the locals would bury *me* in an unmarked grave for *her* past sins. They would thus serve their enemy's further purpose by erasing all evidence in the event of an investigation into my disappearance.

"I believe now there was a second reason: the fear that Villiers and Clarke might learn—as they indeed did—of her resurrection. I am certain this fear was why she chose the anonymity of a guttersnipe's existence for so long. Thus, the need of a new identity—*my* identity—to move more freely about England and reunite her followers.

"Of course, when it became apparent that I was indeed yet another victim of Helen Vaughan, the locals took pity on me and nursed me, though all expected me to die. Even with my preternatural ability to regenerate, a year passed before I was able to leave Caermaen in pursuit of my child. Yet another year went by before I again heard that cursed song from that upstairs window on Great Gualteney Street

"Once before, about six months after I left Caermaen, I had a near reunion with my Annie and Helen. In one village, I learned of the arrival only a month before of a woman of an unsettling mien leading a toddler by the hand. Both were dressed in filthy and disheveled clothing. The authorities were so bold as to take the child from this unfit mother and place her in an orphanage five miles away.

"Naturally, I rushed to the site, and as night fell, I saw the glow of a conflagration on the horizon. I found the orphanage on fire. No children survived the night. They laid on the ground, burned black, some of them so much so that..." here, Becky shuddered, "...that the skin had split open in places."

"Dear Lord," Clarke said.

"I shall never forget," Becky said, "how the pain that would not release them to the relief of death twisted their little faces into the most ghastly of grimaces. It was as though, their voices failing to convey the depths of their pain, the flesh itself was wailing.

"The faces are so etched in my memory, gentlemen, because I did not know—*could* not know—which one of these wretched figures, as I ran from one to the other, might be revealed as my child. I was forced to study each of the agonized little girls in hopes of recognition of a facial resemblance that their disfiguring made impossible.

"I swooned at the news, upon the breaking of day, that Annie had been removed from the orphanage by Helen, and that the witch had set the blaze to conceal her latest abduction of my child by creating the impression she had been consumed in the flames. I had this account from one of the authorities who interrogated the orphanage handy man. Helen had seduced him into aiding her, but he swore he had no idea of her full plan until she put a knife in his back and then began setting the fire. But he survived both blade and blaze. That the woman was Helen was clear from his description of the nasty groove around her neck."

"The Sâr, Clarke, and I, are all very familiar with the events of this last episode in your story, Miss Sharp," Villiers said. "We three have been on Helen's trail since Sâr Dubnotal came to London with his letter from our late, esteemed associate Dr. Matheson. The Sâr wished to examine Helen's remains to add the description of such a creature to his repository of occult knowledge. It was then that we discovered that her body had vanished. Since only Clarke and I knew where she was buried, and the full range of her dark powers were unknown to us, it was all too possible that she had resurrected herself. Our subsequent investigation confirmed this horrible truth.

"That search led us, too, to that orphanage a few days after its burning, after reading in the papers that the villagers were certain it was the work of the 'devil-woman' who sought revenge for the taking of her child. That Helen Vaughan had reproduced was perhaps more frightening to contemplate than her reincorporation.

"Miss Sharp," Villiers continued, going on one knee so that he could look her in the eye as he warmly clasped her delicate hand between his two, "Helen Vaughan is the spawn of a human woman and an entity from that hellish dimension you glimpse on occasion. After hearing your story, we are much relieved to learn that Providence has apparently rendered her sterile. When she saw you were pregnant, and that you could see the satyr—well, those were the circumstances of her own mother and father. When you steadfastly refused to divulge the paternity of your baby, it only confirmed what she already suspected: here was a child of a similarly abominable conception by the same sire, and being of her own perverse lineage—her chance for a daughter.

"Clarke, if you would bring my valise…"

Once his partner had delivered it to him, Villiers opened it and took out a stick with a metal noose on one end. "We thought this sufficient to destroy her, and if Sâr Dubnotal had not arrived with Dr. Matheson's letter, requesting to see the remains of this foul creature, we would have never known she had resurrected. It appears you have paid the price for our folly."

"She suffered by this garrote?" Becky asked, sniffing.

"Much agony."

"*Très bien*," Becky said. "Please, might I hold on to it? It would be such a comfort."

An expression of both puzzlement and distaste immediately registered on Villiers' face at her request. Still, he said, "Of course," folded her hands about the stick, and rose to his feet.

Sâr Dubnotal had listened intently to Becky's tale, and while Villiers talked, he had withdrawn into a deep state of meditation over her story. He suddenly snapped his fingers, as though to awaken himself from his own trance, turning the attention of all assembled upon him.

"Miss Sharp, do you still have Helen's ring on your person? Yes? If you would be so kind as to hand it to me… Ah—thank you."

Sâr Dubnotal held the ring out, pinched between thumb and forefinger, so that the satyr's head could be seen by all. "The nursery rhyme, Miss Sharp. Have you ever thought that it might have some special significance to Helen Vaughan?"

Becky slowly shook her head from side to side. "I must confess I have not."

Dubnotal now examined the inscription inside the ring band. "Here 'tis written, *DEVOMNODENT-MAVORS CAMVLOS*. The first part translates roughly 'Nodens, the god'—of the abyss, in this case. That, then, is the identity of the satyr on this ring, though the name 'Pan' is by far more common. The second part of the inscription gives yet a third and fourth title: *MAVORS CAMVLOS*, or Mars-Camulos.

214

Camulos was a Celtic god sometimes depicted, satyr-like, with the horns of a ram and who, through the syncretism of the Roman invaders, became identified with their Mars.

"As to the significance of that tormenting nursery rhyme, Miss Sharp, it is a palimpsest through which we can still discern the pagan under-text: King 'Cole' is Camulos. We may assume that his pipe is for smoking, but the fact that he calls for three fiddlers indicates it was originally musical pipes—*Pan* pipes.

"If this still seems mere speculation to any of you, let me add this to remove all doubt: the oldest city in England, built by the Romans, was named Camulodonum after Camulos. Today, it still bears his name, though softened—just as in that nursery rhyme—to Colchester. It is inevitable that Helen will retreat to her father's house."

"Then, that is where my child..." Becky began, her voice choking on a sense of hope she wasn't sure she could trust.

Sâr Dubnotal reached down and firmly gripped her by her shoulders. "Be strong, Miss Sharp, for not all of what I'm about to say will be comforting: Helen is taking her to Colchester—to meet Camulos."

IV. Out From the Abyss

"But do not despair," the Great Psychagogue added. "Helen Vaughan's arrogance and manipulative schemes have already given us the keys to her undoing.

"Villiers! Clarke!" he said. "Go immediately to the train depot, and obtain a list of every train station along the railways from Bath to Colchester. Have dispatched a telegram to all the stationmasters describing Helen Vaughan and ordering they place highly visible wanted posters for her, with your names prominently attached to each in large block letters.

"The dispatcher will be reluctant to do what you ask, of course. Therefore, take this signet ring of mine and have him describe it via wire to the County Somerset railway superior stationed at Cad Green. This man is in my debt for services rendered on his behalf in the Affair of the Leprous Bodhisatt-va."

"But… why would we want Helen to know we are on to her?" Clarke asked. "Even if we make it impossible for her to travel by train, and slow her progress…"

"Exactly, but my reason is twofold: you two are the only men Helen Vaughan fears, so she will take every precaution now that you are on her trail, most certainly including a disguise. You see, she does not have the option of turning back. I now recognize our earlier guest Yeats' poem about the return of a beast-man as the record of a prophetic—if distorted—dream. Based on his poem, I suspect this meeting of Helen with her father at Colchester will be a uniquely tangible one. Her cult, which is surely gathering there to join her for this event, will be alerted to expect her arrival incognito.

"Miss Sharp, I return Helen's ring to you. Keep it safe, for it, along with the papers she placed on your person, will aid in your passing yourself off as your enemy, thereby granting us ingress into this vile Sabbat.

"Villiers and Clarke, little Jacques and his Eustache, will go with you. Once that you see the telegram is dispatched properly, all of you will board the next train to Colchester. But first, make a second request of the Somerset railway superior. For my sake, ask if he will prepare an alternate schedule for all trains arriving at Colchester for the next 48 hours. It should place them two hours behind their actual arrival. *This* schedule is to be presented to any who might request it—except those whose duty is to see that the trains arrive safely. Helen's cult will be monitoring your pursuit, and this will grant us an element of surprise. Jacques, I suppose I need not remind you to bring your box? I thought not."

At that point, Naini entered the room.

"Naini, has Rodin received due recompense?"

"He has, master."

"Then justice has been served. Rudolf, Annunciata: normally I would dispense this detail to Naini, but I have need of him elsewhere. To you, I'm afraid, falls the unpleasant task of disposing of Rodin's remains."

A stunned Rudolf opened his mouth but was mute, his face contorting with more and more revulsion as the exact nature of this grim detail settled in.

Annunciata, however, immediately found her voice: "Please, master! Wouldn't I be more useful channeling his spirit—something more along my line?"

"If I may," Aytown injected. "One theory of Basil Hallward's disappearance that we..." he nodded at Randolph and Tate, "...have investigated was that his murderer could have disposed of his body through dissection in a tub and then an application of acid."

"Yes," the Sâr replied. "That was my exactly my idea in having Rodin taken to the room adjoining a water closet with bath. Messers. Aytown, Tate, and Randolph—though I'm sure you wish to personally take the battle to Vaughan—you would best serve all our interests here. But be assured, your friend Beardsley *shall* be avenged, and you all will be witness to it.

"Your investigation into Hallward's disappearance has, no doubt, made you familiar with the milieu of such men who might discretely provide us with such items as we need in the matter of Monsieur Rodin. Will you be so good as to obtain them? And aid Rudolf in their administration? Poor Annunciata over there has actually managed to exceed her usual pallor—altogether, quite remarkable. Feel free to retire to your room, my dear Annunciata. And, for pity's sake, be careful of *which* WC you visit over the next 48 hours.

"In the meantime, Miss Sharp, Naini, and I will board the earliest train to Colchester. Hopefully, the circulation of the wanted poster will force Helen off the railways sooner than later and allow us to arrive first, delaying her inevitable challenge of our ruse. This should give us plenty of time..." here, a smile parted the lips of the Great Psychagogue, a smile which, though slight, was weighted with foreboding, "...to do some damage of the irreparable sort."

The turbaned man who identified himself as "Severus el Tebib" and the cloaked and hooded woman calling herself "Helen Vaughan" strolled through the midsummer's eve twilight that had now enveloped Colchester. A giant draped under cape and cowl followed. Fresh dew shone on the grass, and the stars themselves seemed just minted. The night air was soft and all nature insouciant on the cusp of its dissolution.

"I still do not quite understand," the woman under the hood said, "why Helen has waited two years to deliver my baby to that thing she believes is Annie's father."

The three were passing an ancient oak which the locals had mentioned was 750-years old. At the sight of it, Severus el Tebib thought again of Yeats poem that he had, on more than one occasion over the last 48 hours, regretted not committing completely to memory.

"It was not given to her to choose the moment of his coming," he said. "Take a lesson from the oak, Miss Sharp: should it be sawed off at the trunk, you would see concentric rings, one for each year of its 750 years of growth. The past, you see, is not simply done; it is yet present inside of that tree. Its cross section is both a chart of Time and a symbol of its cyclic nature.

"Camulos, I suspect, was here, in the deep time before men, but at some point was locked out. In the revolving of the ages, it seems there are certain junctures that could be propitious for his return. Among the natives in Africa, there is a similar tradition of *L'mur-Kathulos*, while the South Seas Kanakas look to the gyring consolations as the harbinger of *Tulu*.

"Miss Sharp—are you trembling?"

"Just the chill from the evening dew," she said and even her voice shivered. "Please, go on El Tebib—or should I just say, 'Doctor?'"

"According to Mr. Yeats, the last propitious moment for Camulos was approximately 2000 years ago. But at that point, Camulos was forced into slumber; the human race was granted an extension to allow for the grace of Christ to take global effect—which would have been sufficient to lock out Camulos forever. Well... to see what we did with that opportunity, I submit for your consideration the 'blood-dimmed tide' of 'the war to end all wars.'

"But I rather think this time around we are set against Camulos' coming as God's appointed conspirators. A motley lot to be sure, but then, so were Christ's first disciples."

"I suppose I fill the spot of the woman taken in adultery, then?" Becky asked, her smile sardonic beneath her hood.

The Sâr's cheeks burned under his beard. "It was perhaps... not so much an analogy as an *induction*, Miss Sharp."

"I understand all you have said so far, Doctor—believe me, far more than you could ever suspect. But why are you certain that the cult of Helen Vaughan is gathering at the old castle?"

"Like a tree, a building may retain past time in its present: a phenomenon responsible for more than one haunting I have investigated. Now, that castle is built on the foundation of the burned temple of Claudius, erected contemporaneously with the rise of Christianity, which Yeats sets as the *terminus a quo* of the epoch which the arrival of his 'rough beast' will end. Within Colchester Castle, all time from the beginning of Christianity's spread throughout the world unto this very moment is present: as it contains the *terminus a quo*, it is the most apropos point for the inauguration of the *terminus ad quem*."

Sâr Dubnotal touched Becky's elbow while holding up his other hand at Naini and nodded slightly at one of the Australian soldiers who currently filled Colchester Hospital. The trio stopped to watch the soldier angle up a telescope on its tripod. Nearby a large searchlight set on the ground.

Becky drew the hood down lower so that her eyes were veiled as the Sâr said, "Excuse me, sir. You seem to be surveying the constellations—may I ask you for what purpose?"

"I'm not stargazing, if that's what you mean," the soldier answered without looking at who addressed him, his face grimacing with the effort of keeping his eye properly attached to the viewfinder. "The first Zeppelins that bombed England last year chose a route in this vicinity for their return to Germany. Makes sense they might come back this way."

"I see. Goodnight, sir. And thank you for your efforts on all our behalves."

The soldier grunted something, still without looking at who addressed him, steadfastly intent on searching the skies.

Now, they came at last to Colchester Castle. How they had obtained the use of the facilities, the Sâr did not know, but he felt certain it had more to do with some mundane form of blackmail or coercion than any occult "hostile current."

Bearing electric torches, three muscular men in evening wear were quickly making their way across the lawn toward them. Naini's cape rustled as he began to move it back to give his long, massive limbs freedom, but the Sâr raised the fingers of one hand. "Not yet, Naini. Not until we see there is no other recourse."

Still, the cloaked giant had to do no more than stand there for the men to stop short of the trio. They were armed, and their hands were already at their holstered revolvers in case Naini should begin to encroach upon them.

"Who are you?" the leader of the guards demanded.

Becky alone stepped forward. Her heart was racing, for if Helen had somehow managed to beat them here, things were about to get much more difficult.

She extended her hand from the long sleeve of her cloak, letting her wrist dip to display Helen's ring. "I am Helen Vaughan," she said. "Behold the ring that bears the visage of my great sire, god of the abyss, lord of fortresses. Surely you were told that the pursuit of my mortal enemies Villiers and Clarke necessitated I come in disguise? Was this identifying effect not described to you? Does anyone without my birthright dare wear it? Do any of you fools dare come between me and my father?"

The guards now were more cowed by Becky than Naini. The leader took tentative steps toward her while the other two hung back. He did not dare touch her hand to lift it, but instead bent and held his electric torch near.

"My lady!" he gasped in awe and quickly stepped away. "I will run ahead to announce your arrival. My men will escort…"

"Fool! Do you not see that I already have an escort? And no one shall know I am here until *I* deign to reveal it. All of you return to patrolling the grounds."

"Well played, Miss Sharp," Sâr Dubnotal said when the guards were out of earshot.

The threesome finished their approach without further impediment. Upon entering the main chamber of the castle, they found before them men and women from England's and France's highest societies, dressed as though they were attending the symphony.

"Dilettantes and elitists," the Sâr said, sniffing contemptuously. "These fools all think they are attending nothing more than a glorified version of table rapping or *planchette*. They play with strange fire in the decadent idleness of the privileged, heedless of what they are about to unleash. *Sur vous, le Déluge.*"

From behind Becky, a salutation delivered in an effete, urbane intonation: "Helen! Is it you? Here at last? It has been too long since 'Mrs. Belmont' held court over her infamous Ashley Street salon, eh?"

"Do not turn," the Sâr hissed under his breath.

The immaculately dressed man with his trimmed goatee the color of ash was now upon them. The whites of his eyes were shot through with tiny red tendrils, and the crevices of his crow's feet had reached his cheeks. Still, the wreck of a once devilishly handsome face was discernible under a now sallow complexion.

"Helen! Surely you have not forgotten your most devoted admirer, Harry? It's Lord Henry!" As a jaundiced hand reached for her shoulder to turn her, the Sâr imposed himself between Becky and the aristocrat.

Lord Henry withdrew his hand but did not step back. "Swarthy heathen! You dare come between me and a friend I thought I would never see again?"

"I dare nothing less! You, sir, certainly know of the trauma which she suffered and how she changed form into a writhing obscenity at the point of expiration. Perhaps you have not heard that, since her resurrection, she has not been able to completely assume full human form—and such human features as she retains have been misshapened. Even her vocal chords have thickened. She ventures out, silent and hooded, to spare herself the humiliation of the involuntary shock and revulsion that could not help but strike even the closest of friends."

Lord Henry's hooded pupils shifted from Sâr Dubnotal to the giant who loomed protectively over the turbaned doctor. Still, he stood his ground. "Do you think me a fool? That I would just take a stranger's word?"

"Harry," Becky croaked as she turned and extended her arm, her hand thrusting from the sleeve of her cloak.

Lord Henry gasped. "The ring!"

"Do you wish to examine it?" the Sâr said. "Helen told me beforehand to grant this dispensation only to her closest friends to assure them, under these extreme circumstances, that it is indeed her."

The Great Psychagogue reverently removed the ring from Becky's still extended hand, then placed it in Lord Henry's palm. As he held it close to his bloodshot eyes, Henry said, "This craftsmanship cannot be reproduced today—and there is the inscription of the names of her father. Only she and her nearest associates—of whom I am one—knew what was written on the inside of the band. And she wore it only on special occasions, keeping it at all other times in a place known only to her. It was not on her person when she died. We thought it either pilfered or its location lost with Helen."

He returned the ring to the Sâr, who placed it back on Helen's finger. "My dear Helen," Lord Henry began, "I am so sorry for your misfortunes. Forgive me for adding to your distress. But we must announce your arrival!"

Sâr Dubnotal held up his palm. "It is Helen's wish not to reveal herself until her father restores her former glory at his advent, and she takes her place at his left hand."

"Of course," Lord Henry said. "And please—you are?"

"Severus el Tebib—you may call me 'Doctor.'"

"Quite. Please, Doctor, accept my apology. You and this…" he nodded at Naini, "…giant are her escorts, then? Ha! Few would be inclined to engage in fisticuffs with this bruiser, eh?"

"Villiers and Clarke would be most hesitant to attempt to murder her again with such a bodyguard, yes."

"Our spies have reported they are bearing down on us— in the company of a monstrous hound and its master, a most untoward dwarf I once had the displeasure of knowing. Although it was obviously something of a stretch for him, we of Helen's salon sought to school him extensively in the secret knowledge, but he could only see it as a short subject. When it became clear our investment in him was one of diminishing returns, he—and his flea-bitten cur—were expelled from our company.

"No matter: they will all arrive too late. I assume, now that Helen is here, I may order those who have assembled in the Roman cellar to begin the summoning?"

"Immediately," the Sâr replied.

"Sâr!" Becky said when Lord Henry was out of earshot. "What are you doing? Why are you hurrying this on with Helen and my child not yet arrived?"

"We could only revive his suspicions by not agreeing to what Helen Vaughan has expressly come to do. But be at ease, Becky, and let me concentrate. I have not before attempted hypnotism on quite this scale, but the wills of these people are as thin and pallid as their inbred blood."

Sâr Dubnotal swept his gaze back and forth over the lengthy table where the idle rich had all gathered, until he made eye contact with a dandy. In an instant, the current of mesmeric magnetism rushed across the room, and the man was held by Severus el Tebib's will. After a pause, the man

began arranging his dishes, cutlery, and other dining imple-
ments into diagonal lines, then did the same with the din-
nerware of whom sat at his right and his left. Baffled, they
stared as he rose, compelled to carry on this task around the
entire table, raising ires as more than once his leaning over his
fellow diners put an elbow in someone's face.

Sâr Dubnotal now strolled across the room to the table.
As the rest of the group looked up at him, he threw open wide
the floodgates of his eyes and the rapacious force that swept
out took them all.

In a moment, all returned to their idle chatter, unmindful
of the Doctor as he withdrew and the dandy as he continued
on his mission.

"What exactly did you do?" Becky asked.

Sâr Dubnotal smiled and slightly raised his hand.
"Watch," he said.

Becky noticed that, as people tried to return the dishes
and other utensils back to their proper places, they could not
lift them despite what turned into strenuous efforts.

"Hypnotic suggestion," the Great Psychagogue explained. "Those diagonal lines form sigils wedged into
Camulos' point of ingress. The sigils will snare him between
our world and what lies behind it until his moment has passed,
and he must return fully back into the abyss."

"But if someone you didn't hypnotize enters the room?"

"Other than Helen and whoever accompanies her, no one
else will. Lord Henry would not have begun the summoning
unless the coven was complete. He was only awaiting Helen's
arrival, which you were kind enough to supply. I dare say,
when the real Helen comes, she will not take time to count the
silverware, and those who are with her will be too intent on
their mistress to care how the table is prepared. As for Lord
Henry, upon his return to the chamber, should he move toward
the table, he can be persuaded to do otherwise easily enough."

"*What the deuce does that mean?*"

224

They all startled at Lord Henry's exclamation, but he was still out of earshot of their lowered voices, his attention riveted on the action across the room.

Henry had now reached the Sâr's group. "What on Earth does Monsieur N*** think he is doing? Why, he has become as fantastical in his behavior as Doctor Johnson! I'll put an end to this before he disrupts…"

"*You will do no such thing, Lord Henry*," the Sâr commanded—and the force of his words struck Lord Henry stock-still.

"What the deuce? Who… who are you? Who are you *really*?" Lord Henry said as his voice trailed into a whisper.

"The one who knows all that you have done in public and private over a lifetime that has lingered far too long in this world. I know by name those you have corrupted, and their loved ones to whom you have dealt a lifetime of woe with no cause but to satisfy your vanity and contempt.

"You who have sown the vile seed in the field of innocence, know that the reaping is at hand. *The axe is already laid to the roots*. I will deal with you personally, Lord Henry. Your only choice is this: shall you suffer the fell stroke now or tomorrow, or the day after tomorrow? In a fortnight or next month? But be sure of this: *I shall not tarry!*"

Lord Henry's knees dipped and his face blanched. Even here, amidst the cult, he knew he was not safe.

"Retire to that corner where you will be under the watchful eye of my manservant. Speak to no one, nor move one muscle. Be as still as if you were posing for a portrait. I trust I am clear. Naini, if you will."

"You frighten me, Sâr Dubnotal," Becky said as Naini escorted Henry. "And that is not an easy accomplishment."

He smiled down at her. "Rebecca Sharp, the downtrodden and innocent victim shall never have cause to fear me—only the guilty."

"That is most comforting," Becky said as she withdrew her face even deeper into the folds of her hood.

"*All rise for the Advent of Our Lady of Pandemonium!*"

Four figures stood in the castle doorway which remained open, framing them against the night sky. The stars had gone out in the wake of Helen Vaughan, leaving behind the four a dark void that went on forever. The three men who had intercepted Becky, the Sâr, and Naini made a guard about her. She stood hooded and cloaked, radiating a malicious self-possession. With a haughty toss of her head, her hood fell to her shoulders. Her hair was fire and her face a mask of porcelain most adamantine. And in her arms, she cradled a small child.

Sâr Dubnotal's hand was already reaching to restrain Becky. But he found her to be the epitome of composure. She stood as straight and regal as did Helen Vaughan. Only then did the Sâr think to look for Lord Henry, who, at the announcement of Helen's arrival, had stopped on his way to the corner. Now he was grinning triumphantly at Sâr Dubnotal as he brushed by Naini and strode toward them.

But the Great Psychagogue displayed no concern. It was clear he considered both Lord Henry and his moment of triumph beneath contempt. "Reduced to hiding behind a woman's skirts, Lord Henry?" he asked out of the corner of his mouth as the dissipated aristocrat stopped beside him.

Henry shot the Doctor a sour look, then shouted, "Helen! I have found out three impostors among us! And this wench has gone so far as to dare impersonate you!"

He reached to pull away Becky's hood, but Naini had followed and his hand shot out and enveloped Henry's frail one. He winced as he felt and heard something snap.

"Manners, Lord Henry," Sâr Dubnotal said, shaking a finger at him.

Henry fell back, gingerly working the fingers of his injured hand while cradling it in the other.

Then, for the first time, Helen Vaughan spoke: "All this is known to me."

"It would appear the guards have licked the red off Lord Henry's confection," Sâr Dubnotal murmured to Becky.

Helen put out her arm and flicked her wrist in an imperious gesture that ended with her forefinger pointing at Becky. "Let me see the face of she who has dared try to supplant the chosen daughter of Nodens, the Handmaiden of Chaos!"

All heads turned toward Becky as she calmly drew back her hood and smiled at the woman whose status as an enemy outstripped any adversary she had faced before.

Helen's eyes widened on reflex, and Becky was gratified to see the "chosen daughter of Nodens" look at her with a disbelief that was almost awe. But she quickly resolved her expression into one of a smiling, sinister dominance.

"I see you still have my ring," Helen said, slightly craning her head forward.

"I see you still have my child," Becky said, still smiling.

"Yes," Helen said, making a point to lower her head to the face of the child in her arms and smile as though she might coo. Then Helen looked up at Becky. "I am so happy that, in your final moments—and you may be sure you will most certainly be dead this time—you might see what good care I have taken of your baby. I hope, since your eyes shall close forever on this sight, it might keep your eternal rest peaceful."

Sâr Dubnotal remained silent. He was watching Becky for her reaction. Her shoulders had not slumped, nor had she ceased to smile. Her countenance showed no sign of defeat. Becky was up to something which she had not shared with him. As Helen Vaughan was presently neither concerned with him nor Naini, El Tebib bided his time.

Until the opportune moment presents itself, thought the Great Psychagogue, *discretion dictates that I leave this one to the ladies*.

"Now," Helen continued, "bring me my ring. While I hold your child, you will kneel before me and place it on my finger. Come, wench! And if you fail to keep your hands before you, you will be shot on the spot!"

Becky, serenely obedient, proceeded to do as told and soon stood before her archenemy. But she neither moved to kneel nor to remove the ring from her hand.

"The ring!" Helen demanded.

Becky's gaze bore into Helen's eyes as she continued to remain still and silent.

"Do you want to die now, cow? No—you're too much of a survivor for that. What is wrong with you? *Say something!*"

"I'm going to kill you, Helen."

Helen's head jerked as though stunned by a slap, but immediately she turned this slight tremor into a spasm of a haughty laugh. "I do not die easily," she said.

"Why, Helen," Becky said with a guileless smile, "why ever would you think that I want it to be easy?"

Becky's right arm now dropped to her side, and from its sleeve slipped the end of the stick with the metal garrote which Becky had told Villiers she had returned to his valise. The necessary haste to carry out Sâr Dubnotal's orders had not allowed for reflection on Becky's earlier, odd regard for that instrument of death until he, Clarke, Jacques, and Eustace were on their train to Colchester.

Upon sight of that metal noose, the imperious mask of Helen Vaughan cracked. She looked from the garrote into a face whose expression made clear that, despite her current unwinnable circumstances, nevertheless, Becky would, some-how, inevitably, manage to squeeze her throat by that noose until the wires touched.

Helen's hand went to the scar which the clasp of her cloak concealed. "Kill her!" she screamed at her guards. "Kill the bitch now!"

"*I think not!*"

Sâr Dubnotal's voice stunned the guards as though the mystic had hurled a thunderbolt across the room. In the next moment, they were again grabbing at their weapons. But the moment that the Sâr had purchased was enough.

A large, airborne hound thrust through the still open doorway and struck full on the guard on Helen's left, sending him down before he could remove his gun. The dog's jaws clamped onto his throat. As their trajectory carried them past the guard on Helen's right, the dwarf atop the hound sliced the razor-honed edge of his sword across the man's throat.

Helen, her features contorted by shock, fell back, shoving the remaining guard behind her off balance and out the door. He dropped backward on to the steps and the angle and impact of the fall broke his neck. For the first time, the child in Helen's arms began to cry.

Becky pushed forward, grabbing the staggered Helen by the upper arms. She wrenched her forward, so that, though cradled by her enemy, Becky felt for the first time her baby against her breast. "Let go of my child, bitch!" she snarled.

The jostled Helen cast a desperate glance over her shoulder toward the open doorway, only to see her archenemies, Villiers and Clarke, standing there, shoulder to shoulder. Villiers held a revolver on her.

"You're not going anywhere, Helen," Clarke hissed. "Except when Villiers and I send you back to Hell."

Then all simultaneously heard for the first time a rumbling which, in all the excitement, had begun gathering itself below the threshold of their hearing. Now it seemed a sudden, apocalyptic blast that made the castle around them tremble.

Helen's chin rose as a look of smug satisfaction reappeared on her face. "You hear that, you fools? That is the footfall of Camulos! He has come at last!"

Though worry could be seen in the faces of her enemies, they did not retreat, and she could not pass through the door and the longed-for reunion with her father. Then, with a sneer, Helen threw the tiny Anne over Becky's head.

Wide-eyed, Becky immediately turned her head over her shoulder and Villiers instinctively lunged forward for assistance. This was the opening Helen needed. She bolted out the door. Clarke caught her, but Helen scratched her nails across his face.

Clarke fell back, cursing Helen, as she ran onto the castle lawn.

Becky watched as a squalling Annie landed, knocking her head against the leg of a chair in the process. Livid, Becky bit into her lower lip so that it bled.

"Oh, that's the limit!"

Becky shot out the door, Sâr Dubnotal's shouts to her drowned out by the rumbling that had descended upon them all—not that his commands would have been heeded. She hit the lawn in a run and found Helen standing there looking up, her mouth agape at what she saw:

Three zeppelins, aloft over the castle grounds, like airborne whales migrating through a starless sky. It was the pulse and throb from their engines that shook the castle.

Becky, however, remained heedless of what was above. While her enemy stood slack-jawed from the false note of her demonic father's arrival, Becky tackled her, the momentum behind her run yielding an impact that thrust the air from Helen's lungs.

Becky quickly turned Helen on her back and mounted her. As her knees bore into Helen's ribs, she brought the back of her hand like a cudgel to her enemy's mouth, bursting her lips. Helen winced, as Becky again drew back her hand…

But the sudden flash of spotlights from the ground arrested her, their beams of brilliant white aimed at the zeppelins, but revealing something *more…*

Glimpsed only in diagonal cross sections by the sweeping streaks of light angled into the sky, *Devomnodent-Mavors Camvlos*, the Great God Pan, loomed so large that his goat's head reached the altitude of the zeppelins; it seemed he might catch them on his giant horns and toss them out of the sky, or, by a few quick thrusts, burst them like a child's party balloons.

The sharp, frantic cries in German were faintly audible even over the oppressive droning of the zeppelins. The risk of opening their floodlights to direct their fire meant losing what cover of darkness they retained. And their committed, slow drift combined with a limited ability to maneuver placed them, quite literally, on the horns of a dilemma.

A vicious metallic chattering heralded machine gun fire—their only defense—which followed wherever the beacons from the ground revealed the giant straddling Colchester with one hoof planted on the foothold of the castle. Ground fire followed, but no one could be certain if it was aimed at the Germans or Camulos.

Curiously, whatever parts of his massive anatomy which at any moment were outside the band width of each spotlight were simply *not there*, as though the beams rubbing over him in their passing erased what was seen as soon as it was revealed. There was complete lack of presence in their wake until the lights swept over in cross sections again.

Even in the light, Camulos appeared composed of no more than the motes of dust swarming in the beams. It was said that the world would dissolve with the weight of Camulos' glory as he placed his hooves upon it, but it was *he*, rather, who was rendered ethereal...

...for the diagonal bar Sâr Dubnotal had decreed lodged against the door to the abyss had held!

Helen was forced to glimpse her father's near advent upside down as she lay flat on her back under Becky. "He's not coming through!" she wailed.

"Allow me to offer my condolences," Becky said and brought down upon Helen's mouth a large rock she had found within reach, smashing her front teeth.

"Sauce for the goose, eh, Helen?" Becky said with a smile. She tossed the stone aside and clamped Helen's mouth closed, angling her head back. "Swallow, Helen! I want those teeth lodged in your throat!"

But Helen fought. In her paroxysms, her esophagus swelled and rippled like an engorged boa constrictor.

"Choke!" Becky ordered, digging her knees into Helen's ribs. "Very well, then," she said, withdrawing the garrote from her sleeve, "this has proven fairly effective before..."

Despite her distress, Helen's bulging eyes immediately took note of the garrote, and Becky was rewarded by the sheer fear in her adversary's eyes. But before she could get the noose over the still-convulsing Helen's head, Naini's powerful arms locked around her and yanked her up.

"What are you doing? Let me go, you fool! Are you trying to save her now?"

"Miss Sharp!" Sâr Dubnotal's thunder clap of a voice caused her to immediately cease her struggling. She saw now that, along with the Sâr and Naini, Clarke, Villiers, Jacques and a growling Eustace, had also arrived. The latter two were guarding Helen, who was on her knees, spewing out teeth.

"Why did you stop me?" Becky wailed bitterly.

"Miss Sharp, you must remember you are not the only one Helen Vaughan has sinned against. Others have suffered grievously as well... Would you rob them of their share of vengeance?"

And then, for the first time, Becky noticed Annie was cradled by the Great Psychagogue.

"Annie..." her voice trailed off softly. She slipped free of Naini as he relaxed his grip, and, for the first time, Becky took her daughter into her arms.

"I have examined her," the Doctor said, "but only cursorily so due to the circumstances. I will be much more thorough later. But she seems perfectly sound physically. In fact, she is developed beyond a child of two. It seems little Annie at an early age will blossom into young womanhood, where I suspect she shall remain for an indeterminable period of time. All due, no doubt, to her mother's own preternatural defiance of the aging process.

"Now, my friends, the zeppelins have gone, and Camulos, his moment now passed, has vanished in their wake. It would appear Pan has been cuckholded by an upstart, particularly 20th century kind of evil. In any event, while there is still general confusion, let us remove hence, before the interference of the authorities somehow grants Helen Vaughan a succor she must assuredly does not deserve."

V. The Judgment

Helen Vaughan was transported by surreptitious route to a concealed estate Sâr Dubnotal maintained in Cornwall, his base for whenever his battle against the principalities of darkness brought him to England. It was here, surrounded by those whose friends had been destroyed by Helen Vaughan, that the Great Psychagogue pronounced her sentence.

He sat upon a raised judgment seat, Helen Vaughan bound before him. Standing and watching were her accusers: Becky with Annie in her arms, Clarke, Villiers, Jacques with Eustace—and his little box of tremors—and Aytown, Tate, and Randolph. Seated to the side were Ruldolph, Annunciata, Naini, and three detectives on permanent retainer to Sâr Dubnotal. These three had managed to obtain a list of the names of the children who had perished from Helen's act of arson. At the end of the voicing of the charges against her by those present, each detective, by turn, read aloud the names of 50 silent orphans.

"Helen Vaughan," Sâr Dubnotal said when they were finished, "you have inflicted anguish not only on your victims—whose sufferings were blessedly cut short when death removed them from your hands—but also their survivors, who will endure a deep and abiding anguish for the remainder of their lives. Were we to execute you now, they would still not be free of you. If the end of their suffering will not come quickly, then neither shall yours.

"Therefore, it is my decree that you will fulfill your boast to not die easily. Jacques, come forward. And Naini, if you will now perform what I instructed you to do earlier."

The dwarf commanded Eustace to stay, then approached the throne, bearing the thumping box before him. He stood before Helen and flashed a nasty smile up at her. Naini knelt between Helen and Jacques as the dwarf removed the box's lid.

Up jumped two small, rubicund objects which Naini's great hands snatched out of the air like grizzly paws catching fish leaping from a rapids. Naini rose and turned. At the sight of what the Hindu now held, Helen Vaughan's eyes widened and her face paled.

"I believe you recognize these shoes, Helen," Sâr Dubnotal said coldly.

Thrusting to be free of Naini's hands were tiny red ballet slippers—and within them, tiny white feet. Holding one shoe in the pit of his arm, Naini's fingers dislodged its mate's foot, which hit the floor and skipped frenziedly scattershot over the room. The other foot soon followed.

"Open the door, Rudolf," Sâr Dubnotal commanded. "Allow them the dignity of at least attempting to rejoin their mistress's other remains before the residual enchantment fades and they begin to decompose."

Rudolf did as told, and the feet that had been throwing themselves against every wall in their imbecilic dance immediately ran out.

"*Au revoir, mes enfants*," Jacques said, as his tiny hand rose to a salute, wiping away a single tear in the passing.

The red shoes, now free of the tiny feet, seemed to have grown in Naini's hands. And Helen Vaughan contemplated them in horror.

"Ah," said Sâr Dubnotal. "I see you also recall that whosoever wears these ballet slippers cannot stop dancing until another removes them. Did you think Jacques would not tell me how Minuette's tiny heart failed after you placed them on her feet? How your laughter mingled with that of your guests while she begged you, her most cherished friend, for help? And how, for the amusement of subsequent salons, you would open the trunk in which you kept her corpse and send it prancing even in the advanced stages of decomposition? And that it was only Jacques' sword that released Minuette from this continued indignity, this *violation* to her person.

"In the hour you purposed to commit this abominable atrocity, it was you who decreed your own sentence. These shoes will drive you ever on like a fury, Helen, until your heart stops from exertion. Of course, your heart will beat far

longer than Minuette's little one did under the same duress—
but it's all a matter of proportion, wouldn't you say?

Now Sâr Dubnotal said to Rudolf: "Bring the saddle,
reigns, harness and bit."

"What… for?" Helen whispered.

"Why, Helen—did you actually think we would just set
you loose?" Sâr Dubnotal said. "To be rescued by the first fool
whom you would most assuredly murder at the earliest opportune moment and then begin a new reign of terror—the focus
of which would, no doubt, be innocent Annie there?

"It is my sentence, then, that while propelled by the red
shoes, you be repeatedly ridden 'round the coasts of Britain,
from the drowned lands of Lyonesse to the regions of the Heb-
rides and back again—until you expire."

"Oh, saddle me up!" Becky said and would have passed
Annie into poor Villiers' arms right then, except he was so
stunned by such an instantaneous shedding of maternal instinct that his hands were rendered torpid.

"Miss Sharp!" Sâr Dubnotal said. "You have already enjoyed the privilege of crushing the face of the woman who
crushed yours and taking back the child she claimed as her
own. You must see to Annie and leave to others the administration of justice for Helen's sins that are not against you. Do
I have to ask you which is more important?"

Becky gathered Annie back to her and tucked her head in
token abashment, yet her hooded eyes could not conceal the
gall of resentment therein.

"I already have riders stationed along the shores of this
isle," the Sâr said, as his gaze bore down on Helen like the
most pitiless sun. "You will be ridden until death, at which
point, the shoes will be removed, and you will be dismem-
bered, your body burned, and your ashes scattered into the
ocean.

"Ah, here is Rudolf. You will now be shod and saddled,
and then you will be ridden to the first station by Naini…"

Helen's mouth dropped. "That giant… atop me? How can you expect me to go even five feet under the Hindu without falling to the ground, unable to rise?"

"Helen, the sentence of the red shoes punishes you only for what you did to Minuette. But the children of the orphanage cry out as well for justice from the ground where they lay in prolonged agony. The children for whom a single comforting touch against their blistered skin was rendered into a hornet's sting. Do you dare say you deserve one less such touch of encouragement?

"Therefore, when you fall, you will receive a goad until you rise—one for each child who died in the orphanage to which you set fire. No more; no less."

Helen's jaw dropped. "But there were 150 children in that orphanage! Your sentence is too cruel, Sâr Dubnotal!"

"Helen Vaughan," Sâr Dubnotal's voice roared down upon her so that she dipped at the knees and clasped her hands over her head, "you who never showed mercy to your victims, who mocked them in their agonies that were the fruit of your corruption… you dare accuse *me* of cruelty? Beware lest *having whipped you with whips, I whip you next with scorpions.*

"Yet this mercy I will grant you. If, while you might still rise, you choose to end your torment, whether it be two feet from where you now stand or 20 miles, you have but to lie there, endure how many of the goads remain, and you will be immediately beheaded. And when the goads are finished, upon my word, Helen, you shall have no more or no less than what your transgression has decreed—should you choose to go two feet or 20 miles more—you will have but to say 'enough.' Whether until your heart bursts or while it may yet beat on another day, or week, or month, you, Helen, shall decide the length of your agonies; a dignity you never allowed any of your victims."

"But what… what do you mean by 'goads?'" Helen asked, her voice small and trembling.

"Jacques?" Sâr Dubnotal said and turned his head toward the little man.

236

Jacques again grinned toothily up at Helen as he reached into his pocket and produced a leather pouch from which he took two mean-looking, barbed objects.

"It has been my experience," said the dwarf, "that nothing will drive the Devil out of this woman like a fine set of spurs."

Never has Sâr Dubnotal faced a most momentous decision than when confronted with choosing between the monumental evils of Mr. Hyde and that of Cenobites from Clive Barker's Hellraiser *franchise...*

Matthew Dennion: *A Tale of Two Souls*

Paris 1921

The old man in the back of the taxi groaned, leaned toward the driver, and screamed at him:

"Can't you get this infernal contraption to go any faster?"

The driver sighed and accelerated the vehicle.

The old man grabbed his stomach and said:

"Wait Edward, please wait! You know what awaits you; give me the chance to find help for us both."

The driver glanced into the backseat to see the old man with the oversized suit and cloak continue his conversation with his imaginary friend. He sped up the vehicle even more. He was anxious to get the crazy man out of his car.

As the cab pulled up to the house that was their destination, the old man threw three times the fare for the ride into the front seat and ran towards the building.

He pounded on the door and it was quickly opened by one of the servants.

"I need to see Sâr Dubnotal, immediately!" the old man panted.

Upon hearing the commotion, the Great Psychagogue walked to front door preceded by Annunciata Gianetti and Rudolph, two of his most trusted followers.

When he saw the man standing there, he stopped dead in his tracks. He stared at the man for a moment with an intrigued look upon his face, then chose his words carefully:

"Henry Jekyll, I have not seen you since medical school. What brings you to my house in such a state?"

Jekyll stumbled into the door.

"Sâr, back in school, I remember rumors about an odd case involving the supernatural where you assisted Professor Van Helsing. I pray those rumors are true, as I am in need of assistance against a supernatural threat."

"I can see from your aura that two separate consciousness currently inhabit your body," said the Sâr, nodding. "Has a demon possessed you?"

"It is not a demon that inhabits my body," replied Jekyll, shaking his head, "nor is it any other supernatural creature. The monster that shares my body is a creature of science... from within myself."

Hel stumbled to a nearby couch and fell into it.

"My time is short," he continued. "Edward will be here soon and with him comes my damnation. Let me tell you my tale quickly. In my studies, I attempted to purge myself of evil and, in the process, created a separate personality within my mind. You have perhaps heard of the villainous Edward Hyde? He and I are one and the same. He lives within me."

"I am aware of the actions of that madman," said the Sâr, nodding. "So, the other aura which inhabits your body is that of this monster? Is that why you have to come to my house? To purge yourself of this other self?"

"No," answered Jekyll, shaking his head. "You could no more purge Hyde from me than you could remove my heart. He is me, and I am he. As I said: we are one and the same. When he first emerged, he was a small impish man. He was only able to escape my mind for a few hours when I allowed him to do so by ingesting a formula that I had created. However, in the decades since then, he has grown more powerful, both mentally and physically. He is now a monstrous creature and he can force my consciousness into the dormant recesses of my brain at will. He will run free for days at a time, committing all kinds of heinous acts."

Jekyll took a deep breath, the continued:

"When he is in control, I can see all his dreadful crimes. When my mind is able to claw its way back to surface, I attempt to help as many people as I can with my medical skills, without pay or compensation. Through my efforts, I hoped to do enough good to balance out Hyde's evil. But as Hyde began to control me, I started to see death as my only escape. I prayed that my soul and his will be judged separately as we stand before the gates of Heaven. Hyde has recently taken steps which have put this matter to rest as he has ensured that we will both soon be in Hell."

With his right hand, Jekyll reached into his oversized coat and pulled out a small wooden puzzle box.

"Hyde is a hedonist, as well as madman. He learned of an object which brings ultimate pain and pleasure. He traveled the world and finally found it here in Paris—and activated it."

Sâr Dubnotal eyes opened wide with anger.

"You have dared bring that accursed thing into my house!" he roared. "Do you know the potential danger in which you have placed all of us?"

Rudolph stepped forward.

"Forgive me, master, but what is that box?" he inquired.

The Sâr did not remove his eyes from the artifact as he explained:

"This thing can summon the Cenobites. They are powerful demons in Hell's army who carry out the countless tortures inflicted upon the dammed." He glared at Jekyll. "You say that Hyde activated it, and yet you stand before me. How is this possible? No man can escape the reach of the Cenobites."

"It was providence that saved both Hyde and me from being dragged to Hell," replied Jekyll, shuddering as he spoke. "Hyde had entered an abandoned building to open the puzzle box. He sat on the floor turning it over and over until he found the correct configuration. Suddenly, even the small amount of moonlight that was filtering into to the room grew dark. Then, one side of the room lit up as a door opened into the very wall..." Here, Jekyll closed his eyes. "Then, the most terrifying creature I have ever seen emerged through that door and began to approach Hyde. Seeing the horror, I panicked and, thankfully, Hyde had been in control of our body for a long time that I was able to reassert control and transform back into my normal form. The demon stopped and stared at me with an intrigued look. He said that I was not the one he had come for, but he could still see into my mind and soul. He knew that Hyde would eventually return. He said that he would then drag him body and soul to Hell."

Jekyll feel to his knees at Sâr Dubnotal's feet.

"You understand my predicament now," he begged. "Soon, Hyde will reassert control and the Cenobite will come for him—for me—for us! I am responsible for Hyde. His crimes are a result of my curiosity. One day, I shall have to answer for them, and all I ask is a chance to make my case. If this demon drags us to Hell, I will be robbed of this opportunity. Please, Sâr Dubnotal, help me! Don't let Hyde's actions force us to spend eternity being tortured by that creature!"

The Great Psychagogue helped Jekyll back to his feet.

"You believe that the Cenobite will not return until you revert back to Hyde," he said. "How long do we have until this transformation occurs?"

Jekyll quickly checked his pocket watch.

"He is fighting to get out of me as we speak. I feel that I could hold him back for no longer than an hour at the most."

Sâr Dubnotal addressed Rudolph and La Gianetti:

"The two of you, follow me. Dr. Jekyll, please make yourself as comfortable as possible. I assure you that we shall return with a half an hour."

The Great Psychagogue walked towards his study, his associates behind him. When he entered the room, El Tebib closed the door and addressed his friends:

"I am placed in a unique situation. Typically, we strive to save and protect good people who have been unfortunate enough to be assaulted by dark supernatural forces. But the Cenobites do not attack innocent people; they only pursue those who call them, and usually the people who do so are of the lowest form of humanity, those who care only for themselves and will not hesitate to harm or kill others to attain their selfish goals. Hyde is just such a person. He is a known murder and a madman. He deserves to go to Hell. By summoning the Cenobite, he has only hastened his descent into the pit..."

Rudolph and *La* Gianetti understood that their master was speaking as much to himself as he was to them. They continued to listen without saying a word. Sâr Dubnotal took a deep breath and continued:

"The problem in this case is that Hyde condemned an innocent man in the person of Dr. Jekyll to eternal damnation as well. This is a dilemma. We have two crucial aspects to consider: First, do we attempt to save the two of them, knowing that Hyde will continue to do evil? Even with Jekyll working hard to undo the evil Hyde does, will it ever balance out that monster's crimes? Wouldn't the greater good of humanity be served if we were to let the Cenobite take Jekyll as well as Hyde?"

Annunciata Gianetti bowed as she spoke:

"Master, we can try to limit the evil that Hyde does, and at the same time support Dr. Jekyll in his attempts to be a benevolent power. We must believe in the best of a person, not fear the worst of him."

Rudolph then stepped forward:

"Master, if we let an innocent man like Dr, Jekyll be dragged to Hell, then aren't we worse monsters than Hyde or the Cenobite? They are simply acting as is their nature, whereas we would be making the choice to condemn an innocent man to eternal damnation. We must help this man!"

Sâr Dubnotal bowed to his followers.

"It pleases me to hear both of you respond in this manner. I have chosen well in the people who will someday take my place when I am no longer here."

Tears welled in La Gianetti's eyes.

"Master, why do you speak in this way? Surely, you have confidence that you can defeat this Cenobite."

Sâr Dubnotal placed his hand on her shoulder.

242

"Sadly, my child, I know that I cannot defeat the Cenobite. In Hell, only Lucifer commands more power than the Cenobites. As you have both stated, if we do nothing to help Dr. Jekyll, then we are worse monsters than the foul creatures we fight. I will stand by Jekyll as he changes into Hyde, so that he will not face his end alone, and then, I shall face the Cenobite with Hyde. Perhaps, with his monstrous strength, we can make a good accounting of ourselves against the demon. I need you to get all of our people out of this house immediately. Take them to one of my other houses. Tomorrow, if I do not come for you, then inform the others of my demise, and carry on in my stead."

Rudolph grabbed Sâr by the shoulder.

"Master, I cannot leave you at the mercy..."

"I will not be questioned on this matter, Rudolph!" exclaimed the Sâr. "I cannot possible face the Cenobite if I have you to protect as well! Now obey my commands!"

Rudolph bowed, apologized, and then quickly began to organize the evacuation of the house.

Once they were alone, Sâr Dubnotal addressed Dr. Jekyll:

"Come, we will enter my sanctum. It is the most secure location in the house. There, we will make our stand against the coming horror."

The Sâr's sanctum was a vault located in the cellar of the house; it contained numerous mystical artifacts that the Sâr had collected throughout his adventures, such as the Helmet of Nabu, the Witchblade, the Resurrection Stone, and a multitude other weapons and writings. All of them were destined to be used by other by mystics and warriors in the future. Until they found their way into the hands of their future wielders, Sâr Dubnotal was responsible for safeguarding the world from their destructive potential. To secure these items, he had constructed his vault. It was heavily fortified by both physical and mystical barriers. The Great Psychagogue prayed that these would be able to contain the mystical forces that would be unleashed in the coming confrontation.

Jekyll was sweating profusely as Sâr Dubnotal directed him to the center of the room and instructed him to sit on the floor. The two men sat crossed legged from each other with totally different demeanors. Sâr Dubnotal was calmly meditating and focusing his mental energy and mystical powers. Jekyll, on the other hand, was fighting to keep from changing into Hyde, as he feared that when he did so, he would never revert back to his human persona, until he was suffering in the pits of Hell.

Suddenly, he grabbed his sides and moaned:

"He's coming!"

Sâr Dubnotal opened his eyes to see Jekyll's skin moving and stretching. He watched his friend's clothes, too large for Jekyll, begin to rip and tear as he changed into the much larger Hyde. Muscles and bones grew in length and density, his brow pitched forward, and his shoulders quadrupled in size. Jekyll looked like the sixty-or-so-year-old man he was, but Hyde looked like a massive Neanderthal in the prime of life. Sâr Dubnotal realized that the transformation must have somehow delayed the normal aging process and wondered if some of the chemicals Jekyll had used were derived from the methods that he himself had employed to delay aging.

Then, he pushed the thought from his mind as Hyde stood up and roared through jagged teeth. The man-monster stretched his body to its full height, nearly seven feet tall.

Hyde bent down and droplets of spittle flew into Sâr Dubnotal's face as the madman spoke:

"That fool Jekyll thought that you might be able to help me against that demon? Ha! You look even more pathetic than he does!"

Sâr Dubnotal remained calm.

"You are fortunate that we find ourselves in our current situation. Otherwise, I would show you how formidable I can be, and make you atone for the all the crimes you have committed."

Hyde was about respond when the artificial light in the room began to flicker. Suddenly, a glow began to seep from behind the bricks on the far wall. A door swung open out of the solid wall, releasing a noxious, sulfuric stench into the vault.

Sâr Dubnotal's eyes widened as he saw the horror that emerged from it: It was a man wearing a long, black robe with massive hooks and chains attached to it. His skin was chalk-white, but his most disturbing feature was that his head was covered with long pins sticking out of his skull. This gave him a nightmarish look that would haunt even Hyde's twisted mind for years to come.

The Cenobite strode slowly into the vault. When he reached the center of the room, he stopped and lifted his hand, pointing his finger at Hyde.

"Edward Hyde," he said, "the time has come for you to know suffering as none in Hell has ever suffered before."

Before Sâr Dubnotal could attempt to intervene, Hyde leaped at the Cenobite. He crashed into the demonic creature, smashing his chest with his own massive fist. The vault shook under the impact. Yet, despite the force of the blow, the Cenobite stood unaffected. It was as if Hyde had attempted to punch a mountain. The Cenobite did not reply; he simple stared at the wall. Seemingly of its own volition, a long chain with a hook at the end of it appeared and shot towards Hyde. The hook buried itself in the monster's shoulder, pulling him away from the Cenobite. Hyde fell to his knees and screamed as the chain continued to pull him backwards.

Sâr Dubnotal began reciting an incantation. As he chant-ed, the room shimmered. A wave of distortion cascaded over the vault, seemingly changing it into a dense forest. Once his spell had transformed the room, he ran towards Hyde, grabbed the hook and pulled it out, causing the monster to scream in pain.

The Cenobite turned his head slowly from left to right, surveying the new landscape. Again, he caused another hook and chain to appear and slice through the forest. As the chain cut across the landscape, a portion of the forest disappeared, revealing the vault once more. The Cenobite shifted his eyes from side to side, causing multiple chains to tear apart the illusion. The demonic being then spoke in a deep foreboding voice.

"Sâr Dubnotal, this was your illusion. It is gone now. But be warned, Psychagogue: I only take to Hell those who have summoned me, but if you stand between me and my victim, I will tear your soul apart."

Hyde once more sprang at the Cenobite. The monster lifted both fists over his head and brought them crashing down on the demon's shoulders. The floor under them buckled and cracked, but, as before, the Cenobite was unaffected by Hyde's strength. He simply shifted his gaze, causing another hooked chain to dig into Hyde's thigh. Then, the chain went taunt, causing Jekyll's *alter ego* to crash to the floor. Hyde shrieked as the chain again dragged him along the floor toward the glowing doorway in the wall.

Sâr Dubnotal strode defiantly towards the Cenobite.

"You state that you claim only those who have summoned you, but in Hyde resides the soul of Henry Jekyll. If you take Hyde, you must per force also take Jekyll, an innocent man who did not summon you. On Jekyll's behalf, I ask you to leave Hyde here and return to Hell."

The Cenobite stared into the Great Psychagogue's eyes.

"Since the dawn of humanity, no man has escaped the Cenobites. Edward Hyde has summoned me. His soul belongs to Hell. I would not drag Jekyll to Hell when Hyde was hidden within him, but now that Hyde has reemerged, I will take Hyde. Jekyll's situation is unfortunate; however, it is not my concern. Now I warn you for the last time: stand aside."

"I will not let you take an innocent man to Hell, no matter the cost to me!" replied the Sâr, taking took a deep breath.

He brought the tips of fingers together in front of him. He then separated his hands and thrust them outward. As he did so, the Cenobite was engulfed in flames.

The demon appeared unconcerned; he scanned his body as the flames continued to burn around him.

"Do you think these flames could affect one who lives in Hell's dungeon?" he asked, casually.

The Cenobite reached out and grabbed the Great Psychagogue by the throat, lifting him off of the ground. The flames around the Cenobite's body died down as he looked into Sâr Dubnotal's eyes.

"I warned you not to stand between me and the one I have come for."

When the Cenobite finished speaking, a hooked buried itself into Sâr Dubnotal's arm and started to pull him towards the doorway.

' The Cenobite began walking toward Hyde. In a fit of rage and fear, the man-monster tore his leg free from the chain that held him. He stood up and savagely attacked the demonic being, striking him in the chest and stomach with a flurry of punches and kicks.

Sâr Dubnotal stared in awe that something as powerful and vibrant as Hyde could reside in the feeble body of the elder Jekyll. As that thought entered his mind, a thin glimmer of hope formed as to how to save Jekyll's soul from eternal torment.

Hyde was reaching back to deliver another blow to the Cenobite when another hooked chain dug into his arm. The first hook was quickly followed by three more, which embedded themselves in the monster's other arm and his legs. His massive form was pulled again towards the doorway with his arms and legs outstretched. He screamed in pain and fought to break free as the Cenobite approached him.

Sâr Dubnotal acted quickly. He closed his free hand into a fist and then brought it across his body reciting a mystical incantation. The Cenobite stopped in mid-step as his body became covered in frost and frozen solid.

After completing the incantation, Sâr Dubnotal spoke in a hurried voice to Hyde:

"Mr. Hyde, quickly—do you age as Jekyll does, or does your condition cause you to age differently than the average human?"

"It seems the weaker Jekyll gets, the stronger I become," he growled. "As I have grown in size and strength, I have not aged as that weakling Jekyll did."

"The Cenobite will break free any second," said the Sâr. "When he does, agree to whatever I say. It is your only hope of surviving this encounter."

The air around the Cenobite began to shimmer and the frost encasing him shattered. The creature continued to approach Hyde when the Sâr called out to him:

"Hear me Cenobite! I have a proposition for you that may serve your purposes and yet still save Jekyll's soul."

The Cenobite shifted his eyes causing the chain in Sâr Dubnotal's arm to tighten.

"There is nothing you can offer me, mage. Be thankful that I have kept your suffering to a minimum thus far. Disturb me again and you will incur pain, the likes of which you have never imagined."

The Sâr ignored the threat and voiced his offer:

"How many souls do you claim in year? One or two, at most? What if I could offer you the opportunity to claim three times as many souls in a year as you currently harvest, but only if you partially release your claim in Edward Hyde?"

The Cenobite changed direction and stood in front of Sâr Dubnotal.

"I shall give you exactly sixty seconds to explain your proposition."

"Currently, you must wait until the puzzle box finds its way to someone who desires to summon you," said Sâr Dubnotal, speaking in a measured tone. "What if Hyde here were to operate as your emissary on Earth, facilitating the transfer of the box from one person to the next? Hyde does not age as most people do; he will live long beyond the lifespan of normal humans—and I have methods that might extend his life even further. If he were to fulfill the role, as I have explained, would you not claim much more souls?"

The Cenobite stared at the mystic for moment before responding:

"There is truth in your suggestion, but you have attempted to thwart me and are known in Hell as one who strives to battle our forces on Earth. Furthermore, you purposefully try to alter the lives of those on the path to Hell. Why would you knowingly support a plan that would assure more souls entering our domain?"

"There are souls who are so evil that they are beyond my ability to change them," replied the Sâr, sighing. "Tserpchikof, Fantomas... Even Hyde himself. These are men who have chosen the road to Hell, and there is nothing I, or anyone else, can do to change this. Hyde could seek them out for you; he is one of them; he knows how they think; where to find them... My offer is as follows. Allow him to remain here on Earth and operate in the capacity I have suggested. He will only give the box to the vilest souls—those that are beyond saving. I will see that he adheres to this bargain. Should he deviate from it, I will contact you and you may claim him. While Hyde is serving you, I shall try to discover a method for separating him from Jekyll. If I succeed, I will also contact you and you may claim Hyde's soul without taking Jekyll's."

The Cenobite continued to stare into Sâr Dubnotal's eyes.

"You offer is interesting," he said, "but the soul I desire is that of Edward Hyde. I am disinclined to grant him even a temporary reprieve from the tortures that await him."

"Then let me add an ultimatum to my offer," said Sâr Dubnotal, grimly. "If you claim Hyde today and take Jekyll to Hell with him, I will personally encase the box that grants you access to Earth in concrete and toss it into the deepest depths of the ocean. Yes, it will eventually reemerge and find its way back to land, but it will take centuries to do so, and I shall be waiting to do it all over again. Even if you should slay me, my disciples will carry out this duty in my stead. Are you truly willing to wait so long prior to claiming your next soul, or would you prefer my suggestion of allowing Hyde to bring souls to you?"

The Cenobite stood motionless for a moment and then waved his arm, causing the chains which held Sâr Dubnotal and Hyde to disappear. He turned and began walking back towards the glowing doorway.

"Your offer has been accepted," he said. "However, should you deviate from it, I shall claim Hyde and then subject you to horrors beyond comprehension. Work diligently, Sâr Dubnotal, I desire to claim Edward Hyde and my patience is not without limits."

When the Cenobite walked back through the doorway, it closed behind him and the wall became solid once more.

Hyde leaned against it as blood poured from the wounds inflicted upon him.

"If you think that..." he snarled at Sâr Dubnotal,

"Silence!" roared the Mage. "It loathes me to see you remain on Earth! You are a monster and truly belong in Hell, but today, you are fortunate that it suits my needs to save you. You will adhere to the parameters of my agreement with the Cenobite; you will facilitate the transfer of the box between the murderers and madmen who inhabit your world. As you perform this task, I will find a way to separate you from Henry Jekyll and, at that point, you will answer for your crimes! You have one small glimmer of hope, Edward Hyde, and that is to answer to me rather than the Cenobites. Use the time you have gained wisely. Study the Cenobites as they claim those who call them, and look for weaknesses that we may one day exploit. If you find one, report it at once to me, and I shall endeavor to use that knowledge not only to free you from your fate, but should another innocent soul ever be endangered by the Cenobites, I shall have the means to defeat them. Now, go and fulfill your mission!"

Two Months Later

It was a hot summer day as Irma Vep and the Great Vampire walked through the slums of Paris. The Great Vampire winced as he looked at the misery on display on these streets. He glared at Irma and voiced his displeasure:

"Why are you dragging me through this filthy neighborhood? Why did you not simply bring the objet to me?"

"I was told by the... man... who has it says that it can only be given to the person who most desires it. He said the object would not allow itself to be given to an intermediary, and that I had to bring you here in person."

"You could have just stolen it from that man," snarled the Great Vampire, "and brought it to me. You are supposed to be a master thief!"

Irma rolled her eyes.

"When you see this man in person, you will understand why I would not want to incur his wrath by stealing from him, especially when he was willing to give the object to you as long as you appeared in person."

Irma turned down a refuse-filled alleyway with a small shack at the back of it. A simple metal sheet served as the door to the structure. The Great Vampire stood there as Irma pulled it back. A horrid smell immediately assaulted their nostrils.

"This object had better be a valuable as legend suggests," said the leader of the Vampires.

As he entered the dark shack, he could see a large form squatting on the floor, his back to the wall. The Great Vampire slowly approached the gargantuan figure.

Mr. Hyde held out his massive hairy hand and opened it to reveal a puzzle box. He looked into the Great Vampire's eyes and, in foreboding voice, asked him a simple question:

"What is your pleasure, sir?"

Roman Leary chose to associate Sâr Dubnotal with The Shad-ow, another crime-fighter also forged amongst the ancient mysteries of India and Tibet. It is in New York's notorious Hell's Kitchen district that the two heroes first meet in a tale entitled...

Roman Leary: *The Evils Against Which We Strive*

New York, 1927

I will never forget the day I saw the stranger standing outside Miss Nolan's door. I have made many memories since that distant summer day in 1927, but few are as vivid as the sight of that extraordinary man. His stylish morning coat would have been enough to mark him as a man apart in the Hell's Kitchen tenement where I lived, but it was merely inci-dental compared to the multicolored sash he wore about his waist, or the immaculate white turban that crowned his head. His angular features were framed by a neatly trimmed beard which was only a few shades darker than his deeply-tanned skin.

I was only nine years old, and I had never seen such a man outside of the illustrations in a copy of *Arabian Nights*. I was watching him nervously through a crack in my own front door and wondering what he could possibly want with Miss Nolan, when he suddenly turned and looked directly at me. I felt an ice pick stab of panic, but something kept me from slamming the door and shooting the bolt. Instead, I simply peered back at the man and we regarded one another for a long, silent moment. Slowly, the corners of his mouth turned up in a smile.

"It is all right, lad," he said. "You can come out if you like. I am a friend."

His English was flawless, but heavy with an accent that I was too provincial and inexperienced to recognize. I could only imagine what my father would say if he caught me speaking to this man, one of the "dam' foreigners" he sometimes ranted about in his drunken tirades. Fortunately, Da was passed out on our tattered sofa and I knew from long experience that he wouldn't be awake for many hours yet. So, curiosity overpowering my fear, I stepped into the hallway.

"Allow me to introduce myself," said the man. "I am Sâr Dubnotal, the Great Psychagogue, called by some the Napoleon of the Intangible." He gave a deep bow and then, to my great relief, he added, "But you may call me *Doctor*."

He gazed at me expectantly with his piercing green eyes. I knew I should say something, but I was in such a state of awe that I could only stand and gape. For an awful moment, I almost ran back into my apartment, but then I thought of Miss Nolan and how disgusted she would be if I behaved in such a cowardly way. She had been very impatient with me lately, and I didn't want the stranger to tell her I had been rude to him. I forced myself to stand up straight and hold out my hand.

"It's very nice to meet you, Doctor," I said. "I'm Nick."

"It is an honor to make your acquaintance, Nick," said the Doctor, and he shook my hand as if I were another splendid gentleman like himself, rather than a pale, sickly boy dressed in rags.

Emboldened by his friendliness, I asked, "Where are you from, sir?"

"Many places," he said, "but France is the country I call my home."

I brightened considerably. "I know about France! Miss Nolan gave me a copy of *The Three Musketeers*. It was a hard book, but when I finished it, she took me to the zoo. Do you know Miss Nolan?"

"Should I?"

"I thought you were getting ready to knock on her door."

"Ah," said the Doctor. "As it happens, I do not know Miss Nolan, but I would very much like to meet her. Do you know if she is at home?"

"No, sir, she's at her bookshop."

"*Her* bookshop? She is the proprietor?"

"She used to just work there, but the old lady who owned it died, and she left it to Miss Nolan in her will."

"Remarkable," said the Doctor. "Do you know the name of this bookshop, Nick? Or where I can find it?"

I was about to answer, and then I caught myself. Why was I telling so much to this strange man? What if he wanted to hurt Miss Nolan?

"I promise I do not mean any harm to Miss Nolan," the Doctor said.

I gasped. "How did you know I was thinking that?" I whispered. I was frankly terrified, but too fascinated to turn away. "Are you a genie?"

"Hardly," he said with a smile. "And I did not read your mind. Your thoughts were plainly evident upon your face."

I frowned, and felt the face in question flush with embarrassment. At this, he favored me with a look of mild rebuke. "Come, now," he said. "Do not look so abashed. You are right to be cautious. You are old enough to know there is evil in this world."

I thought of my Da, and then buried that shameful thought before the Doctor could read that on my face as well. "So how can I know that you're a good guy?" I asked. "Why are you looking for Miss Nolan anyway?"

"Those are fair questions," the Doctor said. He gestured toward the nearby stairwell. "Why don't we sit down for a moment and discuss it?"

"OK," I said, and we did just that. I can hardly convey how strange it was to be sitting there with Sâr Dubnotal. Regal though he was, he seemed perfectly at ease in those shabby surroundings, and I could almost imagine that we were sitting together in some exclusive club for wealthy tycoons, instead of on the top step of a filthy stairwell.

"Nick, I am very concerned about Miss Nolan," the Doctor said. "I think that she may need my help."

"How can you know that? You didn't even know her name until I told it to you."

"I will explain." His eyes fixed on a point in the middle distance. "I am here in New York to visit a friend with whom I have been corresponding, a certain Judge Pursuivant. I was meditating in my hotel room when I sensed a disturbance in the astral plane which..."

"The *what*?" I interrupted, thoroughly confused and wondering what Miss Nolan had to do with airplanes.

The Doctor sighed. "Of course," he said, mostly to himself, "silly of me." He looked me squarely in the eye. "Nick," he said in a quiet voice, "last night I had a feeling that something very bad was happening, and my feelings with regard to such things are never, *ever* wrong. Just as one can follow smoke to a fire, I have followed that feeling to this building," he pointed down the hall, "to that apartment. Do you understand?"

"Yes," I whispered, and though it sounded a little crazy, even to the ears of a child, the Doctor was so grave and assured that it was impossible to disbelieve him.

"Excellent," he said. "Now, tell me, do you care for Miss Nolan?"

"She's my best friend in the whole world."

"Do you spend a lot of time with her?"

"She lets me stay with her when my Da..."

"Yes?"

I tore my eyes away from his penetrating gaze. "I visit her a lot."

"I see," he said, and I am sure that he did. "I want you to think very carefully about what I am going to ask you now. Has Miss Nolan done or said anything recently that seemed strange to you?"

"Well...she won't play checkers anymore."

255

"Really?"

"Yes, sir. She used to love it, but now she says it's…" my brow furrowed as I tried to find the word. "*Infantile*, that's it. She's been showing me how to play chess."

The Doctor raised a single eyebrow. "And how are you progressing?" he asked.

"I'm not very good. She yells at me a lot."

"Did she ever do that before?"

"No," I said, and I thought I sounded very small and weak. I looked down at the steps.

"Is there anything else?" the Doctor asked. In my mind, I could hear a faint echo of Miss Nolan's voice, icy with rage: *You insolent whelp!*

"Nick?" the Doctor asked, as gentle and persuasive as a caring father.

You insignificant maggot!

"Please look at me, Nick."

I clenched my teeth and stared resolutely at the floor. Inside me there was a sudden rush of anger toward Sâr Dubnotal. Why was he making me talk about these things? Why wouldn't he just leave me alone? I felt the curses I had learned from my Da curling on my tongue, eager to be spit into his face. Snarling in defiance, I turned to him…and I was immediately struck dumb by what I saw.

The Doctor, his eyes glittering like emeralds, was casually walking a gold dollar to and fro across the knuckles of his right hand. Suddenly, he clenched his fist and the coin disappeared. Then he turned his wrist, slowly opened his hand, and the coin was sitting up on its edge, perfectly balanced in his palm.

I was dazzled by this sleight of hand, and in my amazement I momentarily forgot my anger and pain. My reprieve, however, was short-lived.

"Nick," the Doctor said, "I know it hurts you to discuss these things, but I'm afraid it's necessary. I cannot help if I am not privy to all the facts. However, there is a way you can give me the information I need without having to actually talk about it."

"There is?"

"Yes. Unfortunately, you still have to *remember* it. It will not be a very pleasant experience, but it will be of invaluable assistance to me."

"Assist you how?" I asked, a petulant whine creeping into my voice. "What exactly do you want to know?"

"I want to know why Miss Nolan doesn't like checkers anymore," he said, without a hint of irony or sarcasm. "Will you help me?"

I considered it for a moment. He was such a strange man, but everything about him inspired feelings of confidence and trust. Of course, I knew from my books that all the best villains did the same thing, but I couldn't persuade myself that he was bad. I glanced at the coin, still steady and straight on its edge in the center of his hand, and I made my decision. "What do you want me to do?" I asked.

"Keep your eyes on the coin," he whispered.

Slowly at first, then with increasing rapidity, the coin began to spin. I felt a chill despite the summer heat.

"How are you doing that?" I asked, and my voice seemed to come from some distance far outside of myself.

"I am the Great Psychagogue," he replied, as if that explained it. "Concentrate on the coin. See how it reflects the light. Let everything else around you fall away…"

As he said these words, I felt a sudden lightness, and my surroundings seemed to grow hazy and indistinct. I felt as if I were slipping into a fever dream.

"Do not be frightened by what you are feeling," the Doctor said. "I will be with you on every step of this journey."

The stairs completely disappeared into a dark, grey mist. The air was cool and dry, and I could no longer feel the floor beneath me. All the while, floating before my eyes, the coin continued to spin, flickering like a golden star.

Then, there came a sense of gentle descent, and I could once again feel the wood of the steps. The flickering light began to slow, then ceased. The hall reformed, but retained a certain dim, artificial quality, as if it were an imperfect reproduction constructed from someone's flawed and fading…memory.

I felt a shock of realization. I heard the Doctor's voice, not with my ears but with my mind. *That is correct, Nick*, he said. *We are within your memories.*

There was a creaking on the steps. I looked down and saw Miss Nolan, bundled in a heavy coat and brushing flakes of snow from her shoulders. There was a package with a red bow in the crook of her arm, and I recognized it as a gift she had given me at Christmas, a used copy of *The Book of a Hundred Games*.

She was then, and remains to this day, my ideal not only of feminine beauty, but of Beauty itself. Petite, red-haired and freckled, she was the very archetype of the fair Irish colleen, and seeing her filled me with such love that my heart ached.

She looked up and saw me, and her blue eyes narrowed with concern. "Nick!" she exclaimed. "What are doing out here? You're going to catch your death of cold!"

I wanted to answer, but I couldn't. Startled, I tried to stand up, but my body wouldn't respond. *Do not be alarmed*, I heard the Doctor say. *You are a dreamer, conscious of the fact you are dreaming, but powerless to control your actions. Relax, and let yourself be pulled by the strings of memory.*

Miss Nolan knelt in front of me. "So," she said, "in his cups again, is he?" I slowly nodded. "Oh, well," she sighed, "may as well be mad at the sky for being blue. Maybe if your Ma hadn't died so young…" She shook her head, and then her expression of dismay vanished with a mischievous wink. "Tell you what, why don't we have some hot chocolate?"

At last I spoke. "Can we? With whipped cream?"

She gave an exaggerated scowl. "What do you think this is, my boy, the Waldorf-Astoria?" She laughed and tousled my hair. "Come along, Master Rockefeller. I hope you'll forgive us for not having cream tonight."

Suddenly, the scene changed and we were in Miss Nolan's apartment. I was sitting with her on a couch, a steaming cup of cocoa in my hand. "Have you made any progress on *Robinson Crusoe*?" she asked.

"It's too hard," I whined. "Why can't I keep reading *Tom Swift*?"

"You can, but I want you to read other things, too. I want you to challenge yourself, Nick." She reached over and tapped my forehead. "You have a good mind, so I want to see you use it. I want you to be living better than this when you get to be my age."

"You're not doing so bad," I assured her.

"Think so, do you? Twenty-four years old with no decent man to speak of? Barely scraping by working as a clerk in some old lady's bookshop? And a haunted one at that?"

"Haunted?" I asked. "By a ghost?"

"Well, what else, silly? I've heard it a couple of times coming from the cellar."

"What does it sound like?"

She frowned. "It sounds like a crying child. I've gone down there to look, but I can never find anything. I asked Mrs. Bishop about it, and she says she hears it all the time. 'Pay it no heed,' says she. 'It's just another lost and forgotten soul.' Pretty spooky, eh?" I nodded vigorously, and then the cocoa was gone and Miss Nolan had her arm around me, holding me close. I felt myself drifting into sleep, lulled by her warmth and the sound of her heartbeat against my ear. "I want you to listen to me, Nick," she said. "I'm going to give you a key. Anytime that I'm not here and your old man gets to be a bit too much, you can come over and stay, OK?"

"Yes, ma'am," I said in a drowsy whisper.

"That's a good boy," she said.

Then I was awake again, sitting on the couch alone, reading by a feeble ray of spring sunshine. I was on the last chapter of *Robinson Crusoe*, and consumed with elation at being so near to the end. There was a rattle at the door, and Miss Nolan stepped into the room. "Now there's a handsome man to come home to," she said with a grin. "I was hoping you'd be here. You can help me celebrate!"

"You got a new job?" I said.

"Oh, better than that! Nick, my boy, I deserve a good swift kick for every time I ever complained about dear, sweet, lovable Mrs. Emily Bishop, God rest her soul!"

"What do you mean? You always said she was nasty. When she died two weeks ago, you said..."

"Bite your tongue, my lad! That wonderful lady, that *angel*, has reached out from the grave and delivered me into a better life!"

"How did she do that?"

"She left me everything, Nick! Do you understand? She wrote a will and left me everything she owned!" Laughing, she took my hands and led me in a little victory dance. Then a disturbing thought occurred to me, and I gave it voice: "Does this mean you're going to move away?"

Miss Nolan sat down on the couch and pulled me down with her. "Now, Nick," she said, "sometimes a person's circumstances can change and they...and they..." A far-away look came into her eyes, and then she winced as if in pain.

"Are you all right?" I asked, leaning in close. She roughly pushed me away.

"Yes," she said sharply. "Yes, I'm perfectly fine. It's just my head... Sometimes it hurts." She started rubbing her temples. "It started about a month ago, right after Mrs. Bishop got sick. It always goes away after a few minutes. I just have to... Oh...God..." She gasped and curled into a fetal ball. For a moment I was panic-stricken. She was clearly in agony and I had no idea what to do. I was even considering going to Da for help, when she suddenly sat upright. She looked at me for a moment as if she were surprised to see me, then gave me a peculiar little half-smile.

"Distressed, boy?" she asked. It seemed like such an odd thing to say, and was said in such a mocking tone, that I wasn't sure how to respond. I waited for her to say more, but she just kept staring at me with that strange, impish look. Her eyes, normally so gentle, began to burn with a predatory cruelty. She was scaring me, and must have sensed this, because she blinked a few times and appeared normal again…almost.

"I'm sorry, child," she said. "You must forgive my behavior. It's these dreadful headaches. They can really be quite debilitating. Now, as I was saying, you are clearly concerned that I will be leaving you to your own devices in this…place." She looked around with a sneer, then seemed to force herself to smile. "But you must not trouble yourself. You are very important to me, you see."

"I am?" I said, and my misgivings disappeared at the pleasure of hearing her say this.

"Oh, yes!" she exclaimed. "In fact, I don't think I could live without you."

No one—not even Miss Nolan—had ever said something like that to me before, and I was over the Moon. I rushed forward and hugged her, barely noticing the stiffness and hesitation of her returned embrace. Then she softened and some of the familiar warmth and affection returned to her arms.

"Steady on, Nick," she said with a laugh. "What's brought all this on?"

"You're the nicest person in the world," I said.

"Am I? Well, I suppose I'd be foolish to argue with a thing like that."

I looked up at her, and the strange and unpleasant light that had danced in her eyes was gone. "Is your head better?" I asked.

"My head?" Her eyes narrowed in confusion. "It *was* hurting again, wasn't it?" She brightened a little. "But it's all gone now, thank the Lord."

There was a sudden stillness, and everything around me seemed to freeze; a moment trapped in amber. I couldn't understand what was happening. I felt a rising panic as I gazed into Miss Nolan's now vacant eyes.

We have to go forward, Nick. I heard the Doctor say. *Please release us from this memory.*

But I'm not doing this! I cried out to him, but even as I thought the words, I realized I was wrong. In fact, I was doing it, and I knew why. *Please bring me out*, I implored. *Just let it all stop here.*

I will not force you to continue, Nick. But let me ask you this, do you believe I have seen all I need to see?

I did not respond.

This is the last pleasant memory you have of Miss Nolan, isn't it?

I let my silence stand for a yes, and I refused to say anything more. I expected the Doctor to grow angry at me for my obstinacy, but all I could sense from him was pity, which was somehow worse. *Very well*, he said, and I thought I could hear him sigh. *I will count down from...*

No! I interrupted. *I'll show you the rest. I'll show you everything.* I concentrated...and entered a kaleidoscope of pain.

– I sit, nervous and bewildered, staring at a chessboard while Miss Nolan berates me for an obtuse clod.

– I feel her cuff me on the back of the head. *Cocoa?! Impertinent brat! Am I your serving wench?*

– I see her on the floor, holding her head, writhing in pain. *What's happening to me? Why is this happening to me?* I go to her and looks up at me, frightened and imploring. *I'm losing me! I'm...I'm... Away from me, boy! I don't need your help! Go back to your sod of a father!*

I cried out, whether aloud or only in my mind I cannot say. I felt myself plunging into the black abyss where I had buried the worst moments of my young life. I rushed headlong through the death of my mother; through a hundred beatings from Da; through a thousand cuts of Miss Nolan's increasing and unaccountable cruelties...

...I am standing outside of Miss Nolan's door. On the other side, I can hear a low, guttural chanting, punctuated by a series of small cries. In my hand, I hold the key that she gave me, and I resolve to use it. I quietly step into the apartment. The room is saturated with a dull, yellow glow coming from some indeterminate source. Miss Nolan is sitting on the floor, her back turned to me. She is naked, but her body is covered with symbols and writing I cannot understand. The chanting and the crying is emanating from her, but it does not sound like her voice. She falls silent, and sees me over her shoulder. *You dare?* she says, low and dangerous. *You dare disturb me now?*

My mouth moves but no sounds come out. I want to run, but I am rooted to the spot.

Nothing to say? She rises to her feet and turns to face me. The strange runes and foreign script cover her from head to toe. *Tell me boy, do you like to see me this way?*

I shake my head. I don't like it at all.

No? Why is that?

My mouth feels as if it is full of sand, but I force myself to answer. *Because this isn't you*, I whisper.

She laughs. *That is an interesting observation. Perhaps you are more intelligent than I presumed. If so, then you won't have any difficulty learning this lesson.* She steps forward and strikes my face with the back of her hand. *Look at me, you insignificant maggot!* She grasps my chin and forces me to look into her eyes. They were once blue, those eyes, but now they have darkened to black. *If you ever again come unbidden into my presence,* she says, *I will thrash you until you bleed. Do you understand?* I say that I do, and she strikes me again, hard enough to send me to my knees. *You do not weep*, she observes, standing over me.

It never does any good, I reply.

There is a long silence, and then she is helping me to my feet. *Go*, she says, *and remember your lesson.* She slams the door behind me and...

Please, Doctor...

She slams the door behind me...

Please bring me back...

She slams the door...

Please...

263

…I was once again sitting at the top of the stairs, staring at a spinning coin in the hand of Sâr Dubnotal. For a moment I could not move or speak. The thought occurred to me that I was still trapped in the labyrinth of my memories. I felt a rising horror at the possibility I would have to travel those dark corridors again, but then the Doctor's hand closed. "It's over, Nick," he said. "You have done well."

Relieved beyond measure, I closed my eyes and took a deep, shuddering breath. "Did you find out what you needed to know?" I asked.

"Yes," he said. "I was able to see things through your eyes which were very telling." He turned his head and pointed to the side of his face. It was red and inflamed as if he had been struck. "I felt things, too."

"I'm sorry," I said.

"You have nothing to apologize for. I made you relive those memories. It is right that I should share your pain." He stood up and brushed off his pants. "Now, my lad," he said, "I have to see about some things. I have a very good idea what is happening here, and who is responsible for it. But I need to confirm my suspicions."

I stood up too. "What about Miss Nolan?" I asked, and I could barely keep myself from clutching at his coat like some desperate beggar. "Can you help her? I mean, can you make her…be like she used to be?"

"I do not know, Nick," he said, and my heart fell. "However," he added, "I give you my word that I shall do my best, and Sâr Dubnotal always keeps his word." He held out his hand, and I shook it. "We will see each other again," he said, and he went down the stairs.

I waited until I could no longer hear his footfalls, then sank back to the floor. I was still sitting there, exhausted and consumed with an inexpressible sadness, when I became aware of an object in my right pocket. I reached into it, and when my hand emerged, it was holding Sâr Dubnotal's golden coin. In spite of all I had endured that afternoon, I found myself smiling.

Many hours later, after Da had gone out for his nightly prowls, I sat alone in the apartment listening to the warm wind rattle our single windowpane. There was an occasional flash of lightning, and the rumble of approaching thunder held the promise of a summer storm that, hopefully, would break the suffering heat.

I was staring with listless disinterest at a copy of *Tom Swift and the Land of Wonders*. Ordinarily, I could always count on good old Tom to take me away from my troubles, but that night I couldn't think of anything but Miss Nolan and Sâr Dubnotal. Every few minutes I found myself reaching for the gold dollar in my pocket, holding it up to the light, reminding myself that it was real. In fact, I was doing that very thing when I heard a tapping at the door. I opened it a crack, and saw Miss Nolan smiling at me.

"I owe you an apology, boy," she said sweetly. "I'm afraid I've been quite hard on you lately. Why don't you come over and allow me to make amends?"

I wanted to run to her, but the devastating memories dredged up by the Doctor were still fresh in my mind. I hesitated, remembering the sting of her hand against my cheek.

Miss Nolan kneeled, making her eyes level with my own. "Afraid?" she whispered. "There's no need. Come with me, and all of your pain will end. I promise."

Even at that age I knew that was a vow no one could keep, but I didn't care. All that mattered was the kindness I thought I could hear in her voice. For a smile and some kindness, I would have forgiven her of a thousand false promises. I opened the door and rushed into her arms. I could have cheerfully stayed in her embrace forever, but she quickly pulled away from me and led me to her apartment. We stepped inside and, to my surprise, I saw that the room was illuminated solely by an arrangement of candles spread out over the floor.

"I'm going to show you a new game tonight, boy," she said as she closed the door.

"Is it as hard as chess?" I asked, filled with a sudden foreboding.

"Oh, no," she said with a laugh. "You'll find these rules to be very simple." I gave a sigh of relief, which turned to a gasp as my eyes adjusted to the gloom.

Drawn on the floor were a series of large, interlocking circles, each containing a mad jumble of letters and symbols, which, with horror, I immediately recognized. They were the same ones I had seen painted on Miss Nolan's body.

I turned in time to see her bolting the door. She was still wore a smile, but now it was little more than a thin, red slash across her pallid face. In her right hand she was holding a knife. She walked toward me, and I stepped back until I was in the center of the pattern of circles.

"What are you doing?" I asked, frightened and confused.

"She intends to kill you," said a voice behind me, and the smile disappeared from Miss Nolan's face.

I turned, and saw a patch of darkness shaped like a man detach itself from the shadows. It wore a slouch hat pulled low over its face, and a long black cloak, which, as it moved, revealed a flash of crimson lining.

"Hello, murderess," it said to Miss Nolan, and its voice was like a whisper of wind between forgotten graves.

"Who are you?" Miss Nolan asked in a fearful whisper.

There was a thoughtful silence, followed by a low chuckle. "My enemies once called me *Der Schwarze Adler*," said the living shadow, "The Black Eagle."

Miss Nolan visibly struggled to gather her nerve. She crossed her arms, hiding the wicked gleam of her knife. "Boy," she said, never taking her eyes from the Eagle, "come here to me."

I didn't move.

"Do as I say, boy! This man is dangerous! Get over here, now!"

I looked at the dangerous man. Beneath the brim of his hat burned a pair of black eyes that seemed to smolder like coals. He was the living personification of every night terror I had ever known, but somehow I did not fear him. "Why did you say she was going to kill me?" I asked.

"She has killed many children," he replied, "most of them even younger than you."

"You lie!" Miss Nolan shouted.

The room filled with a hollow, mocking laugh. "Do not waste your breath," the Black Eagle snarled. "I have been to your little bookshop, and I have stood in the charnel house you have hidden behind the walls of the cellar."

There was a flash of lightning outside the window, and Miss Nolan looked as if it had struck her between the eyes.

"Oh, yes," hissed the menacing man in black. "I have seen their bones. In life they were poor, homeless, forgotten. You looked at them and saw the perfect victims for your perverse rituals. You thought you could pluck them from the streets and no one would notice. No one would care. But you were wrong."

The cloak rustled, and a pair of automatic pistols appeared in the Black Eagle's hands.

"*I* noticed," he said. "*I* cared. And tonight I have come for a reckoning."

"No!" I cried out. I stepped in front of Miss Nolan and held up my arms in an attempt to shield her. "You're wrong! She'd never do anything like that! It must have been the old lady, Mrs. Bishop! She told Miss Nolan not to listen to the sounds in the cellar! She said it was ghosts! She was..."

I was interrupted by Miss Nolan, who suddenly lifted me in her arms—and pressed the edge of her knife to my throat.

"Leave us!" she commanded the Shadow.

The Black Eagle laughed. His guns were steady, unwavering. Outside the window, there was a tremendous crack of thunder and the rain began to fall.

I could feel Miss Nolan trembling. "If you shoot, you will hit the boy!"

"No, I won't," the Shadow said, and I closed my eyes.

There was a deafening crash…but not of gunfire. I opened my eyes and there, standing over the shattered remains of Miss Nolan's door, was Sâr Dubnotal.

"Stay your hand, my friend," he said to the Black Eagle, "lest you take the life of an innocent woman."

If the Eagle was surprised by this interruption, he did not let it show. "Hello, *El Tebib*," he said. "Shouldn't you be having dinner with Judge Pursuivant?"

"I informed him that I might be late. Please lower your guns."

"Yes!" Miss Nolan said through clenched teeth. "Listen to him! Or this boy's blood is on your hands!"

The Doctor slowly turned until his eyes met mine. "Have courage, Nick," he said. "This nightmare is almost over." Then he looked at Miss Nolan, and a darkness came into his expression that I had not seen before. "I demand that you release Mary Nolan," he said.

Miss Nolan's arms tightened around me. "What are talking about, you fool?" she said. "I *am* Mary Nolan."

"No, you are not," the Doctor said. "Nor are you Emily Bishop, though you called yourself that for many years while you occupied her body."

Miss Nolan gasped. "How can you possibly know that?"

"It is not for nothing that I am called the Conqueror of the Invisible."

There was a giggling in my ear, and I knew that Miss Nolan was on the brink of hysteria. "You arrogant poseur," she said. "Do you think you impress me? I have conquered death itself, many times over, with only the power of my own indomitable will!"

"Indeed," the Doctor said. "The will to do unspeakable deeds in the service of abominable gods. The will to destroy innocent lives in order to unnaturally extend your own." His lip curled into a sneer. "I stand in awe of your will… *Lady Ligeia*."

Miss Nolan—Ligeia—said nothing. The edge of the blade bit into my neck, and I could feel a warm trickle of blood run down my skin.

"You told Nick that you couldn't live without him," the Doctor said, "and you were correct. Your...sacrifices...were sufficient to give you the power to invade Mary Nolan's body, but your possession could not be complete until you spilled the blood of a child who loved her."

Incredibly, despite the dire peril I was in, I felt an enormous weight lift from my heart. It really wasn't Miss Nolan who had been so cruel these last weeks! It was some evil imposter!

"It is over, Ligeia," said Sâr Dubnotal. "You cannot complete the final ritual."

"I can!" Ligeia shouted. "I will!"

"I think not," said the Black Eagle. "These vile ceremonies take time, do they not, *El Tebib*?"

"Indeed, they do, old friend, time that we will not allow."

Ligeia growled like an animal.

"The game has ended, sorceress," the Doctor said. "Put down the boy. Release the woman. Go to your final judgment. Who knows? Perhaps there is mercy even for the likes of you."

"You know that isn't true," Ligeia snapped. "Even now I can feel Hell's hot arms, opening to embrace me. But I tell you this! If I must go to the flames, I'll go knowing that I defeated you!"

She was going to kill me then, of that I am certain, but she was interrupted by an explosion of gunfire. Screaming, she dropped me to the floor and tumbled against the wall, clutching at her head.

I looked up at the Black Eagle, his eyes blazing behind a plume of gun smoke. "The bullet only grazed her temple," he said. "She will be fine."

I heard Ligeia cry out in rage. I turned to see her holding the knife to her own neck. "You may have saved the pup," she screamed, "but I still claim the bitch!"

I have often wondered if there was anything the Doctor or the Eagle could have done to stop her. They were men of incredible abilities, and it is certainly possible that they could have somehow prevented Ligeia from slashing Miss Nolan's throat, ending both of their lives in a final act of cruelty and spite. But, as fate would have it, I was the one closest to her, and I was the one who acted first.

I leapt forward and closed one of my hands around Ligeia's wrist, and the other around the blade. I felt it cut deep into my fingers, but I ignored the pain and held the knife with all the strength I could muster. Her eyes locked with mine, and I stared into those bottomless black pools of hate.

"You're...not...strong...enough," she hissed. "My will..."

"Has been thwarted once and for all," the Doctor interrupted. He grabbed Ligeia's arm and pulled, adding his strength to my own. By now, the blood was flowing freely from my lacerated hand.

"Blood!" Ligeia cried in a voice choked with panic. "No! Not without the proper..."

Some of the drops landed on her chest, and she cried out as if they were acid.

"No," she whimpered. "It can't end like this...it can't...it..."

"Behold, Nick," said the Doctor. "The storm clouds fade."

The blackness in Ligeia's eyes dissipated and lightened...and turned to a crystal blue. The pressure on the knife eased, and I was easily able to wrest it away from her.

"Nick?" Miss Nolan said. "What's happening? What on Earth...?"

"Sleep," said Sâr Dubnotal. He pressed his forefinger against Miss Nolan's brow and she immediately fell into a swoon. "It's over," he said. "The evil that lurked in her heart is gone."

"I know," said the Shadow. He swept his cloak through the air and the candles went out, plunging the room into darkness.

I could hear voices in the hall, and I realized that some of the neighbors were probably coming to investigate the noise. Then there was the distinct click of chain being pulled on a light, and a policeman was standing in the apartment. He was tall, with a prominent nose and a pair of piercing eyes set deep in a pale, mask-like face.

"Tend to them," the patrolman said to the Doctor, and then he stepped over to the door. "This is the police!" he shouted down the hall. "Some thieves broke into this apartment and attacked a woman and a child, but they fled when I arrived. Everything is under control! Please go back to your rooms and remain there!"

The Doctor chuckled. For the next few minutes, he ministered to the wounds suffered by me and Miss Nolan. "I am very sorry for what you have been through, Nick," he said as he finished applying my bandages. "Miss Nolan will not remember any of these events. I think perhaps it would be best if you didn't either. Look into my eyes and I will..."

"No," said the policeman. "The boy was brave tonight. He deserves to remember that."

The Doctor considered this, then nodded. "My friend is very wise, as usual."

"But I wasn't brave," I protested. "I was scared to death!"

The policeman looked at me. "You stepped in front of two loaded guns to protect someone's life," he said. "That is not the act of a coward."

"He is right, Nick," the Doctor said, gently placing his hands on my shoulders. "There are many evils against which we strive. No man's life is ever completely free of them. As you contend with them in the years to come, remember your courage on this night."

271

He stood up and went to the door. "I believe our work here is done," he said to the policeman. The officer gave him a curt nod, then disappeared into the night.

The Doctor hesitated in the door for a moment, then looked back at me, "You have the heart of a lion, my son," he said, "and you have earned the respect of Sâr Dubnotal."

And then he, too, was gone.

Matthew Baugh returns to depict the final confrontation between Sâr Dubnotal and Herr Doktor Von Meyer...

Matthew Baugh: *Ask Me A Riddle...*

London, 1938

> *Cottleston, Cottleston, Cottleston Pie.*
> *A fly can't bird, but a bird can fly.*
> *Ask me a riddle and I reply:*
> *Cottleston, Cottleston, Cottleston Pie.*
> —A.A. Milne

"Here you are, guv," the cab driver said as he pulled to the curb. "Number thirty-seven, Little Oakfield Street.

Sâr Dubnotal didn't reply; he just waited as the cabbie came around to open the door for him. Climbing out would have been difficult, as sore as he was, even without the sling on his left arm. Nevertheless, he ignored the hand the driver offered. He had to apply all his willpower just to keep from wincing, but he managed.

"Would you like me to wait?" the driver asked, a touch of concern in his voice.

Dubnotal stared at the man, momentarily caught off guard. He hadn't hidden his pain as well as he'd thought. Either the cabbie was unusually perceptive, or he was an agent of the enemy.

"Sir?"

"That won't be necessary," Dubnotal said.

He took out his wallet and paid the fare, adding a generous tip. He sensed no taint in the man's aura. He might be exactly what he seemed, an honest working man with a streak of kindness.

The driver thanked him and drove off. Dubnotal watched from the sidewalk until the vehicle was out of sight, then turned and stared at the handsome Edwardian building. It was an attractive enough setting, especially on a sunny April afternoon, but he didn't let himself relax for a moment. He entered and ascended the stone stair to the third floor.

Normally, this would have been almost effortless, but he found himself aching and out of breath when he reached the landing. He paused long enough to catch his breath and to read the brass plate on the door.

GEES
CONFIDENTIAL AGENCY
Hours: 10 to 5 - Saturdays: 10 to 12:30

Just below the sign a business card had been tacked to the door. It was blank, except for some neat handwriting that proclaimed, "*Initial Consultation—Two Guineas*."

Dubnotal frowned at this. The money was nothing to him, but he wondered about the quality of someone who would be expected to be paid for the kind of work he had in mind. Still, he needed this man's help.

He rang and a moment later, a tall young woman with dark hair opened the door.

"Yes, sir?" she asked in a voice that matched her very proper business outfit perfectly.

"Sâr Dubnotal to see Mr. Green," he replied, handing her his business card. He watched her as she studied the card, and then him. Her hair held faint highlights of red and her features—while not regular enough to be classically beautiful— were quite pretty. She took him in, her gaze lingering for a second on the turban, the cape, the sling, but her face betrayed no surprise at his unusual attire.

"Mr. Green doesn't see anyone without an appointment," she said. "I could arrange one for tomorrow, if you like."

"I'm afraid that's impossible," he said, letting a touch of mesmeric influence flow through his voice. "My business is urgent."

"I can tell him you're here, Mr. Dubnotal," she said with a professional smile. "If he can see you, I'll need the consultation fee."

Dubnotal's eyes widened a fraction of an inch. Normally his influence would have removed all resistance. Either he was even weaker than he felt, or this woman—Miss Brandon, according to the name plate on her desk—was unusually resistant.

"I would like to see him, *now*," Dubnotal said.

Miss Brandon's blue eyes went blank.

"Of course, sir," she said. "Please wait here a moment."

She went through the inner door, leaving Dubnotal to examine the outer office. It was meticulously neat and well ordered, suggesting either business was slow, or Miss Brandon was very efficient. He suspected it was a touch of both. He caught sight of a Charles Williams novel, partially hidden by the typewriter, and allowed himself a small smile. The young woman had a well-ordered mind, but more than a touch of imagination as well. Small wonder she'd resisted him.

The door opened and Miss Brandon emerged. She offered him another professional smile.

"Mr. Green will see you now."

Sâr Dubnotal rose with as much grace as he could manage, gave the young woman a small bow, and proceeded through the door. A man of perhaps thirty rose to greet him. He was tall and lean, with the hands and feet of a much bigger man. His face was only saved from ugliness by a pleasant expression that blended amusement and intelligence in equal measure.

"Mr. Green," Dubnotal said, taking the hand the younger man offered.

"Gregory George Gordon Green," he replied. "That's if you want the whole mouthful. My father had a liking for the Romantic poets and stuck me with it."

"Ah!" said Dubnotal. "So the 'Gees' on the sign…"

"Are all mine, yes. But you're hardly here for anecdotes about the amusing things parents do with their children's names. Please, have a seat and tell me about it."

"I'm in need of a specialist," Dubnotal said, once he had settled into a comfortable leather chair. "I've been told that you are such a man."

"Really?" Gees said. "I've always thought of myself as more of a generalist. If you've seen my advertisements in the paper, you'll remember my motto: '*Anything from mumps to murder*.'"

Dubnotal inhaled deeply and took a moment to let the prana flow through his body calming him. Under normal circumstances, he would probably have found this man and his banter charming, but he was drained in body and soul.

"If you'll forgive me, Mr. Green," he said. "Time is something I do not have in abundance."

"Of course," the young man said, taking a seat behind his desk. "Why don't you tell me what you need done and what special skills you'd like me to do it with."

"I need to find a man—a very evil man. I've been hunting for him for some time. I nearly had him in France, but he eluded me."

"Is that how you ended up looking the worse for wear?"

"I fared better than those who were helping me," Dubnotal said. "The man is as slippery as the very devil, and twice as dangerous."

"Mmm," Gee said. "And what happens when you find him? I ask because I get the feeling there may be blood between the two of you. I'm happy to take on all manner of cases, but not when it leads to murder, or vengeance, or retributive justice, or whatever you may care to label it. I can help you find your man and deliver him to the law—"

"Mr. Green," Dubnotal said. "The law has no power over a man like this. I would go to them, but I know it is useless."

"Very well, then. Perhaps you should tell me what sort of man this is, and why you think I can deal with him better than the police."

"This man, Herr Doktor von Meyer, is a sorcerer; a practitioner of the darkest arts. You—so I am told—can defend yourself from his kind of deviltry better than any policeman."

"Go on," Gees said.

"I have been chasing this man for a very long time," Dubnotal said. "Since before the Great War."

"You're very well preserved, if that's the case."

"Yes…von Meyer is as well. I have my suspicions about the man's true age, but very little to back them up. In any case, it was during the war that he came into possession of an item of great power, a grimoire written by a Medieval French sorcerer named Nathaire. With its power, I saw him turn men to beasts, bring statues to life, and summon the hordes of Hell itself. He was more powerful than I and, had I not found powerful allies, he might have won the war for the Germans, and set himself up as the power behind the Kaiser."

Gees raised an eyebrow.

"I can understand your skepticism," Dubnotal said. "But he has not remained idle since the war. He was the guiding force behind the Thule Society in Germany. They dissolved in 1919, but not before von Meyer had become an intimate of Heinrich Himmler."

"So, he's a Fascist?"

"No, though he finds them useful for his purposes. He serves older forces than National Socialism—older and darker. There are beings, not of this world, once worshipped as gods."

Gees's remained silent but his eyes brightened.

"He has made a pact with one of these beings in particular," Dubnotal continued. "An Unnamable goddess of the extinct Azalean culture."

"Not completely extinct," Gees said.

"You've encountered them?"

"Several times. I'm starting to see why you think I'm your man."

"Good!" Dubnotal said. "I, with several allies, recently tracked the devil to the catacombs beneath Bayonne—"

"Catacombs underneath Bayonne? I didn't think there were any."

"They are a well-kept secret." Dubnotal replied with a touch of irritation. "I lost several friends there and all of us were wounded. Von Meyer fled, and only I was able to pursue him. My arts allowed me to trace him to England, but my further efforts have not yielded any results."

"So you find yourself in need of an investigator," Gees said.

"An investigator who will not be caught off-guard by unnatural methods of discouragement."

"I see," Gees said. "Well, I must agree, I'm rather hard to discourage."

"Then you'll accept the case?"

"I think I already have."

"Excellent!" Sâr Dubnotal said. Reaching into his coat with his good hand he withdrew a thick envelope, which he handed to Gees. "You'll find documents, newspaper clippings, and several photographs of von Meyer in there. I've also included what I hope will cover your retainer. You can deduct the consulting fee from that and let me know if there are any adjustments."

"My consulting fee?"

"I'm afraid I neglected to give that to your Miss Brandon. My apologies."

Gees took the envelope, but the look he offered Dubnotal seemed suspicious.

"We're here, sir."

Sâr Dubnotal had not been at his London home in over a year and had found it unstaffed and closed up, with most of the valuables in storage. It gave the place a strange, still feeling, but that was what Dubnotal wanted just now. He needed the silence to prepare himself for what was coming, and he didn't want to place innocent servants in harm's way. Better to lay low in an apparently empty home until he was ready to strike.

He moved to the salon, picked up the telephone, and asked the operator to connect him to a number in Bayonne. A few moments later a voice answered in French.

"Would you kindly inform M. D'Atois that Sâr Dubnotal wishes to speak with him," he said in the same language.

There was a brief pause, then his friend's voice spoke.

"It's good to hear from you, *mon vieux*," D'Atois said. "I hope your journey was uneventful."

"I have made it this far unscathed, Pierre," Dubnotal replied. "How is your friend?"

"Sidi Abdurrahman is still comatose," D'Atois replied. "I hope and pray that this is some sort of healing trance of his devising. He lies in his home, tended and guarded by his sons. They assure me he lives, but I can see no sign of breath or pulse in him."

Sâr Dubnotal was silent for a moment. The Sidi was a wise and good man, as well as an extremely powerful adept. If he died, it would be one more atrocity to hang on von Meyer.

"What of your two patients?"

Pierre D'Atois gave a loud snort. "They are recovering, though slowly. Thank providence for Dr. Trowbridge. If they were my patients, I should have drowned them both in the sea by now. Two more difficult men do not live on this earth."

"I am glad to hear they are healing," Dubnotal said.

"De Grandin's wounds will trouble him for a time, but the doctor assured me he will recover fully, with rest. That last will take some doing. The little fool is eager to be up and about to join you in the chase."

"What of de Richlieu?"

"He finally woke this morning, just long enough to take some broth and to challenge de Grandin to a duel."

"Are you serious?"

"Sadly, yes. Trowbridge was there and foolishly relayed the message to his friend. I tried to convince him that Mon-

sieur le Duc was delirious, and did not know what he was saying."

"What did de Grandin say to that?"

"That when the Duc de Richlieu recovers from his deliri-
um, I am to ask him if he prefers sabers or pistols."

"Unbelievable!" Dubnotal said. "Do you think it will
come to that?"

"They hate each other," D'Atois said. "If it's not politics
with those two, it's religion, or sports, or… anything that
strikes their fancy. If there's one good thing von Meyer has
done, it's to give them a common enemy. My worry is that
they will both ask me to second them, but that is a problem for
another day. Have you found any trace of our nemesis?"

"Not yet, but I have found an ally to help track him, an
Englishman with an extraordinary number of Gs in his name.
He's an unusual fellow, but he seems very clever, and he has
the right kind of experience."

"Are you sure that will be enough?" D'Atois asked. "I
could be there by tomorrow."

"No, it would be too risky to leave our invalids unguard-
ed. M. Green and I should be enough."

Pierre D'Atois fell silent and Dubnotal knew what he
must be thinking. He had already faced the German necromancer once, with three of the world's most seasoned investigators of the occult, plus the skills of Sidi Abdurrahman, on
his side. They had driven von Meyer away, but had barely
survived the encounter.

"Promise you will let me know when you have located
him, at least," D'Atois said.

"You have my word."

After the two had said their goodbyes, Sâr Dubnotal
moved to the bath, where he turned on the hot water and
sprinkled some powders, into the tub. Straightening, he re-
garded the mirror for several moments. His reflection looked
weary and unhealthy. As steam filled the room, his image
blurred, ironically looking better as details were obscured. In

fact, it almost seemed as if the reflection stood taller than he did, and had a ruddier complexion...

Dubnotal wiped away condensation to reveal the leering red-bearded face of von Meyer. He started back as the sorcerer reached for him. The surface of the mirror rippled like water as the arm emerged. The thick fingers caught him by the throat and began to squeeze.

Before his breath was cut off entirely, Dubnotal reacted. Catching the wrist with his good hand, he wrenched it while twisting his body away. To his surprise, the choking fingers came free and the arm fell to the marble floor with a dull plopping noise. He backed out of the bath as the arm, no longer connected to the mirror, writhed on the floor. As he watched, its motions grew more coordinated and it began to hump toward him, moving like a grotesque inchworm.

Dubnotal continued to back away, his good hand fishing in his pocket. A moment later, he drew out a small phurba with a two-inch blade. Holding the ritual knife high, he sank into a crouch and waited. The arm drew near and shifted position, the forearm rising like a cobra, the fingers flaring like the serpent's hood.

As the arm struck, Dubnotal's own hand came flashing down. The phurba pierced the back of the hand and drove through it, into the carpet and the floorboards beneath. The arm began to thrash violently but was unable to free itself and remained nailed to the floor.

Sâr Dubnotal began to chant in Sanskrit and the arm fell still. As he continued, the limb began to evaporate into ectoplasmic smoke. At the pommel of the little knife, the three carved faces of the god, Vajrakīla, opened their mouths and began to inhale the vapors. As the images drew in the last wisp of ectoplasm, Dubnotal ceased his chanting, and the tiny mouths snapped shut.

Leaving the knife embedded in the floor, he returned to the bathroom and wiped the mirror with a towel. The reflection was his own again, still pale but now with red finger marks on his throat.

"A clumsy attempt, von Meyer," he said.

It was half past noon when Sâr Dubnotal's meditations were interrupted by a loud knocking at the front door. Rising, he went to the door and opened it to find Gees standing there.

"Please come in, Mr. Green," he said. "I apologize that I don't have anything to offer you."

"Quite all right," Gees replied stepping inside. "As it happens, I have something to offer you."

"So quickly? I'm impressed at your efficiency."

"I don't know where your man is, but I know who does," Gees said. "I don't think he'll give von Meyer up willingly, but you might be able to influence him."

"I do have some skills that could help."

"I thought you might. In fact, I suspect they're the same skills you used on my secretary yesterday."

"Mr. Green, I..."

"You see, Miss Brandon has worked for me for several years now," Gees continued. "I've never known her to look so…blank when introducing a client, and I have certainly never known her to let anyone slip past without collecting the consultation fee."

"You are correct, Mr. Green, but I needed to see you. And what I did caused the girl no harm."

"I beg to differ," Gees said coldly. "Miss Brandon is an intelligent and independent young lady, who does not need anyone to do her thinking for her. Mucking about in someone's mind is a nasty business, especially when the person is Eve Madeline Brandon."

Sâr Dubnotal bowed his head.

"It was thoughtless of me," he said. "I apologize. I will not repeat the offense."

"I'll take you at your word on that," Gees said.

It was another unusually lovely day and Sâr Dubnotal had to work to keep his mind focused as the Rolls-Bentley navigated the lush country roads.

"Reginald Spode," he said. "It does make sense that von Meyer would seek assistance from a leading Fascist, but how can you be certain?"

"I wasn't until a spoke to an old acquaintance this morning," Gees said. "Rather, I spoke to his valet. Bertie's not terribly useful, I'm afraid, but his man, Jeeves, is highly intelligent. More importantly, he has his finger on the pulse of servants' gossip, which includes Spode's household. Anyway, he said he'd heard of Spode smuggling a man matching von Meyer's description off his estate several days ago. Unfortunately, he didn't know where the man was being taken."

"But Spode knows," Dubnotal said.

"Precisely."

Spode's home was a sprawling country house which boasted a beautifully kept lawn, on which about twenty men of varying ages, heights, and builds were drilling under the supervision of a large, red-faced man with a bellowing voice. The men were all dressed in khaki shirts with arm bands bearing a symbol that looked like a cross between a swastika and a capital S, and black shorts.

Dubnotal and Gees were greeted by a butler who ushered them into a sitting room.

"Whom shall I say is calling?" he asked.

"Gregory George Gordon Green and Sâr Dubnotal," Gees said, handing the butler his card.

The man left and Dubnotal studied the room, noticing that, though the books were mostly rhetoric and pseudo-science, the decor was exquisite. Spode, it seemed, was a man of contrasts.

Several moments later, the man who had been leading the drill strode into the room. He was as tall as Gees, but considerably broader and wore an expression that made Dubnotal think of a petulant gorilla.

"Which one of you is Green?" he bellowed. "And what's this foolishness about mumps and murder?"

"I'm Green," Gees said. "I apologize about the card. It's a bit of whimsy I came up with to aggravate my father, the General."

"The General?" Spode blinked several times rapidly and his expression softened a bit. "You're General Green's son?"

"Guilty," Gees said. "I apologize that the General couldn't come with me today. He's terribly busy."

"Of course! Of course!" Spode said. His attempt at a smile didn't work well with his face. "Is the General interested in our program?"

"Not as interested as I am, though I may be able to warm him up to it a bit more."

"That would be wonderful! A man of his stature."

"But that's for a later date. I'm here today to ask your assistance on a business venture."

"Business venture?" Spode looked warily from one man to the other.

"You have a reputation as an expert on fine jewelry," Dubnotal said, producing a shiny bauble. "We were hoping you could give us an appraisal of this."

He held the object out for Spode's inspection. It was a swastika with curved arms, giving it the profile of a circle about an inch and a half in diameter. It was made of beaten gold and studded with a number of half carat diamonds.

"By the Great Harry," Spode whispered. "I've never seen anything like it."

"It's quite wonderful, isn't it?" Dubnotal said, moving the swastika so the sun caught the diamonds. "See how it sparkles?"

"Sparkles…" Spode said.

"You want to watch the sparkles, but you're so sleepy."

"Sleepy…" Spode remained standing, but his eyes closed and his chin fell to his chest.

"That was fast," Gees said.

"Extremists tend to have the most susceptible minds," Dubnotal replied. "Spode, was von Meyer a guest in your home recently?"

284

"Yes."

"Where did he go?"

"Kent."

"Well, that's helpful," Gees commented.

"Where in Kent?" Dubnotal asked, ignoring him.

"Don't know," Spode answered. "Has a friend out somewhere on Romney Marsh, I think."

Dubnotal tried a few more questions, but it quickly became apparent that Spode had nothing else of use to tell them. They left Spode sleeping, with instructions to forget about them and their conversation.

"Romney Marsh is a big place," Gees said.

"Don't worry," Dubnotal replied. "Once we're that close, I have a way to find him. We'll just use the phurba to…" He trailed off as his hand encountered an empty pocket. "Blast!"

"What is it?" Gees asked.

"It's a small ceremonial knife from Tibet. I used it to soak up some of von Meyer's essence, which means it should be able to track him when we get close. Unfortunately, I left it in my home. I must be more tired than I thought. I never make mistakes like this. We had better go back to London to get it."

"Where, exactly, is this phurba?" Gees asked.

"It's in my home in Cheyne Walk," Dubnotal said. "I left it sticking in the floor."

"And therein hangs an interesting tale I am sure. Don't worry. There's no need to go back. When we get to Romney, I can telephone Miss Brandon and have her bring it to us."

"Yes, that would be best," Dubnotal agreed. "I feel so unprepared."

"You seemed prepared to me back at Spode's. Do you always carry a diamond studded swastika in your pocket?"

"I knew where we were going and thought it might be helpful. Besides, it was a sun symbol in India for millennia before the Nazis co-opted it. By the way, I noticed you didn't seem to have any moral objections to me influencing Spode's mind."

Gees stared at the road.

"Perhaps I do have a double standard," he said. "But it's one I can live with."

"Romney Marsh?" Pierre D'Atois said.

"It does seem an unlikely place," Sâr Dubnotal replied. "But perhaps that's why he chose it. Who would think to look for the darkest of sorcerers in Kent?"

"It is not as mundane a place as you might think," D'Atois said. "I've been there before, and I'm familiar with its many legends. In addition to the usual black-dogs and boogie men, they tell of a demon-scarecrow and his army of ghosts who haunt the marsh."

"Such legends don't help us," Dubnotal said.

"Then here is something that might. While I was there, I met a man who was an expert on the region and all its macabre stories. His name is Charles Hogarth and he lives at the place called the Old Palace of Wrotham. I think you'll find him a great help, even if only in providing a base for your investigations."

After Dubnotal hung up, Gees used the telephone to contact Miss Brandon. If she was taken aback at being asked to fetch a Tibetan dagger which was stuck in the floor of Dubnotal's home, she gave no indication. The plan was for Gees to meet her at the 6:10 train at Maidstone—the closest station to Wrotham. Once that was arranged, they telephoned Hogarth, who was delighted to put up friends of D'Atois. He only required them each to offer up a macabre story in return for his hospitality.

The Old Palace was a grand place made of gray stone, which looked as if it might once have been a monastery, at least in part. It was off the beaten path, but still took them less than half an hour to find. They were greeted by an old servant named Hoadley, who wore a quaint black outfit that made him resemble a dean's verger of a Cathedral more than a valet. He led them to a well-stocked library, the most distinctive item it held was a glass case filled with sundry trophies including a pair of skulls, a curved oriental dagger, and a single dead moth with white wings.

The master of the place, a lean fellow who looked to be in his fifties, clean-shaven with neat white hair rose to greet them with the help of a crutch and shook their hands.

"Gentleman," he said. "This is a genuine pleasure, I assure you. I haven't heard form Pierre D'Atois in many years. I remember him with singular affection. Hoadley, will you see to the gentlemen's bags?"

"I'm afraid we haven't any," Dubnotal said. "Our errand here is of some urgency and we left London without packing."

"I see," Hogarth replied. "Well, we shall do our best to accommodate you, regardless."

"Thank you," Dubnotal said. "I hope we shall not have to inconvenience you for very long."

"But there is no inconvenience at all," Hogarth protested. "You gentlemen are welcome to stay as long as you like. I'm afraid I'm rather incapacitated at the moment by what Hoadley calls 'neuritis.' Still, I'm happy to offer any assistance I may be capable of. Pierre D'Atois has an admirable habit of championing the right, and coming away with the most wonderfully macabre stories. I suspect the same may be true of his friends.

"But forgive me for my bad manners. You're clearly weary from your journey. I'm sure you'd rather rest then listen to my prattling."

"That is very kind," Sâr Dubnotal said, "but there will be time to rest when our mission is completed. Until then..."

"Actually," Gees interjected, "there's really nothing we can do until Miss Brandon arrives, is there? I think it would be an excellent idea to rest and gather your strength while there is a chance."

"Yes, I suppose you're right." Sâr Dubnotal closed his eyes, feeling suddenly weary.

"Have you prepared some rooms, Hoadley?" Hogarth asked.

"Indeed, Master," the manservant replied. "I suggest the young gentleman take the tapestry room, and the other should be most comfortable in the chapel."

"Very good," Hogarth said, steadying himself and making an expansive gesture with both arms. "This place, gentlemen, it is what remains of a grand palace for the archbishops of Canterbury. The old chapel is the most comfortable room, and has an excellent tub if you want to soak your wounded arm. That is, if you don't mind the fact that the tub was once a marble crypt. Though now that I think on it, I wonder if your wounds are more of the body or of the soul. You strike me as a man oppressed by a heavy burden of the spirit."

"Perhaps so," Dubnotal said. "I do not feel myself, and the problem is greater than mere physical exhaustion can account for. I think I should accept your kind offer."

"In that case," Hogarth said, "I think we should change the room arrangement. Mr. Green should take the chapel, and Mr. Dubnotal the tapestry room. I'm afraid this old place has a reputation for ghosts. Some guests, sleeping in the chapel, have found their dreams disturbed by the shade of a long dead abbot. The ghost of the tapestry room, on the other hand, is that of a beautiful young novice, whose presence is much more soothing."

"Your pardon, sir." Hoadley's voice sounded hesitant and full of awe.

Dubnotal let his body settle to the floor before opening his eyes.

"Yes, Hoadley?" he said.

"Dinner, sir…if you'd care to join us."

"Thank you, I think I shall."

"If you don't mind my asking, sir…"

"Yes?"

"Were you levitating?"

"I was," Dubnotal said, allowing himself a faint smile. "I find that freeing oneself from the bonds of the earth is very helpful in achieving the emptiness I need."

"I imagine it would be, at that," Hoadley said. "Very sensible, sir."

"Your master's suggestion was a good one," Dubnotal said. "I didn't encounter any restless spirit, but I found the room calming."

"I'm happy to hear it, sir."

Charles Hogarth was seated at the head of the great table in the dining hall. He rose, somewhat painfully, when Dubnotal entered. The Sâr's gaze took in the whole room, and he noticed that the drapes were drawn.

"Is it dark already?" he asked. "I must have been at my meditations for longer than I realized."

"It is quarter-past-eight," Hogarth replied. "I didn't feel right asking Hoadley to wait dinner any longer."

"Where is Mr. Green?"

"That has me somewhat concerned," Hogarth said. "He left several hours ago to pick up his secretary at the station, but I've heard nothing from him."

Dubnotal frowned, wondering if he should go to search for his ally.

"I think it best to dine before we take any action," Hogarth said, as if reading his thoughts. "If you share your story, I may be able to offer some assistance."

"Very well," Dubnotal said, sitting.

As Hoadley served them a splendid meal, he told Hogarth about two decades of pursuing von Meyer, on and off. He finished with the climactic battle in the catacombs of Bayonne, his pursuit of the villain to England, and how Gees had helped track him to Kent.

"Hmm…" Hogarth said. "I can't be sure, but I think I have a good idea where your sorcerer may have gone to ground. One of our local aristocrats, Sir Cecil Pembury, fancies himself an adept of the dark arts. He's always going about dressed all in black, and saying portentous things. I don't think he's one of Spode's lot, but he's certainly sympathetic. Likes to go on about how Herr Hitler is our natural ally against Bolshevism."

"If that's who von Meyer is taking refuge with, he's come down in the world," Dubnotal said. "Where does this Pembury live?"

"Lympne Castle. I can take you there tomorrow."

"Not tonight?"

"It would be a difficult journey without Mr. Green's motorcar. All I have to offer are several horses."

At that moment, the sound of a powerful engine came from courtyard. A moment later, a grim-looking Gees came striding into the dining hall.

"She wasn't there," he said. "Miss Brandon wasn't on the train."

"Perhaps she mistakenly got off at an earlier stop," Hogarth said.

"I thought of that. I've spent the evening checking every stop half-way back to London. There's no trace of her."

"Then our enemies have taken her," Sâr Dubnotal said.

"Why do you say that?" Gees demanded.

"It is an intuition, but my intuitions are generally correct."

"Do you have any way to find them, without your phurba?" Gees asked, his shoulders slumping.

"Actually, Sâr Dubnotal and I were just discussing that." Hogarth rose and hobbled over to his case of odd trophies. He unlocked it and removed an ancient and massive iron key. "With any luck, we not only know where Miss Brandon may be, we even have a way in."

"I think this is it," Gees whispered.

Dubnotal stared intensely at his companion, but only had the impression of a black silhouette hunched in front of a black hillside in a black wood. The night was wonderfully clear, but he found that a crescent moon and a sky full of brilliant stars did next to nothing to help him find his way. Fortunately, Gees seemed to have a slightly easier time of it.

"This feels like it must be the door," Gees said, "only I can't find the blasted keyhole. We'll have to risk using a light. Do you have any matches?"

"I believe I can do better than that," Dubnotal replied.

He held his hand out, palm up and slightly cupped, then murmured a chant in Sanskrit. A ball of faint blue flame sparked to life an inch above his skin. In its glow he could see that Gees had uncovered a round iron door set into the side of a hill and covered with heavy undergrowth. Gees stared at the phantom flames for a moment before shaking his head and returning to his task.

"Aha!" He said in a low voice. Raising the large iron key Hogarth had given them, he inserted it in a hidden slot. The key turned slowly and made a loud click. Gees pressed the door and it swung inward. He looked at Dubnotal, drew a deep breath, and climbed into the passage. Dubnotal followed close behind, keeping his spectral light blazing. Its illumination was only about what a cigarette lighter would have given them, but they were glad of it.

For the first dozen feet the passage was so tight they almost had to crawl. After that, it broadened to roughly six feet high by six wide. They paused for a moment and Gees took out a revolver that Hogarth had given him. He studied the weapon for a moment, then smiled at Dubnotal.

"Do you suppose our host has a story to go with this pistol that matches the one he told us about the key?"

"Perhaps we should ask him later," Dubnotal replied.

"Perhaps I'll ask you how you do that, as well." Gees nodded at the flame. "It's an awfully handy trick. Why don't you go first, and I'll cover you?"

Dubnotal took the lead and the two pressed forward silently. Their progress was slow, and he found his mind wandering a bit. Hogarth had indeed given them quite a story to go with the key. It involved this long-forgotten secret entrance, a young woman held captive, a heroic vicar, and a living scarecrow. Dubnotal might have called the man a romantic, but the tunnel showed that his story was at least partly true. Now they found themselves playing the parts of the young lover and the vicar of Dymchurch, though they couldn't be sure the young woman they hoped to rescue was actually here.

The passage ended in a landing large enough for the two men to stand upright. A heavy metal door, with a large ring set into it, pulled open easily, admitting them into a dark cellar.

"Looks like no one's been down here in years," Gees said, indicating an undisturbed layer of dust on the floor. Dubnotal nodded and pushed the door back into place. It blended almost perfectly with the rest of the stonework.

"I was hoping we might find Miss Brandon down here," he muttered.

"Did you expect to find her locked in a dungeon cell?" Gees asked. "That would be a little cliché, even for someone like von Meyer." Dubnotal could hear fear underneath the man's banter.

"In my experience, it's a mistake to underestimate how cliché people like this can be," Dubnotal said.

The two headed up the stairs to find a heavy oaken door in a bad state of repair. Pistol at the ready in his right hand, Gees gently threw the latch, and gave the door a gentle shove. It creaked loudly as it moved, and he grabbed it to keep it from making any more noise.

"I don't suppose you have a lubrication spell in your bag of tricks, do you?" he asked.

Sâr Dubnotal shook his head.

"Then, I suppose we'll have to just take our chances." Wincing at the noise, he pushed the door enough that he could slip it through the opening. Dubnotal followed a moment later, to find himself in a sitting room lined with the portraits of many generations of Pemburys. The house, as nearly as Dubnotal could see, was dark. Despite the stillness, he had a persistent sensation of being watched, though even his mystically attuned senses could not pin the feeling down.

A sound came to them, borne on the perfect stillness of the house. It was a woman's voice but with no words—

perhaps a gasp or a whisper. Dubnotal felt the prickling of instinctive fear skitter up his spine and neck.

"Eve Madeline," Gees whispered. Before Dubnotal could say anything, the young man was on the move, pistol at the ready. Dubnotal followed silently, his anxiety growing with every step.

"Green!" he whispered as loudly as he dared. "Don't rush in like a fool!" But the sound came again and Gees pressed on as if he hadn't heard a word. They moved through a hallway, which Dubnotal judged to be in the east wing of the castle. A left turn brought them into what looked like a darkened ballroom. There, on a divan, illuminated by a single candle on a side table, lay a pale form.

"Green!" Dubnotal hissed, but the young man was already moving to the center of the room. He followed, his eyes trying to pierce the shadows that surrounded them. As he moved closer, he closed his hand, extinguishing the blue flame. If this was a trap, he didn't want to do anything that made him an even easier target.

As they reached the divan, the electric lights snapped on, revealing five armed men. The lights were fairly dim but Dubnotal found himself dazzled just the same.

As his vision cleared, he saw that three of the men appeared to be servants—the sort of servants who are useful when heads need to be cracked and threats needed to be made. All of them held automatic pistols, and looked very familiar with their use. The fourth, a short, corpulent young man who dressed all in black and fit Hogarth's description of Sir Cecil Pembury, also carried a pistol. The fifth, von Meyer, shocked him. When he had seen the sorcerer a week ago, he had been a big, powerful man, seemingly in the prime of life. Now, von Meyer look to be at least eighty. His hair had gone white and his body had shriveled. He sat in a wheelchair with his right arm hanging useless. His left trembled with palsy as it caressed the large book in his lap.

"Don't try anything," Sir Cecil said. "My lads will fill you both with lead before you can move."

Dubnotal froze in place. Gees stood slowly, hands raised and pistol hanging loose in his grasp.

"Drop that!" Sir Cecil said.

Gees obliged and the revolver hit the carpet with a soft thump.

"Oswald, get his gun," the aristocrat commanded.

One of the servants started forward but stopped when von Meyer spoke.

"No. I have been greatly weakened by my struggle with Sâr Dubnotal and his allies, but I still have some power. Miss Brandon, stand up!"

The young woman rose, blue eyes wide.

"Bring your employer's revolver to me," he said.

Without hesitation, or a trace of emotion on her face, Eve Madeline Brandon picked up the weapon and walked over to stand next to the German sorcerer.

"Miss Brandon," Gees said. "Snap out of it. Don't let him control you."

"Useless, Mr. Green," von Meyer said. "It is still child's play for me to control a lesser mind; certainly that of a girl."

"You have us, von Meyer," Dubnotal said. "I'm surprised you haven't already told your lackeys to shoot us."

"Unfortunately, I need you," von Meyer replied. "You and your thrice-damned friends have broken me, body and spirit. I still possess the grimoire of Nathaire, but lack the strength to cast anything more than the most elementary spells. That is unfortunate, because my weakness has signaled the Unnameable that our agreement is at an end. Now she comes for me, and the suffering that I have caused will be as nothing compared to what I will endure in her embrace."

"Do you expect sympathy from me?" Dubnotal said. "Why should I care one iota what kind of Hell you have consigned your black soul to. Knowing what you have done to so many innocents, I rejoice at the thought of you suffering eternal torment."

"Pitiless bastard," von Meyer said. "You pretend to be so righteous! But I know your kind! You're full of spite and venom!"

"Shoot me then!" Dubnotal replied. "I am not afraid of the next world or what I shall find there."

"I'll oblige most happily," Sir Cecil said.

"No, you imbecile," von Meyer shouted. "How is he going to help me if you shoot him?"

"I won't help you under any circumstances," Dubnotal said.

"Just a minute," Gees said. "Let's hear him out. He may be a vile, disgusting, repellent toad of a man, but if he has a plan to resolve this without anyone getting shot, I'd like to hear it."

Von Meyer glowered at Gees for a moment before speaking.

"Your mind has been befuddled for several days, has it not, Dubnotal? That is a spell of my own making. However, you still retain your considerable occult power. That, combined with a ritual gleaned from this grimoire, shall save me from the Nameless One. This spell shall transfer my consciousness into your body, and yours into mine. When the goddess arrives to carry me into her realm, body and soul, it shall be the body of von Meyer, but the soul of Sâr Dubnotal."

"That's insane," Gees said. "Even if you can do this, do you really imagine you can fool the goddess of the Azaleans with that kind of cheap trick?"

"Perhaps not," von Meyer said, "but as it is the only option open to me, I must hope for the best."

"I will not help you," Dubnotal said.

"I think you will," von Meyer replied. "Otherwise my men shall be forced to do some very unpleasant things to Miss Brandon and Mr. Green."

Before Sâr Dubnotal could reply, Miss Brandon took two quick steps to her right and placed the barrel of Gees' revolver on Sir Cecil's back.

"Drop your gun," she said.

Cecil complied. "I thought she was under your control," he said.

"She was!" von Meyer said. "She is! Miss Brandon, drop that pistol and come back here. You cannot resist my will. I command you to drop the pistol."

Dubnotal saw Miss Brandon close her eyes and silently mouth words he could not make out, but the revolver never wavered. Looking astonished, von Meyer fell silent. Miss Brandon took a deep breath and opened her eyes again.

"Tell your men to drop their weapons," she said.

"N-now, see here, young woman—"

"Sir Cecil," she interrupted, "if I pull the trigger, the bullet will blast through your spine and most likely lodge in your liver. It will make for a rather unpleasant death."

Dubnotal thought he heard a bit of a tremor in her voice—not surprising—but he was certain she wasn't bluffing. Apparently, Sir Cecil came to the same conclusion.

"Drop your weapons," he commanded.

The men did as they were told. While Gees gathered up the pistols, Sâr Dubnotal snatched the grimoire from von Meyer's hand.

"No!" the sorcerer screamed. "It is my last hope."

"Then, for you, hope is gone," Dubnotal said. He held the grimoire over the candle until its pages burst into flame.

"Remarkable," Charles Hogarth said over dinner that evening. "But, Miss Brandon, weakened as you were, I don't understand how you were able to resist von Meyer's control."

"I wouldn't have been able, if Sâr Dubnotal hadn't done the same thing to me," she replied. "After that experience, I found a method for resisting mental domination in one of Mr. Green's books. It suggested focusing on something memorable and nonsensical with all your might."

"Memorable?"

"And nonsensical. I decided to recite *Cottleston Pie* over and over to myself."

That drew a peal of appreciative laughter from Hogarth.

"Saved by a poem from Winnie the Pooh!" he said. "I gather my neighbor, Sir Cecil, is enjoying the hospitality of the local police, but what became of von Meyer?"

"If you gentlemen will excuse me," Miss Brandon said, rising. "I think I'll take a breath of fresh air and leave you to your discussion.

The men stood as she left the room."

"Von Meyer is dead," Gees said. "With his book destroyed, he was consumed by his fear of the Unnamable. He begged us to kill him—Miss Brandon finally gave him a pistol with a single bullet."

"A mercy he did not deserve," Dubnotal said.

"She didn't do it because he deserved mercy," Gees said. "She did it because...well, because she's Eve Madeline Brandon. It wasn't an easy thing for her, either."

"I imagine not," Hogarth said. "Perhaps you should check on her."

"I think I shall," Gees said rising. "Thank you gentlemen."

"He's a good man, but a bit of a fool," Dubnotal said when Gees was gone.

"I don't know," Hogarth replied, smiling. "For my money, he's only a fool if he doesn't marry that girl."

Stuart Shiffman's tale takes Sâr Dubnotal right into the swinging 60s and brings together the Great Psychagogue with both Craig Rice's and Mark Phillips' Malones for this amusing supernatural yarn...

Stuart Shiffman: *True Believers*

Shangri-La, 1967

There was a large white room relieved by red and yellow terracotta tiles and a beneficial breeze from the lattice-framed window, the only sound being that of the birds singing outside.

"If Mr. Conway says that there is a guest for me, young Wang, then I must surely receive him."

Sâr Dubnotal rose in a smooth movement from his seat on a thin mat. The acolyte nodded and gestured for a man in the shadows to come forward.

"This is the pilgrim Simon Ark, Sâr, who has come to the Shangri-La in search of you."

The stranger stepped into the bright Himalayan light. He was a large man with his head shaved bald, dressed in what looked like Scandinavian woolen and flannel skiing clothes and stout leather climbing boots. He was heavy-set and appeared vigorous and youthful, but, on closer study, his face was revealed to be covered in a crackle-finish of fine wrinkles. He might pass for an active man of 75. *But then*, Dubnotal thought, *I appear to be a man in his forties...*

The direction of the breeze changed and brought the scent of tuberose to him. When he had first come to Shangri-La, Dubnotal had been told by Father Perrault that in China it was called the "smell of moonlight."

"Welcome, Brother Simon."

Simon Ark came and took the hands that the Sâr held out to him in greeting.

"I have heard of you as the Coptic priest who intervenes in matters of possible occult peril," said Dubnotal. "Is it true what is said of you: Are you really almost two thousand years old, brother? I presume that you have a metaphysical puzzle that requires my aid."

He sent Wang off for tea and led his guest to lacquered table and chairs.

"Thank you, brother," replied the newcomer. "It is true that I am the one about whom such things are murmured; I make no such claims for myself. You know yourself how such legends accrue over time."

"You have obviously had plenty of time then. What do you wish of me?" asked Dubnotal.

"I have come to take you to the United States where the grand-daughter of your acolyte, the medium Annunciata Gianetti, is in great spiritual danger." Ark's eyes held a look of great age and expectation.

"Annunciata had a child...? So much for my Visualization of the All..."

"No doubt, you were contemplating in the other direction, worthy colleague. Yes, she married your assistant Rudolph Arcati after you left to retire to Shangri-la. Rudolph was captured by the Gestapo during the occupation of France and Annunciata, now Madame Arcati, escaped to England with their son to work for the Diogenes Club. Her son, Alphonse, joined the British Security Coordination and the Special Operations Executive training agents in Canada at Camp X, where his daughter Josette was born in 1948."

"If this young person, a descendent of my dear Annunciata, is in danger, I have an obligation to leave my Visualization of the Cosmic All. Tell me more, brother."

The acolyte returned with two rough ceramic cups of aromatic tea.

"Josette Arcati is currently a university student in Chicago in the United States," said Simon Ark. "She has been pulled into the orbit of a new cult there, led by a young and charismatic leader. Many young people in America have become seekers of new spiritual paths, disillusioned by the crass materialism and hypocrisy of their elders, but there are many snares for the unwary and this one is a path to darkness."

"Can't you help her, Master Simon? I have not left this sanctuary in a very long time."

"I would face this myself," said Simon Ark, "but I have a prior obligation of my own. It will take me to Collinwood Manor, which seems to be located over a Hellmouth... I must do something about it. Alas, I must leave the Josette Arcati affair to the Great Psychagogue himself to solve."

"My last visit to America was before I came to Shangri-La," said Dubnotal. "My former contacts there, like Prince Abduel Omar, known as Semi-Dual, are surely long gone. Can you make suggestions for new allies?"

"Ah, I remember Semi-Dual... There are some modern white magicians in New York's Greenwich Village that would be of immeasurable aid to you and might point you in the right direction in Chicago." Ark reached into his pocket and took out a white pasteboard business card, which he handed to Sâr Dubnotal. "You will probably need this too."

Sâr Dubnotal looked at the face of the card: *John J. Malone, Attorney at Law. Chicago, Illinois*. This did not sound like a master of white magic or psychic sciences.

Chicago, 1967

The inside of Joe the Angel's City Hall bar was a mob scene, shoulder to shoulder from the narrow entrance back to the 1890s mahogany bar and the booths. The sounds of clinking glasses, beer taps, and laughing patrons filled the space. The fog of cigarette smoke made visibility near impossible, but the stranger in the white suit and turban managed to follow the traces of cigar fumes back to a booth occupied by two men, an attractive blonde and a brunette.

"I think that I finally got this figured out, Pop!" said the younger man, Kenneth J. Malone, a handsome brown-haired fellow in his early twenties. He wore a tweed sport coat over chinos and a button-down madras shirt. "There is always a perceived menace in every period: In 1914, it was the Boche; in the 1930, it was the Nazis. Now it's the Commies with an atomic sword of Damocles over all of us. No wonder a lot of my generation are looking for new answers anywhere they can!"

"Oh, Kenny, I think that you're still your father's boy, operating on hunches and instinct," said the brunette. Maggie Cassidy was his father's long-suffering secretary and his own surrogate mother. She wore a powder blue cocktail suit with a pillbox hat and white gloves, the Jackie Kennedy "tasteful lady" ensemble now a few years past its sell-by date. "We're just so proud of you, passing the Illinois Bar and getting accepted to the FBI Academy!"

"Yes, that's my boy!" agreed the short, dark-haired but graying man hoisting his whisky glass high. His red face was blazing with enthusiasm and alcohol. He was Chicago's legal eagle, John J. Malone, with the map of Ireland on his face, and the vest of his dark suit generously covered with cigar ash. He was ballyhooed as Chicago's noisiest and most noted criminal lawyer.

"If only my pal Danny von Flanagan were here!"

"He's off fighting crime," said Kenny, "that's what cops like Captain von Flanagan do, Dad. They stand between the darkness and the light."

Malone blessed that night that he had staggered to his door long after midnight to find one of his former chorus girl friends clutching the hand of a five-year-old. He'd looked into that boy's face and saw his own and that of his parents. The woman had disappeared with a clipped mutter of "He's yours now" and he'd never remembered which of his former intimate lights of love she had been, Dolly Dove (known as "the mouse who built a better man-trap") or Dawn O'Day, or some other statuesque blonde candidate. There had been many such fitting the profile over the years.

It hadn't mattered to Kenny or to Maggie Cassidy when she stepped in to help raise the child. In many ways, Maggie was Kenny's real mother. And that is only one of the many, many, fine reasons why John J. and she were going to be married after so many years.

"This is a wonderful night," yelled the blonde half-pint, Kenny's law school friend Lily Thrown. She was dressed up for the celebration with the Malones since she had no family of her own in town. She wore an attractive black silk blazer over a red dress that was very flattering to her figure and set off her peaches and cream complexion.

"I am so proud, Kenneth! I could just eat you up!" she whispered in his ear.

She'd also passed the Illinois Bar and was going to work as counsel for a religious organization in Chicago. Lily hadn't mentioned which, but the Malones had jumped to the conclusion that it was the Catholic archdiocese.

They would find out later that their conclusion was not accurate.

The stranger was passing through the crush at the bar without effort, the rowdier clients reflexively opening a path before him. He was dressed all in white, like a pair of linen p.j.'s, with his feet in sandals, and a large pugaree-style turban on his head. He caught a barman's attention, Joe the Angel himself, and ordered a drink, a cranberry juice. His eyes watched the booth.

"Are you sure about that, mister? If you get jostled, it'll make a heck of a mess on your nice white clothes," asked Joe the Angel.

"That is not going to be a problem, Giuseppe de Angelo."

The black and white Motorola television over the barman's shoulder showed the face of UBS news anchorman Howard Beale in his coverage of today's space spectacular. Astronauts Anthony Nelson and Maurice Minnifield would in turn be conducting a "space walk," which Beale and veteran girl reporter Jane Arden explained in NASA-speak as an "extra-vehicular activity," or EVA, from their Apollo space capsule.

No one in the joint seemed to be paying attention.

Sâr Dubnotal made his way to the Malone family's booth, his glass of cranberry juice held in his long ascetic fingers, with nary a drop spilled. He had a perfect bump of direction. A path opened effortlessly before him.

"To the law faculty of Compass University," called the senior Malone in salute, and all drank. Suddenly he noticed the man in white. "Oh, can I help you, mister? Are you lost?"

"No, Mr. Malone—you are the one found." The man squatted down on his heels beside the table and explained his problem and search for his "grand-daughter" Josette Arcati. "You may call me the Doctor, or El Tebib, or Sâr Dubnotal," he concluded.

"*Czar*? Does this mean that you are emperor of all the Russias?" said John J. Malone giggling; he had taken more than a few drinks.

"No, it is an ancient Sumerian title," replied Dubnotal.

The younger Malone muttered something into his glass about one swallow not making a Sumer.

"Gosh, you need a detective, not me, Mr. Doob-nottle. There's plenty of detective agencies in Chicago, like Continental or Nathan Heller's A-1, if you like a smaller organization."

Sâr Dubnotal corrected his name and title again for Malone's benefit. While he was explaining his need for just the type of legal assistance typified by Malone, Lily Thrown excused herself and frantically pleaded an incipient headache and an early morning at her new position.

"This is weird… Please don't go yet, Lil," pleaded the younger Malone. He looked stricken and reached for her hand to halt her progress. She avoided his clutching fingers but snatching her own back.

"No! I'll call you really soon, Ken, I promise you! Bye, folks, and thanks for everything!" was her reply as she blew him an airborne final kiss and disappeared into the crush.

Sâr Dubnotal looked back over his shoulder at her receding form. A lovely young woman, but there was something about her aura that he did not like. He'd seen auras like it before and it was seldom a good sign. That was how he and Judex had met at Notre-Dame in the course of the gargoyle adventure. The Malones exhibited strong bright auras from a lighter side of the spectrum, which greatly encouraged him.

He arranged with the attorney to meet the next day at his hotel, the classic Palmer House.

The Malones arrived early the next day with a black overcoat, red cardigan and penny-loafer moccasins for their client.

"You have to stop this pajama game, sir. You make us feel cold just looking at you."

The Sâr accepted them with appreciation for their feelings.

John J. Malone drove them away from the hotel in his late fifties Ford Fairlane (restrained in aquamarine and white, with modest chrome-edged fins) heading to Compass University in order to question Josette's roommate, Lacey Raintree. Kenny had the advantage of knowing all of these young people, had even dated Lacey at one point, and would serve as guide. On the way, John J. Malone discoursed on the subject of historic crime figures of Old Chicago.

"There's been a lot of change from the days of Mr. Dooley's Chicago and the 1893 World's Columbian Exposition. Over there is the old garage that was the site of the massacre by the goons of 'Spats' Colombo under the orders of Little Bonaparte," he proudly pointed out to his guest. "Two musicians accidentally witnessed the hit and lit off on the lam to Florida, even disguised themselves as women in an all-girl band."

"Oh, dad," said Kenny, "that's just musicians for you." He wore a red windbreaker over a black turtleneck and black pants.

"It's all different now from the old days when I was a kid, when the town was dominated by gang bosses like Little Caesar and Scarface during the corrupt administration of Big Bill Thompson. It was all wide-open back then, full of public enemies free to have their way in plenty of speakeasies. At least Robbo and his Robbo Foundation gave a lot of cash to orphanages and other needy institutions until Reform came in and suppressed them."

"I see," said the Great Psychagogue, without really understanding the attorney's references.

"As a kid, I wanted to be a defense attorney. And eventually, I did become one."

"You bet, dad."

"Then the Crash and the Depression came and the town was still wide-open with a different cast of characters and a thick odor of desperation among the populace. Crime was the only industry that was thriving. The Big Boy had it organized until he came up against detective Tracy's investigative team."

"It must have been harrowing to grow up in such an environment, Mr. Malone," said the Sâr.

"It's better now. Mayor Daley has things under control. That's why the Democrats are having their convention here next year…"

Compass University, Chicago

After parking in the guest parking, Kenneth J. Malone led the trio across Compass U's quad towards the dorms, which took them past the Student Union building. He sighted a friend manning one of the rows of tables outside the Student Union.

"Hey, there's my buddy, Jeff. He was a good friend of Lacey and Josette too. We need to talk to him."

The attractive young man with long fair hair, dark eyebrows and a nascent beard and mustache was seated behind a table with petitions on clipboards in front of him. The table bore a sign reading *Stop the War*. He wore an embroidered shirt of white Indian cotton, well-worn bell-bottom denims and Keds sneakers. He looked like a surfer washed up in the Windy City. A large poster was plastered behind him for the University Film Society, illustrated in the San Francisco psychedelic style. In front of the table was a pretty young woman with waist-length carrot-red hair, clutching a tattered copy of *Siddhartha*, wearing a white peasant's blouse with Kelly green macramé vest and a matching mini-skirt.

"...I remember when I helped write the Port Huron Statement..." Jeff leaned in close across the table, making deeply meaningful eye contact with his subject.

"Oh, come off it, dude, you were only 15-years-old in 1962." The younger Malone was laughing at his friend while the young woman stalked off.

"Kenneth J. Malone," replied Jeff, "your timing is execrable as usual. How do you do that?"

"A special talent that I have as master of time and space. Gents, this poor example of today's radicalized youth is Jeff Lebowski of the Compass campus committee to stop the war. Jeff, this is my dad, and his client, Sâr Dubnotal." Hands were shaken enthusiastically. "We need some help. The Sâr's grand-daughter is Josette Arcati and she's gone missing."

"Ah," said the Great Psychagogue on taking Lebowski's hand, "don't worry about the carpet. Other things in your life will tie it all together." His Visualization was enhanced. This was obviously another case of coincidence and luck benefiting the Malones.

"What, what, that makes no sense at all! Oh no," replied Lebowski. "Look, I've been on this table all day and I'm starved. Let's go over to the deli and you can fill me up with hot dogs while I try to fill you in."

Malone led the foursome away into a storefront housing *Klaw's Best—Jewish Delicatessen*. Dubnotal was hit by a full sensory wave of steaming spiced meats, triggering a sense-memory of a visit to a charcuterie in Paris's *Pletzel*, the Yiddish name for the old 13th century Jewish quarter found in the Marais district.

Behind the register stood a darkly handsome teenage girl, with long black hair that was much curlier than she would have preferred, wearing a white bib apron over a man's white tuxedo shirt and a leotard, and a bored expression.

"Hi, Iris, where's the boss?" asked the lawyer.

"The sleeping prince is taking fifteen in the back. Can anyone else help you, counselor?"

"Always a good question. We'll see your father when he emerges. In the meantime, a round of kosher franks, Dr. Brown sodas and keep'em coming. And get a cool brew for me too, please."

"OK, remember you asked for him."

Iris turned away and yelled, "Dad! Get the celery tonic and get out here!"

A tall spare man in his forties came out, rolling out a flat of Dr. Brown's Cel-Ray soda cans on a hand-truck. He wore a black rayon skullcap on his graying hair, a white nylon short-sleeved shirt with a Black Watch clip-on bow-tie and gabardine trousers with wear at the knees.

He hauled the soda cans into a glass-fronted refrigerator and then turned to the senior Malone with a deep sigh.

"Oy, John J. Malone, I knew that you were coming but why do you have to afflict me today?"

"I wanted to introduce you to my friend here. Sâr, this is the occasional kabbalist, dream detective and master of cuisine, Maurice Klaw."

"A pleasure," said Dubnotal. "Did I hear correctly that Mr. Malone referred to you as a 'dream detective'?"

"Yes, I get it by way of my paternal grandfather, Moris Klaw, who according to family lore kept a musty curio shop near Wapping Old Stairs in London, filled with all sorts of broken statuary, old books, and assorted fauna, including an ancient parrot that guarded the door. It called out 'Moris

Klaw! Moris Klaw! The Devil's come for you!' whenever a customer entered. Crazy stuff like that which can't have been good for his business. He was a bit eccentric and claimed to be a master of Odic photography."

"What's that when it's at home?" asked the lawyer.

"It's as obsolete terminology as mesmerism now, with Rhine's modern studies in hypnotism and telepathy, but the theory of Odic force—the name is derived from the Nordic deity Odin—was developed by Baron Karl von Reichenbach," replied the Great Psychagogue, "in the mid-19th century. According to this theory, every human being has an unknown source of power that produces rays. These not only inhabit the body, but also radiate from it, so that a person is surrounded by a virtual field of this Odic force, as von Reichenbach called it. Odic photography is like a snapshot of the phenomena by a psychically sensitive person giving insights into the inner problems, what we might better call *clairvoyance*."

"That supposedly was Grandpa Klaw's talent that he used to help his 'clients'," Klaw sighed. "My parents got fed up with his nonsense and came to America in the early 'teens and my brother Stephen and I grew up here. You'd like my brother Stephen, Kenny. He became an FBI man and a member of their special 'Suicide Squad' in the thirties and forties."

"I'm impressed, Mr. Klaw—that had a reputation as a rough and tough elite unit."

"Did you have a vision of anything besides Mr. Malone's advent, Mr. Klaw?" asked Dubnotal.

"Yes, beware of the winged cephalopod and the pretty priestess—she is not what you expect. Watch for the malefic influence of the *mazikim*. After midnight, the powers of evil are exalted."

"Oh, that's oracular," quipped Jeff Lebowski. "What's a *mazikim*—and whatever happened to those hot dogs? Can I get a black cherry soda too?"

"*Mazikim* are demons, I am afraid. I'm sorry, kid, but I'm not Edgar Cayce. I leave the interpretation to others."

"The Talmud says there are 7,405,926 demons, or *mazikim*, in the world," said Iris. "That seems to be more than a bit excessive to me."

"Now, Mr. Lebowski," began John J. Malone in his cross-examination mode, standing over the young man. "Do you know anything about the whereabouts of Josette Arcati, or can you point us to the whereabouts of her roommate Lacey?"

"I know what happened to Lacey; she's changed her name to Lakota Rainflower to embrace her Sioux ethnic heritage. She started working as a secretary for Dr. Spektor and who knows where they've gone off to now."

"Do you know where Josette is, Mr. Lebowski? Can you help us pull it all together?" asked Dubnotal. "She may be in danger both physical and spiritual."

"I remember that Josette was getting into a weird spiritual head space; somebody she met put her on to some old cult called the Ordo Templi Occidentalis," said Lebowski, scratching his nascent beard.

Dubnotal was distressed at his answer. He knew the name and history of the Ordo Templi Occidentalis from its original British roots in the Golden Dawn to its twisted destinies. It went back to the Arcane Order of the Black Sun, the creation of the man then known as Aloysius Trelawney, later Rowley Thorne, whose later Californian disciples raised the Temple of the Dark Truth in Pasadena and Berkeley in the 1940s. Even ignoring its embrace of the dark side, it was significant that it was used to funnel technical intelligence to the Axis.

"This is not good news, gentlemen," said the Sâr. "Mr. Malone, do you recall hearing about the Temple of the Dark Truth spy ring that was broken by the FBI during World War II?"

"My brother worked on that case," said Klaw. "Pretty dramatic case and high profile indictments."

"Sure I remember, they claimed an oath of fealty to the 'Lower Lord'," replied John J. Malone. "Just the usual run of California pop-diabolism. Before the G-men broke up the

309

racket, they are supposed to have conjured up a wolf demon out of thin air. Later they traced the cult's links to Los Angeles and that big-time rocket experimenter Hugo Chantrelle at CalTech."

"I've got a hunch that temple is where we'll find Josette," said Kenny. "Dude, do you know where their sanctuary is?"

"I know it. It's in a part of Chicago undergoing major urban renewal," replied Lebowski, "and currently is an urban wasteland—used to be a local picture palace, the old Metropolis theater."

Lebowski guided them on a fairly quick trip to the blasted heath where the old Chicagoan Theater was located. It stood alone on the street except for a soda fountain and an isolated barbershop. On one exterior wall of the theater, one could still barely make out the partially effaced remains of a large 1940s Chicago *Times* tip-line ad that advertized *Call Northside 777*. A dozen hard-ridden Harley motorcycles were parked in the empty lot next door.

They entered beneath the marquee, modernized in 1963 with new neon and aluminum structure, past a closed box-office and through the brass door into the lobby. The Great Psychagogue noticed the bronze dedication plaque immediately, showing that the 1931 theater building had been designed by the architect Ivo Shandor. The design was like a modern rendition of the Alhambra. He remembered Shandor very well, whose buildings remained ticking time-bombs of eldritch purpose.

Dubnotal moved deeper into the lobby and the Central Asian patterns of the carpet, followed by the two Malones and Lebowski. Kenny Malone became to softly sing W. S. Gilbert lyrics under his breath:

"*With cat-like tread,*
Upon our prey we steal;
In silence dread,
Our cautious way we feel."

310

They were not alone in the lobby although the press of silence made them feel that they were. There were a half-dozen young men and women dressed in red boiler suits cleaning the lobby with broom and dustpan, brush, wash-cloths and carpet sweepers. They made no conversation and no eye contact.

"What the heck," whispered Lebowski, "these dudes have got to be stoned and they missed it."

"No," replied Dubnotal, "they are zombies. Not the undead, but sapped of their willpower."

"I don't like this," quipped John J. Malone. "For zombies, I should have had another beer and charge more per hour."

"Let's check the offices and perhaps we can find out some more there," advised Dubnotal.

They passed beyond the refreshments stand and found the old theater's management suite. The brass inlaid door held a signed reading *Private* below a roundel enclosing what looked like an Art Deco squid with cherub wings. The door was unlocked and they pushed in.

The outer office looked like a place of work, with a reception counter and old wooden desk. A couple of framed film posters decorated the walls. What struck Dubnotal was the obviously recently purchased new technology: Mandarin red IBM Selectric typewriters and Swingline staplers, a Varityper, Gestetner Stencil Duplicator and GesteFax Electronic Scanner. This equipment allowed cheap and readable copies to be made and distributed quickly. Virtually every school, office and union hall had a mimeograph in the back room, usually surrounded by reams of paper and the unmistakable odor of fresh solvent.

Dubnotal went immediately to see the large glass-fronted oak library cases and an antique text strapped down on a map table. His heart sank. It looked to be bound in an organic material of dubious origin.

"Look here, gentlemen," he said, "this is a private research library of iniquity." The others rushed over to him.

"These are the magical prescriptions of Nephren-Ka, probably a later Gnostic creation. Here are the *Egyptian Secrets of Albertus Magnus* and *The Ruthvenian*, the so-called 'vampire's bible'; the horrid *Cultes des Goules*, attributed to the Comte d'Erlette. Only a handful of copies are in existence, one of which is locked and sealed in the restricted section of the Vatican library. I also see the more 'mundane' works of Montague Summers on magic, and Reverend Baring-Gould on werewolves, as well as the modern oeuvre by Sidney Redlitch, *Magic in Mexico* and *The Witches of New York*." He held up a smaller book with limp violet pages. "This slim, pale purple volume is the Psychical Society's report on the horrific 'Honeysuckle Cottage' and 'Bludleigh Court' manifestations. The presence alongside them of Dr. Rhine's studies is more surprising."

That was when they heard the Mighty Wurlitzer open up in the Auditorium and they all experienced a *frisson* of awful anticipation.

Dubnotal and the younger members of the party left via a doorway to the auditorium and viewed a stage set with memories of Nuremberg rallies in mind. Peeking through the curtains, they saw long black and red banners and an audience filled dressed in boiler suits. In the center of the stage stood initiates in crimson robes and pointed hoods covering their faces, like Klu Klux Klanners whose laundry whites would have been mixed with a red sweater. They wore the heavy hob-nailed boots of bikers and chanted a round in base voices which was heard as *Huggum squamish, nictzin dyalhis, squamish huggum.*

The initiates framed an altar bearing a nude female figure, sedated, with long brunette hair crowned with foxglove and nasturtium blossoms, behind which was a huge transparent column of space-age plastic, containing an alien creature whose form shifted, sometimes appearing to the human mind as related to the cephalopods and sometimes reptiles or humanoids.

"Oh, Godhead," whispered the Great Psychagogue, "It's an Arisian!" The alien was bounded in its prison by what he recognized as an electrical pentacle, whose distinctive blue glow suffused the contents. Its vacuum tubes had been updated to transistor and solid-state technology. "How foul—who would bind a beneficent being like an Arisian?"

Dubnotal knew from the ancient knowledge that he had studied that the Arisians were benevolent to human and other species fighting to build civilizations of law and peace. Their enemies had destroyed Atlantis and Lemuria, and here one was bound and being drained of psi power. Was this how the cultists had taken psychic control of their followers? Was this what was planned for Josette Arcati?

The focus was now on a shorter figure, the officiating adept in long crimson velvet robes and wearing a golden mask evoking the so-called Mask of Agamemnon found by Schliemann at Mycenae in 1876. However, this mask, instead of the bearded face of Agamemnon, showed the bullet-head and hatchet nose face of Rowley Thorne. Around its neck was an amulet of the Seal of Cagliostro, depicting a serpent with an apple in its mouth, impaled with an arrow. This officiant seemed to sense Sâr Dubnotal and companions, and turned violently to where they peeked through the curtain. It turned towards them and removed its mask.

"Lily, is that you?" said Kenny as he stepped through the curtain, with his father and Jeff Lebowski following. That was his last word. They were all frozen in place with a flick of her hand. It was all that the Great Psychagogue could do to slip mental shields around the minds of his associates and put their consciousnesses to sleep.

Lily Thrown stamped her feet, causing her floor-length scarlet robe to open in the front to reveal her more prosaic white tennis dress and PF Flyers training shoes on her feet.

"Kenny, what are you doing here? You interlopers dare intrude during my ritual? I am Lilia Destrue Pedibus Thorne, the Daughter of Rowley Thorne, the Beast himself! This cult that my father founded in an odd moment is all mine now. My father wanted to obtain power by entering into compacts with outside entities, but I find that psionic power gives me all that I need..." Her purple aura blazed and obscured her figure temporarily. "What we are witnessing is a shift of total consciousness in America, the dawning of a new Age!"

"Miss Thorne, you obviously are an *esper* of startlingly high functionality," said Dubnotal. "Today, you intend to drain Josette Arcati of her psychic power, inherited from her grandmother Annunciata. I had already suspected that you were attracted to Kenny Malone's psychic potential as well, but I have shielded him from you. I cannot allow you to have further use of this psionic energy. I am reliably informed that a man named John Thunstone once defeated Rowley Thorne. What one man can do, another can emulate..."

"You should not be able to do this," cried Lily Thorne, seeing the Sâr free himself from her spell.

She extended her left arm out of her robe, displaying a gold identity bracelet with a sinister black lens.

"I have drained the psychic power of hundreds, as well as that of my alien captive. If that power cannot hold you, perhaps this will." She stamped her sneaker-clad foot in frustration and motioned her initiates to step forward.

"Ah, but I am the Napoleon of the Intangible, the Conqueror of the Invisible, my dear..." replied the Sâr, raising his hands.

"This is the Chicago Police Department," suddenly called an authoritative voice via megaphone, interrupting their exchange. "You are all under arrest for violations of statutes prohibiting witchcraft, devil worship, and involuntary psychic servitude. Please let yourselves be taken into custody and no one will be harmed."

Homicide cop Daniel von Flanagan strode down the center aisle, accompanied by several dozen of Chicago's Finest dressed in white helmets and riot gear. Several reached the stage and removed bicycle chains and switchblades from the initiates.

"The wheel turns, does it not, Miss Thorne? But who alerted the police?" asked Dubnotal

While two officers secured her wrists in the cold iron of handcuffs, after removing her power bracelet, John J. Malone picked himself off the floor and brushed himself off as much as possible.

"Sorry I hadn't mentioned it before, but I called before leaving the theater office. I thought that we would need back-up."

Kenny and Lebowski freed Josette from the altar and wrapped the altar cloth around her.

"My dear," said Dubnotal to her, "your grandmother, Annunciata, was very dear to me. I would be proud if you re-garded me as a grandparent."

Josette grabbed him and hugged him tightly and began to weep softly.

A husky senior plainclothes officer in a trench-coat over a black suit walked over and was introduced by Captain von Flanagan:

"This is Lieutenant Samms of the Chicago P.D. secret division, Special Unit 2, which handles all cases involving monsters, alien and domestic. He'll take custody of the, uh, extraterrestrial and make sure that it gets its one phone call."

Samms was a big man with red hair. On his right hand, Dubnotal saw a bright green malachite ring and a Navajo sil-ver bracelet with a huge bright opalescent moonstone rather than the usual turquoise—items of power and protection. The aura was beneficial and his Visualization was able to perceive that matters were in good hands.

"Glad to meet you, Sâr. Looks like the Seventh Cavalry was in time."

Samms then faced the being in the Lucite cylinder.

"Sorry about any delay, sir or madam, but we do have procedure to observe before we can release you back to outer space. In the meanwhile, we do have a Dirac communicator if you'd like to send a message for a ride home."

SÂR DUBNOTAL

«Faut psychologue! charlatan!» rugit Sâr Dubnotal. «Je vais donc te démasquer enfin!»

Credits

Clash of the Titans

Co-Starring:	Created by:
Captain Nemo	Jules Verne
Moby Dick	Herman Melville
Cthulhu	H.P. Lovecraft

The Treasure of the Ubasti

Co-Starring:	Created by:
Banks	Jules Verne
Henry Jones	George Lucas & Steven Spielberg
Captain Hood	Jules Verne
Mowgli	Rudyard Kipling
Cult of Ubasti	Harry Earnshaw & BarryBarringer
Behemoth	Jules Verne
Bandar-Log	Rudyard Kipling
Cold Lair	Rudyard Kipling
Helmet of Nabu	Gardner Fox & Howard Sherman

The Swine of Gerasene

Co-Starring:	Created by:
John Silence	Algernon Blackwood
Thomas Carnacki	William Hope Hodgson
Count Magnus	M.R. James
Magnus Greel	Robert Homes
The Hog	William Hope Hodgson
Swine Things	William Hope Hodgson
Sheila Crerar	Ella Scrymour
Aylmer Vance	Alice & Claude Askew
Tong of the Black Scorpion	Robert Holmes

Judge Pursuivant	Manly Wade Wellman
Dr. Omega	Arnould Galopin
House on the Borderland	William Hope Hodgson
Blood of Belshazzar	Robert E. Howard
Kor	H. Rider Haggard
The Faltine	Stan Lee & Steve Ditko

The Gargoyles of Notre-Dame

Co-Starring:	**Created by:**
Judex	A. Bernède & L. Feuillade
Doktor Von Meyer	Seabury Quinn
Gargoyles	Clark Ashton Smith
Blaise Reynard	Clark Ashton Smith
Mitra	Robert E. Howard
Viritrilbia	C. S. Lewis

The Hounds of Saint-Augustin

Co-Starring:	**Created by:**
Inspector Maigret	Georges Simenon
Jack Clayton/Korak	Edgar Rice Burroughs
Paul d'Arnot	Edgar Rice Burroughs
Griffin	H.G. Wells
Boroff	Barry Shipman & Franklin Ardeon
Drago	Earl Kenton & Jackson Barr
Colonel Bozzo-Corona	Paul Féval
Chantecoq	Arthur Bernède
Superconn Crystal	Earl Kenton & Jackson Barr
Marovania	Barry Shipman & Franklin Ardeon

What Rough Beast...

Co-Starring:	**Created by:**
Hugo Danner	Philip Wylie
Judex	A. Bernède & L. Feuillade

Doktor Von Meyer	Seabury Quinn
Colossus	Clark Ashton Smith
Ghouls	H.P. Lovecraft
Ape Demon	E. Hoffman Price
Tentacled Demon	Seabury Quinn
Abednego Danner	Philip Wylie
General Broulard	Humphrey Cobb
Nathare of Vyones	Clark Ashton Smith
Tom Shayne	Philip Wylie
Joiry	Catherine L. Moore

Slouching Towards Camulodunum

Co-Starring:	**Created by:**
Helen Vaughan	Arthur Machen
Becky Sharp	William Makepeace Thackeray
Clarke	Arthur Machen
Villiers	Arthur Machen
Jacques Courbé	Clarence A. "Tod" Robbins
Francis-Aytown	Bram Stoker
Randolph	Lloyd C. Douglas
Richard Upton Pickman	H.P. Lovecraft
Charles Delaware Tate	Dan Curtis, Sam Hall
	& Violet Welles
Pierre Rodin	Micah Harris
	based on Robert Bloch
Dr. Robert Matheson	Arthur Machen
Basil Hallward	Oscar Wilde
Dorian Gray	Oscar Wilde
Lord Henry Wotton	Oscar Wilde
Judge's House	Bram Stoker
Kadath	H.P. Lovecraft

A Tale of Two Souls

Co-Starring:	**Created by:**
Dr. Jekyll/Mr. Hyde	Robert L. Stevenson

Cenobite (Pinhead)	Clive Barker
Abraham Van Helsing	Bram Stoker
Witchblade	Marc Silvestri & Brain Haberlin
Helmet of Nabu	Gardner Fox & Howard Sherman
Resurrection Stone	J.K. Rowling
Fantômas	P. Souvestre & M. Allain
Irma Vep	Louis Feuillade
The Great Vampire	Louis Feuillade

The Evils Against Which We Strive

Co-Starring:	Created by:
The Shadow	Walter Gibson
Ligeia	Edgar Allan Poe
Nick	Roman Leary
Judge Pursuivant	Manly Wade Wellman

Ask Me A Riddle...

Co-Starring:	Created by:
Eve-Madeline Brandon	Jack Mann
Greegory George Gordon Green aka Gees	Jack Mann
Pierre d'Atois	E. Hoffman Price
Dr. Trowbridge	Seabury Quinn
Jules de Grandin	Seabury Quinn
Duc de Richleau	Dennis Wheatley
Doktor Von Meyer	Seabury Quinn
Sidi Abdurrahman	E. Hoffman Price
Bertie Wooster	P.G. Wodehouse
Jeeves	P.G. Wodehouse
Reginald Spode	P.G. Wodehouse
Charles Hogarth	Russell Thorndike
Hoadley	Russell Thorndike
Nathaire	Clark Ashton Smith
The Unnameable	Jack Mann
Dr. Syn/The Scarecrow	Russell Thorndike

Cecil Pembury	based on Russell Thorndike
The Azalians	Jack Mann
The Catacombs of Bayonne	E. Hoffman Price
Dullchester	Russell Thorndike
Old Palace of Wrotham	Russell Thorndike
Lympne Castle	Russell Thorndike

True Believers

Co-Starring:	**Created by:**
Simon Ark	Edward D. Hoch
Joe the Angel	Craig Rice
John J. Malone	Craig Rice
Maggie Cassidy	Craig Rice
Kenneth J. Malone	Randall Garrett
	& Lawrence M. Janifer
Jeff Lebowski	Joel & Ethan Coen
Maurice Klaw	based on Sax Rohmer
Lily Thorne (aka Thrown)	based on Manly Wade Wellman
Josette Arcati	based on Noel Coward
Arisian	E.E. Smith
Captain Von Flanagan	Craig Rice
Lieutenant Samms	based on E.E. Smith
Special Unit 2	Evan Katz
Robert Conway	James Hilton
Father Perrault	James Hilton
Madame Arcati	Noel Coward
Prince Abduel Omar	J. U. Giesy & J. B. Smith
Dolly Dove	Craig Rice
Howard Beale	Paddy Chayefsky
Major Anthony Nelson	Sidney Sheldon
Colonel Maurice Minnifield	Joshua Brand & John Falsey
Jane Arden	Monte Barrett & Frank Ellis
Continental Op	Dashiell Hammett
Nate Heller	Max Allan Collins
Judex	A. Bernède & L. Feuillade
"Spats" Colombo	Billy Wilder & I.A.L. Diamond

Little Bonaparte	Billy Wilder & I.A.L. Diamond
Little Caesar	W. R. Burnett
Scarface	Armitage Trail (Maurice Coons)
Robbo Foundation	David R. Schwartz
Dick Tracy	Chester Gould
Big Boy	Chester Gould
Lacey Raintree (Lakota Rainflower)	Donald F. Glut
Doctor Spektor	Donald F. Glut
Aloysius Trelawney	R. A. LaFevers
Rowley Thorne	Manly Wade Wellman
Hugo Chantrelle	Anthony Boucher
John Thunstone	Manly Wade Wellman
Ivo Shandor	Dan Ackroyd & Harold Ramis
Sidney Redlitch	John Van Druten
Comte d'Erlette	Robert Bloch
Shangri-la	James Hilton
Visualization of the Cosmic All	E.E. Smith
Diogenes Club	Sir Arthur Conan Doyle
Collinwood, Collinsport	Dan Curtis & Art Wallace
Hellmouth	Joss Whedon
The Ruthvenian	Donald F. Glut
Le Cultes des Goules	Robert Bloch
Honeysuckle Cottage / Bludleigh Court	P. G. Wodehouse
Call Northside 777	Jerome Cady
Dirac communicator	James Blish

SF & FANTASY

Adolphe Alhaiza. *Cybele*
Alphonse Allais. *The Adventures of Captain Cap*
Henri Allorge. *The Great Cataclysm*
Guy d'Armen. *Doc Ardan: The City of Gold and Lepers*
G.-J. Arnaud. *The Ice Company*
André Arnyvelde. *The Ark; The Mutilated Bacchus*
Charles Asselineau. *The Double Life*
Henri Austruy. *The Eupantophone; The Olotelepan; The Petitpaon Era*
Barillet-Lagargousse. *The Final War*
Cyprien Bérard. *The Vampire Lord Ruthwen*
S. Henry Berthoud. *Martyrs of Science*
Aloysius Bertrand. *Gaspard de la Nuit*
Richard Bessière. *The Gardens of the Apocalypse; The Masters of Silence*
Chevalier de Béthune. *The World of Mercury*
Albert Bleunard. *Ever Smaller*
Félix Bodin. *The Novel of the Future*
Louis Boussenard. *Monsieur Synthesis*
Alphonse Brown. *City of Glass; The Conquest of the Air*
Émile Calvet. *In a Thousand Years*
André Caroff. *The Terror of Madame Atomos; Miss Atomos; The Return of Madame Atomos; The Mistake of Madame Atomos; The Monsters of Madame Atomos; The Revenge of Madame Atomos; The Resurrection of Madame Atomos; The Mark of Madame Atomos; The Spheres of Madame Atomos; The Wrath of Madame Atomos* (w/M. & Sylvie Stéphan)
Félicien Champsaur. *The Human Arrow; Ouha, King of the Apes; Pharaoh's Wife; Homo-Deus; Nora, The Ape-Woman*
Didier de Chousy. *Ignis*
Jules Clarétie. *Obsession*
Michel Corday. *The Eternal Flame*
André Couvreur. *The Necessary Evil*; *Caresco, Superman; The Exploits of Professor Tornada* (3 vols.)
Camille Debans. *The Misfortunes of John Bull*
Captain Danrit. *Undersea Odyssey*
C. I. Defontenay. *Star (Psi Cassiopeia)*
Charles Derennes. *The People of the Pole*

Georges Dodds (anthologist). *The Missing Link*
Charles Dodeman. *The Silent Bomb*
Harry Dickson. *The Heir of Dracula; Harry Dickson vs. The Spider*
Jules Dornay. *Lord Ruthven Begins*
Alfred Driou. *The Adventures of a Parisian Aeronaut*
Sâr Dubnotal *vs. Jack the Ripper*
Odette Dulac. *The War of the Sexes*
Alexandre Dumas. *The Return of Lord Ruthven*
Renée Dunan. *Baal; The Ultimate Pleasure*
J.-C. Dunyach. *The Night Orchid; The Thieves of Silence*
Henri Duvernois. *The Man Who Found Himself*
Achille Eyraud. *Voyage to Venus*
Henri Falk. *The Age of Lead*
Paul Féval. *Anne of the Isles; Knightshade; Revenants; Vampire City; The Vampire Countess; The Wandering Jew's Daughter*
Paul Féval, *fils. Felifax, the Tiger-Man*
Charles de Fieux. *Lamékis*
Louis Forest. *Someone is Stealing Children in Paris*
Arnould Galopin. *Doctor Omega*; *Doctor Omega and the Shadowmen* (anthology)
Judith Gautier. *Isoline and the Serpent-Flower*
H. Gayar. *The Marvelous Adventures of Serge Myrandhal on Mars*
G.L. Gick. *Harry Dickson and the Werewolf of Rutherford Grange*
Delphine de Girardin. *Balzac's Cane*
Léon Gozlan. *The Vampire of the Val-de-Grâce*
Jules Gros. *The Fossil Man*
Edmond Haraucourt. *Illusions of Immortality; Daah, the First Human*
Nathalie Henneberg. *The Green Gods*
Eugène Hennebert. *The Enchanted City*
Jules Hoche. *The Maker of Men and His Formula*
V. Hugo, P. Foucher & P. Meurice. *The Hunchback of Notre-Dame*
Romain d'Huissier. *Hexagon: Dark Matter*
Jules Janin. *The Magnetized Corpse*
Michel Jeury. *Chronolysis*
Gustave Kahn. *The Tale of Gold and Silence*
Gérard Klein. *The Mote in Time's Eye*
Fernand Kolney. *Love in 5000 Years*
Paul Lacroix. *Danse Macabre*
Louis-Guillaume de La Follie. *The Unpretentious Philosopher*

Jean de La Hire. *Enter the Nyctalope; The Nyctalope on Mars; The Nyctalope vs. Lucifer; The Nyctalope Steps In; Night of the Nyctalope; Return of the Nyctalope; The Fiery Wheel*

Etienne-Léon de Lamothe-Langon. *The Virgin Vampire*

André Laurie. *Spiridon*

Gabriel de Lautrec. *The Vengeance of the Oval Portrait*

Alain le Drimeur. *The Future City*

Georges Le Faure & Henri de Graffigny. *The Extraordinary Adventures of a Russian Scientist Across the Solar System* (2 vols.)

Gustave Le Rouge. *The Mysterious Doctor Cornelius* (3 vols.); *The Vampires of Mars; The Dominion of the World* (w/Gustave Guitton) (4 vols.)

Jules Lermina. *Mysteryville; Panic in Paris; To-Ho and the Gold Destroyers; The Secret of Zippelius; The Battle of Strasbourg*

André Lichtenberger. *The Centaurs; The Children of the Crab*

Maurice Limat. *Mephista*

Listonai. *The Philosophical Voyager*

Jean-Marc & Randy Lofficier. *Edgar Allan Poe on Mars; The Katrina Protocol; Pacifica; Robonocchio; Return of the Nyctalope;* (anthologists) *Tales of the Shadowmen 1-11; The Vampire Almanac* (2 vols.)

Xavier Mauméjean. *The League of Heroes*

Joseph Méry. *The Tower of Destiny*

Hippolyte Mettais. *The Year 5865; Paris Before the Deluge*

Louise Michel. *The Human Microbes; The New World*

Tony Moilin. *Paris in the Year 2000*

José Moselli. *Illa's End*

John-Antoine Nau. *Enemy Force*

Marie Nizet. *Captain Vampire*

C. Nodier, A. Beraud & Toussaint-Merle. *Frankenstein*

Henri de Parville. *An Inhabitant of the Planet Mars*

Gaston de Pawlowski. *Journey to the Land of the 4th Dimension*

Georges Pellerin. *The World in 2000 Years*

Ernest Pérochon. *The Frenetic People*

Pierre Pelot. *The Child Who Walked on the Sky*

J. Polidori, C. Nodier, E. Scribe. *Lord Ruthven the Vampire*

P.-A. Ponson du Terrail. *The Vampire and the Devil's Son; The Immortal Woman*

Georges Price. *The Missing Men of the Sirius*

Edgar Quinet. *Ahasuerus; The Enchanter Merlin*

Henri de Régnier. *A Surfeit of Mirrors*

Maurice Renard. *The Blue Peril; Doctor Lerne; The Doctored Man; A Man Among the Microbes; The Master of Light*

Jean Richepin. *The Wing; The Crazy Corner*

Albert Robida. *The Adventures of Saturnin Farandoul; The Clock of the Centuries; Chalet in the Sky; The Electric Life; The Engineer Von Satanas*

J.-H. Rosny Aîné. *Helgvor of the Blue River; The Givreuse Enigma; The Mysterious Force; The Navigators of Space; Vamireh; The World of the Variants; The Young Vampire*

Marcel Rouff. *Journey to the Inverted World*

Léonie Rouzade. *The World Turned Upside Down*

Han Ryner. *The Superhumans; The Human Ant*

Pierre de Selenes: *An Unknown World*

Angelo de Sorr. *The Vampires of London*

Brian Stableford. *The New Faust at the Tragicomique;The Empire of the Necromancers (The Shadow of Frankenstein; Frankenstein and the Vampire Countess; Frankenstein in London); Sherlock Holmes & The Vampires of Eternity; The Stones of Camelot; The Wayward Muse.* (anthologist) *News from the Moon; The Germans on Venus; The Supreme Progress; The World Above the World; Nemoville; Investigations of the Future; The Conqueror of Death; The Revolt of the Machines; The Man With the Blue Face*

Jacques Spitz. *The Eye of Purgatory*

Kurt Steiner. *Ortog*

Eugène Thébault. *Radio-Terror*

C.-F. Tiphaigne de La Roche. *Amilec*

Simon Tyssot de Patot. *The Strange Voyages of Jacques Massé and Pierre de Mésange*

Louis Ulbach. *Prince Bonifacio*

Théo Varlet. *The Golden Rock. The Xenobiotic Invasion; The Castaways of Eros; Timeslip Troopers* (w/André Blandin); *The Martian Epic* (w/Octave Joncquel)

Pierre Véron. *The Merchants of Health*

Paul Vibert. *The Mysterious Fluid*

Villiers de l'Isle-Adam. *The Scaffold; The Vampire Soul*

Gaston de Wailly. *The Murderer of the World*

Philippe Ward. *Artahe ; The Song of Montségur* (w/Sylvie Miller) *Manhattan Ghost* (w/Mickael Laguerre)

Victor Margueritte. *The Bacheloress; The Companion; The Couple*

MYSTERIES & THRILLERS

M. Allain & P. Souvestre. *The Daughter of Fantômas*
A. Anicet-Bourgeois, Lucien Dabril. *Rocambole*
A. Bernède. *Belphegor; Judex* (w/Louis Feuillade); *The Return of Judex* (w/Louis Feuillade); *The Shadow of Judex*
A. Bisson & G. Livet. *Nick Carter vs. Fantômas*
V. Darlay & H. de Gorsse. *Arsène Lupin vs. Sherlock Holmes: The Stage Play*
Séamas Duffy. *Sherlock Holmes in Paris*
Paul Féval. *Gentlemen of the Night; John Devil; The Black Coats ('Salem Street; The Invisible Weapon; The Parisian Jungle; The Companions of the Treasure; Heart of Steel; The Cadet Gang; The Sword-Swallower)*
Émile Gaboriau. *Monsieur Lecoq*
Goron & Émile Gautier. *Spawn of the Penitentiary*
Paul d'Ivoi. *Around the World on Five Sous* (w/Henri Chabrillat)
Rick Lai. *Shadows of the Opera: Retribution in Blood; Sisters of the Shadows: The Curse of Cagliostro*
Steve Leadley. *Sherlock Holmes: The Circle of Blood*
Maurice Leblanc. *Arsène Lupin vs. Countess Cagliostro; Arsène Lupin vs. Sherlock Holmes (The Blonde Phantom; The Hollow Needle); The Many Faces of Arsène Lupin; The Island of the Thirty Coffin; 813*
Gaston Leroux. *Chéri-Bibi; The Phantom of the Opera; Rouletabille & the Mystery of the Yellow Room; Rouletabille at Krupp's*
Richard Marsh. *The Complete Adventures of Judith Lee*
William Patrick Maynard. *The Terror of Fu Manchu; The Destiny of Fu Manchu*
Frank J. Morlok. *Sherlock Holmes: The Grand Horizontals; Sherlock Holmes vs Jack the Ripper*
Jean Petithuguenin. *The Adventures of Ethel King*
Antonin Reschal. *The Adventures of Miss Boston*
Frank Schildiner. *The Quest of Frankenstein*
P. de Wattyne & Y. Walter. *Sherlock Holmes vs. Fantômas*
David White. *Fantômas in America*
Pierre Yrondy. *The Adventures of Thérèse Arnaud*